Blood Children

The Bodies Of Dead Bankers

Rick Williams

Publisher:	One Difference Press Los Angeles, CA 90067 www.onedifferencepress.com
Author Website:	www.rickwilliams2016.com
Blood Children Trilogy:	www.bloodchildren.com

ISBN– 13: 978– 0692255940
ISBN– 10: 069225594X

The Blood Children Trilogy

One Difference Press
Los Angeles, CA
www.onedifferencepress.com

EXCERPTS FROM BIBLICAL GENESIS

GENESIS 1

In The Beginning God created the heavens and the earth

* * *

Then God said, "Let us make mankind in our image, after our likeness"

* * *

God saw all that he had made, and it was very good.

GENESIS 2

And the Lord God planted a garden eastward of Eden,
and there he put the man whom he had formed.

* * *

And the Lord God took the man,
and put him in the garden of Eden
to dress it and to keep it.

* * *

And the Lord God commanded the man saying,
"of every tree in the garden though mayest freely eat;
but of the tree of the knowledge of good and evil,
thou shalt not eat of it;
for in the day that thou eatest thereof
thou shalt surely die."

GENESIS 4

And Eve said, "I have gotten a man from the Lord!"

PRELUDE

A Tale of the Ancients

This is the story of how it all began. The story of the Blood Children, and Level Z, and the start of the Banker Wars. Our tale is far from over– Enlil and his Igigi are still among us, and the wars continue on. But the Blood Children are looking forward to better days ahead . . . because this is the time when we cast off the chains.

It started on New Year's Eve, with the death of Harlan Bloom. And then we saw TEOTWAWKI . . . the end of the world as we knew it. Some of my younger colleagues like to say it was SHTF– the moment when shit hit the fan– but whatever we might call those earlier days, one thing is for sure: our old world was gone once the bankers started turning up dead. I know it's true . . . I was there when it happened.

This book is written twenty years later, in 2041, and it's all so different now. Everything changed after I left Los Angeles– even who I am. Back then Randolph Blaine was a respected lawyer in a Century City law firm, but today that man no longer exists. I'm a soldier now, with Tanner in the 42nd Remnant. We fight in lands that were part of the country once known as the United States of America.

Over the two decades since TEOTWAWKI, seven different regimes have sought to rule this area, but none of them lasted for long, and the current group won't either. The charlatans who lust to be our Overlords are thieves and murderers– a tiny collection of parasites, seeking to feed off the blood of the many. But we've learned their secrets . . . we know these people have nothing of value to offer.

The creeping darkness was well on its way during those last few years in Los Angeles. I would have seen it if I'd cared to look– the twenty first century was the time of decline; the time when ordinary men and women became like animals; the time of tyranny; and most of all, the time of the bankers. The Overlords had their moment of glory in those years . . . when people were mindless sheep. Including me.

I was a partner in the law firm Hazeltine Phillips & Blaine LLP. The "Blaine" in the firm name was my grandfather, Harrison Blaine, one of the founders back in the 1920s. Los Angeles was growing rich in those days on unlimited oil and eternal sunshine, and my father, Edwin Blaine, followed in my grandfather's footsteps. Dad spent his entire fifty year career at the firm, so it was only natural that I would come back to LA after law school at Harvard and join the firm that my family had started. I did what was expected, and HP&B was the place I called home when Victor Desert walked into our lives.

Young Victor was fresh out of law school; he was interviewing for a job. Victor Desert had a good academic background– an editor of the law review at UCLA– but more than that, he had something even as a brand new lawyer that set him apart from the other young hopefuls who sought work at the firm. I'm not quite sure how to describe it: charisma; innate confidence– call it what you will. But whatever the driving cause, Victor Desert lifted himself up, and avoided the fate of his fellow graduates who spent their time writing legal memos that no one would ever read.

I was 40 years old when I first met Victor, and I knew right away that he would be a major asset to HP&B. And so it was– Victor Desert developed clients; he quickly became a partner in the firm; and I was the one who helped him along the way. When we talk about the spreading darkness of those earlier days, it was runaway debt; a collapsing middle class; counterfeiting bankers; the surveillance state– a collection of creeping unpleasantries that I didn't even know existed. Oh, I was vaguely aware that our financial people had gotten kind of excessive, but I viewed such things as minor matters that a few smart folks from Harvard and Yale would straighten out easily enough. I was earning plenty of money– what difference did it make if some of the young people were falling behind, and going broke, and losing their houses to the bankers? I went to church every Sunday; I paid my taxes; I supported the right political causes; and most importantly of all, I was a contributor. Not at all like those losers who get too deep in debt and then start complaining about how unfair everything is. I still believed back in those days that our Overlords would make it OK– it wasn't my nature to stray from the herd.

I have to admit that some of us were a bit jealous of Victor Desert. Here was this handsome guy– already a key player in Hazeltine Phillips & Blaine at the age of 28; taking home a big income; living with a hot young singer; and just in general enjoying his Hollywood life to the max. Victor was quick, and smart– seemingly on top of the world. But in the important things he was every bit as clueless as the rest of us . . . he didn't see what was coming any more than I did.

Everything seemed easy, and we wanted our lives to continue along just as they were. Victor Desert and Randolph Blaine liked the world we lived in– finding clients and making bunches of money were good things. Good for Victor; good for me; and good for the other partners at HP&B who were only too happy to divide up the extra dollars that Victor brought to the table. The lawyers at Hazeltine Phillips & Blaine were doing fine;

we paid no attention to such mundane things as bankers creating money out of thin air.

It's not my purpose in this book to place blame, or lament the events of the past. Most of the bankers from that era are dead by now anyway, and when you think about it, shouldn't they get some perverse recognition? Let's give credit where credit is due– the bankers did something twenty years ago that was entirely unique in human history. They managed to build an entire worldwide financial structure on phony money, and it actually survived for a few years before reality came calling and everything fell to pieces. Quite an achievement they had going– in an upside down sort of way.

I still have my journals from the earlier days, and I'm going to write a couple more of these books if I can keep from getting killed or stuck away to rot somewhere in a prison cell. The regimes are always on the lookout for subversives like me; so I move around to stay ahead of their assassins. It's like a game– I leave a series of false trails, and they follow leads to nowhere and squander their resources along the way. It's been like that for years, and they haven't caught on yet. I can tell you from personal experience that our wannabe Overlords aren't actually very smart.

* * *

The tale of the Blood Children first appeared on Mesopotamian clay tablets nearly 5000 years ago. The tablet writings– in modified form– later found their way into Biblical Genesis, and various of the apocrypha and midrashes written at the time of the Old Testament. The Bible tells us that multiple gods were involved in the creation of man ("Let us make mankind in our image, after our likeness"), and this tale from Genesis is a much abbreviated version of earlier tablet writings about two Mesopotamian gods named Enki and Enlil. We learn from the ancient tablets that these two half–brothers had very different views about the destiny of man, and their competing philosophies remain with us to this very day. Are men slaves, or free? Are we destined to learn and grow, or must man remain forever unknowledgeable? Back when I was a lawyer I didn't think about such things . . . but that all changed when Theresia Anjau came into Victor's life, and mine. Once you meet Theresia, you begin to see.

Theresia Anjau was an actress, and she played the role of Ninhursag in the film epic of the Blood Children. The screenplay for the movie was derived from a grand poem written on twelve clay tablets by a young author named Callien. The Callien tablets– buried for thousands of years in the sands of Iraq– resonate today with the message of freedom from slavery just as they did in the time of the ancients. His tale of gods and man will never die.

We know a few things about the author of the ancient tablets. Callien was a Sumerian– he lived in the most advanced civilization of the time. Sumer thrived in the area of the Tigris and Euphrates rivers, and the secrets of that extraordinary place took the world by storm in the 1800s when some of the Sumerian clay tablets were translated for the first time. Pretty soon there were thousands of transcribed tablets, and modern scholars were discovering that these pre–Biblical writings spoke to the great questions that are still with us today. How did life begin? Where did humans come from? Why was man created? Callien's epic poem of the Blood Children has taken a leading place among the ancient writings, and once you grasp what Callien is saying, there can be no going back to whatever it was you believed before.

The Blood Children tablets tell us that Enlil and his Igigi set out to create a race of lowly humans to do the work of the gods. This was Enlil's purpose for early man– to dig canals, and work in the mines, and build cities for the ruling Overlords of the day. Slaves to the gods . . . Callien tells us that the early humans– he called them the Eljo– were created to serve Enlil.

But that isn't the end of the story. Callien writes of Enki, Lord of the earth and the protector of mankind. Enki fathered the Blood Children to live among the Eljo and one day raise them up from their lowly status as slaves. The message of Callien in the Blood Children tablets is the message of Enki himself. Stand up, slaves! Cast off your chains! Get off your knees, and flourish as free men!

Not surprisingly, our modern day Overlords didn't like what they were seeing as tablets of Callien and other early writers began to emerge from their desert hiding places. Long established truths about God, and rulers, and the politics of obedience were being called into question by the words of the ancient writings, and the privileged class didn't appreciate the notion that twenty first century Eljo might come to learn the freedom values embodied by Enki and his Blood Children. The Overlords called it treason, and when the movie *Blood Children* threatened to carry Enki's words into popular culture, our rulers sensed danger. This was how it started.

* * *

So twenty years have passed, and the world is not as it was. We're still living in turmoil, but the Blood Children grow stronger every day, while Enlil and his Igigi grow weaker. We are winning, and one day these wars will be over. A new and better day is soon to dawn.

Randolph Blaine
Written on the Road
2041

PART ONE

The Mysterious Death of Harlan Bloom

I.

The actor was making his way along Sunset Boulevard on a drizzly Los Angeles night. There was a storm coming, but the club creatures were out in force anyway. Young girls in ultra– short black dresses and platform heels; boys in baggy jeans and leather jackets. These were the night people, and Harlan Bloom watched with interest as they passed in front of his Porsche while he waited for the light to change. The girls on the street were about the same age as Theresia Anjau, but all similarity ended there. Harlan's dinner companion from earlier that evening would never be found in the grunge hangouts of Hollywood. It wasn't her style.

Harlan Bloom had been trying for months to convince Theresia to marry him. The dinner tonight at La Pastiche was his latest attempt, but it had been no more successful than his previous efforts. Christmas was only three days away, and Harlan had resigned himself to the fact that he would be spending the holidays alone. The problem Harlan Bloom faced was simple and straightforward– Theresia didn't love him the way he loved her. She was willing to be friends, but nothing more than that.

Harlan Bloom had come to acting by an unusual path. He was a college graduate– from the University of Southern California, no less. His family had wanted the best for their son, and they had prepared him well. Harlan's degree was in economics– he didn't fit at all with the common stereotype about actors being stupid. Harlan Bloom in college was a very smart guy, and he was all set to launch his career in corporate finance when an acting opportunity came knocking at the door. A friend from the USC film school told him about a role being cast for a new television series and convinced Harlan that he would be right for the part. Bloom went to the audition on a lark– but much to his surprise he landed the role. The world of finance had lost him forever.

Harlan Bloom was twenty six years old, and handsome in a leading man kind of way. He had thick black hair and a winning smile, but for whatever reason the breakout acting role had yet to come his way. Harlan worked– he landed parts on television, and occasionally in a feature film, but he had never approached the pinnacle among his Hollywood peers– until *Blood Children* entered his life, that is. Harlan Bloom auditioned for the role of Enki before Sydney Anjau himself, and the famous producer made the decision that Harlan was right for the part. With Anjau's two daughters cast opposite him as Ninhursag and Naamah in the female leads, the production of *Blood Children* was Harlan Bloom's opportunity of a lifetime. He was living his finest moment– Harlan was entirely convinced that this major film about the ancient gods and goddesses was destined to be a huge hit.

As he drove through the Crescent Heights intersection, Harlan noticed a flashing red light in the mist behind him. A police car– was it pulling him over? For what? Harlan knew he hadn't been speeding, or doing anything to bring attention to himself. He was simply moving along with the flow of traffic on an ordinary Thursday night. He looked again in his rear view mirror, and this time there could be no doubt. It was a police car, and the car was following him. Harlan considered his options, but there weren't any good ones. He stopped at the side of the road.

Harlan sat in the Porsche and waited. The car with the flashing red light was close behind him, but the light had been turned off as soon as Harlan pulled out of the line of traffic.

Two men got out of the car. Harlan watched in his mirror as they approached the Porsche, one on each side. The men were wearing business suits, not police uniforms. The man standing at the driver side window displayed a badge inside a clear plastic holder– the insignia on the badge said "Federal Reserve Police, New York."

"Would you get out of the car, please?" The man at the driver's side did the talking. Other than the badge there was nothing about him that would indicate he was a police officer.

"I don't understand," said Harlan. "Who are you? And what right do you have to pull me over?"

"We have every right," said the man in the suit. "Federal Reserve police have nationwide jurisdiction, and we're authorized to enforce local and state laws when an infraction is committed in our presence. We were watching you drive, and you were weaving all over the road. You're being pulled over on suspicion of driving under the influence. If you'll get out of the car please, I'm going to administer a standard field sobriety test to you. It will only take a few minutes of your time."

Harlan was confused, and trying to think fast. "Am I required to take the test?"

"We've been following you and observing your erratic driving, so that gives us the right to detain you on suspicion. If you decline the field test, we'll take you into custody, and then you'll be required by law to undergo blood testing. So the choice is yours– do the field test now, or we take you to the station for a blood exam."

Harlan considered his choices. He knew he hadn't been driving erratically, and he certainly wasn't drunk. He and Theresia had each had only a single glass of wine that night with dinner– neither had felt much like drinking after their long day on the set. Harlan wasn't a drug user, so he had no concerns there. Nevertheless, the prospect of being taken into custody seemed threateningly real, and that was far and away the least favorable of his available options. "OK," said Harlan, "I'll take the test."

"Get out of the car please, and follow me to the sidewalk." Harlan complied. In the meantime, the second officer had moved around to the driver's side door and gotten into the car. The officer was laying on his back on the floor of the driver's side, looking upwards behind the dashboard.

"Hold on a minute. What is that man doing?" Harlan was deeply shaken at the sight of the second officer entering his car.

"He's searching the car for drugs. If you don't consent, that's your right. But in that case, we'll impound the car and get a warrant to search it at the station."

Harlan knew he didn't have anything illegal in the car, so once again he chose what he thought would be the lesser of two evils. He consented to the search of the Porsche, and joined the first officer on the sidewalk to go through the process of field sobriety testing. Harlan Bloom felt humiliated and alone as he was forced to go through his paces: standing on one leg; doing the horizontal eye gaze; submitting to the walk and turn. It was standard procedure, the officer told Harlan as he marched him through the exercise.

After a few minutes, the second officer joined them on the sidewalk. "He's clean. Nothing in the car."

The first officer smiled broadly at Harlan. "OK, you're free to go. You've passed the field tests, and there's no contraband in the car. We appreciate your cooperation; drive carefully on your way home."

Harlan was shaking as he got into the Porsche and drove away in the direction of Cahuenga Pass and his North Hollywood apartment. It had been a frightening confrontation, but Harlan felt at least some degree of relief. I made the right decisions by complying with the field test and the search, he thought to himself. The officers had found nothing to use against him, and he had avoided being taken into custody. Harlan Bloom believed the incident was over– but he would turn out to be wrong. Dead wrong.

II.

The old man came to the intersection of Broadway and Maiden Lane and paused for a moment at the busy corner. This was the older part of New York's Wall Street area, and the man hadn't visited for awhile. But he knew his way around.

He turned off Broadway and walked down the gentle slope of Maiden Lane in the direction of the East River. It was a brisk and blustery December day in New York, and the man turned up the collar of his overcoat for some extra protection against the biting wind. The sun was out, but it was blocked by the tall buildings– no warmth or sunlight could make its way to the narrow street below. A mass of people was moving along the crowded sidewalk in tandem, heads bent low against the chilly breeze. The old man was smiling as he walked– he was close to his destination now.

After making the turn down Maiden Lane the man had reduced his pace to a leisurely stroll. Maiden Lane was one of the most historic streets in downtown New York. By the 1700s the street was lined on both sides with smart shops and elegant houses, and later it became a center of the New York jewelry district. The dawn of the twenty first century changed all that, and Maiden Lane by 2020 had become a focal point of Wall Street finance, with its latest and largest addition being the gleaming ninety seven story headquarters tower of LawbridgeTrimble, Ltd. The building stood at the location where Thomas Jefferson had once rented a house during his time as Secretary of State under George Washington, and the bankers at LawbridgeTrimble paid appropriate tribute. A small plaque on an entry pillar marked the spot where Jefferson had lived, and what a grand irony it all was. The largest and most powerful investment banking firm in recorded history had located its headquarters on the spot where America's greatest anti–bank president had once made his home. LawbridgeTrimble, it seemed, had a sense of humor.

Across the street from the tower stood the headquarters building of the Federal Reserve Bank of New York. It was an imposing structure which filled the entire block between Liberty Street and Maiden Lane, but the mammoth Federal Reserve headquarters was aging and squat in comparison to the gleaming LawbridgeTrimble edifice. It was certainly remarkable– not to mention convenient– to find the two most important financial institutions in the world living comfortably across the street from one another. If the leaders of LawbridgeTrimble and the Fed wished to get together for a friendly chat, they could do so quietly, and privately, with minimal interruption in their busy schedules.

There were always tourists around– staring in awe at the great buildings of the Overlords. The New York Fed liked to show off its gold, and the visiting tourists were an eager audience. Back in the days before SHTF, the basement vault of the Fed was reputed to hold the largest reserve of gold in America, and gullible visitors would look at the gleaming collection of gold bars on display in the visible vault area and believe there were endless mountains of similar bars in the deeper bowels of the great storehouse.

The Fed bankers, after all, were telling us the gold was there, and back in 2020 people still believed what they had to say about such things. We now know, of course, that the gold had long since been moved to greener pastures. It was taken away– a little bit at a time– to personal storage locations in the Cayman Islands, and Antigua, and other such secure places where gold in the possession of important persons was lovingly welcomed without a lot of silly questions being asked.

Back on Maiden Lane the gold was long gone, but busy bureaucrats at the Fed still carried out their daily counterfeiting activities right up to the end. This was the New York Fed headquarters– the home of the central bank money creation machine. Anything was possible here, because this was the place where money was conjured up from nothing. It was the alchemist's dream of endless riches come true, and it was at this location– directly across the street from LawbridgeTrimble– that the old man found a place on the sidewalk with a clear view of the giant tower. It had the appearance of a great arrow rising endlessly into the sky. Impressive, the old man thought to himself . . . if you care about such things, that is.

The old man had arrived at his destination a few minutes early, and he settled in to wait. At his back was the Fed, and across Maiden Lane, rising above an open plaza, was the tower. The architect for LawbridgeTrimble had created a glass and steel profile that was slim and streamlined– everything the great firm pictured itself to be. Ninety seven shining floors– all bustling with people making money for the reigning Overlords of global finance. This was the place of Enlil, and his ever present Igigi were gathered closely around their leader.

A black stretch limousine pulled to a stop on Maiden Lane in front of the tower entrance. The old man watched with interest as the limo waited for its precious payload to emerge from the high ceilinged lobby and make their walk through the crowded courtyard area. There were hundreds of people milling around on the sidewalks along Maiden Lane, and many more in the open courtyard area outside the tower entrance. The old man was an indistinguishable face in the crowd . . . he pulled his hat low over his eyes for added warmth and watched the tower entrance. He waited.

Four burly men came out of the giant glass doors of the LawbridgeTrimble building and pushed their way toward the limousine on Maiden Lane. These were the bodyguards, from Mirrorprobe, and their task was to clear an open pathway through the crowd in the courtyard. All wore sunglasses, and dark suits with no overcoats. The bodyguards gave no credence to the wintry air.

It was the week before Christmas in New York, and the old man had been enjoying his annual holiday visit to the great city. He always liked to get away from LA during the Christmas season– and there was no finer sight in the world than the store windows of Fifth Avenue in their holiday splendor. The old man had never tired of the New York experience– it brought back pleasant memories from his days as a young boy growing up in the city.

The four bodyguards shared no such spirit. These were men of authority, and almost as if by magic the milling crowd in the courtyard saw what they wanted and stood aside to open a pathway. It was like the parting of the Red Sea in *The Ten Commandments*– the crowd created an open area which extended all the way from the entry doors of the tower to the waiting limousine on Maiden Lane. Everything was in readiness now, and the old man standing across the street watched the drama with an amused smile.

The glass doors of the tower opened again, and a second collection of suited men entered the courtyard. They walked briskly through the crowd of curious onlookers in the direction of Maiden Lane. The limousine was for these five men.

This second group was completely different in appearance from the burly security guards. The new five were shorter, more compact than the bodyguards, and they all wore tailored woolen overcoats appropriate for the season. The five were trim to a man– and all appeared to be costumed in exactly the same uniform. The old man couldn't see beneath the overcoats, but he was entirely confident that each of the five was wearing a finely cut gray suit and a conservative tie. These were bankers, and that was how bankers dressed. Well polished shoes completed the ensembles.

The five sported the signature look of the time. Bald heads on top, with neatly trimmed greying fringe about the ears and above the rear neck area. Beards– cut very short to create the impression of one who hadn't shaved for the past several days. The overall effect was of a shiny dome completely encircled front, sides and back by a hedgerow of closely trimmed grey hair. This was the favored appearance of the Overlords for public display to the outer world.

Lawrence Yasgar was one of the five. Yasgar was the Chairman and CEO of LawbridgeTrimble, and despite his small stature and unremarkable face there was no meaningful doubt about who the leader was in this group of important men. Lawrence Yasgar walked first in line as the team of five made its way down the narrow Red Sea corridor leading to the limousine. The crowd recognized him, and knew who he was.

Lawrence Yasgar was a public figure . . . a celebrity in his own right . . . the visible icon of Wall Street. Yasgar prided himself as a man with no weaknesses, and a man without fear. The lord and master of all he surveyed.

Lawrence Yasgar had been born into a family with money. He was raised on the Upper East Side in a neighborhood populated by other families of similar social and financial stature to his own. His father, Halston Yasgar, had been a senior level banker at Suffolk Trust, and his mother Errika was the unchallenged leader of New York society in her time. Young Lawrence had all the advantages, but that didn't mean he wasn't hard working and committed to his own success. Lawrence Yasgar may have been a trust fund baby– but he was driven by ambition, with a craving for recognition. Smart and ruthless, young Lawrence (never Larry, even to his closest friends) had all the tools, and he knew how to use them.

Lawrence Yasgar graduated from Harvard Law School, but didn't practice law. Instead, he went to work in the commodities trading arm of LawbridgeTrimble– the firm he was destined never to leave.

One step at a time, Lawrence Yasgar worked his way up the ladder at LawbridgeTrimble, and by the time he reached the top he was taking home more than $100 million per year. I'm sure if you asked he would tell you he was worth every penny of that. And probably he was. For it was during Yasgar's tenure that the other investment banking houses on Wall Street all collapsed, leaving LawbridgeTrimble as the sole remaining firm on the street. Lawrence Yasgar's time was LawbridgeTrimble's monopoly moment, and his giant firm was up to the test. Under the leadership of Lawrence Yasgar, the firm amassed a global reach that allowed it to have a hand in every important financial transaction of the era. LawbridgeTrimble was everywhere– and the lucky outside partners who participated in the deals paid handsome tribute to their benefactor. By the year 2020, LawbridgeTrimble had achieved such stature that the entire financial system we once called capitalism was largely managed and controlled from their single sparkling tower on Maiden Lane.

LawbridgeTrimble didn't magically appear on the Wall Street scene from nowhere– the firm had a long and storied history in the affairs of global finance. The activities which caused this firm and others of its kind to rise to positions of prominence and untold wealth can be traced back to medieval times, in England. It all came about as a result of the business acumen of a small group of people we remember today as the goldsmiths.

The goldsmiths were in the business of storing gold for their customers in safe rooms and vaults. They would issue paper receipts for the gold, and over time the receipts began to be traded as if they were themselves gold. The new paper was convenient; much more so than carrying around heavy gold and silver coins for transactions and trade. As more time went by, the goldsmith paper receipts were made payable to "bearer" rather than the individual depositor of gold, and the era of paper money was born. Bearer paper was readily transferable without need for a specific signature, and after awhile the paper lost any tie to a specific or identifiable deposit of gold in the vault of a smith.

Honest goldsmiths in the community knew, of course, that it would be fraudulent for them to issue more bearer paper "receipts" than they could actually redeem in physical gold. But human nature is what it is, and pretty soon the goldsmith fraternity began to figure out that depositors only rarely appeared at their door to withdraw the physical gold. Since only a tiny fraction of the total storehouse of gold was likely to be demanded by customers at any given time, why not take just a modest bit of liberty and issue receipts for amounts greater than the value of the actual gold that was available to back the receipts up? This exciting new business practice was quite literally the creation of money out of thin air by the goldsmiths, but as long as the general public continued to believe the bearer paper receipts were actually backed by real gold no one would be the wiser.

As time went by, the paper issued by the goldsmiths lost any character as a receipt. It became a loan; the goldsmiths had become the early lenders, and pretty soon they issued debt paper to borrowers who had no gold on deposit at all. Money from nothing . . . plus interest . . . the goldsmiths of medieval England had discovered the secret of what we would later come to call fractional reserve lending. And just like fractional reserve bankers in more modern times, the medieval goldsmiths had found a way to make astronomical amounts of money for themselves through the simple act of making a loan. They were handing out fraudulent receipts for gold they didn't actually possess, but nobody could stop it. The system grew and grew.

It went on like this for hundreds of years, finally culminating in 1694 when English political leaders were forced by their runaway spending to go hat in hand to the bankers asking for a loan to cover government debts. The bankers agreed to make the loan, but only on the condition that they would be allowed to organize and maintain their own privately owned bank which could issue money out of thin air. The Bank of England was the result– a central bank that lent newly created money to the government. Needless to say, English politicians of the day found endless uses for these funds.

Central bank money in England seemed to appear like magic . . . for free. The Bank of England grew by leaps and bounds, and the net result was that England emerged for a time as the leading power of the world. But of course it couldn't last. By the end of World War II, the English model had become the paradigm for central banking failure: a once great nation . . . hopelessly mired in debt.

As the Bank of England emerged in the 1700s, one gentleman in particular came to stand above all the other goldsmiths. His name was Jacob Reddick Cambridge, and his London–based firm was known as Cambridge Gold Holdings, Ltd. Jacob Reddick Cambridge was a relative latecomer in the goldsmithing business– he lived at the time when England's central bank was beginning its rise to prominence. Jacob was a smart and savvy man– his Cambridge Gold Holdings firm was able to acquire many of the smaller goldsmith houses, and the firm soon stood as the largest and most prominent of its kind in London. Cambridge lived in the elegant Estinghman Castle with his wife Verna and children Kromwell and Vassi– all surrounded and supported by an appropriate array of servants, supplicants, and hangers–on. Jacob and his family seemed to have it all.

But a problem was looming, and it was not the sort of thing that Cambridge was equipped to handle. Goldsmithing, it seemed, had fallen out of favor in England. People had figured out the trickery of the smiths, and the very word "gold" was becoming a badge of ill repute. Jacob Reddick Cambridge was seen by many as a parasite, and the man didn't have a clue about how to stem the negative tide that threatened to bring down his firm. All looked lost for the once–admired Cambridge family. It fell to Jacob's daughter Vassi to save the day. She found a young up and comer in London finance named Seymour Law, and soon the two were husband and wife. Once ensconced in the Cambridge family, the brash newcomer proposed a radical change. No longer would the family business be known as Cambridge Gold Holdings, Ltd. From then on it would be Lawbridge, Ltd. – the disfavored Cambridge name and the tainted reference to gold would disappear entirely from the public masthead of the firm. Seymour Law became the head of the newly christened entity, replacing his aging father in law, who was suffering mightily from the ravages of gout anyway. "Lawbridge"– the name carried the connotation of majesty inherent in Lady Justice herself. All references to the disreputable goldsmiths of old were soon eliminated from the recorded history of the firm, and when Oscar Trimble joined in 1746 from Amsterdam, the merged LawbridgeTrimble, Ltd. found its place as the leading financial house of the era. The firm had reached the top of the heap, and there it was destined to stay.

* * *

Lawrence Yasgar was a man with highly developed instincts. As he neared the waiting limousine, a sixth sense told him that something was amiss. Yasgar hadn't experienced this feeling for a very long time . . . but he recognized in an instant what it was. Yasgar was sensing the physical presence of his ancient enemy, and he scanned the crowd with sharp eyes. There . . . across the street . . . Lawrence Yasgar saw him. An old man . . . standing in front of the Federal Reserve building, wearing a worn overcoat and a hat pulled low over his forehead. The enemies stared at each other for a long moment across the crowded expanse, and Yasgar saw that the old man was mocking him. Smiling, with a look of contempt in his eyes.

Yasgar grabbed one of his followers roughly by the shoulder. "There, over there! The old man in the gray coat with the hat! Go get him, and bring him to me."

Nelson Bartell was Vice Chairman of LawbridgeTrimble, and over the years he had grown accustomed to this sort of peremptory outburst from his superior. Bartell's job was to do what Lawrence Yasgar told him to do . . . immediately, and without any backtalk or questions. But on this occasion, Nelson Bartell didn't know what Yasgar was talking about. He looked in the direction across the street where his superior was pointing, and saw nothing out of the ordinary. There were many people gathered on the other side of Maiden Lane in front of the Federal Reserve building– some walking briskly to get somewhere; others enjoying the entertaining spectacle created by the parting of the Red Sea in the LawbridgeTrimble courtyard. Bartell saw an ocean of gray overcoats as he quickly scanned the chaotic scene.

"Where?" Bartell said. "I don't understand what you're asking."

"The old man," Yasgar was pointing as he spoke. "Directly across the way! He's laughing at us! Take two of the guards and get over there. Bring him to me!"

Bartell recognized all too well the tone in Yasgar's voice– this was a moment for action, not quibbling. He turned to the two bodyguards standing closest to the limousine, and started yelling out commands. "You . . . and you . . . come with me! Across the street– now!"

Like most bodyguards, the Mirrorprobe team assigned to protect Lawrence Yasgar had nothing to do most of the time. So when the man standing next to Yasgar started yelling orders, their initial reaction was confusion, and uncertainty. They froze in their positions. What was this underling talking about? One of the guards was able to get out a few hesitant words in the confusion of the moment, "What did you say?"

Bartell wasn't going to just stand there at a time when Lawrence Yasgar was demanding action. "Follow me," he said to the two guards with a tone of anger in his voice. Bartell reached out and grabbed one of the guards roughly by the arm and started to pull him away from the limousine.

The guard shook off Bartell's hand. "What are you doing?" he said. Nelson Bartell wasn't his boss, and the guard had no responsibility to take orders from anyone other than Lawrence Yasgar or a superior officer in the guard detail. He didn't know how to respond to an order from Bartell.

But then the guard saw for himself the look on the face of Lawrence Yasgar. It was a strange mix, like nothing he had ever seen before. There was fear there, and surprise, but most of all a look of loathing that was deeper and darker than anything the bodyguard could even begin to contemplate. Seeing Yasgar's face, the guard grasped the urgency in Nelson Bartell's commands. He turned to his fellow officer: "Come with me! Something's wrong across the street! We need to check it out."

At just that moment a large truck was passing by the limousine on its way up Maiden Lane toward Broadway. Several jaywalkers in the crowd walked in front of the slow moving truck, causing it to come to a complete stop immediately adjacent to the limousine parked at the curb. The truck blocked the way . . . there was no place for Bartell and the two bodyguards to go. By the time the truck had moved on, the old man in a gray overcoat and hat was nowhere to be found.

Nelson Bartell returned to the limousine and started to tell Yasgar the news. But there was no need– the failure was obvious. "Let's go," said Yasgar in a flat voice as he climbed into the limousine. In a moment, the big car had pulled away, and the courtyard area resumed its usual pattern of people bustling in and out of the gleaming LawbridgeTrimble tower. The parting of the Red Sea was over, and business on Maiden Lane returned to normal.

The old man was smiling as he watched the limousine pull away from the curb. He had won this encounter, and in his mind he thought to himself, "Your days are numbered, Enlil; your entire structure is about to fall. Be ready, brother. They'll be coming . . . and sooner than you know."

The old man walked slowly in the same direction toward Broadway that Lawrence Yasgar's car had just taken. Sydney Anjau thought about his beautiful mother as he walked, and how much she used to enjoy the New York holiday season. Sydney hadn't gotten many opportunities to see Errika Yasgar while he was growing up, but mother and son had shared an unbreakable bond. She knew her first born son was destined for greatness, and Errika Yasgar had a mother's pride.

Sydney couldn't be there on the day his mother died– Errika and Sydney had an unspoken agreement that Halston Yasgar was never to learn the secret of Sydney's existence. But Errika's last thoughts on her deathbed were of her first born son. Lawrence Yasgar looked on with horror as she spoke the name "Sydney . . . Sydney . . . Sydney" over and over again with her final breaths.

The old man pondered for a moment how he would spend the rest of his time in the city. He could catch a subway back to midtown, and rest for awhile at his hotel. There would still be time to do some Christmas shopping after a nap– then a nice dinner would be in order. Sydney Anjau's holiday visit was complete– he would be catching the early flight to Los Angeles in the morning.

III.

Victor Desert grudgingly reached over to the side table and stifled the noise of his buzzing alarm clock. The clock read 7:00 a.m., and it was the Tuesday morning after a three day New Year's holiday weekend. Victor wasn't thrilled about the idea of getting up and going to work– he had enjoyed this brief time away from the office. Most of all, he had enjoyed spending the holiday with Katy Hooper. A weekend like that didn't happen often anymore– she was in high demand and never seemed to have any time these days.

Things had changed since they'd first started living together. Back then, it was always Victor who didn't have the time, and Katy who was seeking attention while she waited around for her big break. Now that it was here, everything seemed upside down. Katy Hooper had a hit song– and that was what she'd wanted. *Serpent's Seed* had been sound tracked in a movie, and everyone was saying it would get a Best Song nomination for an Academy Award. If that happened, Katy would sing at the Awards ceremony on Oscar night in front of a worldwide television audience. Katy Hooper was about to be a very hot item in the Hollywood scene.

Victor and Katy had been living together in the Curson house for a little over a year. It had been a good time for Victor– Katy had filled a void. Back in the early days she had talked a lot about getting married, but Victor had put her off. Now that her career was running strong, Katy seemed to be taking a step back, and Victor found himself spending time alone. They were a young couple having a lot of early success, but was this relationship something that would last? As the new year dawned, neither Victor nor Katy had any way to know.

Victor's shower felt good to him– washing away the hints of a lingering hangover. He had spent much of the weekend partying with Katy's music industry friends, and the hot water was clearing his senses. One of the things Victor particularly liked about the Curson house was his oversized shower/bath combination that the decorator had insisted upon as one of her first improvements. The house was still under renovation– it had been in an endless state of construction ever since he had moved in. But it was all worth it, Victor thought to himself. Curson Avenue was one of the premier streets in Hollywood, and fixing up the house was an important part of his still–fresh life as a successful Century City lawyer. Victor was redoing the house as a Mediterranean– annoyingly expensive, but Victor was convinced it would turn out to be a good investment one of these days.

The morning sun was shining in from the bathroom window, and Victor took a moment to relax under the hot spray and check out the open hillsides up the street. Curson Avenue was located just off busy Hollywood Boulevard, and it mattered to Victor that the hills were so close. His small town background in Millford was never far beneath the surface– and a man from the northwest enjoyed the out of doors.

Young Victor had attended a state college near Millford, and he was all lined up to start work as an accountant when he decided on a whim to take the law school admission test. He was in for a surprise– scoring in the 99th percentile on the LSAT, and suddenly there were law schools all over the country offering scholarships and welcoming him with open arms. He ended up at UCLA because his mother had been an actress in her younger days, and she knew people in the Hollywood community. People who remembered Joanne Desert, and would one day help her personable son get his start as a lawyer. Pretty soon he was working at Hazeltine Phillips & Blaine . . . Victor Desert was on his way.

Victor and Katy Hooper were a couple that looked good together. Victor was tall and lanky– six foot two, and two hundred pounds, while Katy was built like the gymnast she'd been in high school– short and muscular, but in a curvy and very feminine kind of way. Katy's dark hair and blue eyes gave her a striking look– it was no surprise to Victor Desert that this woman was having a breakthrough in her singing career. She had a style of her own, and it was backed up with some genuine talent. Katy's producer was a man named Camelhump, and he had been featuring her in some edgy new videos. Witchy stuff– really sexy. It was a big change for the preacher's daughter from Bakersfield who was new in town and just getting started when Victor met her one night at Club Jaxx. Katy had come to Hollywood as a country singer, but that was all in the past. Under the guidance of Camelhump, she was a rapper now.

There were no scheduled court appearances for Victor on this first business day of the new year, so he chose to dress casual. Black slacks and a sport shirt would be fine. Like most LA firms, Hazeltine Phillips & Blaine had long since moved on from the olden times when lawyers and the staff wore suits and dresses in the office.

Victor slipped into the bulky black shoes that he liked. He called them his Bolshevik shoes, and they were a replica of work shoes found in the long dead Soviet Union of earlier days. Victor told anyone who asked that he wore the Bolshevik shoes to prove his standing as a man of the people. It was all a joke of course, but underneath the surface humor there was actually a part of Victor that carried quite a considerable revolutionary edge. Look below, and there it would be.

Victor Desert's nickname in the law firm was the Facade. He got it because he never seemed to be bothered by setbacks. Most lawyers obsess all the time about winning or losing, but Victor was different. He understood from the start that his career as a lawyer would require him to accept any outcome in a hotly disputed case– an enormous insight for a young lawyer to have. Most of us reach that level only after losing a bunch of times, but for Victor it came naturally. Winning or losing didn't seem to affect the Facade . . . he was the same either way. It wasn't that Victor didn't care– he did, and deeply. But it never showed.

Katy was still asleep when Victor left for the office. The drive to Century City from the Curson house took about 20 minutes, and Victor followed his usual route that morning– a right turn at Sunset Boulevard, heading west through Beverly Hills.

This was the most expensive residential real estate on the planet. The houses along Victor's route were mostly hidden behind tall green hedges– but occasionally one of the monstrous castles showed through just enough to let a visitor know he'd arrived in the promised land. This was the part of Los Angeles where vendors sold maps showing locations of the stars' homes, and buses filled with tourists combed the neighborhood streets. Everyone loves the rich and famous– and their turf was right here in Hollywood and Beverly Hills.

Victor pulled his Jaguar into the garage at 1820 Century Way East and handed the keys to a waiting attendant. The shiny new Jag was yet another sign of Victor's fresh success. Only a few short years before, he had been driving a dated Toyota. Times had changed since law school days.

Lawyers from Hazeltine Phillips & Brant were spread around the fourteenth and fifteenth floors of the 1820 building. Victor's office was on the higher floor, with a view to the northwest overlooking Century Park Country Club. It was 9:30 a.m. when Victor arrived at his office, and his assistant Caroline was already there.

"Good morning, Victor. ETB came by a couple of times– he wants to see you right away. As soon as you come in, he said."

ETB was Adrian Garfinkle, a recent Pepperdine law graduate who had been with the firm for a year. Victor was his mentor. Everyone called him ETB because Adrian spent endless amounts of time monitoring and operating a website known as EndtheBailouts.

ETB was immensely proud of his Internet creation– and rightly so. EndtheBailouts put forth the writings of a growing collection of edgy young political activist bloggers, and the website was developing quite a considerable public following among people who liked to read every day about freedom, and sound money, and other such discomforting topics. My partners Jack Hazeltine and Roland Phillips disapproved of the website, of course, but our firm tried to maintain at least a surface appearance of tolerance and open–mindedness where political views were concerned. No one felt strongly enough about ETB's Internet creation to actually insist that it be shut down; so Jack and Roland were left only with a hope that the thing would fizzle out over time.

In fact, the opposite was occurring. In barely a year, EndtheBailouts had picked up eyeballs from all around the country, and ETB was developing a considerable personal following as a result of his own blogging. Victor found amusement in Adrian Garfinkle's website operation– he liked to visit the site himself on occasion and read some of the firebrand writings that ETB and his young activists were posting. Other than wearing his Bolshevik shoes, Victor wasn't much into politics in those days– but he enjoyed what Adrian was doing with EndtheBailouts.

"Give him a call," Victor said to Caroline as he stood near her desk outside his own office. "Tell him to come by in about 20 minutes. I want to check out my emails and messages first."

"OK," said Caroline, "but he said it was about a new client. I think he's pretty excited." Caroline Sikes had a warm feeling for Adrian Garfinkle– she was taken with his enthusiasm, and the eager enjoyment he found in the process of learning how to practice law. Like Victor, ETB was a lawyer who genuinely cared . . . Caroline thought that was special.

Victor went into the office and opened his email inbox. As expected, there were fifty or so new messages that had piled up since close of business on Friday. There were *always* fifty or so new messages for Victor Desert– and on some days many more. Victor had a significant law practice, with a sizable collection of clients. In any law firm, there are finders, minders, and grinders where client relationships were concerned, and Victor was a finder. The clients, not surprisingly, expected instant response, and Victor Desert was acutely aware that a paying client hasn't the slightest interest in what his or her lawyer might be doing for someone else in that moment of time when the client wants to reach him. Armed with a fresh cup of coffee, Victor got ready to plow through the backlog of weekend messages.

ETB couldn't wait. He burst into the office before there was time even for Victor to pick up his phone and listen to the voicemails. Victor smiled at Adrian's wide–eyed excitement– it was quite apparent that there would be no business as usual until ETB's special new case was dealt with first.

"So what have you got?" Victor's casual comment was accompanied by a wave of his hand for ETB to sit down in one of the leather client chairs opposite his desk. But ETB didn't need the encouragement– he rushed into his report while still standing.

"OK, here's the deal. Have you heard of an actor named Harlan Bloom? Well guess what– he died on New Year's Eve in a car crash. Saturday night. Supposedly running away from the police, or that's what they're saying anyway." ETB was really wound up.

"And you think . . ." said Victor, but ETB wasn't about to be interrupted. He had a full head of steam.

"It's not what I think," said the younger lawyer, all in a rush, "it's what Theresia told me this weekend. You know . . . the actress . . . Theresia Anjau. You've seen her."

Actually Victor hadn't seen her, but he vaguely recalled the name. ETB had mentioned her before. "Isn't she one of your EndtheBailouts people?"

"That's right," said ETB, unable to hide the hint of pride in his voice. "She's been reading my stuff on the blog. Harlan Bloom too. I met both of them that way. I told you about Theresia a couple of months ago, but I think you were busy at the time."

Victor was trying to picture the actress in his mind, but he couldn't come up with a face. "You've actually met her . . . in person?"

ETB was growing prouder by the minute. Tall, skinny, and not particularly good looking, he didn't have much of a track record with the opposite sex. Adrian Garfinkle had always been the egghead; an odd man out where women were concerned. But EndtheBailouts, it seemed, was changing all that. "Not only have I met her, but we actually had dinner together one time. Theresia's really something special; she's way into my freedom stuff on the website, and she's even written a few pieces of her own. Not using her real name, of course."

"OK, so what does your screen lover have to do with Harlan Bloom and his New Year's Eve car wreck?"

ETB was momentarily flustered by Victor's comment. "Don't get me wrong, she's not actually my lover . . . it's nothing like that at all. I've only met her couple of times, and she's way out of my league. Anyway, she and Harlan were dating. They were shooting this movie together over the past six months or so. Harlan and Theresia were the stars, and her sister Sarah– she had a major role too. So they were all working together– Harlan, Theresia, and Sarah– and the project was pretty close to being finished. Now, all of a sudden, Harlan Bloom is dead. It's a big loss for Theresia and a huge setback for the movie."

"Theresia Anjau– what's her connection to the car crash?" ETB's story had caught Victor's interest, and the younger lawyer had his full attention.

"She called me. The first time was Sunday morning . . . two days ago. And she was all shook up; crying, and scared. She'd just learned about the car wreck, and she said there was something wrong. She'd heard about it on the news, and the news people were talking about a high speed chase, and how Harlan Bloom had smashed into a freeway abutment, and how the police were after him, and how he had alcohol in his system. The news reports were making it sound like the crash was all Harlan's fault."

"So was it?" asked Victor. "What does Theresia say?"

"She says she was with Bloom for dinner on Saturday night, and they were hardly drinking at all. They didn't even stay out 'til midnight, and she says he was fine when he left her. She says he's a really good driver– no way he was going to smash into a cement pillar at 100 miles an hour. It just wasn't like him."

"What does she think happened?"

"Well that's the part where it gets interesting. Theresia says Harlan was being followed around. He had some kind of police team after him, making his life miserable. They were putting all kinds of pressure on him, and he owed some money to a bank. And the bank was pressuring him too. Theresia thinks these people had something to do with his accident . . . if it was an accident. She thinks there's something going on here that the people on the news aren't telling us."

Victor pondered for a moment, then said, "I don't get it. Why would some actor be followed around by the cops? What would they want from him? And if he owed money to a bank, I don't see why they would want anything to happen to the guy. Pretty tough to collect on a debt from a dead man."

Adrian tried to explain. "There's more to it than that. Theresia tells me this movie they're making is all about ancient gods, and how the gods created a race of slaves, and how the movie was urging the slaves to stand up against their masters. That's part of what got Theresia involved in EndtheBailouts– the movie was sparking her interest in our revolutionary stuff on the site. And Harlan Bloom was really into it. He was convinced that the bankers are modern day slave masters who create counterfeit money and use debt to keep the slaves in line.

"Harlan had started a group in college called Level Z that went around criticizing the banks, and he gave speeches and interviews calling for the bankers to be thrown in prison, and how we needed to fire up the guillotines again . . . that sort of thing. Harlan Bloom believed the bankers were creating this giant economic collapse that's about to fall on all of us and wipe everybody out. That's what he was going around saying, and that's why the bankers were all pissed off. Theresia thinks the bankers were the ones who sent cops out to harass him– to scare him, so he would shut up. Well they scared him, all right. And Theresia too. She's scared to death, and she thinks the people following him around had something to do with his death."

Victor was all business, now . . . he looked intently at Adrian Garfinkle. "Where do we go from here?"

"I tried all weekend to get Theresia to meet with me, and talk about this thing some more, but she wouldn't do it. So finally, yesterday, I told her, 'why don't you come into the firm and talk to one of the partners? We do a lot of entertainment work, and he'll know what to do.' That kind of thing– that's what I've been telling her. So anyway, she finally agreed. I've made an appointment for her to come in this afternoon and I was hoping you might see her and talk to her. Maybe it's nothing . . . maybe it's all just an accident like the news people are saying. But if you would meet with her, I think it would really mean a lot." Garfinkle looked at Victor and waited for an answer. It came immediately.

"Of course I'll meet with her. Reserve the conference room, and set it up with Caroline. What you're telling me seems very unusual– let's get to the bottom of it."

Adrian Garfinkle's relief was obvious. "OK, thanks. I'll call her right now– I told her about 1:30 this afternoon if that works for you. I hope she hasn't changed her mind."

"Let me know if anything changes," said Victor, "but I'll go ahead and put it on the calendar. So you mentioned this film they were making, and how it might have had something to do with the people who were following Bloom around. Tell me a bit more– what's the movie about?"

"I don't really know much, other than the slave uprising stuff. They're keeping it under wraps while the filming is going on. About the only thing Theresia would tell me was the title. They call it *Blood Children*."

IV.

Theresia Anjau was used to it by now . . . the reaction she caused whenever she walked into a room. People stared– particularly the men, of course. Usually with their mouths open. Theresia had that effect, and there was nothing she could do about it.

Her look was extraordinary; something entirely unique. Long red hair, green eyes, tall and curvy– and with no visible effort or affectation. Theresia belonged in the countryside even though her entire life had been spent in Beverly Hills and Hollywood. A woman from a different place and time– or at least she seemed that way to people meeting her for the first time. In a single word . . . goddess.

Theresia Anjau arrived at our office alone, right on time for her meeting with Victor and ETB. She was dressed informally in a simple flowered blouse and dark brown skirt, with flat heeled sandals. Long bare legs completed the look.

Minnie Larren was our receptionist in the main lobby on the fifteenth floor, and two of our young associates were standing in the open hallway behind Minnie's desk when Theresia made her short walk from the elevator lobby into the reception area. They couldn't take their eyes off her.

"I'm here to see Adrian Garfinkle."

Minnie, always the consummate professional, tried to not sound as flustered as she actually felt. "Your name please?" Theresia answered, and Minnie managed to get things together well enough to place a call to ETB's office and tell him the visitor had arrived. Then Minnie spoke to Theresia: "Please follow me. I'll show you into the conference room. Adrian will join you shortly with Mr. Blaine and Mr. Desert."

Minnie rose from her chair behind the entry desk and led her visitor past the two gaping associates and down the hall to a large, glass–walled conference room near the entry reception area. We called it the Board Room– the conference table which filled most of the space in the room was large enough to seat 25 people at a time, and there were more chairs lined up along the wall area and under the long row of windows for use in the event of an overflow crowd.

Theresia took a seat at the conference room table facing the windows that looked out over the golf course across Santa Monica Boulevard. Minnie offered coffee, water or tea, but the visitor declined. She had a carry bag with some papers which she placed on the table to her left. Theresia waited . . . but only for a moment. ETB had come quickly from his office on the fourteenth floor below, and he eagerly joined the visitor in our Board Room. The two young people exchanged smiles and a brief kiss on the cheek.

"I've asked two of our partners to join us," said ETB with an excitement that he was not entirely successful in hiding. "I think they'll be interested in what you have to say. So how are you? Are you feeling any better? I know how tough this must be . . . are you doing OK? Can I get you anything?" ETB was having difficulty stopping the flow of words.

"I'm fine," said Theresia with a weak smile. "A little shaky, maybe, but mostly I feel so sorry for Harlan and his family."

ETB didn't know Harlan's family, so he wasn't quite sure what to say to that. He chose the safe course. "Well, I certainly wish them the best in this difficult time. It's a tragedy, no doubt about that. But I'm sure we're going to get to the bottom of things once we take a close look at what actually happened. We'll work it through . . . don't worry. Victor and Randolph Blaine will know what to do."

Theresia favored the young lawyer with another smile. "I hope so," she said.

Victor and I joined up in my office, and walked to the Board Room together. It wasn't clear to me at that point how this death of an actor in a car crash translated into paying legal work for Hazeltine Phillips & Blaine, but I liked to maintain an open mind about such things until I learned the facts and circumstances of the engagement. It was lawyer thinking– listen first, figure it all out, tell the client how much it's going to cost, and then go take care of everything. That's how it was supposed to work.

I was no better prepared than any of my other colleagues for the vision waiting for us in the conference room. What a strange and striking creature this woman was. I stared at her, most likely with my mouth open, just as our two young associates had done in the hallway. But I recovered quickly, and mumbled my name in greeting. Victor followed, and we joined ETB facing our visitor across the conference room table. This was to be a legal meeting– something I was used to. My initial sense of disorientation passed, and I fell into the familiar posture where I was ready to hear whatever it was that the prospective client had to say. I sat back to listen.

Victor led off. "So, Theresia . . . if I may call you Theresia . . . thank you for joining us. Our colleague Adrian has told me a bit about Harlan Bloom and his unfortunate death on Saturday night. My condolences. As I understand it, you have some concerns that the full story about his death might not be coming out in the news reports you've been seeing, and I understand the two of you were working together on a movie production. But at this point, that's about all I know– so perhaps we can begin by you telling us why you're here, and then we can decide what we might do to help. Does that sound right to you?"

Theresia may have been only twenty one years old, but she was a trained and articulate actress, and it showed. She launched into a concise report. For the first few minutes she told us the background– who Harlan Bloom was, and what he was involved in at the time of his death. It started with the film.

"Harlan was chosen to star in *Blood Children* by my father," she explained. "None of us were exactly sure why, since this would be his first starring role in a film of this size. I had expected the movie company to choose someone more established, but my father knew best about things like that and Harlan was the choice. He was doing a very good job by the way, and in a challenging role. My father was right . . . but now this . . .".

Theresia told us about Sydney Anjau. "My father was born and raised in New York, but he came to LA as a young actor when he was eighteen years old, and he never left. He's seventy six now . . . but you would never know it to see him. To me he looks about fifty– but maybe I'm biased because he's my father. Anyway, he was a successful actor back in those early days; you can still see some of his movies on TV. But his real career came as a producer. His pictures have won several Academy Awards, and he's drawn big audiences. His movies have a kind of added depth. It's difficult to explain . . . but if you've seen *The Dispossessed*, or *Monarchy*, or *The Dark Threads*, or any of his other really outstanding films you'll know what I mean. *Blood Children*– the film Harlan and I were working on– I'm sure will be his best."

Harlan Bloom, she explained, had fallen in love with her during the shoot. "He wanted me to be the mother of his children," she said. Such quaint terminology, I thought to myself, but Theresia carefully explained that she and the actor were only friends. Their evenings out weren't for romance, she told us. Not even their date on New Year's Eve.

"You were with him the night of his death?" asked Victor.

"Yes," she said with a troubled look, "we had dinner that night at Carousel in West Hollywood." The memory was obviously uncomfortable for her, but she continued on, "We were doing an early evening; I left around eleven o'clock. That's what seems so odd to me. Harlan was fine when we went on our way. He wasn't sad, or depressed, or anything like that. And he certainly wasn't drunk, like they tried to insinuate in the news reports. Something just doesn't fit."

Victor asked her about Harlan's public speaking, and the bankers.

"His background was in economics, and he was always speaking out about the bankers . . . for as long as I'd known him, and even before that. He believed the bankers were a bunch of crooks, and he gave speeches and talked to groups. It had been going on for Harlan since he was in college. Maybe he wasn't so smart to be speaking out, but Harlan really meant it."

"Was he making threats?" asked Victor. "When you start talking about throwing bankers in jail and bringing back the guillotine, there's a pretty good likelihood that someone important is going to pay attention. That's probably why he was being followed. They were keeping tabs on him . . . like some kind of terrorist, or something."

"Harlan was always telling me he didn't advocate violence," said Theresia with a thoughtful look, "but he had a way of saying things that was close to the edge. He was smart enough not to make any direct threats–but was he angry? About the bankers, I mean? You bet he was. As far as he was concerned, they were a gang of counterfeiting criminals. So . . . was he wrong?"

Theresia's question was a pointed challenge to Victor's comparison of Harlan Bloom to a terrorist. But my colleague didn't rise to the bait.

"Whether he was right or wrong about the bankers, the issue I'm concerned with is what happened on the night of the car crash. I know you said earlier that you went home before midnight. So is there anything you can tell us that might shed some light on what happened after you and Harlan went on your way?"

"It wasn't just that people were following him," Theresia explained. "There was more to it than that. Barely a week ago, they pulled him over at night when he was driving home after dinner. They made him get out of his car, and do a field sobriety test, and they searched his car looking for drugs or something. Really creepy stuff. And they were threatening him. They had meetings with him, and they would say things like, 'Harlan, pay attention; listen to us; we're not joking around. You need to do what you're told.' That kind of thing. Like they owned him or something."

Theresia told us about a night at the Tiger Lounge a few weeks earlier. "I was sitting in one of their booths along the side wall waiting for Harlan. And all of a sudden these two guys in suits come walking over and sit down at the table with me."

"You mean they actually just came and sat down? No introduction or anything?" I asked a question that came to mind because it was so difficult to picture anyone acting that way where Theresia Anjau was concerned.

"That's exactly what I mean. And they started talking to me– like tough guys, you know? They weren't yelling or anything like that, but they said thing like, 'Look at us, Theresia; we've been trying to talk to Harlan, but he won't listen. He's out there threatening our clients, and we can't stand for it. He needs to stop . . . and right now.' That kind of talk– scary."

"Were they police?" asked Victor.

"I don't think so. They never showed me badges, and they didn't seem like cops. They were . . . smoother . . . than police guys. More professional. Like hired killers, if I were to let my imagination run a little wild."

"Have you ever seen them again?"

"I never talked to them again, but I saw them. And I know Harlan met them several times. They called him into his banker's office. Right down the street here– Turn of the Century Bank. You probably know it."

"Of course," I said, "they're one of the biggest banks in LA. And probably nationwide, for that matter. They really took off during the big housing boom in the early 2000s."

"Yes, that's them. Anyway, Harlan owed them some money. A lot of money, actually. More than $100,000 he told me last week– mostly from left over student loans that he took out when he was at USC. The interest and service charges on those kinds of loans just keep adding up, and these bankers from Turn of the Century were telling Harlan they were going to call his loan unless he cut it out about the bankers. And the two professional killer types were there, and they were telling him he needed to drop out of *Blood Children.* They didn't like the movie– it was subversive, they said. Not something they wanted him to be involved in. It was like they thought they could just tell Harlan what to do and then he was supposed to do it."

Victor was puzzled by what he was hearing. "Why would these people possibly be unhappy about something like a movie? It's only entertainment– not real life or anything. I can understand how Harlan might have been smarter to not be out there making threats about the bankers, but I don't get what the movie has to do with it."

Theresia smiled at him. "I think if you knew the story of *Blood Children* you might have a different view about that. It truly is revolutionary, and Harlan was all caught up in his role as Enki. I don't know how to explain it so you'll understand . . . but Harlan started seeing himself as the protector of mankind– that sort of thing. He already had his Level Z group, talking about how they were going to throw the bankers in jail, and the movie made it all so real to him. This was the time when he found EndtheBailouts, and started reading the stuff on the blogs that Adrian and his writers were posting. That's how I met Adrian, by the way, through Harlan discovering his website. And with Harlan already focused on how the bankers had been stealing everybody blind and ruining the country for ordinary people, it all just fit together with the movie.

"I saw the men in suits one time when they were with Harlan at Martin & Bernie's, sitting in a booth together. I was supposed to join Harlan for dinner. When I came over, the two men got up and left, but it was creepy. They looked at me in a way that wasn't even human. They're sociopaths– Igigi– and they can't relate to us at all."

"Igigi?" asked Victor. I had the same question.

"Igigi. The followers of Enlil."

"Tell them how the script came to you," suggested ETB, who had mostly been quiet up to then.

"I found it in my mailbox one day, but it had been placed there by hand. There was a manila envelope, and it had my name on it, and I opened it up, and there was the *Blood Children* screenplay. With a note. I brought it with me, if you're interested."

Theresia took a well–used script out of her carry bag and placed it on the conference room table. Along with a handwritten note, that read:

> To Theresia Anjau:
> I've seen your work, and I want you to play the role of Ninhursag in *Blood Children.* Please read my script; you'll understand why I've sent it to you. If you decide to take the role, the script is yours to do with as you choose.
> With admiration,
> Callien

"My sister got the exact same letter except that Callien was telling her to play the part of Naamah. And Callien was right– whoever he is. Sarah is perfect as the young Naamah, and the role of Ninhursag is the best thing I've ever done in a film. I don't know how to explain it exactly– but it's as if I've almost become the character. The whole thing seems real to me– Callien's screenplay is that compelling. I've never been involved with anything quite like it before."

Theresia had no idea who Callien was, or where the script for *Blood Children* had come from. But once she had read it, Theresia knew she wanted this movie to be made.

"I took it to my father. Of all the people I know, he more than anyone would understand just how good this script was. And of course he saw it right away. So he showed it to the lawyers, and they told him we were OK as long as Sarah and I played the two female leads. So here we are."

"What I don't understand is why Harlan's bankers would be unhappy about him acting in the movie." I was still trying to grasp what Theresia was telling us on that point. "What could possibly be wrong with an actor taking a movie role?"

"Because it was more than just an acting role. He actually believed he was Enki; he knew it for a fact, and no one was going to convince him otherwise. The bankers didn't like that. They're the cronies of Enlil, and they don't want anyone to be out there in the public eye telling people what they've been doing. Once the movie came out, and Harlan became a big star, people were going to start listening to him. Much more than they'd been listening up to that point. If the movie took off, Harlan Bloom could all of a sudden become a genuine threat to the bankers. So I think they were trying to cut things off before that happened– and that's why they killed him."

It was eerie that Theresia could be telling us outright that Harlan Bloom had been murdered, and that two long forgotten gods from thousands of years in the past were the reason why.

"Was he Enki?" Victor asked his question with a completely straight face.

"No, of course not," said Theresia. "Harlan Bloom wasn't Enki; he was only an actor playing a role."

"How do you know? Maybe Enki came back to life after all these years, and chose Harlan as his new persona." Victor was trying to make a joke, or so it seemed.

But Theresia's answer to Victor was entirely serious. "I know Harlan Bloom couldn't possibly be Enki," she said, "because my father is Enki. And my sister Sarah is Naamah."

* * *

Victor wasn't convinced that anything improper had happened to Harlan . . . not even close. His thinking at that point was that Harlan Bloom had been in an accident, probably one that he brought on himself. All this talk about bankers owning Harlan Bloom, and following him around, and killing him because they didn't like his movie seemed like tinfoil hat stuff to Victor Desert. But Victor was first and foremost a lawyer, and he wasn't going to jump to conclusions after only a single meeting. "So what is it that we can do for you, Theresia? What do you want from us, and how can we help?"

"I want you to find out why Harlan Bloom is dead. I've talked to my father about it, and he's willing to have the production company pay your fees to look into the crash and figure out what happened. My father says the filming of *Blood Children* can go on to completion even without Harlan for the remaining shots, but there's going to be a lot of extra expense, and he'd like the company to be able to recoup that money if possible. More importantly, though, my father simply wants to know how Harlan died, and who's responsible. And so do I. So that's what we want your firm to do."

Victor pondered her request. "Here's what I propose. We have a private investigator that Adrian and I are very high on. A young guy– his name is Frank Paladin, and I think he's the best in the business. My advice is that we bring Paladin on board, and let him dig around and see what he can find. He's your man for this job– and of course we'll be working with him and keeping tabs on the legal end."

Theresia's face was filled with relief as we showed her out to the elevator lobby.

I'll call Paladin and get him started today," said Victor. "We'll keep in touch." Theresia gave each of us a brief kiss on the cheek– then she was gone.

V.

Three days had passed since Theresia's visit, and Victor, ETB and I were gathered again in the Board Room. Frank Paladin joined us to deliver his initial report.

Paladin wasn't a tall man, but he had a presence. Black hair and dark eyes; he had a kind of easy and sincere smile that was disarming, and took you off your guard. The investigator was an outgoing sort– a useful trait if you're looking for information. And he knew how to dress– Paladin looked sharper than any of the three lawyers in the room with his European cut suit and designer tie. The investigator was only in his early 20s, but he made an impression– no doubt about it.

"So have you all been reading your Bible?" Paladin was smiling; amused by his opening comment.

"No . . . should we?" Victor had seen the twinkle in the investigator's eye, and he responded with some humor of his own. "I wasn't thinking the Bible would be the place to find answers about this pesky killing of Harlan Bloom."

"Don't be so sure." Paladin held up his copy of the *Blood Children* script. "There's a bunch of Biblical stuff in here that you're going to enjoy reading. Except it's all different in this earlier Mesopotamian version than what we find in the Bible. I'll bet you didn't know that Adam and Eve were created in a laboratory in Northern Iraq, did you? From Neanderthals– by mixing their dumb DNA with the essence of the gods to create a new man that would make a good slave. That sort of thing– this screenplay is full of it. Cain and Abel; Noah's Ark . . . it's all here. And in a whole new package . . . ready for the silver screen."

"So is this all a bunch of crap, or are you thinking people are actually going to pay money to see the movie?" asked Victor.

"It's revolutionary, so it's not going to sit well with some people. But it's certainly interesting. Different, I guess would be the right word."

Victor was ready to get to the point. "You're supposed to be an investigator . . . so tell us something we don't already know. Theresia told us the other day that there's a bunch of Genesis– type mythology in the script, but what does any of that have to do with the death of Harlan Bloom?"

Paladin was ready– he'd been doing his job. He told us about an outreach he made to Talmadge University, a private college in Philadelphia that was noted for having the largest collection of Mesopotamian artifacts and clay tablets in the world.

"I talked to the curator at Talmadge yesterday, a man named Evelyn Walthers, and I told him a few things about the screenplay. Just to see if he'd heard of the movie, and might know something. And what he said was pretty interesting. Your screenwriter Callien, it seems, is a real person. The only problem is that he lived 4500 years ago, not today. Since the mysterious Callien who wrote the movie *Blood Children* is going by that name, then either he's a really, really old guy, or else he isn't Callien at all and he picked up that name by reading it somewhere. There was a Callien back in the ancient days; he was a poet in a place called Sumer. There are some clay tablets in the collection at Talmadge that contain his writings and bear his name. He was apparently fairly well known back in his time."

"So where does that get us?"

Paladin paused for a moment before answering, and when he did speak again, his tone was deadly serious. "Where it gets us is that I don't believe for a minute that this *Blood Children* screenplay is something that our modern day Callien just dreamed up one day while he was flipping burgers over at Carl's Jr. I think he got his ideas from someplace– from some ancient tablets is my guess. So I asked the Talmadge guy about that– whether he was aware of any old writings by Callien that had themes like we find in *Blood Children*. And what do you suppose happened? All of a sudden our friendly and helpful curator got all flustered and tongue tied. All of a sudden he wasn't such an expert after all– but he gave me the name of another group to follow up with– have you ever heard of the Mezo Institute?"

None of us knew the name, so Paladin filled us in. "The Mezo Institute is based in New York. On East 78th Street. They operate a museum there– and it turns out that Mezo is the leading organization in the world for the collection and translation of Mesopotamian cuneiform clay tablets, particularly the ancient Sumerian writings. They have hundreds of thousands of these things; all dug up in the Iraqi desert over the past 150 years or so.

"For a long time, the experts couldn't figure out the language– they couldn't tell us at first what the writings meant, but after awhile they began to catch on. About a hundred thousand tablets have been translated so far, and they're working on more of them all the time. Mezo has a whole staff of translators who do nothing else but decipher Sumerian tablets and translate them into English. That's how the Callien poems were found."

"So did you find some tablets that tie in to the script for *Blood Children*?"

"The short answer is no," said Paladin. "At least not yet. But I was just scratching the surface in my initial phone call with these Mezo people. There's a lot more we need to find out– particularly because if you look at the Mezo website, they explain very proudly how most of the archeological digs that are going on in Iraq today are funded and carried out by Mezo teams. It's like these people from Mezo took over the whole country after the Iraq War, and nobody else is doing anything on the archaeological sites. Mezo has the money, and they're controlling the whole process from digging these things up all the way through translating the tablets and placing them in museums or storage locations. No other group is even close. If the screenplay came from Sumerian tablets, then Mezo is where we're going to find them."

"Where does their money come from?" I asked, with genuine curiosity.

Frank Paladin was smiling again, but his eyes were cold. "You'd never guess. It turns out that our friends at Mezo are funded by none other than LawbridgeTrimble, Ltd. Do you know them?"

We all nodded our heads yes. Everyone knew LawbridgeTrimble back in those days before SHTF.

"Well LawbridgeTrimble is also the owner of Turn of the Century Bank. It looks to me like the same investment banking firm that was pushing Harlan Bloom around through Turn of the Century is also the owner of the Mezo Institute. I can't tell you what LawbridgeTrimble's direct involvement is, but it sure seems like more than a coincidence to me."

The lawyers pondered Paladin's point, and he moved on to the rest of his report.

"I stopped by to see the wreckage down at the LA County Sheriff's garage. It looks like what you'd expect– a Porsche Carrera all crumpled up like an accordion in the front end. We're talking about a head– on crash here, and obviously a high speed impact. I wasn't surprised by what I saw– but I was surprised by what I learned about the car chase. The two cops in the Sheriff's Department responsible for the investigation think there might have been a second car involved. Three different witnesses describe a dark gray sedan with no markings driving fast up Cahuenga not far behind Bloom's car. The Sheriff's Department officers don't know what to make of it. It wasn't a police unit from LAPD or the Sheriff's office, so they're assuming it wasn't a police chase at all. They think it might have been some sort of street drag racing maybe. Or perhaps there was no connection between the two cars. The Sheriff's deputies I talked to said they don't have enough information to suspect foul play– so they're telling the news people it was an accident. I don't think they're entirely comfortable with that story– but it's what they're going with for now."

"That seems odd," said Victor with a quizzical look on his face. "And it confirms Theresia's story, that's for sure. Sounds to me like someone else was involved that night. And from what Theresia says, they're either some kind of plainclothes cops, or private security types."

Paladin explained that he was still at early stage, and he would need to do a lot more investigation if we were ever going to get to the bottom of what happened. He had some recommendations.

"First, you should all read the screenplay. I'm convinced this screenplay– one way or another– had something to do with Harlan Bloom's death. Theresia says Bloom got all caught up with these bankers, and when you look at the script you'll understand why. Anyone who thinks of himself as one of the Overlords isn't going to like what he sees in this movie– it's subversive stuff, no doubt about it.

"Second, I'd like to arrange a trip for Victor and me to go out to New York and Philadelphia and meet with the people from Mezo and Talmadge University. I can't get any kind of good read on those people if we don't go out there and see them in person. I think they know more than what they were willing to tell me on the phone– we need to sit them down face to face for some serious conversation about what's going on here.

"And the last thing is that I'd like to bring in an expert. A specialist in accident reconstruction– I've worked with him in the past, and he's the best in the country. He works out of Des Moines, Iowa, and I've already spoken to him. He's interested in the case, but he needs to take a look at the wreckage to learn anything. So I'd like to bring him out here. His name is David Kincaid, and as far as I'm concerned we should get him on a plane in the next few days so he can nose around before the evidence starts disappearing. Give me the OK, and I'll bring him on board."

We gave Paladin the OK.

VI.

Barbara Langsden had reached the end of the line– literally. She was doing some family food shopping at her neighborhood food store– the upscale Ralphs on Beach Street in San Lomas– but she faced a problem. And the problem was money. Barbara Langsden was trying to put together a week's worth of food for her husband and two children, but she only had $42.91 in her purse. That was her entire bankroll . . . anywhere. Barbara Langsden had run flat out of money.

Standing in the checkout line, she quickly tabulated the total bill for the paltry collection of food items in her cart, and what she found was that her tab was coming in about $20 over. Even with some relief from the food coupons in her purse, she wasn't going to make it– so she pulled out of the line and moved to a nearby open aisle to decide on the next step. Credit card? No, all the cards in her purse were maxed out. Write a check? Nope– the family checking account was already overdrawn. Call her husband at home and have him come down with some extra cash? Bad idea– Scott was out of work, and hadn't had a paying client in his architecture practice for more than three months. No help there. So Barbara did the only thing she could– she began removing items from her cart one at a time until she was back within the limit of her small reserve of cash. She left the store with a single bag of groceries and 73 cents remaining in her wallet. But her family would eat for a few more days at least.

Being flat broke was something entirely remote from anything Barbara Langsden had ever experienced in her thirty eight years. Barbara was the second daughter of middle class parents, an attractive and well-mannered woman who grew up in a time of what appeared on the surface to be ample family wealth. Her father complained about taxes, of course, but the family had lived in a nice house in Costa Merra. Until their recent bankruptcy when their house lost all its value, Barbara's parents had always seemed to be the model of prudent financial planning.

The house in Costa Merra was gone now, and pretty much everything her parents had ever owned was gone with it. Barbara and Scott had taken her parents in at their home in San Lomas for a couple of years, but once Scott lost his job at the architectural firm the family strains became too great. Barbara's parents had moved out– and she didn't know where they were living at the moment. With friends, Barbara hoped. It hurt to be out of touch with her parents, but Barbara knew there was nothing she could do to help them. Or for that matter, help herself.

Everything had seemed to be moving in the right direction even as recently as two years before. The house on Alta Vista was still looking good as an investment– Scott and Barbara had paid $1.9 million for the house with 20% down and they'd managed to do a refinancing and pull some cash out. It all seemed possible on their two salaries– Scott at the architectural firm and Barbara as a successful mortgage broker at Turn of the Century Bank. But then the crash came– and everything changed. The Alta Vista house was suddenly worth only $1.2 million, with a mortgage against it for $1.7. The Langsdens– like so many other middle class families of the time– were underwater, with no way out. And when Scott lost his job, it was over for them. They couldn't make mortgage payments without an income to count on, and the bank started foreclosure proceedings. Barbara and Scott Langsden had only a few months left before the house would be sold. Then they would be in the street, with two children and no place to go.

Barbara knew she wasn't alone in her predicament. Many of her loan customers at Turn of the Century were in the same boat she was. Hundreds of families in the coastal area around San Lomas were in foreclosure on their once–prized homes. Their pleasant community had turned into a living nightmare, and there was no end in sight.

Barbara had started up a network for meetings and discussion sessions with her underwater loan customers . . . but none of them had a clue about what could be done. She spoke to a couple of local lawyers– but they said a loan is a loan, and it needs to be paid back. Nothing encouraging there. She talked to the people at the bank– they were all smiles, and had lots of pleasant words, but the bottom line was that either she and Scott bring their mortgage current or they would lose the house. The bank held a mortgage, so the Alta Vista house belonged to them. End of story.

Or was it? Barbara Langsden discovered an unusual website one day while she was surfing the net looking for ideas. It was a social network blog, and the name of the site was EndtheBailouts. Barbara Langsden was seeing something new here. Something she wasn't hearing from the lawyers, or the bankers, or the TV talking heads . . . or anyone. The usual sources were all saying the same thing– pay up, or get out. But EndtheBailouts had a different message. One blog piece in particular caught Barbara Langsden's eye. It was written by an author who called himself ETB. Here's what he had to say:

CREATING MONEY OUT OF THIN AIR

Have you ever considered where your friendly neighborhood banker got the money he loaned to you for purchase of your house? You probably think the loan dollars were sitting there waiting for you in a closely guarded bank vault– ready to be extracted from safekeeping and handed over to fund your mortgage loan once you signed on the dotted line. That's probably what you were thinking all right . . . but you couldn't have been more mistaken.

There were no dollars sitting around in the bank vault. In fact, the bank never loaned you anything at all when you took out your mortgage and handed over the rights to your future income. It was all just a banker trick, and you were the sucker who fell for it. You gave the bankers a mortgage on your house– a legal right to foreclose and kick you out if you didn't make payments on your so–called loan. But what did the bankers give you in return? Nothing. That's what the bankers gave you when you took out your loan . . . nothing. They never funded your loan. They didn't put up anything of their own. Your friendly neighborhood banker never puts up anything of his own when he makes a loan to a borrower. Instead, he creates the loan dollars out of thin air! From nowhere! With a simple accounting entry on the books of the bank! It's . . . magic!

The very act of signing you up for a mortgage makes the bank a whole lot richer. That's because they're able to conjure up brand new money out of thin air, and use that new money to fund your loan. The new money comes from no one. The new money comes from nowhere. A banker's loan dollars appear from the mists– the money doesn't exist at all until the instant the banker makes the loan. Money from nothing– loaned to you at interest. Quite a nice business . . . for the bankers. But not for you.

I suspect you've never heard anything like what I just told you. Well the reason you've never heard about it is because our leaders in finance, and law, and politics don't want you to hear about it! Creating money out of thin air is a banker scam . . . and the greatest fraud in all recorded history. Our wealthy bankers and the political leaders who benefit from the scam don't like it at all when ordinary people figure out what's happening, so they keep real quiet about it. As long as we don't know what they're doing, their fraud can go on and on. Forever.

But every once in awhile, ordinary people do catch on, and they spread the word. One of the most famous unveilings occurred in a court case known as *First National Bank of Montgomery versus Jerome Daly.* Martin V. Mahoney was the Presiding Justice of the Peace in the case, and it went to a jury in Minnesota back in December, 1968. You can check it out for yourself on the Internet– it's all there waiting for you if you simply take the time to look. Justice Mahoney ruled that a bank creating and loaning money out of thin air had no legal right to foreclose. He threw the bankers out of court. Why? Because in the now–famous words of Justice Mahoney, the banker practice of creating money from nothing "sounds like fraud to me."

A shocked jury agreed, and Justice Mahoney ruled that actual and legal consideration must be tendered by the bank if it's going to claim some right to foreclose on a loan. Money out of thin air just didn't measure up. In the words of Justice Mahoney: "The money and credit first came into existence when they created it . . . The jury found there was no lawful consideration and I agree. Only God can create something of value out of nothing." End of case.

> Nothing much has changed in the years since Justice Mahoney's decision in 1968. Business as usual by the "money out of thin air" bankers is still going on, and banks are foreclosing on fraudulent loans every day. Want to put a stop to the scam? Join with us; send me an email at etb@endthebailouts. I'll get back to you about what can be done, and how we can do it.

* * *

Barbara Langsden read this blog piece over and over again. She did some Internet research of her own– googling "Credit River, Justice Mahoney" and sure enough she found the actual court records from the Minnesota case. So didn't the same logic used by Justice Mahoney apply to her foreclosure circumstance– today? Barbara knew she had to find out.

On the night after her trip to Ralphs, Barbara Langsden clicked "New Email" on her computer and sent a note to ETB at EndtheBailouts. She might have reached the end of the line financially, but Barbara Langsden wasn't the kind of woman who would lay down for the bankers without a fight.

VII.

The Sheriff's Department garage on Western Avenue was a grimy and dusty place– not a spot you would want to be on a January day in Los Angeles. Frank Paladin had been on the phone all morning with his contacts in the department to get access to the Porsche wreckage, and his efforts had finally paid off. Paladin, Desert and David Kincaid arrived at the garage promptly at 2:00 p.m., and after yet another round of phone calls to get verification, the Deputy in charge led the investigators to a corner location in the bustling facility that was loosely secured with yellow hazard tape. Inside the closed–off area the three men could see the crumpled remains of a white Porsche Carrera. It was the Harlan Bloom death car.

Victor Desert was glad he'd left his suit coat in the Jag. Once the group was inside the hazard tape, Victor loosened his tie and watched with interest as Kincaid opened his oversized briefcase. The expert took a handheld device of some kind out of the case, and attached it to an electrical cord which he plugged into an outlet on the back wall of the garage. Paladin lent a hand as David Kincaid ran the lengthy cord to the door on the driver's side of the car.

The door was stuck– the front and side panels of the Porsche were crumpled from the crash. Finally, after a lot of coaxing and hard effort by the two men, the door was sufficiently ajar to allow Kincaid to access the interior. Once inside, he ignored the visible components, choosing instead to lie flat on his back on the floor of the car in front of the driver seat. His head and shoulders were pointed in the direction of the damaged front end, and he was able from this awkward position to see behind the dashboard. His lighting came from a military style flashlight that had emerged from his bag of tools.

It didn't take long for Kincaid to locate what he was looking for. Reaching into the area above his head, Kincaid used the USB port connector of his handheld device to marry with some interior component of the vehicle which wasn't visible to Victor standing outside the car. Suddenly, the device in Kincaid's hand lighted up, and a stream of codes flowed across a screen on the unit. The streaming code display continued for about thirty seconds, then the screen went blank.

Kincaid disconnected his handheld device from underneath the dash, and extricated himself– with considerable difficulty– from the floor of the Porsche. He crawled out of the semi–open driver's side door, and stood next to Victor and Paladin for a moment while he stored his equipment away in the briefcase. Next, he took a well–used camera from the case and moved gracefully around the car to capture photos of the wreck from all angles. After the photo shoot Kincaid turned to his companions and said,

"We can go now. I've done everything I need here." The inspection of Harlan Bloom's car had taken only ten minutes.

David Kincaid had been in Los Angeles for less than a day. Paladin had met him at the airport the night before the garage visit, and the two men connected up with Victor for dinner at San Terra's on Canon Drive in Beverly Hills. Victor's first impression of Paladin's expert was less than favorable– the lawyer was not excited by the sight of a such a young man sitting across the dining room table. In Victor's view, an expert witness should have gray hair and gravitas– Kincaid looked like he just came from a high school band practice.

In fact, David Kincaid was young– only 29, and he wore a simple sports shirt and slacks of the sort one buys at the discount pile in the local Walmart. Small in stature– he was no more than five feet four inches tall– David Kincaid was about as unprepossessing in appearance as anyone could possibly be. Only his bright and sparkling eyes set him apart from the ordinary man in the street. Victor felt a keen sense of disappointment– but Paladin's recommendation carried considerable weight, and the lawyer elected to reserve judgment about his dinner companion.

"So I hope you had a pleasant flight," said Victor.

"Very nice, thank you. I don't get a lot of occasion to fly anymore, so I took the opportunity to immerse myself in a good book. Herman Wouk's novel *The Lawgiver*– have you read it?"

Victor had no idea who Herman Wouk was. "Too bad," said Kincaid. "He actually was quite a noted author back in his day. *The Caine Mutiny* was his breakout book– terrific movie too, with Humphrey Bogart, and Fred MacMurray. One of the greatest movie lines ever– the lawyer played by Jose Ferrer turns to the MacMurray character and says 'Here's to the *real* author of the Caine Mutiny'– then he throws a glass of wine in MacMurray's face." Kincaid's eyes sparkled at the long ago movie memory.

But Victor could only say, "I don't think I've seen it."

"Of course. From a different era. Anyway, Wouk went on to write some other great novels– *Marjorie Morningstar* and *Youngblood Hawke*– and he just kept on writing after that. He wrote *The Lawgiver* when he was 97 years old, and it's all about life in the crazy world of a Hollywood movie. I'd think you might find the book interesting. Anyway, I'm happy to say that my pleasant little airplane ride provided an opportunity to read it. With so many people my age sitting around doing nothing, it's a relief to find an oldie like Herman Wouk writing a book at the age of 97. If a few more of us would stand up and actually do something about the problems in this country, we could get things turned around easily, so seeing a 97 year old man still being active like that was just what I needed to put me in the right frame of mind for a new assignment."

Kincaid told Victor and Paladin about his background as the three men waited for dinner to be served. He'd been working for the National Security Agency since he graduated from college, filling various top secret positions. At first he was a true believer– fighting for freedom and democracy as part of the global war on terror. After a time, however, that initial warm feeling about what he was doing fell away and Kincaid began to see his activities for what they truly were.

He stopped being a tool to the regime– one day he just stood up and quit. David Kincaid went home to Des Moines and started his own investigative firm. His experience as an intelligence operative had given Kincaid exactly the training he would need as an accident reconstructionist where foul play or cover–up was suspected. He turned out to be what Frank Paladin said he was– a unique genius in the business of determining how accidents actually happened.

"So what will you be looking for tomorrow when we see the wreckage?" asked Victor.

Kincaid smiled. "Nothing visible. Anything we're going to learn about this accident will come off the telematics."

"And those are . . .?" Victor wasn't familiar with the term.

"Onboard ECU computers– electronic control units– there are probably 70 or so in a Porsche Carrera that manage the various operating and communications components in the car. The telematics record will tell us whether there was any sort of compromise in integrity of the electronic devices."

"Are you saying you're going to be able to read the onboard computers? And that the telematics might have some useful information about how the accident happened?"

"Well, I don't know what I'm going to find, of course. . . . Who can say at this point what sort of damage occurred to the ECUs in the crash. But basically what you say is right– if we can access the telematics and read the operating output from the electronic control units we'll get a pretty good idea about how the accident came about."

Victor had never heard anything like this before. "How on earth do you get access to electronic control units– is that the right term? – in a car that's been involved in a high speed, head–on crash?"

"Actually, it's not complicated at all. I'll be doing exactly the same thing your Jaguar mechanic does when you take your car in for servicing. There's an entry port under the dash of all modern cars that provides access to the internal automotive networks. It's called the Onboard Diagnostics Port– OBD–II is the technical name– and assuming I can plug into the port and run my download software system I'll be able to track everything that's happened to the car since the day Harlan Bloom drove it off the showroom floor. It's all there, and just waiting to be accessed. Of course, the key is that my software will interpret the data for me so it doesn't just read like a bunch of gibberish. My software will need to figure out what the ECUs are telling me– otherwise I won't be much use to you, I'm afraid.

But I'm pretty confident about this case. A crash where there's no fire usually leaves the telematics record in readable condition."

"What are you going to be looking for? Can you find what caused the accident by a readout of the ECUs?" Victor was keenly interested by this point.

Kincaid looked at Victor Desert quizzically, and said with a smile: "Isn't that the reason I'm here?"

* * *

Over coffee, the conversation turned to the financial system, and David Kincaid talked for awhile about his views on the economy. Kincaid, it turned out, had a wealth of knowledge on the subject of survival in a collapse scenario.

"A lot of people these days call themselves survivalists, or preppers, or something cute like that– but most of them are a bunch of boobs who won't last more than a couple of months once the electrical grid goes down. They're stocking up on food, and they've bought a first aid kit to keep in the basement, but once the electricity stops working, they're finished. Urban survivalists think they'll be OK in their McMansions, but they're living in a dream world. I was just reading the other day about a guy and his wife in Orange County who have a nice big house, and what they've done is replant their flower beds in raised boxes off the ground around the perimeter of the McMansion. Their planters are bulletproof, and by raising them up like that, they think they've gained some extra protection for a firefight. These people are nuts, I'm telling you."

"So what should people be doing when TEOTWAWKI comes?"

"Not bad . . . not bad at all," Kincaid was smiling. "You're up to date on the prepper lingo."

"I try to keep my finger on the pulse," said Victor. "Need to be ready when the world goes all WROL."

Kincaid pondered for a moment: "Got me with that," he said.

"Without Rule of Law," said Victor, happy to add a little something of his own in a conversation where he was feeling out of his element.

"Good one. So anyway, when the shit hits the fan all their prepper supplies, and storehoused food, and tinfoil hats will be used up in a matter of weeks. Then what? Most of the survivalists still believe somewhere in their heart of hearts that the big boys in the system are going to bail them out if things get really serious. Despite all their talk about anarchy and such, most of the preppers don't grasp that the saviors aren't going to be there; the whole thing is actually going to collapse for real, and there's going to be nothing that any so–called leader can do about it. The survivalists who storehouse food are thinking the crash is going to be something that causes trouble for a little while, but then pretty soon the problems will go away and the regime will get us all back to what we were before. Absolute nonsense."

"So what do you think is going to happen?" Victor was genuinely interested in what Kincaid would have to say– the visitor had obviously given the topic some considerable thought.

"It's going to be the breakdown of money that triggers it. That's always the way– take a look at your history. All the great wars are Banker Wars, and the collapse cycle we're seeing today has happened over and over again whenever the financial system of the era falls to pieces. The difference this time is that the breakdown will be worldwide– it's going to be bigger . . . and people will be dying everywhere. By the billions they'll die . . . including at least tens of millions right here at home."

Victor pondered the dark vision offered by his dinner companion. "What are you doing to get ready?"

"My family has a farm outside Des Moines. We grow corn, and a bunch of other crops. We have eleven water wells on the property, and there are a fair number of animals. We've tried to set things up with all the essentials we'll need to be self-sufficient on the land. It may not mean anything in a truly worldwide collapse, but it's the best anyone can do."

"Do you actually believe things will get that bad?"

"Take a look around. Can Los Angeles survive a breakdown? Of course not. Or our grandiose nation's capital in Washington DC? Not a chance– Washington will be one of the first to go. Civilization is a fragile thread, and once the food, and water, and power stop flowing into our cities your beloved legal system in all its glory will disappear in an instant of time. That's when our preppers will learn what survivalism truly means. Because if they're still hanging around in LA or any of the other big cities when the time comes, they'll be dead."

On that happy note, Kincaid and his colleagues called it a night.

VIII.

As a name partner in the firm, it often fell to me to open a meeting and make the introductions.

"OK, I think we can get started now." I waited a moment for the people around the table to wrap up their private conversations and turn their attention to me. "I want to welcome our newcomers that I see with us today, and I know we have some investigative reports to share as well. So on behalf of Hazeltine Phillips & Blaine, let me begin by introducing myself– I'm Randolph Blaine– and now perhaps we can go around the table and each of us can identify themselves, starting here on my right with Victor."

"Victor Desert. Partner at Hazeltine Phillips & Blaine."

"Adrian Garfinkle. Associate in the law firm."

"Theresia Anjau. Actress; Ninhursag in *Blood Children*."

"Sarah Anjau. Naamah in *Blood Children*."

"Frank Paladin. Investigator."

"Bella Bloom."

"Samuel Bloom."

"Jonathan Silverstein. President of Eanna Pictures, for *Blood Children*."

"David Kincaid. Accident reconstruction."

We had gone completely around the table. "OK. Glad to have everyone here. Let me turn it over now to my partner, Victor Desert, who can bring all of us up to date on what's been done so far."

"Thank you, Randolph." Victor stood up and walked to the whiteboard at the end of the room. "Let me make just a couple of notes about what we've been doing." Victor picked up a red marker pen and began scribbling on the board.

"Our first meeting was a week ago Tuesday– the Tuesday after the New Year's holiday. Theresia came in; she gave us some background about the difficulties Harlan had been dealing with; and she raised the question whether Harlan Bloom's death was an accident in any meaningful sense of that word."

"So here are the issues." Victor had completed his list on the board, and he pointed to each red bullet point as he spoke.

"First, what was Harlan Bloom doing on New Year's Eve driving 100 miles an hour up Cahuenga Pass?"

"Second, what do we know about the car that apparently was chasing him that night?"

"Third, what does *Blood Children*, the movie, have to do with Harlan's death . . . if anything?"

"Fourth, we've heard from Theresia that Harlan was dealing with some bank debts– so what did his financial difficulties have to do with Harlan's death . . . if anything?"

"Fifth, do we have any indications of wrongdoing in connection with Harlan's death?"

"And finally, sixth, where do we go from here . . . and specifically is it worthwhile to allocate time and money to further investigate what happened that night?"

"With that, I'm going to turn things over to Frank Paladin, our lead investigator, who can fill us in on what he's found out so far. Frank . . ."

Paladin took Victor's place at the whiteboard. "Thanks, Victor. I have quite a bit to report, so let me just go ahead and take things in the order that you've posted them up here."

"All right . . . so what was Harlan Bloom doing that night? Well, we know he left Carousel at around 11:00 p.m. Despite some early news stories that said he had a high blood alcohol reading, it turns out that his reading was only .05– well within limits. The police report is completely negative on marijuana usage, so I think we can rule out intoxication as a cause of the crash. The early media reports were just flat wrong– that's my first conclusion."

"The car that was chasing him? I've talked to three witnesses that saw a second car, and they all tell pretty much the same story. The car was a dark gray sedan, with no police markings or lights. It wasn't directly behind Harlan, and wasn't going as fast as Harlan was. So maybe it was chasing him, or maybe not. The Sheriff's Deputy leading the investigation hasn't turned up anything about the car, and I don't expect he will. He's not really viewing that second car as a live issue– he thinks Harlan was simply going too fast for the conditions and lost control of his vehicle.

"At this point, we don't have anything solid about the second car, but here's what I've found out that looks interesting. We know from Theresia that the men who were harassing Harlan weren't regular LAPD cops or Sheriff's Deputies. So who were they working for? Harlan told us himself– they were Federal Reserve police. And apparently out of New York. So we have to ask the obvious question– what were they doing here in LA?

"I'm no expert about the Federal Reserve, but I did some searching and found out that they have their own Law Enforcement Units with officers deployed all around the country. Including right here in Los Angeles. The Federal Reserve office in downtown LA has a police unit, and one of the things they do is investigate threats against the bankers or the banking system itself. Remember that Harlan told Theresia about the special badges the officers showed him, and how they wore plainclothes and drove unmarked cars? Well it turns out that Federal Reserve cops are authorized to do that. They can go undercover, and wear plainclothes– pretty much anything they want. I'm highly confident that Federal Reserve police were involved in the harassment of Harlan Bloom– probably from both New York and Los Angeles."

Paladin had another point to make. "I've also looked into the possibility that private security guards were involved. Theresia tells us that she was confronted by men she believed were private, and Harlan apparently had one or more meetings with those same people. The big banking houses have a lot of bodyguards in place for their senior management, and I believe some high end private detectives– if I can use that term loosely– were likely involved in the Bloom case. Harlan was a borrower from Turn of the Century Bank here in Century City, and Turn of the Century is owned by LawbridgeTrimble. I guarantee you that if LawbridgeTrimble is involved there's going to be a private security presence. LawbridgeTrimble is completely paranoid– everyone in the investigative business knows that– and they own and operate their own nationwide investigative company, a firm called Mirrorprobe. The Mirrorprobe people are real cutting edge . . . they have all kinds of specialty units that do spook business of one kind or another, but most of all, Mirrorprobe specializes in personal security and investigative work. They're like a private army for LawbridgeTrimble and all the companies they own and operate– including Turn of the Century Bank.

"I believe Mirrorprobe people were the ones who tried to intimidate Theresia and Harlan. That would be their style. And when I say they operate like a private army, that's exactly what I mean. They have their own SWAT teams, and high tech weapons, and communications capability that ordinary police like the LAPD and the Sheriff's Department can only dream about. If Mirrorprobe was hooked up with Harlan Bloom, he would have plenty of reason to be afraid."

Paladin stopped for a moment to get a bottle of water. Then he resumed his report at the whiteboard.

"The police report doesn't really tell us much about how the accident happened. Basically, it just says the Porsche was driving east on Hollywood Boulevard, and then turned left on Highland and accelerated up Cahuenga Pass heading north. When Harlan got to the freeway underpass his car swerved off the road to the right and hit a concrete abutment head on. Harlan apparently died instantly on impact."

Paladin paused to let his comments thus far sink in. The people around the conference room table were looking at him with full attention.

"Now we come to another really puzzling part– how does the movie tie in to Harlan's death? Theresia tells us that the bankers from Turn of the Century were giving Harlan Bloom a hard time about *Blood Children*, ordering him to drop out of the project . . . treating him like they owned him and they could just boss him around– that sort of thing. That sure sounds like LawbridgeTrimble to me, but what would be the reason why they would care?

"The explanation I've come up with is that LawbridgeTrimble, for some reason, doesn't want this *Blood Children* movie to be completed and released. They may well have thought that it would be a death blow to the film if Harlan couldn't complete the shoot. They were wrong, as it turns out, but my hypothesis is that they actually believed the film would have to shut down if Harlan pulled out. This doesn't mean they murdered him– I'm not ready to draw that kind of conclusion– but I do believe they thought the film would be knocked off track without Bloom." Paladin turned to the movie producer for comment, "Jonathan– what's your view on that?"

Jonathan Silverstein was less than thrilled to find himself in a room full of lawyers and investigator types. But he was a pro, and he didn't hesitate to step up and speak to Paladin's question. "I don't know what the LawbridgeTrimble people might have been thinking, but the bottom line where the movie is concerned is that we're going to be able to complete the filming without Harlan. We're actually much further along than anyone outside the production might have believed– we've been keeping the shoot under wraps. The movie is going ahead, and nothing is going to stop it."

Paladin picked up again with his report after Silverstein was finished. "In looking at why Harlan Bloom found himself being pushed around, I think it has something to do with a nonprofit foundation out of New York known as the Mezo Institute.

"Mezo is shorthand for Mesopotamia– cute, huh– and the Institute arranges for archaeological permits and provides funding for nearly all the important dig locations that have been a source of discoveries in Sumer over the past forty years. Mezo collects the artifacts in Iraq; they catalogue the pieces; and then they warehouse these treasures in the hands of interpreters and experts at Talmadge University in Philadelphia. Talmadge has the largest collection of Sumerian historical pieces in the world– by far. The Iraq National Museum is second, and the British Museum is third– but those locations are actually rather modest compared to the Mezo collection at Talmadge."

"So now I come to the important part. Our modern day Callien, it turns out, didn't prepare his screenplay from the ground up. He had a model– your screenwriter took a poem consisting of twelve clay tablets written by an ancient author named Callien, and converted it into the script for your movie about Enki and Enlil. My conclusion is that the essence of *Blood Children* was initially recorded by the ancient Callien back in 2500 BC."

Theresia spoke up. "How can you be so sure? Maybe the screenplay simply talks about some of the same events that the ancient Callien wrote about separately. How can you necessarily tie the two together?"

"Excellent question," said Paladin. "And the reason I'm so sure is because I found an article from about two years ago that spoke in detail about the tablets. I compared what the article said with what I found from reading the movie script, and there are some close matches– it isn't coincidence or chance. Your screenwriter was drawing from a translation of the twelve tablets."

Paladin had a handout that he passed around to the group. "Here's the article I found. It's from the *Journal of Middle Eastern Studies*– it went defunct, not long after this article. Most of you are familiar with the screenplay– take a few minutes to read the article, and you'll see what I'm talking about where similarities are concerned."

Paladin sat down to relax while the group read the *Journal* article. This is what they saw:

A TALE OF THE ANCIENT BLOOD CHILDREN
By Karen Ashley

Mark Greenlee is a Senior Fellow at the Mezo Institute who specializes in the process of deciphering and translating ancient Mesopotamian cuneiform writings. Hundreds of thousands of clay tablets containing these writings have been located in the desert sands of modern day Iraq, and Mark Greenlee is one of a small group of experts who understand the language and can tell us what these ancient writings actually have to say. Most of the writings Greenlee works with date back to 2500 BC or thereabouts, and describe events that occurred in the first great civilization– the place we now know as Sumer. Our own Karen Ashley recently sat down with Mark Greenlee at the Mezo Institute offices in Manhattan to talk about his latest discoveries.

Ashley: Mr. Greenlee, good morning. We appreciate your taking the time to visit with us today.

Greenlee: Happy to be here, Karen.

Ashley: So I understand something quite new has come up in your work– can you tell us about it?

Greenlee: Well Karen, as you know, the Mezo Institute is a worldwide leader in deciphering ancient Sumerian cuneiform writings. The range of writings is very broad, but my personal expertise is in the translation of Sumerian poetry– the often epic tales that describe the culture of their times, and sometimes provide mythological stories about earlier days many thousands of years before the writers actually lived. We haven't found a lot of these epics– the story of Gilgamesh is probably the most famous– so when a new poem of that sort surfaces to my attention as a translator, I try to focus in on it. Most recently, I completed the translation of an epic by a poet named Callien that told the story of ancient gods and their human offspring. Callien called these people the Blood Children, and we were very fortunate in the case of the Blood Children tablets to find an entire collection in good condition. The twelve Callien tablets only recently came to light . . . and what a find they've turned out to be.

Ashley: What was it about the Blood Children tablets that caught your interest?

Greenlee: Think of the Hollywood saying about the requirements for a good movie script: it's content, content and content. That's what I found in the Blood Children tablets– interesting content, and lots of it. Callien's writings track quite closely to stories found in Biblical Genesis, but place a unique perspective on the familiar stories which causes the reader to think about them in a different way than is typically encouraged by establishment religious scholars. It's quite a challenging experience– seeing the familiar tales of Genesis recorded on clay tablets thousands of years before the Bible was written, and interpreted in an entirely different way.

Ashley: So give me an example– are you saying that the Callien tablets contradict the Bible?

Greenlee: Not at all– I'm telling you that Callien's writings affirm what we see in Biblical Genesis. Callien describes the creation of man in terms that will be readily familiar to anyone who has read Genesis. Let's consider the Biblical story of man in the Garden of Eden, for example. The Bible tells us that man was placed in the garden to be a worker– "to dress the garden and keep it"– and Callien's tablets use similar phrasing. Also like the Bible, Callien writes about knowledge of good and evil in his Blood Children poem. Biblical Genesis tells us that God commanded man that he was not to eat of the tree of knowledge of good and evil . . . on penalty of death. The Blood Children tablets also say that the god of the garden denied his human creations access to knowledge of good and evil, so we see striking parallels in the factual basis for the stories. Where Callien stands apart is in his interpretation of the events. Callien depicts early man as a slave, and he says it was wrong for Enlil and his Igigi to create man as a lesser being whose only purpose was to serve as an unknowledgeable worker for the benefit of the gods themselves.

Ashley: Isn't it inconsistent with Biblical Genesis for Callien to speak in terms of multiple gods as opposed to a single Supreme Being?

Greenlee: Not if you accept Genesis in its own words. In Genesis 1, the Bible says that man was made "in our image, and after our likeness," and most Biblical scholars now agree that the stories of Genesis were drawn from earlier writings that were shortened and modified when they were placed in the Bible. The ancient tradition of multiple gods still existed in the minds of the scribes at the time the Bible was written.

Ashley: You've mentioned Enlil, and the Igigi. Who were the other gods that played a role in the creation process?

Greenlee: In Callien's telling, there were two gods involved: half–brothers known as Enki and Enlil. Callien tells us that a council of the gods– the Overlords of their time– collectively decided that they needed some cheap labor to build canals, and work the mines, and create the cities of Sumer back in the early days. The Overlords were getting tired of doing all the hard work themselves, so they came up with the idea of creating a slave worker– what Callien called an Eljo– to take over the burden. The new creature would be less than the gods, but a big step up from its beastly predecessors. Enki was their greatest scientist so the council put him in charge of creation, and there we find Callien's version of the story of Adam. What differs from Biblical Genesis is the motivation and intent of the gods.

Ashley: So what does Callien have to say about Eve?

Greenlee: Again, the creation of Eve in Callien's tale is comparable to what we see in the Bible. In Biblical Genesis, Eve was cloned– it's the story of Adam's rib as told in the Bible. In Callien's telling, Enki created Eve through a somewhat similar process, but then we come to the part of the Blood Children tablets that truly sets them apart from Genesis. Enki, it seems, wasn't happy with the idea of creating a race of slaves. He felt compassion for his human creations, and he wanted the Eljo to have the opportunity to upgrade themselves and eventually leave behind the lowly status that Enlil and his Igigi had in mind for them. As recorded in Genesis 4, Eve herself tells us what happened next . . . she says: "I have gotten a man from the Lord!" Eve was impregnated with the "essence" of one of the higher gods– an "essence" implanted in Eve's womb by Enki as part of his effort to elevate mankind above the status of slaves. In Callien's telling, Eve's firstborn son Cain was a child of the high blood– standing well above the lesser sons Abel and Seth. Cain was created by Enki to frustrate Enlil's plan for a slave race.

Ashley: But didn't Cain turn out to be one of the great villains in Biblical Genesis? He killed his own brother.

Greenlee: His half–brother, actually. Cain was not the son of Adam– he carried the "essence" of a high blood god chosen by Enki. But your point is well taken– Cain and his offspring are vilified in the Bible– even though Genesis tells us that these descendants were the builders of early cities and the creators of the civilized world of their time. Again, we find an interpretation by Callien which differs from the Bible where the story of Cain and Abel is concerned. In Callien's version, Cain was hated by Enlil, the Overlord god who knew that Enki had created Cain to foil his plan for a race of slaves. When Cain killed his brother in response to Enlil's taunting, Enki was disappointed, and he realized that Cain wasn't strong enough on his own to raise mankind above the level of the Eljo. Something more was needed, so Enki took the next crucial step. Callien tells us in the Blood Children tablets that the young Enki and the high blood goddess Ninhursag had a child together, a daughter they named Luluwa. The goddess Luluwa was the highest of all high bloods, and after Cain had killed Abel, Enki shielded him from the wrath of Enlil by giving him Luluwa as his wife. The goddess Luluwa became the Biblical "mark of Cain" that we find discussed in Genesis– she was Cain's salvation and protector. Because of Luluwa, the descendants of young Enki and Ninhursag would forever after be known as the Blood Children– the hope of mankind living down through the ages.

Ashley: Does Callien tell us where the creation process took place?

Greenlee: Not directly, but I think we can piece things together pretty easily from some of the clues in the Blood Children tablets. The creation chamber was a manmade structure– a laboratory identified in the writings as the Shem iti, which translates literally as the 'House Where the Wind of Life Is Breathed In.' Callien tells us that the Shem iti was in the mountains, with access to a ready supply of clean water. Since the whole purpose of the laboratory was to create a slave race for Enlil and his Igigi, the mountain location was surely near to Mesopotamia– the place where the newly created slaves would do their work. This almost certainly leads us to the Zagros Mountains and a remote area of northern Iraq that is now known as modern day Kurdistan.

The other thing needed, of course, was a supply of Neanderthals to be utilized in the creation process. The Zagros Mountains were the home to many of these creatures; the Neanderthals were cave dwellers, and the Zagros Mountains are riddled with caves suitable for human habitation. If I were to make an educated guess about the location of the Shem iti, I would put it in the area of Shanidar Cave, a highly significant archaeological location where collections of Neanderthal skeletons have been found.

Ashley: You've told us that Callien described Enki as the friend and protector of mankind. What are the attributes that Callien ascribes to Enlil?

Greenlee: Callien's primary characterization of Enlil is that he didn't want humans to gain knowledge, and particularly the knowledge of good and evil. As long as mankind accepted their servitude and obeyed their masters without question they could continue to live and their material needs would be met. But there was one unpardonable sin where Enlil was concerned: mankind was forbidden to eat from the tree of knowledge, because knowledge was the thing that set the gods apart from their slave creations. Knowledge of good and evil was the one attribute which would enable man to break his bonds of slavery, and the defining characteristic of Enlil was his single minded determination to maintain the slaves as a lesser race; unknowledgeable, and beneath the gods.

Ashley: Our guest today has been Mark Greenlee, Senior Fellow at the Mezo Institute and a leading scholar on the times of ancient Mesopotamia. Mark, thank you for being with us.

Greenlee: My pleasure.

IX.

Sarah Anjau hadn't said anything during Paladin's report, but she was the first to comment about the *Journal* piece. "Isn't this extraordinary! Our script was actually written 4500 years ago. Bless our Callien, whoever he might be . . . he gave us a gift from the ages. I wonder where he got the translated version."

"We don't know yet," said Paladin. "In fact, there's not a whole lot we do know. I don't have any doubt our modern day Callien had access to a translation of the twelve tablets this fellow Greenlee is talking about– but how he got them . . . we don't know."

"Do you have any idea yet who Callien might be?" Theresia asked. "The modern day Callien, I mean."

"I suspect there must be some connection to Mark Greenlee, but we don't know that yet. I did make a few calls about Greenlee, but I couldn't find anything on the guy. He left Mezo a few months after this article came out, and tracing him in detail is an area where I didn't want to start spending money without authorization."

Silverstein was the man writing the checks. "How much are we talking about to do a trace on Callien and Greenlee? To make sure we have full rights to the script?"

Paladin had a plan in mind. "I think what we should do is start with Talmadge University and Mezo Institute. I've had a couple of phone calls with the curator at Talmadge, and my suggestion is that Victor Desert and I should go out east and talk to him in Philadelphia. And Mezo too . . . in New York. These are the people who had the tablets– let's find out what they have to say."

"What do you mean: *had* the tablets?" Silverstein had picked up on Paladin's careful choice of words.

"The curator at Talmadge told me he wasn't aware of any Callien tablets about Blood Children– or anything like what Greenlee describes in his *Journal* interview."

Silverstein was seeking some answers. "So what is it specifically that you propose to do? Obviously, I want to make sure that we've got proper rights to the screenplay . . . that's my number one concern. And it seems to me that we'll all feel a lot better about that if we're able to locate the author– whoever he is. I don't know how else we're going to get a comfort level strong enough to release the movie. I say that Paladin and Desert should follow up, like Frank says. Let's get to the bottom of this . . . if we can. And if we can't, at least we'll have done our due diligence on this new information, and– hopefully– that will help to protect our rights."

Sarah Anjau was confused. "Wasn't the script a gift to Theresia and me? I don't see how anyone could claim otherwise."

Victor responded with a lawyer viewpoint. "You're assuming the handwritten notes from Callien to you and Theresia are genuine. That they actually were sent by the author, and that the author himself genuinely had the right to develop the script in the first place. If Callien was drawing from intellectual property that belonged to someone else, his notes to you and Theresia won't matter. There are some legal complexities here, but basically I agree with Jonathan– I think it's worthwhile to do some further investigation and try to get to the bottom of this at Talmadge and Mezo. If the group wants me to go out to New York and Philadelphia with Frank, I'll go. And we should do it sooner rather than later, if we're going to do it at all."

"Can I come?" said Theresia with a smile. "It sounds really interesting, actually." Victor looked at the actress– was she making a suggestion? He couldn't tell. "I think they might be a bit distracted if you were to show up. Better two stiffs in suits than a movie star."

"I'm glad to hear about the film and all, but I don't understand what any of this has to do with my son." Bella Bloom had spoken for the first time in the meeting.

"Of course," said Victor. "We've spent so much time talking about the script and the Blood Children that we haven't gotten to the real meat of the report about Harlan– the very thing that brought us together in the first place. Frank, let me turn it back to you."

Paladin had been thorough in his preparation for this meeting. "We know where and when the 'accident' happened. And I use the word 'accident' in quotes– at this point we don't have anything substantive as to the cause. It may be one of those situations we've seen before– the cops try to pull someone over; he runs away; there's a high speed chase; then the runner smashes up his car and gets killed in the process. Like I say– I've seen these kinds of scenarios– so the question is whether this is one of them. Does it fit the profile? David, maybe you could tell us what you've found out so far."

David Kincaid turned first to Theresia: "Miss Anjau, could I ask you a question before I talk about my findings? It has to do with something attorney Desert said to me– that Harlan had told you about an occasion not too long ago where he was pulled over by a couple of plainclothes cops, and they made him do a sobriety test while one of them searched the interior of his car. Did that actually happen?"

"It did . . . or at least Harlan told me it did. I definitely remember the conversation– he was pretty shaken up by the whole thing. It was just a week or so before he was killed, and after that he started getting really paranoid . . . with good reason, as it all turns out."

"Do you by any chance remember the date when it happened?"

I remember exactly when it happened. Harlan took me out to dinner the week before Christmas. It was December 22nd– Harlan and I had dinner at La Pastiche, and he told me the thing happened on his way home after dinner."

David Kincaid smiled slightly and turned to the group, all of whom were looking at him with close attention waiting to hear what he had to say.

"Thank you, Theresia. Let me take a moment and talk about why the date is important. As most of you probably already know, Frank and attorney Desert were able to get me in to see the wreckage of the Porsche at the Sheriff's garage over on Western Avenue. It was pretty smashed up– the front end was all crumpled in– here are some pictures I took of the wreckage." Kinkaid passed around his photographs.

"But the relevant point in this investigation isn't the condition of the wreckage– we know how the accident happened. What matters is *why* the event happened in the manner that it did. Why did he lose control of the car so that it smashed into the freeway abutment? Answer that question, and we'll know what we need to know about the death of Harlan Bloom."

The listening group waited expectantly while Kincaid took a few moments to boot up his laptop computer.

"At the garage, I was able to connect with the Porsche telematics through the Onboard Diagnostics Port. Nothing magical about it– OBDs have been standard since the 1990s. But the more complex our cars have become, the more onboard systems there are, and the more our basic inputs to operate the vehicle are computer controlled through electronic signals. It's supposed to work without the driver even knowing what's happening . . . and most of the time that's exactly the way it occurs. You apply the brakes, and the braking system computer sends out its message to the operating components. Same for the steering, and the gas pedal, and dozens of other things that cause the car to operate in the way that it does. The telematics instruct the operating systems about what they're supposed to be doing. Many of the mechanical operations in a car these days are actually computer controlled.

"When your mechanic attaches his diagnostic equipment to your car's OBD, he actually takes control of the onboard computer systems. It's kind of like how a computer mirroring software system can take charge of your laptop from a remote location if you allow it to do so. Same thing here– a repairman can test and manipulate your car's onboard computers through the entry connection. That's how he finds out if anything is wrong."

"But doesn't that mean he has to actually be there? A repairman needs to have an actual physical connection through the OBD port to manipulate the systems." Silverstein had asked exactly the question that had come into my mind. I was beginning to get the idea of where David Kincaid was heading with this discussion.

"Quite right– when you're talking about an auto repair shop. Their equipment isn't set up for remote usage."

When I heard this, I knew for sure what was coming next.

"But there are more sophisticated systems out there that are capable of operating remote," Kincaid continued. "Systems that can interface with the onboard computers of your car even from a remote location thousands of miles away. Systems that can transmit and receive data through wireless communications technology– and can operate the onboard computers on your car through remote keyboard control. It's the same technology used in drone aircraft that are flown by wireless– your car can be operated from a distance in exactly the same way. But one thing is needed– the telematics in the car need to be programmed through implanted software to recognize and respond to the remote wireless signals. And to do that– to install the software– the person who wants to operate the vehicle remotely needs to connect physically with the OBD port for the purpose of putting the software in place. The connection point is right there under the dashboard– an installer needs about five minutes to get the software loaded. And once that's done, a remote operator can take control of the car any time he wants. His remote instructions will override whatever manual inputs the driver tries to implement."

Victor spoke for everyone in the room. "So on the night of December 22nd– when Harlan was pulled over and his car was searched– they were installing remote operating software while he was out on the pavement doing a field sobriety test."

"Exactly right," said David Kincaid. "The night of December 22nd." The expert in reconstruction had our full attention. "That was when the people who killed Harlan Bloom set up a remote control capability in his Porsche. Here's a printout with the connection date and time– 10:38 p.m." Kinkaid handed around his data record. "We know for a certainty that someone accessed Harlan's onboard system that night– and I rather strongly suspect it wasn't some auto mechanic, unless Harlan had a very special guy who did repairs at night for him on the open road.

"Of course this access record is only a starting point. We're going to need proof of an actual remote control takeover– a record of when and how it occurred, and evidence that the car was being controlled remotely at the time of the crash. If you look at my printout, you'll notice that there is no data entry indicating any sort of unusual activity in Harlan's telematics on the night of the accident. Everything looks normal."

"That sounds like a bit of a stumbling block," Victor said dryly.

"Perhaps. But we know that the latest versions of remote control software have features that erase any unwelcome footprints that might be left behind for an investigator like me to find. Or so their software creators like to believe."

"Are they wrong?" I asked.

Kincaid smiled again; he was enjoying this moment. "Of course they're wrong. My software detection system in Iowa can reconstruct the erased footprint. In my opinion, Harlan Bloom was killed by a remote control driver who took over the operation of his car and caused it to crash . . . and I'm going to prove it."

X.

Victor Desert was looking at a long day ahead as he packed his briefcase with papers he would need for the east coast trip to Talmadge University and the Mezo Institute. Victor was scheduled to catch a 1:00 p.m. flight out of LAX to New York with Frank Paladin. The *Blood Children* script sat on the corner of Victor's desk, and he put it in the briefcase. Some reading for the airplane.

Victor had one remaining appointment before he could get away from the office. ETB was bringing in a new client group today– another of his EndtheBailouts website finds. Well, Victor thought to himself, the last EndtheBailouts lead had turned out pretty good– maybe ETB was on to something with this blogging of his. Today's group had something to do with bank foreclosures– Victor wasn't up to speed on the potential new matter. He'd only received a bare bones briefing, so he headed down to the conference room a bit uncertain about what he was going to find.

Adrian Garfinkle and the client group were already there when Victor arrived. Adrian made the introductions– Scott and Barbara Langsden were with the young lawyer, along with a third person named Alan Butler who looked like an accountant type. Which is exactly what he turned out to be.

ETB asked Barbara Langsden to tell her story, and she started off slowly, obviously a bit uncomfortable in her role as spokeswoman for the group.

"Well, Scott lost his job with the architectural firm about a year ago and hasn't been able to find paying clients. And I was let go by Turn of the Century Bank six months after that. I've looked at a few things, but there's just nothing out there. I was a loan placement officer at TCB, and there isn't much of a market anymore for loans in this real estate downturn. So we're stuck– Scott and I– and the kids; and we've flat run out of money. I don't know what to do. We have a house in San Lomas that's underwater, and Turn of the Century has us in foreclosure on our mortgage. Unless something happens in the next month or so we're going to be out in the street."

"Have you tried to negotiate for an extension?"

"Of course, and the bank gave us a couple of extensions after Scott first lost his job. But we still couldn't keep up the payments. So they started up a foreclosure proceeding."

"How much do you owe, and what's the house worth?" Victor wasn't an expert on loan foreclosures, but he knew enough of the basics to ask the right questions.

"About $1.7 million is owing on the mortgage, and the house is worth probably a million two, maybe a little more than that. We bought the house for $1.9 million, but the value has dropped through the floor in this bad market. It's a great property– but there just aren't any buyers out there."

"So what can we do to help?" Victor was a bit impatient– he had to leave for the airport soon, and this case didn't sound like anything worthwhile. Suburban family gets in over its head and the bank forecloses on the house. Happens every day, Victor thought to himself.

"I came to Adrian because of a blog piece he wrote over at EndtheBailouts," said Barbara Langsden. "All about Judge Mahoney's Credit River decision, out in Minnesota, and how bankers commit a fraud every time they make a loan. It really opened my eyes."

Victor wasn't familiar with the Credit River case, and he had no idea what the woman was talking about. Adrian saw Victor's bewilderment, and the younger lawyer spoke up to cover for him. "It's a case from Credit River Township in Minnesota. The judge and jury held that a bank foreclosure could be barred because the bank had created its loan funds out of thin air . . . so there wasn't any legitimate consideration flowing from the lender. The judge ruled that the bank couldn't foreclose because the bank never put up any money at the time the loan was taken out."

"And you think we can apply that case here– in California– is that what you're saying?" Victor was speaking with some irritation in his voice– this concept about a bank not putting up money was something that Barbara Langsden and Adrian seemed to understand, but Victor wasn't grasping it.

Alan Butler spoke up in his accountant–like way. "Perhaps I could shed some light. I used to be a financial officer at Turn of the Century Bank– Barbara and I worked together for several years– and a bit of background about how bank lending actually works might help you understand what the Credit River case is about. I've read the case, by the way, and I agree completely with Judge Mahoney's analysis. Poor man."

"Poor man?"

"Yes, I'm afraid so. He was murdered six months after his decision in the case."

"Oh, I see."

"Yes, quite. It seems to happen a lot where the bankers are concerned. Those kinds of mysterious deaths, I mean. Anyway, perhaps you could tell me what you know about Turn of the Century Bank? That's the place to start."

Victor pondered for a moment. What exactly did he know . . . "well, I know they're owned by LawbridgeTrimble, the New York investment banking firm. And I know they have an office down the street here. Beyond that, they're just another bank to me."

Butler smiled at Victor's response. "Just another bank? Not in the slightest, Mr. Desert. Turn of the Century has been the banking phenomenon of the twenty first century. They first opened for business in 1999– Turn of the Century, get it?– and over the past two decades they've been the fastest growing financial institution in the world . . . by far. We did it on home loans– and particularly in the sunbelt states: California, Nevada, Arizona, Florida. All the places that crashed when the bust came. Turn of the Century led the boom . . . and they've been the main player in sweeping up houses in foreclosure during the bust."

"Is there anything wrong with that?"

"Of course there is," said Butler. "The boom was artificial, driven by the lenders, and it pushed home prices through the roof. So everyone started thinking houses were some kind of great investment instead of a place to live. When the home buying mania was at its peak, Turn of the Century was the largest source for residential mortgages in the country. We were making a fortune."

Victor still didn't see any problem with this. "OK, I'll accept what you say. But so what? What on earth is wrong with a bank making home loans? Isn't that what we want them to do?"

"Mr. Desert, I'd like you to try for a moment to put aside everything you think you know about lending, and banks, and foreclosures, and listen to what I say with an uncluttered mind. Like you're hearing about bankers for the first time. Can you do that for me?"

Victor was a bit annoyed with the pedantic tone coming from the accountant– not to mention in a hurry to get out of the meeting and catch his plane. But he managed to say the right thing: "I'll try."

Good," said Butler, warming to his task. "So first things first. Number one to understand is that banks don't actually loan you anything that actually belongs to them when you come into the bank and borrow some money. They don't go down to the vault and get a fistful of cash for you, and they don't dig into their depositor accounts and transfer over to you any depositor funds that are in checking accounts or savings accounts. Now with that in mind, let's start by asking a simple question: where does a bank get its money when it makes a loan to a borrower?"

Victor thought about it for a moment. "I can't say I know. From their reserves on hand I suppose– some loan account fund or something. At least that's what I would imagine."

"Excellent answer. You just said what 99% of all people in America would say if I asked them that same question. But if I may suggest something that might seem unusual to you, what you just said is not the way things work at all. Banks don't have 'loan account funds' or 'reserves' sitting around waiting to be loaned out to people. And even if they did have such things, that's not the source of funds they would ever use when a loan is made."

"OK. So where does their loan money come from?"

"It comes from nothing. And from nowhere. The bank creates its loan money out of thin air by making a few simple computer entries. It's their magic trick, and it's going on around us every day. We call it fractional reserve lending."

"I've heard the term," said Victor, as he began to understand the lesson, "so explain it to me– tell me how it works."

Alan Butler was up to the task. "Fractional reserve lending is exactly what its name implies: to lend money with only a fraction of the face value of the loan on reserve. For example, a bank that loans you $100 is only required to keep a reserve of $10. Hard to believe, I know, but it's actually true– a bank can loan you $100 even though it only has $10 available to stand behind the loan if anything goes wrong. Wouldn't it be nice if you could do that? Well, to the extent it's legal at all, it's a privilege that exists only for banks. If anyone else tried to get away with a scam like that they'd be immediately thrown in prison as a counterfeiter, and the judge would quite rightly throw away the key.

"The point of all this is that banks engage every day in the process of creating money out of thin air, and none of it is backed by anything meaningful at all. But it gets even worse. Once interest is added in, the price extracted from the borrower goes through the roof. Here's an example to illustrate the point: consider that a bank makes you a 'fractional reserve loan' of $100 and retains $10 in reserve as required by current Federal Reserve regulations. In real economic terms, the bank that appears to be lending you $100 is actually only lending you $10– the amount that the banker is required to reserve. This means that a 5% interest rate on the loan is actually 50%– ten times the nominal rate amount. It's the kind of return that would make a loan shark look like Mother Theresa– the mafia could never get away with it, that's for sure.

"So let's try some arithmetic from the real world to bring it all together. Let's suppose that a bank loans Barbara and Scott $1,000,000 to purchase a home on a 30–year note at 5% interest. The bank earns about $50,000 per year in interest on a loan where they only had to reserve $100,000 to begin with. And since they never put up $1,000,000 in the first place, every principal reduction payment by Barbara and Scott is pure profit to the bank. Over the total 30 year life of the loan, Barbara and Scott will pay $1,000,000 in principal and about $900,000 in interest for a loan the bank made without going out of pocket with anything at all.

"In this example, the entire $1,900,000 is profit to the bank from nothing. It illustrates the key point: that creating money is the most lucrative business in the world. So whenever you hear banks with their sanctimonious talk about the duty to pay debts, and their inviolable right to foreclose, keep in mind a simple point: why should they end up owning the house when they never put up anything of value to begin with at the time they made the loan? I'm not a lawyer, but isn't that unjust enrichment?"

Adrian chimed in: "This is what the Credit River decision was all about. Justice Mahoney heard testimony from the bank president in that case about how the bank created its loan money out of thin air, and Mahoney's words as written in the judgment were "it sounds like fraud to me."

Alan Butler summarized, "The bottom line is that banks who utilize fractional reserve lending– and all the big ones do– are counterfeiters every time they make a loan. Compare it to a personal loan: if I loan $10,000 to my son–in–law, I haven't counterfeited anything. The loan dollars came out of my pocket, and if my son–in–law doesn't pay me back, I will have suffered a real, out of pocket loss. We call that a hard money loan, and it's something completely different from a phony money bank loan. With a bank loan, the bank never put up any consideration in the first place."

Victor Desert was no dummy: "OK, I've got it."

Barbara Langsden was encouraged by Victor's reaction. "After I read Adrian's article on EndtheBailouts, I started doing some investigation of my own. It didn't take long for me to figure out that everything Alan told you is true. Back in the days when I was at Turn of the Century I was their number one loan producer, but I never knew anything about what Alan just said. I thought they were legitimate, and I was placing my loans with all the best realtors. That's how Scott and I were able to make enough income to qualify to buy our house in the first place. A top loan producer in those boom days could make $600,000 a year, or even more, and I had several years when I made that kind of money.

"I was actually chosen to be 'Miss Century' by the senior executives of the bank. Two years in a row! They would drive me around town in a Turn of the Century convertible wearing a crown and a short skirt– people flocked around like I was a movie star or something. Quite an experience– I was on top of the world."

Victor looked at Barbara Langsden closely– she was an attractive woman; he had no difficulty picturing her sitting in the back of the car. But Victor noticed that Scott Langsden was frowning as he listened to his wife describe her exploits as Miss Century. Apparently Barbara's husband hadn't enjoyed those glory days as much as his wife had.

"So after I figured this out," continued Barbara, "I decided to check with Alan. I called him a couple of weeks ago, and sure enough he told me that Turn of the Century was doing everything he just told you about. They've been doing it for years.

"All those loans I was placing for them– I had no idea they were just conjuring up the money with computer entries. I thought they were legit; and I look back now at the big run–up in house prices that all this phony money lending created, and it makes me sick to have been a part of it. My customers were my friends, and now they're losing their houses in foreclosure just like Scott and me. So I made up my mind to do something about it."

Victor waited for Barbara Langsden to continue.

"I started calling around. To my customers, and the realtors I used to deal with. To find out how many of my former loans had gone into foreclosure. I couldn't believe what I heard. There are thousands of them; underwater loans, placed by me, where the families holding the mortgages are about to be wiped out and kicked into the street by Turn of the Century. Thrown out of their houses by a gang of counterfeiters . . . it's disgusting.

"So over the past couple of weeks, I got on the phone and put a group together. I've lined up more than a hundred families so far, and I'm barely getting started. We all want to file some sort of lawsuit together to put a stop to these foreclosures, and I can promise you that once we get started there will be thousands more who'll join us. Turn of the Century was huge in Las Vegas– right there we're going to find a ton of underwater homeowners. And Phoenix . . . and more places that I haven't even thought about.

"I'd like to put a lawsuit website together, and write updates, and share ideas, and find new people to join us. One family like Scott and me probably can't stop the bankers– but I bet a thousand families would; or ten thousand; or even more. These bankers are a bunch of crooks trying to throw people into the street and steal their houses, and I'm not going to stand for it. And since Adrian was the one who got me started on this, I'd like your firm to be our lawyers."

Victor Desert thought for a long moment about what Barbara Langsden had just told him. The lawsuit she wanted to bring might cause a bunch of trouble for the bankers– but would a court actually enter a legal ruling that the system of fractional reserve lending was a scam and a fraud? It was a tall order, and Victor had no illusions about just how difficult this sort of litigation would turn out to be. And expensive. So he asked the key question, "Do you have funding? Large scale litigation against one of the richest banks in the country is going to require a lot of resources."

Barbara Langsden looked at her husband for encouragement, but his eyes were turned downward. Finally she said, "We're broke. If we get kicked out of the house, I don't even know where we could go to put a roof over our head. But there are plenty of people in our group who do have money. There were a lot of wealthy people in my service area, and I know we can get the money together that's needed. Maybe not everything you'll want, but enough to get started, at least."

"How much are you talking about?" Victor asked.

"Maybe a couple of hundred thousand from the first hundred families; maybe more if we need it. And your firm would get a partial contingency fee. No one is asking you to work for free."

Victor knew that $200,000 would barely scratch the surface for litigation funding purposes, but he decided he'd heard enough to look into it a bit more.

"Let's do this. I've got to run and catch a plane, but why don't we try to get together again next week. In the meantime, Adrian can do some research about what the courts are doing in the foreclosure cases that have been filed in California over the past couple of years and try to make a judgment about how tough this sort of lawsuit will likely turn out to be. Let's figure out if this is going to be worth the effort– then we can talk about the specifics of the money issues next week. OK?"

The meeting was over, and Victor showed the group out to the elevator lobby. As he was walking back to his office, something occurred to Victor about the events in the conference room. Something that struck Victor as very odd. Scott Langsden hadn't said a word during the entire meeting.

XI.

Talmadge University had the look of a place that was named for a Revolutionary War general. Because it was. Roger Tweed Talmadge was the second eldest son of one of Philadelphia's leading families of the day, and he was a young man with a lot to live up to. Roger's older brother, Miles Talmadge, was the first of George Washington's officers to die in the battle of New York. The elder Talmadge had been killed in a friendly fire incident when several of his inexperienced fellows had mistaken him for a British agent of some sort– the precise details were never exactly clear. But however the incident occurred, the net result was that Roger inherited the burden of carrying forward the family name.

Newly minted Brigadier General Roger Tweed Talmadge was ready and willing to take on the task of avenging his dead brother. The pursuit of military glory was the way of a Talmadge, but unfortunately for Roger, the battlefield victories he sought never seemed to come his way. A few minor skirmishes in backwater locations were the most he was able to achieve during his stint in the continental army.

The college that bears his name was founded in the year 1804. Roger Tweed Talmadge was the first school president, and not coincidentally, its largest donor. Roger founded his namesake next door to the sparkling University of Pennsylvania campus near downtown Philadelphia– a wise choice for an unknown private college seeking to make a name for itself.

The liberal arts curriculum at Talmadge was innovative for the time, and during its early years the school was able to carve out a niche in the shadow of its much more prominent neighbor. By the 1860s, however, the University of Pennsylvania had relocated to larger quarters in the suburbs, and Talmadge University was left behind to make its way on its own. Easier said than done– it never really took off after Penn had abandoned the area. Talmadge University was left in the backwater, barely scraping by on a stagnant student population and a modest group of donors.

In 1985, however, all of that changed. Like a traveling circus of old, the Mezo Institute came to town, bringing money, and scholarly people, and a whole new lease on life for Talmadge University. Just like that, the school was financially secure for the first time in decades. Mezo provided the funding to create a brand new Department of Middle Eastern Studies, and Talmadge became the leader in the field when Mezo transferred a large collection of artifacts and cuneiform tablets to the school for warehousing and scholarly analysis. It was a new day– Roger Tweed Talmadge would have been proud indeed.

* * *

Victor Desert and Frank Paladin had flown into New York the day before their scheduled meeting at Talmadge. They were staying at the Prince Hotel in midtown, a favorite of Victor's. The Spruce Bar at the Prince was an icon of old world New York that Desert found particularly intriguing. The Spruce dated back to an era of freedom, and entrepreneurship, and the Industrial Revolution– an era of wealth creation that fell by the wayside over the course of the twentieth century. The Industrial Revolution of the 1800s had helped spark the fortune of Victor Desert's early family in Millford, and he felt a strong affinity for those lost days of economic opportunity. The Spruce was from that era.

A meeting at the Mezo Institute corporate headquarters in New York was on tap for the day after the Talmadge gathering, so Victor and Paladin had elected to stay in Manhattan and catch a train to Philadelphia. Very east coast– there were no such things as city to city trains in the west anymore, except for tourist attractions. Victor and his investigator took the opportunity to climb aboard an olden days train at Penn Station for the short trip to Philadelphia, and almost before they were fully settled into their comfortable seats the two men reached their destination and were climbing into a taxi for the ride to the Talmadge campus. They arrived well before their 10 a.m. scheduled meeting with the curator, so Victor and Paladin had time for a cup of coffee in the Student Union building. The investigator brought Victor up to date on what he had put together for the day.

"Evelyn Walthers is the man's name– he oversees the middle east curriculum and the research and warehousing operation for Mezo artifacts and tablets. Walthers has been here for awhile– more than 20 years. So he knows what's going on."

"Have you actually spoken to him?" Victor asked.

"A couple of times. And I sent him the *Journal* article with the Mark Greenlee interview. Greenlee was a faculty member here at Talmadge– an adjunct professor who taught middle eastern languages. How to decipher the old tablets, that sort of thing. Walthers knew him fairly well, but he says they've lost touch since Greenlee left Mezo and Talmadge. He resigned both positions about two years ago and seems to have completely dropped out of sight."

"So what are we looking to accomplish here?"

"I'd say two things. First, of course, is to find out about the Blood Children tablets that Greenlee was talking about in his *Journal* interview. Where are they? Can we get a look at them? And where can we see a transcript of the tablets in English? These are the main questions. I told Walthers by phone that this is what we wanted, and he said he'd look into it. So we'll see."

"And your second point?"

"Find Greenlee. Or anyone else who was involved in deciphering the Callien tablets. So far the only evidence I've seen that the tablets even exist is the *Journal* interview. That interview standing alone doesn't give a writer enough detail to generate a full blown screenplay– the movie script has way more substance and depth than anything Greenlee said to the *Journal* editor who spoke to him. I'm convinced there's a written translation floating around somewhere for the twelve tablets– either that or our modern day Callien has quite the hyperactive imagination."

All of this seemed to Victor like a simple misunderstanding rather than some great mystery. Victor fully expected that the meetings with Talmadge and Mezo would clear up any lingering questions about the Callien tablets, and his assignment from Jonathan Silverstein and Eanna Pictures would be finished. Or so he thought at the time.

The administration building stood at the end of the main road leading into the heart of the campus. Talmadge was typical of the "urban" campus of the day– it pretty much stood as a fortified prison where no one could get in or out without proper paperwork and the approval of one– or sometimes several– entry guards. Talmadge was an oasis of trees, manicured lawns and old buildings in a surrounding outer neighborhood of blight and decay. The world we live in, Victor had thought to himself. The curator's office was on the second floor.

If you can bring to mind the stereotypical picture of a professor of ancient middle eastern studies, you would have Evelyn Walthers properly categorized. He was in his early sixties or thereabouts, with thinning gray hair and a pinched–looking face that bore an expression of preoccupation. The curator was fussing over whatever it was he'd been reading in the moment before his two visitors entered his office, but Walthers was nothing if not a proper gentleman. He put away his project and rose to welcome the visitors with his best imitation of a friendly smile.

"Gentlemen– come in, come in. Welcome to Talmadge. I hope you had a pleasant trip from California– such a long way to come– we're honored by your interest in our program. Honored."

"Thank you Mr. Walthers," said Paladin. "We appreciate your taking the time to meet with us. And you're quite right– we are interested in the middle eastern studies program. As I told you by phone, Mr. Desert here is an attorney for a motion picture production company that is in the process of completing a feature film which draws on some of the ancient Mesopotamian themes that you and your colleagues are knowledgeable about. So we were hoping you might give us some information."

"Of course; of course." Walthers had an affectation which caused him to say the same thing twice in his speech pattern. "We can certainly get to that, and I'll be more than happy to answer any questions you might have. More than happy. It isn't often that the Hollywood community takes an interest in our little corner of the world. We're a bit too academic for your kind of audience, I'm afraid. Not a lot of movie stars around here– but we do the best we can."

Victor had the impression that Walthers was ever so slightly making fun of the two Southern California visitors, so he responded in kind. "Well actually, there aren't a lot of movie stars out and about where we come from either. Mostly lawyers, and accountants, and the occasional private investigator in our neck of the woods, sorry to say. I hope you're not disappointed."

"Not at all; not at all," said the curator still smiling. "I can easily understand why the stars might want to stay out of sight if there are lawyers around. Easily. What's the old joke about the lawyer who moved into the small town in the Midwest where he was the first attorney to open a practice? The poor fellow was starving for his initial year, but then another lawyer came to town and hung out his shingle down the street. The next thing you know, both lawyers had more business than they knew what to do with."

The curator gestured for his two visitors to take seats at the round conference table near the window that looked out on the central courtyard of the campus. He went to his desk and picked up an accordion file folder that was partially filled with papers, then joined the two men. "I took the liberty of doing a bit of research in advance of your visit. Let me show you what I've found out so far."

"Thank you. We'd appreciate that," said Victor.

The curator was searching through his papers, and located what he was looking for about halfway through the stack. "Ah, here it is. The transfer report about the tablets that were sent along to Mezo in New York." Walthers put on his reading glasses, increasing even more the classic look of the egghead academic at work. "March 17th, two years ago. This record shows that 976 tablets were transferred to Mezo– here are the identifier numbers of the individual tablets." Walthers passed the transfer document to Paladin for review.

"And here in this column we have a description of the transferred tablets. As you can see, they're mostly accounting records and the like– that's what the vast majority of the ancient tablets consist of. But I did find a couple of references here to 'Enki poem' and 'Callien'– those were two of the computer search terms I used to try to find what you were looking for. They only reference three of the tablets– not twelve tablets like you were looking for– but at least it was something. And I'm afraid it's all I've been able to locate."

"Can you tell me how your inventory of tablets is accounted for?" Victor was puzzled by the record keeping process.

"Our record keeping system for the tablets is something of a mix. As to the tablets acquired from other sources, the only thing we do is adopt whatever record was maintained by the prior owner. And since only a small percentage of those tablets have been translated and deciphered prior to finding their way here, the former owners of the tablets often failed to record accurate descriptive identifiers for the individual items in their collections. The tablets were usually numbered in the records system, but even that accounting device created difficulty since many of the purchased collections utilized duplicative numbering systems.

"I suppose what I'm saying in a roundabout way is that there are many tablets in our warehouse that are what I might call unknowns– where we have no idea what they say; or who the author was; or when they were recorded, or in some cases even where they came from. It's only after a tablet is translated that we are able to attach precise record identifiers for purposes of inventory control. A bit of a long winded answer– but do you understand what I'm saying?"

"I think so," said Victor. "You're telling us that your records for translated tablets are much more definitive and complete than what you have for the untranslated tablets, right? For the tablets that haven't been deciphered yet, you only have an identifier number in most instances, with no information about the content or author of the tablet."

"Exactly. We have difficulty identifying our inventory by content until the tablets are translated and we learn what they say. And that's the problem I found in trying to locate the twelve tablets you are looking for. We don't show a record of a translation of any sort of poem or epic writing by an author calling himself Callien which relates to the gods Enki and Enlil. I didn't find any records showing translation of anything called 'Blood Children' tablets either, and without being able to pinpoint a translation, I have no way of telling you where such tablets might be, or even whether they exist at all."

"What about the *Journal* interview with Mark Greenlee? And this record you just showed us about the tablets sent to Mezo? Doesn't that tell us something?"

"Not a lot, I'm afraid," said the curator. "We don't have any transcription document or record with respect to the statements Greenlee made in his interview. It's not that I doubt the man– perhaps he was working on something at the time and never turned in a written report of translation. But whatever it was that Greenlee did, we don't find a written record of it in our translations inventory. And since I don't have any idea where Mark Greenlee is, or how to reach him, I can't ask him about it.

"I suggest you focus on finding him– I'm sure he could tell you if he actually deciphered some tablets that we don't know about. And as far as the transfer record is concerned, I'm afraid it isn't specific enough to tell us much. It seems possible that the references to Enki and Callien have something to do with the tablets you're looking for– but then again, maybe not. Our inventory records don't show anything definitive about twelve tablets of the sort Greenlee was talking about in the *Journal* interview. We just don't show anything like that in our file."

"Do you have other writings by a poet named Callien that you've identified?" asked Paladin.

"We do." Walthers searched through his collection of documents again and located several pages which he handed to Frank Paladin for review. "Here are the inventory records on the Callien poems which have been deciphered to date. We have three translated collections– and we think there may be more Callien works that haven't surfaced for translation yet– our researchers believe he was quite prolific in his day.

"But none of these translated Callien writings are anything close to what you're looking for. All three collections are poems which depict love stories in the time he lived in– around 2500 BC. They have nothing to do with ancient mythology, and the activities of the early gods. The Blood Children tablets you describe aren't similar to translated tablets we've been able to identify with Callien so far."

Victor looked at the translations of the Callien tablets that the curator had provided. The writings were difficult to follow– there were gaps reflected by missing or broken tablets. But the thrust of the pieces was as Walthers had described them– love poems set in the era when the author lived. "How do you know Callien is the scribe?" Victor asked.

"His identifying mark has been recognized on one or more of the tablets in each collection. Callien signed his work– much like a modern day author will do with his creations."

There wasn't anything more to be learned in the curator's office, so Walthers escorted Victor and Paladin to a sprawling three story building in the rear part of the Talmadge campus. The building was modern– it stood out as a structure quite distinct from the older buildings located in that area of the grounds.

Middle Eastern Studies was engraved on a signpost in the entryway, and Evelyn Walthers proceeded to lead Victor and Frank Paladin into the building and down a long hallway which was largely populated with rows of small cubicle offices for faculty and staff. Two thirds of the way down, the three men arrived at their destination. "Karen Ashley" was the name on the door, and inside the small office was a pleasant looking woman in her mid-30s who rose to meet her visitors. She had been expecting them.

Walthers made the introductions– Victor and Paladin recognized the name right away, of course. Karen Ashley was the interviewer of Mark Greenlee in the *Journal* article uncovered by Paladin in his investigation. After the curator had turned the visitors over to Ashley, she explained to them that she had been one for the founders of the *Journal of Middle Eastern Studies*– and ultimately its lead content editor. But the publication had eventually died away due to lack of interest and subscribers.

Ashley remembered Mark Greenlee. "We worked together a fair amount over the years," she said. "He lived in New York, but he usually came down here to the campus two or three days a week to teach a class or work on his translation projects. Mark had a lot of freedom in setting his schedule. He was a Mezo fellow, not a regular faculty member here at the university, and that meant he didn't have to follow any of the scheduling rules that the rest of us live by. Working for both Talmadge and Mezo like he did allowed him to do pretty much whatever caught his interest– he had the freedom to set up his own projects and conduct his own research without any real responsibility to report to the university hierarchy. Lucky guy– smart too."

"What sorts of projects did Greenlee work on?"

"Oh my gosh, it would be so hard to put it into any specific categories. Certainly the deciphering and translating of tablets– he spent quite a bit of his time on transcriptions, I know that for sure. And dating of artifacts and tablets. He was very interested in timing questions– when these artifacts and tablets were created, that sort of thing. Like any good historian, he was always trying to get things organized into some sort of chronological order."

"So how did it happen that you came to interview him for the *Journal* article?" Victor asked his question while Karen Ashley was leading her visitors to the elevator at the end of the hallway.

"I knew he was working on a project involving the gods Enki and Enlil, and I asked him about how it was coming. Mark was pretty excited about it. He told me he was deciphering some tablets, and he had come across this really interesting mythology. The things I eventually asked him about in the interview.

"Mark always had an interest in middle eastern religions– particularly the interrelationships between the polytheism of the older cultures and the monotheism of Judaism, Christianity and Islam. Mark cared a lot about that part of Middle Eastern history– he was always on the lookout for artifacts and tablets that shed light on religious practices, and how they developed over time. Ancient Sumer was polytheist, and Mark was quite intrigued by the idea that the Old Testament seemed to encompass more than one godly personality. When he discovered the story of Enki and Enlil that runs so parallel to Biblical Genesis, it became a source of deep interest for him. That's why I wanted to do the interview– because he seemed so passionate about what he was finding in the tablets he was working on."

Ashley led her visitors out of the elevator and into a large warehouse space in the basement of the building. There were tablets and artifacts everywhere.

"This is our primary storage location for matters of immediate interest and study. There's a second warehouse off campus where we keep the rest of the inventory– the pieces that we think are of lesser significance. And as you can see, we have enough here to keep us busy for a long, long time to come."

"How does the translation process work?" Victor looked around at tens of thousands of untranslated tablets, and was genuinely puzzled as to how researchers would ever get the job of deciphering done on all this material.

"It's pretty much what you would expect. Individual translators who know the ancient Sumerian language sit down with the tablets and decipher them one tablet at a time. Or at least that's the way it's worked in the past. There are so many subtleties in the language that we have had only minimal success in trying to mechanize the process through computers. But we're getting there. We have some new software programs that are coming out– software generated right here in our department, by the way, that we hope will lead to computer transcription capability. The software works– but it's still very rough. Translating the ancient cuneiforms of the Sumerian language is an art, not a science, and so far at least we're not there yet in getting it done on any sort of mass production basis. Give it a few more years, and then we can talk again."

"So that's what Greenlee did? He transcribed individual tablets that caught his interest?"

"Yep. That was his first love. No doubt about it. He really enjoyed the ancient languages."

The group found seats in the warehouse area around a small table, surrounded by an endless array of artifacts. The warehouse was deserted except for Ashley and the two visitors.

Victor got right to business. "As you may have already heard, I represent a motion picture development company that is currently in production on a movie about Enki, and Enlil, and the conflicts between the two brothers. The movie script has some similarities to the story that Mark Greenlee talked about in his interview with you. We're investigating whether the Blood Children story in the movie script may have come from the collection of Callien tablets, so we'd like to know what you can tell us about those tablets, and where they might be. By the way, have you had a chance to read the interview recently?"

"Yes. Evelyn passed it along– from your investigator as I understand it."

Frank Paladin spoke up. "I'm the one who located it and called the school. I didn't know you were working here, though. A nice surprise."

Karen Ashley smiled. "I certainly remember that Mark was talking in the interview about a collection of tablets, but I never actually saw them. Mark had a working office on the third floor of this building that he used when he came down from New York. That's where he did his deciphering of tablets. He had open access to this floor, and he could pretty much check out any tablets that he wanted and take them with him to his office. For that matter, he was free to take tablets and artifacts to New York or pretty much anyplace else– this inventory all around us belongs to the Mezo Institute, and if the Mezo people want to move things around they have every right to do that. We don't tell them what to do. So I never actually saw Mark working on the Callien tablets."

"How about a written transcription– did you ever see one for the tablets Greenlee talked about in his interview?"

"Nope. Never saw a translation document. And since there's no record of the Blood Children in our translations library, I assume nothing like that exists. I was actually the one that did the records search for Evelyn prior to your coming out here. Didn't find anything except for that one record entry about the units sent to Mezo in New York. I assume Evelyn told you we're not sure whether that record is actually a reference to the Callien tablets you're looking for."

Victor was puzzled by what Ashley was saying. "Do you think something might have happened to the tablets? Lost– or stolen– anything like that?"

"No way to know except to ask Mark Greenlee about it. And I don't have any idea where to find him. I know back in the 1800s when Sumerian tablets first started popping up, there was a lot of resistance to any word getting out about the Mesopotamian gods. It upset a lot of people that the Bible stories might turn out to not be accurate . . . that sort of thing. I kind of thought we were past the idea that certain tablets needed to be stifled– but maybe I'm wrong."

"Are you saying there was a negative reaction to the tablets in the 1800s?"

"Isn't it obvious? A suggestion of multiple gods is heresy, and persons who might be interested in religious traditions involving polytheism are pagans . . . or worse."

"I don't know anybody who feels that way," Victor protested.

Karen Ashley looked at Victor with amusement. "Are you sure they're Christians? Some of the most heated monotheism debates in history occurred within the Christian faith– have you ever heard of the Arians?"

"Can't say that I have."

"Well back around 320 AD, there was a charismatic Christian priest named Arius whose sermons attracted a large following. Arius was one of those speakers who could reduce his teachings to simple phrases and catchy tunes, and the high clergy of the day came to look upon him as a dangerous rabble rouser. His crime was teaching that Jesus is the Son of God, but is not God himself. By emphasizing this point, Arius was making it seem as if Christianity was polytheist. And particularly so when you add in the Holy Spirit to form the Trinity. It caused quite a stir."

"OK. I can see the point."

"When Arius started suggesting that Christ and the Holy Spirit were somehow separate from God he was condemned as an arch–heretic and banished from the Church. Was Jesus begotten by God, as the Arians insisted, or was he one and the same as God? This question sounds simple on its face, but in fact it divided the Christian Church for centuries in ways we can barely conceive of today."

"Yes," said Victor, "but isn't that exactly the point? These issues may have mattered at one time, but they have nothing to do with the world of the twenty first century."

"Are you so sure about that?" Karen was smiling as she asked her question. "Monotheism has a strong political overtone to it. Belief in a single God can be a very useful tool for ruling over others. Centralized religious thinking leads comfortably to centralized political thinking, and an infallible Supreme Being fits nicely with the concept of an infallible earthly ruler who works hand in hand with God as His human representative. The bottom line is that people are much easier to control if they can be made to accept that sort of unitary thinking."

"True, I suppose, but let me ask you another question that's a bit more relevant to what we're trying to learn here today," said Victor. "Mark Greenlee disappeared not long after his interview was published. Do you think there was some relationship . . . that the timing of his disappearance was more than coincidence?"

Karen Ashley paused for a long moment before answering. "I've thought about that. I asked myself at the time whether I was doing Mark a disservice by publishing his views. I think there were people in his circle who didn't want him talking about Enki and Enlil and the stories of Genesis in the way that he did. I hope it isn't true that he got attacked for speaking out, because I know for sure that Mark was genuinely excited about his scholarship. It would never have occurred to him that he was doing something wrong by reporting publicly on his findings."

Victor thought a lot that evening about what Karen Ashley had said. She had told him that she didn't know where Mark Greenlee might be found, and Victor believed her. Nor did she have any idea where the Callien tablets might be located. In a way, the visit to Talmadge University had been a dead end– Victor and Frank Paladin were no closer to their goal of finding the Blood Children tablets than they were before they visited the college. But somehow Victor knew that the time spent in Philadelphia hadn't been wasted. Something was amiss– he was sure of it. Perhaps a day with the people at the Mezo Institute might shed some light. And that day would be tomorrow.

XII.

Victor thought the cabbie had made a wrong turn. They were heading south on Broadway toward downtown instead of going north toward the Upper East Side. The Mezo Institute operated on 78th Street– where was this guy going?

Frank Paladin cleared up the mini–mystery. "The Mezo corporate office for the nonprofit is located down in the Wall Street area. High rent district– that's where we're heading."

High rent indeed. The taxi carrying Desert and Paladin pulled to a stop outside the LawbridgeTrimble tower on Maiden Lane. Even Paladin was surprised– and almost nothing surprised the investigator. "Are these people crazy . . . meeting with us here?" Paladin was stunned by the hubris of the bankers. LawbridgeTrimble apparently had no concerns about having Desert and his investigator visit the Mezo people in the headquarters building itself.

The visitors walked across the open courtyard fronting on Maiden Lane and entered the tower through the plaza doors. Inside the main lobby, the giant structure was almost completely bare of furnishings or objects of any kind. One large security desk stood in the center of the lobby area– but there was nothing else that was identifiably human in the vast space. The entire three story lobby was empty– even though it bustled with activity as busy looking people made their way to and from the tower elevators. The space had the feel of a giant cavern– a grand tomb of the dead.

Paladin and Desert approached the guard desk and the investigator announced their business to an officious looking attendant. She handed them entry badges complete with instant photo ID's, and the two men found their way to the elevator bank which serviced the 42nd floor. Since the tower was so pencil thin, the elevators operated with a complex array of sky lobbies. Passengers took an express to the sky lobby floor which serviced their segment of the tower, then transferred to a local to take them to the specific floor they were actually going to visit. The sky lobby on the 42nd floor was almost an exact duplicate– in miniature– of the entry lobby below. Marble, granite . . . lots of that. Life and spirit– none to be found. Victor and Paladin dutifully transferred to their designated local and were whisked to the 58th floor where the meeting with Mezo was set to take place.

The two visitors had found their way to the inner sanctum, and they were alone. But only for a brief moment. As if by magic, an attractive young woman appeared in the elevator lobby and announced in a pleasant voice that they were to follow her. Victor and Paladin trailed along as she made her way quickly along a corridor of offices– all of which had closed doors– to a glass walled conference room where two men and two woman sat waiting. The meeting at LawbridgeTrimble was about to begin.

Victor couldn't quite catch all the names during an effusive round of introductions, but it didn't make any difference. Each member of the waiting team had a high gloss business card to present:

Peter Takhar– President of the Mezo Institute
Sharon Perelman– Vice President Research and Development
of the Mezo Institute
Ricardo Massinet– Partner in the law firm of Kessler & Abramowitz
Georgina Doan– Partner in the law firm of Kessler & Abramowitz

Takhar led off the meeting by making a genuine effort to come across as pleasant and helpful. He welcomed the visitors with enthusiasm, a cheery fellow who told them how pleased he was that important people in the entertainment community were taking an interest in ancient Mesopotamian life and culture. His comments were almost a word for word repeat of what the visitors had heard the day before from Evelyn Walthers at Talmadge. Either these people had worked together to plan an opening set of remarks for the visitors from LA, or their standard welcoming lines were so well coordinated and rehearsed as to be second nature. Takhar and Perelman were wearing the sort of interested and appreciative faces that Victor perceived could be trotted out for show on any occasion when a visitor of significance expressed interest in the work of Mezo.

The lawyers, however, offered an entirely different look. Pleasant smiles, to be sure– but Victor Desert knew right away that this would be one of those meetings where his counterparts across the table would be using the tried and true negotiating approach of "good cop, bad cop" for any sort of exchange that might occur at the meeting.

"So if I may say so, we were all a bit surprised by your inquiry." This was Peter Takhar's way of getting things rolling. "It isn't often that Hollywood gets involved with the ancient Mesopotamian stories. Your movie people tend to stay close to the Bible with their epics. A *Ten Commandments* with Charlton Heston as Moses– that kind of movie can get made. *Or a Greatest Story Ever Told*, or a *King of Kings* remake– Jesus always brings in an audience. But a feature film about Enki and Enlil, and the early days of Biblical Genesis? I'm no movie expert, but if I may say so, a film about the Sumerian gods doesn't strike me as the typical formula for a hit. I'm happy to see the interest, of course– and you have my very best wishes for success– but I've been with the Institute for more than ten years, and this is the first time anyone has tried to make a movie about our field of study. So you'll perhaps understand why I might sound a bit surprised by your venture."

"I understand fully," Victor said with a smile. "And I have to admit I thought the same thing myself when I first heard about the project. No disrespect intended, but only a few weeks ago I had never heard of Enki, or Enlil, or Sumer– or frankly much else about Mesopotamia. I'd always thought civilization as we know it got started in Egypt– with the pyramids, and the Sphinx– things like that. Monuments we can see with our own eyes. Trying to learn about an ancient civilization from a bunch of clay tablets dug up in the desert was something new to me, I must admit. Interesting though– and I can certainly see how it is that you must enjoy your work." Victor looked at Sharon Perelman as he spoke, and offered a winning smile even while he was mildly insulting the hosts in response to Takhar's taunt about his client's business judgment in making the film.

"We do indeed enjoy our work," said Perelman, taking her cue from Victor's comment. "The ancient civilizations can really get to you once you dig below the surface a bit. Pun intended, by the way. All of us at the Institute feel deeply blessed to be involved in this project of bringing the ancient civilizations to life, and what's so amazing is how new it all is. A hundred and fifty years ago no one had ever heard of Sumer– it was a civilization that had quite literally disappeared. The people who made the early discoveries were actually looking for Assyrian and Babylonian artifacts– not some civilization called Sumer that they didn't know existed. We've come a long way in a short period of time in our discoveries about the ancients. Cutting edge stuff, but you would be amazed at how many people don't even know it's happening."

"Put me in that category, I'm embarrassed to say," said Paladin. "I'm like Victor– never heard of any of this until a few weeks ago. If you'd asked me last month who Enlil was, I'd have drawn a complete blank. But now it's all different– I see his works all around me– everywhere I look."

Takhar and Perelman weren't quite sure what to make of the investigator's dry comment, so they took the light approach in response.

"You're quite right," said Peter Takhar, "and that's why the subject matter of your client's motion picture is of interest to us. We want people to find out the truth about the ancient middle east, not a lot of nonsense like we've been seeing with all the alien astronaut stuff on TV. Sometimes I wonder whether the alien talk has pushed aside our scholarship completely– no one cares what we have to say . . . what they really want to hear about are Anunnaki gods flying around in spaceships."

"Anunnaki?" It was a new term to Victor.

"That's the name a lot of people use to describe the ancient gods of Sumer," said Sharon Perelman. "They were from outer space, supposedly. The name means 'Those who came down from Heaven to Earth'– or at least that's how the alien astronaut writers interpret it. Anu was the great god of the skies, and the Anunnaki are supposedly his godly children."

So far the lawyers for Mezo hadn't spoken up. But it was Ricardo Massinet's turn now, which meant it was time for the meeting to get serious.

"So we were quite interested in your movie, as Peter told you. But from a lawyer perspective for Mezo, my interest is perhaps a bit different than what Peter and Sharon have said so far. I looked at what Paladin sent us– the *Journal* interview with Mark Greenlee– and my reaction was to ask myself the question whether your movie production company might be using intellectual property that belongs to Mezo. That's what I was thinking. After all, if Greenlee's transcription was involved in this screenplay for *Blood Children* and he derived his story from tablets that properly belong to the Institute, hasn't the Institute been harmed? That's kind of where I started in my thinking about all this."

Victor pondered for a moment. Clearly the ball was in his court, and he took his time in framing the right response. "Thank you for your candid comments, Ricardo, and let me answer this way. First, of course, we don't know whether Greenlee or Mezo had anything to do with the creation of the movie script or not. You're just guessing at this point about whether Mezo has some sort of intellectual property right– and I don't think there's any basis for guesswork when we don't know the facts at this early stage. Candidly, your rather threatening talk about intellectual property seems out of place in a meeting where our purpose was to hopefully get some questions answered that might put any infringement issues to bed once and for all.

"For example– do the twelve tablets that Greenlee talks about in the *Journal* article actually exist? And if so, where are they? And have they been translated? And if so, where's the transcription? Those are the things we would like to learn as our takeaways from this meeting, and once we know the answers to those questions, that would be the time to talk about intellectual property issues . . . assuming there are any." Talking directly to Massinet, Victor said, "You've basically just assumed that Mezo has some sort of intellectual property right here. Aren't you jumping to conclusions?"

"Ah, not so at all." Massinet appeared confident, and spoke smoothly as he responded to Desert's point. "I've looked into the facts on our end, and I think we have enough information to say with a pretty high level of confidence that the Institute has a strong possibility of a claim . . ."

"That's a bunch of nonsense," said Victor, interrupting the New York lawyer. "You haven't sent us anything in response to Frank's numerous inquiries– so where's your evidence? If you've got something, now is the time to put it on the table for me to look at. I didn't fly all the way out here just to listen to a bunch of groundless threats about litigation."

"Gentlemen, gentlemen . . ." Peter Takhar didn't like the turn the discussion was taking. "Let's all stay calm. And of course, Victor, we didn't expect you to come to this meeting without a clear understanding that we were going to answer your questions as best we could. The Institute has nothing to hide. The opposite is true– we are more than willing to make a full disclosure. So perhaps if I might turn things over to Georgina at this point, and she can bring you up to date with what we've found out so far. She and Sharon have been looking into the Callien tablets, and pulling together what we know about the matters discussed in the Greenlee interview. Georgina, why don't you tell attorney Desert and Mr. Paladin what you've come up with."

Georgina Doan could have been a model for what it was that young women lawyers of her time tried to look like. Shoulder length chestnut brown hair– expensively cut and colored. Just the right length to drape over the shoulders of a dark suit, tailored very trim to emphasize womanly curves in only the most subtle and understated way. Minimal makeup; no jewelry– a young woman who wore an expression of bland indifference to all that was happening around her. Could you call Georgina Doan feminine? Perhaps, in a "check the boxes" kind of way– nice figure, shapely legs– the physical pieces were there. But something important was missing, and Victor had noticed it the moment she introduced herself. It was life– Georgina Doan was a dead person. The kind of woman who would always be on her own . . . alone.

"OK," she said brusquely, "first things first. We've tried to track down Mark Greenlee to ask him about the things he was talking about in the article. No luck at all– and I've had a pretty good investigative firm working on it. He's disappeared, as of a couple of years ago, and there isn't a viable lead that we've turned up so far. Maybe our investigators will find him eventually– but nothing yet."

"Who are you using? For the investigation, I mean." Paladin asked.

"We use Mirrorprobe. Their New Jersey office." Paladin made a quick note on his yellow legal pad.

Doan continued with her report. "We've checked out the Talmadge connection. Since you were there yesterday, you probably have already learned what they have to say. No record of a set of twelve Callien tablets that meet the criteria you're looking for. No transcription of any such tablet collection in the Talmadge portfolio. The one thing we got from them is this transmittal record of 976 tablets being shipped to Mezo in New York that mentions the words Enki and Callien."

Doan showed the record to Victor and Paladin. It was the same document they'd seen the day before in Philadelphia. "So we followed up on the Institute's end. They show a receipt for the 976 tablets." Doan produced the Institute's receipt document for review by the people sitting around the table. "It doesn't tell us much about the specific tablets that were actually included in the delivery, so we followed up to find out where the tablets were physically located after the transfer from Philadelphia. What we found was that the 976 tablets were disposed of in a routine destruction process along with a couple of thousand other tablets from the Mezo New York location on 78th Street."

Victor had difficulty grasping what he had just heard. "Disposed of? You mean these historical tablets were taken out and thrown away? Is that what you're telling us?"

"Pretty much. The process varies depending on what it is that's being destroyed, but the end result is that these 976 tablets don't exist anymore, and if we assume that the references to Enki and Callien in the transmittal record actually tie back to the Callien tablets Greenlee was talking about in his interview, this means those tablets no longer exist."

There was a long moment of silence at the table as Victor Desert tried to mentally process what Georgina Doan had just said. She had spoken calmly– as if there was nothing unusual or improper about the destruction of 976 historical tablets dating back thousands of years. She had spoken as if this sort of thing happened all the time, so Victor asked the obvious question– whether such destruction of tablets was indeed business as usual at Mezo.

"I wouldn't actually use that particular term– I wouldn't say business as usual," said Doan with a hint of discomfort. "But it certainly happens from time to time that the Institute disposes of tablets."

"Why?" asked Victor.

"Well . . . there could be many reasons. Duplicative tablets is one. Or tablets that are damaged or degraded to the point that they are indecipherable. There can be many reasons why particular collections are disposed of."

"But these twelve tablets that Greenlee talked about weren't damaged at all. He specifically mentioned how they were in pristine condition. And he said he'd never seen anything like them before. Why on earth would the Institute choose to dispose of tablets that had such uniqueness?"

"We don't know for sure, but I talked to the head of inventory control at the Institute and she told me they sometimes dispose of tablets that they believe are outside the mainstream of Sumerian thinking, or contain erratic information that doesn't fit with everything else we know about the Sumerians. Anyone could write on a clay tablet back in those days, so the inventory control team tries to keep an eye out for political rants by disengaged individuals. They red flag meaningless kinds of writing that are subversive and disconnected from the body politic as a whole."

"And you think the Callien twelve tablets fall into that category?" asked Victor. "Subversive . . . disconnected?"

"It appears that way from what Greenlee said about the tablets. If he actually did a translation, and the deciphering is what he says it is, then there's a pretty strong inference that can be drawn that Callien was writing a terrorist rant as opposed to something that actually expressed the views of the people. Callien didn't have any grounding for what he wrote– he was simply creating a myth. The twelve tablets– at least as Greenlee describes them– appear to have been written in a revolutionary spirit– with a political agenda to inflame the populace against their rulers and legitimate religious authorities. Very simply, Callien was a rabble rouser who appeared to be trying to inspire a slave uprising in Sumer. This sort of tablet writing– highly politicized, and not based on actual experience of the author– the Institute sometimes uses its own good judgment to make the decision that such inflammatory writings won't be published as part of the overall collection."

Victor, speaking slowly and with emphasis, said, "So you don't actually have the tablets anymore, and you don't have a transcription. Is that what you're telling me?"

Attorney Massinet exuded self-confidence, "Don't start sounding too sure of yourself, Mr. Desert. Our experience has been that the courts are entirely willing to protect intellectual property rights, and you've readily admitted on your part that you don't have any idea where your client's script came from. It certainly seems to me that a trier of fact could find on the basis of circumstantial evidence that your mysterious author did indeed have access to a historical work that belonged to the Institute, and that he or she used that intellectual property in the writing of your client's screenplay. My advice is that you stop production on your movie until you get all this sorted out. Your client is producing a movie without owning the rights to the artistic content, a risky course, in my view. Bordering on the foolhardy if I may respectfully say so."

* * *

Paladin did some Internet research about the LawbridgeTrimble tower on the long plane ride back to LA. He found that the Mezo Institute was a tenant at the tower, occupying half of the 58th floor. They shared space on the floor with the other historical research institutes funded by LawbridgeTrimble: the Amerosa Institute, which specialized in archaeological explorations and artifact holdings from sites in the western hemisphere; and the Eurosa Institute which carried out the same functions in Europe and Asia. By the time the plane touched down, the investigator was telling Victor Desert that LawbridgeTrimble controlled pretty much the entire historical record of the developed world.

So that became the takeaway from the east coast meetings. Paladin and Victor had learned on their trip that the Overlords at LawbridgeTrimble controlled the past, and had the power to delete records whenever and wherever they chose. The history of human existence was being written, edited and shaped on Maiden Lane, and if a company like Mezo were to decide that Callien's writing about the Blood Children didn't fit with what they wanted people to learn about, they would simply destroy the tablets. Rabble rousing to strike popular discontent in the masses– that's how Georgina Doan had described Callien's epic poem about the Blood Children. Victor Desert, for the first time, began to grasp the depths that these people were willing to go to in their effort to control the message that would be heard by ordinary people.

Victor started his process of perceiving on that day. He began to grasp that Theresia Anjau's suspicions about the death of Harlan Bloom might actually turn out to be true. It was a chilling thought for the lawyer to accept, but if the ancient words of Callien struck such fear in the hearts of the Overlords, why not the modern words of Harlan Bloom? Words, it seemed, were a threat, and Harlan Bloom had chosen to ignore the edicts of the bankers. Such decisions, Victor was learning, had consequences.

XIII.

It was Oscar night in Hollywood, and Victor Desert was getting ready to play his assigned role as best supporting man. Katy Hooper would be singing her Best Song nominee during the program, and Victor on this occasion was to serve as escort to the star. Heady stuff for a lawyer– but Victor had his facade in place. He would fit in.

Katy looked smashing. The young woman who had learned to sing in the choir would emerge tonight as a full blown rapper with the persona to light up a room. This would be her first introduction to the big stage, and Katy Hooper planned to take full advantage of the opportunity. She had some special treats in mind for this television moment– and Katy's dark hair and blue eyes and . . . whatever . . . were soon to be on full display around the world.

The Academy Awards were Hollywood's way of paying tribute to itself. The awards were first presented in 1929 at the Hollywood Roosevelt Hotel, and by 2021 were being broadcast live on television to more than 200 countries. The golden statues handed out on the big evening weren't actually gold– as with so many other things in Hollywood they were all for show. Gold plating on a black metal base– that's what the Oscar was actually made of.

The Academy voters liked to honor songs that shake things up, and Katy on this night would be only too pleased to oblige. Her costume for the performance of *Serpent's Seed* was the female pop artist outfit of choice– she would dress as the devil's whore. Then at the end of the performance, she would do a pole dance with a broomstick and be burned at the stake. Her lyrics for *Serpent's Seed* went like this:

Your serpent smile is so enchanting
Could I please feel the sting?
Your sliver eyes are so inviting
Won't you please invite me in?
Are you the devil . . .want to know
So you can teach, and I can grow.
Embrace me dark angel
I'll give back for sure.
Tell me your stories
Your seed is my cure.

Katy Hooper left her seat early in the show to go backstage and prepare for her performance. Multiple earrings in each ear, and a beast with

Moloch horns tattooed on her neck and below. It was temporary body paint, of course; Katy wasn't so stupid as to irretrievably deface her exquisite chest. A black thong body suit and fishnet tights completed the look. Tonight's show would not be performed with her former church group in mind.

Victor and Katy had been together for more than a year by the time the Oscar ceremony rolled around in March. They were a bit of an odd couple– the rising lawyer with a girl who didn't graduate from high school. But they had something together, and in a strange way their relationship had worked so far.

So was Victor ready to watch her do a pole dance with a broomstick in front of a television audience of millions? I'm not so sure. Victor was happy for Katy Hooper's success, but somewhere deep inside I suspect he wasn't entirely comfortable with the new persona she was creating for herself. Victor was no prude, but he didn't strike me as the sort of man who would stay happy for long as the escort to a pop princess doing pole dances and spouting satanic lyrics. It just didn't seem to fit.

Their red carpet entrance to launch the evening had gone like clockwork. The fans in the grandstand got the full treatment from Katy Hooper– poses, smiles, bumps and grinds for the cameras. Victor wasn't a star; so he didn't exist in the eyes of the masses.

Theresia Anjau arrived on the red carpet shortly after Katy and Victor had made their entrance. She was on the arm of a much older man that night– a man Victor hadn't seen before. He had the look of a quite proud father as he walked Theresia past the crowded grandstand– because that's exactly what he was. Theresia was being escorted to the Oscars by Sydney Anjau, the reclusive producer who so rarely showed himself in public. He had created three Oscar winning films over a period of the last two decades, and he still had the look of a star, even at the age of 76. Theresia was a later in life child for the storied film maker– and tonight he was doting on her blossoming success.

Sydney Anjau had a full head of grey hair, and he looked fit enough to dominate a movie set that very day. He was a tall man, and he exuded a presence. For a brief moment his eyes locked with Victor's, then he and Theresia were swallowed up by the media crowd. Victor felt from Sydney Anjau's look as if the older man knew who he was, even though the two had never met.

Katy's musical performance that night went off without a hitch, although her song didn't take home the Oscar. Then it was off to the after party hosted by Chartreuse Magazine at the art deco Fountain Plaza Hotel. It was the party of the year– the place in Hollywood this night to see and be seen. The ballroom at the hotel was nearly full when Katy and Victor made their entrance, and Katy was immediately swept up by the celebrity worshipers. Victor found himself shunted off to the side of the room. Not a problem– he was perfectly happy to stand alone and watch the goings–on. But a woman came up to him– a tall blonde in an evening gown that was very low cut, but ever so slightly demure at the same time. It was Sarah Anjau, and she was alone.

“"It looks like your young lady is enjoying her evening," Sarah said with a smile as she watched Katy Hooper basking in the attention of the guests.

"Yes, it's an important night for her. First time she's had the chance to perform in front of that sort of audience. I think it went off pretty well– so I'm not surprised that she's a highlight of the evening. She deserves it."

"And indeed she does," said Sarah. "But that has seemed to leave you somewhat alone. I hope you're not feeling left out."

"Oh, not so at all. I never really cared much for that kind of attention anyway. Hollywood stuff, you know."

"And you're the lawyer– so I understand. The antics of my fellow actors and film makers take place a respectable distance apart from the world you live in."

Victor looked intently into Sarah Anjau's eyes. He couldn't tell if she was making fun of him or not. "Maybe not so far apart as you think. I'm a trial lawyer, so every time I'm in front of a jury, there's an act to be put on. A lot like the movies when you think about it. Movies aren't real life– they're a visual representation of life, just like a courtroom trial is a presentation of the same sort. We don't have scripts, or sound stages, but other than that is there really such a difference?"

"Perhaps not," said Sarah with a smile. "And certainly not for you, it sounds like. It's all about how we approach such things, and if you're an actor in the courtroom, so be it. And good for your clients, I assume. Judges and juries are looking to be entertained too."

"Everybody loves Hollywood," agreed Victor. "Entertainment capital of the world."

"Have you seen my sister yet? And my father?"

Victor had forgotten for a moment that Sarah and Theresia were sisters. "Not here. I saw them briefly when we were all walking into the theater. I've never met your father– outside the theater was the first time I'd seen him."

"Well come with me, I'll introduce you." Sarah took Victor's arm and began to lead him out of the ballroom, and away from Katy Hooper who was still holding court surrounded by suckups and hangers–on. She won't miss me, Victor thought to himself.

Theresia and Sydney Anjau were sitting at a table in a side bar area off the main ballroom. Two other couples were at the table with them, and Sydney was engaged in an animated conversation with one of the women– an attractive blonde in her mid–50s who was clearly enthralled with his every word. Theresia sat quietly as her father spoke to the woman. She smiled when she saw Sarah and Victor approaching.

"So, Sarah, you found yourself a date for the evening after all," said Theresia to the approaching couple.

"Unfortunately not, I'm sorry to say. I'm just borrowing our lawyer for a moment while the ever–lovely Katy Hooper entertains the glitterati. We'll have to send him back before the evening's over, I'm afraid."

Theresia gently pushed away the couple seated next to her to create a space for Victor and Sarah to pull up chairs and join the group at the table. "There now, isn't this more fun than that fake witchy stuff Katy's selling these days?" Theresia's infinitely catty comment was delivered with humor, but Victor had the distinct feeling she was speaking what she actually thought about Katy's routine. And she was right– Katy's witchery was contrived, and Victor knew it. But he stood up for his girlfriend.

"Oh, I wouldn't put much stock in all that. It's just for show. Is it really any different from you playing Ninhursag in *Blood Children*? Acting the part of a sexual goddess from thousands of years ago. Or Sarah playing Naamah? The two of you are doing the same thing Katy does, aren't you?"

Theresia looked at Victor with a wide smile. "Of course . . . you're right. I take back my snide comment, and if Katy joins us later I promise that I'll be the first to compliment her on her fetching performance. I enjoyed her song– sleeping with the devil, and learning from the serpent. She and the Igigi must be finding a lot in common these days."

But Victor was ready this time. "Igigi, eh? So you think her *Serpent's Seed* piece is the work of Enlil and his minions? You're giving her a bit too much credit, it seems to me."

"Not at all," said Theresia. "If you think about the world we live in, you'll see Enlil and the Igigi everywhere you look. With Eljo slaves worshiping the ground they walk on. Isn't that what your friend Katy is doing this very moment? Running with the Igigi and basking in the adulation of the slaves? It's the modern world, Victor . . . don't you know?"

Sarah Anjau broke the spell of the moment. "Father," she said loudly enough for the older man at Theresia's side to turn and take notice. "Come over here! Meet Victor Desert while we're holding him captive from his date. Come now . . . he'll soon be gone."

Sydney Anjau rose from his chair and moved over to sit next to Victor at the crowded table. Theresia moved a bit to the side to create a space.

Sydney shook Victor's hand with a firm grasp. "I've heard of you, of course. You're my lawyer– Silverstein has told me about you and the ownership rights issues where *Blood Children* is concerned. Glad to meet you." Sydney Anjau had been holding Victor's hand the entire time he was speaking.

"Thank you, Mr. Anjau. It's a pleasure to meet you too."

"Please, please . . . call me Sydney. And you've met my daughters, of course. I saw you when we were walking in. With that singer, I believe."

"Katy Hooper, that's right. She's a friend."

"Indeed. Quite a show she put on tonight. I'm impressed. She captures the times we live in, it seems. And isn't that the true mission of the artist?"

Victor had never thought of it in quite that way. "Actually, I'd like to think that the role of the artist is to create something timeless. But I appreciate your comments about Katy– and she does have an excellent sense of the modern world."

"Something timeless, indeed!" said Anjau with enthusiasm. "Like we're trying to do with *Blood Children*. Gods and goddesses that lived thousands of years ago springing to life on the great silver screen for the entertainment of our modern day multitudes! This will be my finest picture– I hope you know that. That's why we can't allow ourselves to be distracted or shunted aside by these legal issues about the rights."

"I understand."

"I'm sure you do. But the real question is whether you understand the depth of this movie. Harlan Bloom understood it perfectly; that's why I chose him for the lead. He knew all about the bankers, and what Enlil and the Igigi have been doing in our modern world. But the question is . . . do you?"

Victor thought it was an odd thing to be asked at an Academy Awards party and he wasn't quite sure what Sydney Anjau expected to hear in response. So he took the lawyerly course: "I suspect I don't understand the film in all of its levels. At least not in the way you suggest. My attention has been on the legal issues– Bloom's death; and the rights to the script– so I probably haven't given as much time to the content of the movie as I should, sorry to say."

"Nothing to be sorry about– you've been busy. Come by my house this week for dinner and we'll talk some more . . . in detail. It will be a chance for us to get to know one another . . . I promise it won't be boring, will you come?"

"Of course– I would enjoy the opportunity."

"Tuesday night then. At 7:00 p.m. My assistant will send you the address and directions to the house. Just the two of us. Fair enough?"

"I'll be there."

Victor left the Anjau group and went back into the main ballroom to locate Katy. She was pinned against a wall by the time he got there– surrounded by sycophants and well–wishers. Some of her enjoyment with the adulation seemed to have worn off, so Victor went ahead and pushed through the crowd to extricate his date from her position of entrapment. After all, that's what an escort is for.

Katy had words of thanks as she and Victor made their way to the waiting limo. It had been a good night for her, but she was grateful to Victor for arriving when he did. She spoke about being a damsel in distress, and the pleasure of a knight's rescue. Katy Hooper's appreciation carried right on through for the rest of the evening, so it was Victor's turn to be grateful.

XIV.

Victor knew that his Tuesday in the office would be a busy day. His schedule extended late into the evening– dinner that night was with Sydney Anjau in Beverly Hills. Minnie Larren was already at her desk in the reception area when Victor arrived at Hazeltine Phillips & Blaine at 8:00 a.m.

"Good morning Mr. Desert." Minnie favored the old fashioned approach in her greetings to the lawyers in the firm.

"Good morning, Minnie. You're in early today. Lot's to do– it's going to be an overload. We have multiple client groups coming in."

"You'll handle it– no problem. Caroline is already here– she's waiting for you."

Victor made his way back to his office, and said hello to Caroline on the way. He turned to his computer, and quickly scanned the overnight email messages. The usual array.

Caroline was standing in the doorway of the office. "I have a conference call set up for you with Paul Cutter and his banker at 8:30, and we're scheduled for Samuel and Bella Bloom coming in at 10:00. You have the conference call with David Kincaid and Frank Paladin at 10:30 with the Blooms, and lunch with Randolph Blaine at noon. At 2:00 p.m. I have Scott and Barbara Langsden scheduled for a meeting with you and Adrian. Alan Butler will be joining you for the meeting with the Langdens. Then dinner tonight with Mr. Anjau.

That's what's on my calendar– do I have everything?" Caroline was conscientious– she never liked to miss anything or make a scheduling mistake. Victor was relaxed and easygoing about such things– Caroline's fussing was a welcome counterpoint.

"Sounds like that covers it," said Victor. "Could you please bring in the Silver Bay file for me to look over before the call with Cutter?"

Paul Cutter was Victor Desert's cousin– a couple of steps removed. Paul was the descendent of Josephine Desserte– the sister of the first Victor Desserte who came to America from Alsace in 1870. Josephine had a daughter who grew up to become the wife of William Cutter, a lumberman who went on to develop several of the major forest properties that surrounded Lake Ponderosa in Northern Idaho.

William Cutter's legacy to his family was a 186 acre parcel of land located on Silver Bay– one of the premier frontage locations on the great expanse of the lake. The Cutter family had owned the property for more than a hundred years, dating back to the days when the mining magnates of Idaho and Montana had built their summer homes in the area. The grand mansions had dotted the shoreline of Silver Bay for generations, and the area for awhile had been one of the richest in the inland northwest. But time changes everything, it seems– the mansions had fallen into disrepair, and Silver Bay had lost its glory.

The Cutter property sat on the north side of the bay looking across the expanse of water toward Spinnaker Retreat– a self-realization center from the 1960s that had been out of business for more than twenty years. The Retreat property never seemed to attract a suitable new owner– it could only be accessed by boat, and the launch area immediately to the east of the Cutter property had not seen any usage for a long time. There was a faded sign on the disintegrating Spinnaker dock that sadly captured its legacy: "Spinnaker Retreat: Set Your Sail and Ride with the Wind!"

The Cutter property featured a lakefront marina, and the Silver Bay Lodge. The complex included 96 rooms in the main lodge building, accompanied by 78 rustic cabins spread among the trees. It had once been the playground of visiting millionaires– the mining and lumber friends of William Cutter held their gala parties there in the earlier time of glory. But wealthy people didn't come around anymore, and the Silver Bay Lodge had been forced to close during the real estate collapse. Paul Cutter had tried to keep the property alive, but there just never seemed to be enough paying customers to make a go of it. The economic reality for the lodge and surrounding property seemed far from favorable, but Paul Cutter was an optimist, and he had come up with a fresh plan to bring things back to life. That's why he and his banker from Idaho Neighbor Bank were calling Victor Desert this Tuesday morning. They were looking for money, and they wanted Victor to put together a group of California investors to revive the estate.

Victor reviewed the Silver Bay file with his morning cup of coffee. He was familiar with the Cutter property in an overview sense– his mother had taken him there for summer vacations when he was a boy. Victor hadn't been to Lake Ponderosa for many years, but seeing the glossy photographs of Silver Bay Lodge and the marina complex brought it all back. The warmth of a summer day in the tall pines was a memory that could never completely be lost, and Victor could almost feel the soothing water of the magnificent lake. He remembered those days– Lake Ponderosa was a unique place, thirty six miles long, and fronted on both sides by rolling hills covered with towering pines. It regularly turned up on lists of the most beautiful lakes in the world, and Paul Cutter's property on Silver Bay was special indeed. But what could be done with it to make any money?

The photographs in the file told a grim story of economic decline. The main lodge was all boarded up, and the marina boat slips stood empty. The cabins were in long term hibernation, and there didn't seem to be much financial incentive to bring them back to life. Resort real estate wasn't worth much anymore– the recent crash had seen to that. Paul Cutter's grand property had been flattened in value along with everything else, and

Victor could see from the file that his cousin was barely hanging on. If there wasn't an infusion of investor money, the property would disappear into the hands of the bank on a defaulted mortgage.

Victor sensed in the conference call that Paul's banker was just stringing his cousin along. Idaho Neighbor Bank had been doing business with the Cutter family for generations, but now that Paul needed a refinancing in hard times, the banker seemed to be coming up with all kinds of reasons why it just couldn't be done. What was really needed, the banker said, was for Victor to deliver some fresh California investment dollars to stand in front of the bank loan. Then there would be no problem . . . and Idaho Neighbor would be right there with them.

"So how much are you looking for?" Victor asked.

Paul Cutter didn't like to talk about money– he was an old fashioned kind of guy who paid his bills on time, and never owed anything to anybody. But times had changed– and Paul was not a stupid man. Unless he came up with some investor cash– and soon– the legacy property of William Cutter would be lost.

"I'd say we need to raise about $500,000 to bring the mortgage and back taxes current and get the lodge and marina operations up and running. There's some deferred maintenance in the dining room and kitchen, and the hotel rooms and cabins will need some sprucing up, but once we're back in operation the property can carry itself on a cash flow basis. The problem is that we've got to get out of the hole this real estate downturn put us in."

Victor addressed the banker from Idaho Neighbor, "Mr. Handler– would you be so kind as to give me an idea of the bank's view on this property."

"Of course, Victor. And please call me Nathan. As I'm sure you know, we've been doing business with the Cutter family for decades. And we think the property on Silver Bay is one of the finest on the lake. You simply couldn't ask for a better location, and the layout of the lodge and cabins is just what you would want. Old William Cutter knew what he was doing when he put that property together– no doubt about it. But the problem is cash flow and collateral. Idaho Neighbor is very reluctant to make a loan on lakefront resort property in this down market. There's just too much risk involved for a banker to stand in a first position with no fresh equity capital ahead of us. As I'm sure you know, a bank is a lender, not an equity player– and we at Idaho Neighbor try to always live by that distinction."

Victor wasn't fooled by the phony talk of the banker, but he said nothing and waited for Nathan Handler to complete his thought.

"So when Paul said you might be in a position to perhaps raise some equity money, we were of course interested. $500,000 would go a long way toward solving everyone's problems, and I'm sure the bank would be with you if that kind of new equity was to be brought to the project."

Victor wanted to get a feel for what was actually involved. "Paul, you and Nathan have both said $500,000. Is that the smallest number that will work? So for example, could the thing get done for– let's say– $300,000 in cash with some sweat equity along with it? After all, it sounds like a lot of what's needed is cleanup and refurbishing of the rooms and the cabins. Some old fashioned hard work might be a big help."

"I think we could get it together for under $500,000," said Paul after taking a moment to weigh his words. "The back taxes and mortgage need about $300,000 total– with repairs and maintenance accounting for the rest. Maybe we could do some kind of blended deal– and I know I could get some skilled people together to do the work. Nathan, what do you think?"

"Obviously, the more fresh equity, the better," said the lender smoothly. "It's never a good idea to go into a project like this on the cheap, but we're open to anything you might come up with. The bank has just over $800,000 on its existing mortgage, and we need some fresh equity in front of that if we're to consider rolling the loan over. Otherwise there's just too much risk, and the bank wouldn't be able to continue in a default posture. I'm sure you can understand our position."

That's the way things were left. Victor promised to think about it, and he and Paul would talk later. In the meantime, for Victor Desert there was no break in the schedule. It was on to the next meeting.

Victor was joined by Samuel and Bella Bloom in his office, along with Adrian Garfinkle. Desert briefed the Blooms about his trip to the east coast with Paladin.

"Not much new to report about how your son died, I'm afraid. At this point we're pretty much counting on David Kincaid and his investigation– so let's find out what he's come up with." Victor asked Caroline to connect up the conference call, and he and ETB made small talk with the Blooms while they waited for Kincaid and Frank Paladin to come on the line.

"OK," said Victor, leading off the group discussion, "let's get started. We have Adrian Garfinkle and Victor Desert in Century City, along with Samuel and Bella Bloom. Frank, I've filled the Blooms in on our trip to the east coast– so why don't you tell us what you've come up with since we got back into town."

"Nothing major so far. I'm still not finding anything on Mark Greenlee. Whatever happened two years ago, the bottom line is that he simply dropped out of sight. I think he may be out of the country. Or dead. I just don't have any active leads at this point, and without hearing from Mark Greenlee it's pretty tough for us to talk about any sort of wrongdoing where LawbridgeTrimble or anyone else is concerned. I'm convinced these people are all tied in together, and my gut tells me that somewhere in that group we're going to find some important leads about the death of Harlan Bloom. I don't have it yet– but I'll get there. . . . I'll find Mark Greenlee. People don't just disappear without a trace."

Paladin's report was a bit disappointing to the group in Century City– but not unexpected. The key at this stage of the investigation was David Kincaid, and he spoke next from Des Moines.

"I've been working on this thing for two months now, and here's what I've found so far. First, there's definitely a data block in the Porsche that's masking the telematics readings from the night Harlan Bloom was killed. I can see the blockage– and I'm confident the data stream readouts are still there underneath the block. But I can't seem to access them. My software platforms aren't set up to address this sort of highly advanced data block that I'm finding. So I'm having to rewrite my own software to get it to work. A little bit at a time– I have to use trial and error. It's a slow process, but sooner or later I'll get through the blockage. A day . . . a week . . . a month– no way to tell how long it's going to take."

"Are you telling us that you're definitely going to get through the blockage," asked Adrian, "that it's only a matter of time?"

"I think that's what I'm telling you . . . but I can't say for sure. This is without a doubt the most sophisticated data blockage I've ever seen. It's something new– no question about it. And developed by some genuine experts. I think it came from that Periscope group at Mirrorprobe– they're doing this sort of cutting edge private sector stuff. It's advanced– but let's keep in mind that it's been done by humans, and that means it can be undone by humans. Specifically . . . by me. I'll get through the blockage."

* * *

Victor and I met for lunch at Castino– a neighborhood Italian place on Santa Monica Boulevard. My young partner was a very busy man these days. He briefed me on his east coast trip and the latest reports from Paladin and Kincaid. But, of course, what I really wanted to hear about was Katy Hooper, and Theresia, and Sarah, and the Academy Awards show that Victor and Katy had so prominently attended only two nights before.

"Randolph, you've got to cut me some slack here," Victor said with a smile. "Katy is all over the place these days– she doesn't have any time for a lawyer like me. And as far as Theresia and Sarah are concerned, you're talking like a star–struck tourist. I barely had a chance to talk to them on the night of the Awards."

I was enjoying myself. "You're protesting too much, Victor. Way too much. Here you are, this ultra-successful lawyer with new cases and clients piling up everywhere, and you're off at the Academy Awards hanging out with three of the most beautiful women on the planet. I'm jealous, and with good reason. Theresia has a crush on you– and don't try to tell me I'm just making things up. Here's my evidence . . . who was her date for the Academy Awards on Sunday? Her father, that's who. Don't be thinking I'm too old to notice such things."

Victor understood I was only joking with him, but there was one thing I knew for sure that wasn't a joke in my mind– if Katy Hooper was smart she would hang onto Victor Desert as tight as she could. I kept my mouth shut, though– it wasn't for me to say.

Victor told me about his cousin's property on Lake Ponderosa. It sounded interesting– I told him to pass along the financial materials so I could take a look at the numbers. Then it was time to move on to my real purpose in inviting Victor to lunch.

"So tell me about this anti–foreclosure group that you're seeing this afternoon," I said.

Victor wasn't quite sure what my interest was, but he told me the story without hesitation. "Scott and Barbara Langsden are coming in, and I believe they've lined up a whole collection of families who want us to represent them in foreclosure proceedings against Turn of the Century Bank." Victor went on to explain about the Credit River decision, and bankers creating money out of thin air, and how that meant there was no consideration given by the bank for the loan . . . he had a whole theory worked up in his mind.

"Do you really believe a court will support that kind of argument?" I asked in a skeptical tone. I was worried that Victor might be getting in over his head.

Victor had obviously given that some thought. "If the homeowners don't pay the money back, they'll be unjustly enriched– no doubt about it. But what happens if you look at the same question from the other side? The real unjust enrichment would occur if Scott and Barbara did pay back their loan. Or if the bank was allowed to foreclose on their house. If the loan is paid back, the bank would be getting money that it never put up in the first place. And if the bank forecloses, it will end up owning a house that it never paid any money for."

Victor asked for my opinion whether the other firm partners would have any concern about his bringing the anti–foreclosure litigation into the firm. He was asking me to clear it with Jack Hazeltine and Roland Phillips, and I agreed to run it by them. I didn't think it would be a problem, and I told him so.

Back in the law firm, Victor met with the Langsdens and Alan Butler that afternoon. They had a list of 123 homeowners who wanted to join in the litigation, and each participant had agreed to put up $5000. With that kind of financing in place, Victor was ready to proceed . . . and for Scott and Barbara Langsden there were no options left. The homeowners in the Langsden group were at the end of the line. Either they litigated– to win– or they would be out in the street. For this group of deeply troubled clients, it was no more complicated than that.

XV.

Victor arrived at the Anjau estate in Beverly Hills promptly at 7:00 p.m. The house on Oxford Way was within walking distance of the Beverly Hills Hotel, and was surrounded by a tall wall which entirely concealed the property from the street. Victor pulled the Jaguar up to the entry gate and pushed the button. The large iron gate swung inward, and Victor drove forward up a sloping driveway that curved slightly to the left. After what seemed like a long distance, the tree lined driveway opened up to an old fashioned Southern mansion which had tall white pillars supporting an eave overhanging the front porch. A dark Mercedes was parked in the driveway, and Victor pulled in next to it. Theresia Anjau waited at the door.

"I wasn't expecting you to join us tonight," said Victor with a warm smile for the actress.

"And I won't be. I've been meeting with my father going over some business and such, but it's time for me to run along and leave the two of you alone. So you can have some guy talk– my father enjoys an evening like that."

Theresia showed Victor into the entry lobby and picked up a collection of books and file folders that were stacked on the hallway table. She gave out a call, "Father! Your guest is here."

Victor wanted to say something sophisticated, but for whatever reason he found himself tongue–tied in the presence of Theresia Anjau. She looked at Victor with an amused smile– waiting for him to speak. A long and uncomfortable moment of silence passed, and she finally took things into her own hands: "Well, I'm going to be on my way. I'll see you again soon, I'm sure . . . love you– bye!" A last quick smile, and the girl was gone.

Victor was alone in the hallway, feeling much the fool after his bumbling performance with Theresia. He wandered for a few moments, examining the collection of large oil paintings that decorated the two story entry hall. The artwork all had an antique look– men and women cavorting in open fields; elves and fairies at play . . . that sort of thing. Victor was a bit surprised . . . it wasn't the sort of decoration he would expect to see in the home of a movie producer. The paintings were ethereal and medieval in tone– not at all the ego pieces one might imagine in a Beverly Hills estate.

Sydney Anjau appeared at the head of the winding staircase. "Victor my boy. Thank you for joining me." Anjau was making his way down the stairs with considerable speed and coordination for a man of his age. "Let's not waste any time. Come in, come in." Sydney was leading his guest into the main living room off the entry hall. "What can I make you to drink? A scotch, with soda? You look to be a scotch drinker to me."

"Scotch and soda will be fine, thank you."

Anjau poured each of them a scotch over ice and led Victor to large chairs that framed a marble coffee table which appeared to Victor to be ancient, and priceless. "Beautiful table," he said.

"Indeed. A piece from France. Your home country I understand."

"Yes. Several generations back. My Desert family relatives came from Alsace."

"I'm always interested in such things," said Anjau. "You can know a lot about a person if you understand where they came from. So tell me about Millford– and how it was that you ended up in Los Angeles."

"It was my mother's doing. She was a young actress in Hollywood, and I'm sure if you asked her she'd tell you that her California years were the most interesting of her life. So I suppose it was only natural that I would have an affinity for the place. I came here to go to law school– and never gave any thought to leaving."

"And your father– what does he do?"

"Actually, I've never met my father. I don't really know anything about him, except that my mother knew him while she was living in Hollywood. One of those brief romances, I suppose. My mother is married to a Millford man– he was the commander of the local air force base on the outskirts of town, and I was raised by the two of them. That's why I have the 'Desert' name– my mother gave me her maiden name and never changed it after she was married."

"Ah, so we have something in common then," said Anjau with a smile.

"Like you, I never met my father. Except I knew who he was– my mother told me that much. His name was Brian Finnegan. Have you heard of him?"

"Of course. The author of *The Midianites*. I read it in high school– my English teacher used it as one of the assigned books of the time."

"Yes– it was his masterpiece. The coming of age book that we all grew up with. Never to be duplicated, unfortunately. My father, it seems, was living proof of the old view that a fiction writer is capable of only one great book. *The Midianites* was his– and he was dead by the age of forty. Drunk and broke– he died of a broken heart."

"So how did you become Sydney Anjau?" asked Victor.

"That was my mother's work. Errika Rubens was her name, and she was quite widely noted in her day for having the figure of a female character from one of the grand paintings of her famous namesake. Anyway, my mother had a way of getting what she wanted in life, and when I was born, she managed through some special magic to have me adopted by one of the leading families in New York. My adoptive parents– Charles and Sarah Anjau– raised me with all the finer things, and I am forever grateful to them and their lovely family. My daughter Sarah is named in honor of my adoptive mother."

"And if I might ask, what became of your birth mother?"

"The beautiful Errika? She went on to do all sorts of wonderful things, of course. Errika married a banker– his name was Halston Yasgar, and they had a son together. She was the leader of New York society in her day, and her son . . . my half–brother . . . has become something of a celebrity in his own right. Lawrence Yasgar is his name– perhaps you've heard of him. The Chairman and CEO of LawbridgeTrimble in New York."

Anjau was watching Victor's reaction with amusement, as for the second time in the evening, the lawyer was at a complete loss for words. After a long moment, Victor managed to regain his composure enough to say, "Are you telling me that Lawrence Yasgar– the head of LawbridgeTrimble– is related to you? That he's your half–brother?"

"That's exactly what I'm saying, and I assure you it's quite true. Small world, is it not? The earthly representative of the great god Enlil– our lord and master of worldwide finance– shares a mother with me. If Errika was still alive, I'm sure she would find the entire circumstance to be immensely entertaining. She had a grand sense of humor, my mother did, and the life and career of Lawrence Yasgar certainly qualifies as one of the amusing ironies of our time."

"I'm not sure I would look upon LawbridgeTrimble as a source of amusement."

"Ah," said Sydney Anjau, "but why not? Their desperate escapades to control a crumbling financial empire cause me to laugh every day. Surely you can appreciate the clownlike buffoonery. My brother actually believes he runs the world, but of course he and his colleagues are doomed to fail. They're quite blind, these bankers, but such hubris! The day of reckoning is nearly upon us, and they haven't a clue about what's happening. In a way I almost feel sorry for my half–brother. Lawrence Yasgar lives in the past . . . and I, for one, wouldn't want to be in his shoes when the Eljo come for him."

"Have you met Yasgar?"

"We've never formally been introduced, if that's what you mean. But I've known who he is for a very long time, and he knows of my existence, even though he doesn't know who I am. The story of my birth was a secret between Errika and me– but Lawrence Yasgar isn't a fool, and I'm quite sure he learned the truth somewhere along the way. I can feel his hatred whenever we're near to one another– he senses my presence. It's quite eerie, actually. Lawrence Yasgar is a descendent of the gods– my mother was a Blood Child to the core. Unfortunately, his destiny was to be on the wrong side."

"So if you're convinced Lawrence Yasgar is Enlil, I take it you believe in Enki, and the rest of Callien's story about the Blood Children?"

"Of course I do– I'm heavily invested in a film about them. But enough of this sort of talk– we must move to the dining room for dinner. Arthur will be deeply upset if we aren't at the table when his food is ready."

Sydney Anjau led Victor into the large dining room at the front of the house where two place settings awaited the men. Victor took his seat across the table from his host.

The film maker told some delightful Hollywood stories from his own life while the two men finished their drinks and awaited their dinner. Arthur and his wife Courtney were about– seeing to their every need. The English couple ran the Anjau household, and made sure Sydney had what he wanted at all times. The older man was enjoying his storytelling, but after a time he turned the conversation back to the business at hand.

"So I've been following the saga of this possible defect in our title to the screenplay. Interesting, I suppose, but only in a small way. Jonathan Silverstein is all worked up about it, but I don't share his concern. I'm quite confident that our young screenwriter Callien fully intended that the script come to us, and I don't believe that anyone will turn up with any kind of legitimate claim to prove otherwise."

"What makes you so sure?" asked Victor.

"Because of the manner in which the script was delivered. And to whom. Our Callien– whoever he or she might be– obviously did some careful thinking to figure out that Theresia and Sarah would be the ones for the roles of Ninhursag and the young Naamah. This tells me that Callien knew exactly what was needed for the script– the young author wanted my production company to do the movie, and wanted my daughters to star in it. We're doing nothing more than fulfilling the wishes of the author."

"Perhaps so," said Victor, "but I would feel better if Callien– assuming that's his real name– or hers– would actually come forward and tell us that his work is truly original and wasn't derived from something that didn't belong to him."

"Derived from the twelve tablets, you mean? Actually I fully believe that the screenplay is derived from the mysteriously missing tablets. But those tablets don't belong to the Mezo Institute, or anyone associated with Mezo. Our friends at Mezo and LawbridgeTrimble think they can control the course of history by destroying tablets, but they're soon to learn differently. They aren't in charge any more, and when LawbridgeTrimble goes down, their front organizations like Mezo and Talmadge University will go down with them. When the day of reckoning comes, this legal dispute won't matter at all."

Victor didn't know quite what to say to the rather strange and unexpected turn that the conversation had taken. So he fell back on some lawyer talk: "Perhaps you're right, but until that day of reckoning is actually here an entity like Mezo can send us a written demand that we cease and desist in production of the movie because they're the owner of the Blood Children tablets. And I expect that's exactly what they're going to do."

"Cease and desist, you say?" Sydney Anjau was amused at the thought. "Coming from an Institute that destroyed the tablets because it didn't want people to know what the tablets had to say? I don't think so. Once Mezo made the decision to dispose of the Callien tablets, whatever ownership rights they had went into the trash bin."

The men sat in silence for a few moments while Arthur served a watermelon and arugula salad with specks of blue cheese as a garnish. Sydney Anjau continued with his running commentary.

"So tell me, Victor, have you enjoyed working with my daughters on this intriguing little mystery of the screenplay? I hope they've been of assistance in your quest for answers."

"Very much so– they've cooperated with everything I've asked of them. And it would be difficult to imagine two more charming and beautiful women to play the leads in your film. I can say with confidence that they've been of great assistance in the effort."

"Beautiful, indeed. You realize, of course, that Sarah and Theresia are Blood Children themselves? And of the highest level."

Victor didn't know how to respond to what Anjau had said. A long moment passed, then Anjau spoke again.

"You seem bothered that I would say that, but you shouldn't be. Their mother Tamara was my grand and magnificent wife and I miss her to this very day. But she left me with her legacy– two beautiful daughters who are entirely worthy of their high blood mother. Theresia and Sarah believe in the *Blood Children* project– not just as actors, but in the content of the film itself. Their belief is the very thing that will make their performances so very special when the movie finds its way into the theaters. My two daughters have become their characters– which is exactly what any great actor should aspire to do. It's the same thing that Harlan Bloom did, poor man. I hope you can see the importance of that."

Victor answered carefully. "I can understand the point you're making about an actor. It's clear to me that an actor who believes in his character is going to deliver a stronger performance than one who lacks conviction about who he's supposed to be. But you seem to be saying something more than that, and Sarah and Theresia say it as well. They don't merely say they're acting a part– they say they have actually become the characters in some mystical way. That they are Ninhursag and the young Naamah in modern day incarnations. I hear what they say, but to me this whole idea of Blood Children actually existing in real life in the modern world seems quite far removed from reality. That's where I have difficulty when we talk about the Blood Children."

Sydney Anjau smiled at his guest. "Your struggle is understandable, but I can assure you that Enlil and the Igigi don't share any of your modern day views about things like equality. They look down on the entirety of humanity as a class of slaves and underlings barely worthy of shining their shoes. And without the existence of the Blood Children, that's exactly what we would all be– slaves, underlings– a herd of cattle grazing mindlessly under the direction and control of a corrupt group of Overlords. I say we're better than that."

Arthur delivered the next course– filet mignon in a red burgundy mushroom sauce with scalloped potatoes. Victor pondered this most unusual conversation while he ate a steak that quite literally melted in his mouth. And by the time dessert and coffee were served, Victor was ready to try some questions of his own.

"So should I take it that you believe the Blood Children tablets are grounded in fact? The stories about Cain, and Luluwa, and Enki's creation of the high blood race. Do you actually think those tales have relevance today in anything other than a mythological sense?"

"Relevance? Hardly an adequate word, my scholarly friend. The modern day existence of the Blood Children is the single most essential hope we have that control of the slaves by Enlil and his Igigi will one day be broken. The Blood Children aren't just relevant, Victor– they are the future of mankind, and the only thing that matters. Without modern day

Blood Children there will be no one to lead the way in the breaking of the chains. The Eljo won't do it on their own . . . they can't . . . they're not capable of it. So either we adopt the premise that Blood Children exist, or we give up, and accept that mankind will always be under the control of Enlil and will never rise above its status as slaves. Those are the choices, Victor . . . and they're the only choices."

Sydney Anjau returned again to the events he saw coming.

"You're not convinced, I can see. And it's easy to know why– you've lived your entire life in the dream world that Enlil and the Igigi have so painstakingly created for people like you. It's difficult to let it all go . . . but you'll see soon enough. I'm certain of that.

"The breaking of the chains is coming soon, Victor– get ready for it! Don't fear the changes that are coming . . . embrace them! This will be our moment, Victor . . . the moment for us, and most surely of all, the moment for you."

"Moment for me?" said Victor skeptically. "How could you know something like that?"

"I know because I'm Enki," said Anjau. "And I know because one of these days soon a new Enki will emerge to take my place. And that new Enki, Victor, is going to be you."

XVI.

They called it the Bourse, and it opened for business in 2008. Not just an ordinary oil marketplace– this was the Iranian Oil Bourse, located on the Persian Gulf island of Kish. The Bourse was founded to create a direct challenge to America's petrodollar hegemony, and it grew in size and significance all through the 2010s. The Iranian Oil Bourse was becoming a genuine threat to US dollar control as the world's reserve currency, and many approved. All around the planet, it was good riddance to the bankers and their phony money.

By 2021, the Iranian Oil Bourse was selling large volumes of crude to China, Japan, Russia, and India– major buyers in the emerging new economy. The Bourse traded in multiple currencies– but the American dollar found no welcome on the Kish exchange. The bankers at LawbridgeTrimble and the Federal Reserve watched, and plotted, and waited for their opportunity. They weren't amused by what they were seeing.

* * *

Everything was becoming too expensive for the Eljo– food, and housing, and gasoline, and clothing– all were skyrocketing in price as TEOTWAWKI approached. Fingers began to be pointed, and more and more ordinary people were finding their solace by placing blame on the bankers. The views of Harlan Bloom were no longer so extreme– others were saying what the actor had once said, and a strange legacy had begun to grow. After Harlan's death, a mushrooming army of protesters emerged, and they called themselves Level Z.

It was the time when money was dying– inflation could no longer be hidden with phony numbers and false words. The wealth of ordinary Americans from all walks of life was draining away to nothing, and a kind of madness was spreading across the land. Millions upon millions were finding themselves destitute in the merciless economic decline of the late 2010s.

The mainstream media told us we were turning the corner, but it never actually happened. It was all a big lie, and pretty soon only the diehards believed it anymore. Things weren't getting better as the 2020s approached . . . they were getting worse. Drip, drip, drip– the ordinary working men and women of America were disappearing into that empty place where forgotten people go to die. Middle class America was growing poorer, but somehow, magically, the bankers were getting richer. Many saw, and voices were calling for change. There was little time left for those who were still living in the old ways.

* * *

Victor and ETB had been beaten down by the sheer physical task of preparing 123 cases on behalf of the Langsdens and their fellow homeowners. But then, finally, it was lawsuit day, and the mass of paper was transmitted for filing to the Southern Magisterial Court. Victor and his team breathed an enormous sigh of relief as the complaints were filed and their clients were launched on the search for courtroom justice. Adrian and Victor were taking a moment to relax in the conference room.

"The hardest part was making the clients understand that Judge Mahoney's decision in Credit River was overturned on appeal," said Adrian. "They just can't bring themselves to acknowledge that the case was actually lost, and that the appellate court in Minnesota went out of its way to ensure that there was no precedential effect. They ask me over and over again: how could the appellate court fail to see the obvious? I've tried to explain, but I don't think they're listening."

"Maybe they just don't care," said Victor.

Adrian didn't understand, so Victor explained his meaning.

"Maybe they've reached the point where they have nothing to lose. They're like the protesters at Level Z, the end of the line as Harlan Bloom would have put it. So this lawsuit is the only thing left for them."

Adrian sensed the resignation in Victor's voice. "I hope what we're doing ends up being good enough."

"There's no turning back now," said Victor. "We just keep going, with our basic points in mind. The banker trick isn't rocket science– no need to get cluttered up with a bunch of extraneous details."

Scott and Barbara Langsden joined the lawyers in the conference room while Victor was talking. Victor could see the renewed sense of hope in their eyes . . . it felt so much better to actually be doing something. The lawsuit meant a lot to Scott Langsden– more than any of the homeowners, he had grasped the deeper meaning of the filings. Scott Langsden in his quiet way had emerged as a leader, and he had been instrumental in convincing others to join the group and put up money to fund the legal fees. Scott Langsden understood the issues, and he was the leading salesman for the legal concepts.

Barbara knew what the filings would mean: “So will we be ready for the onslaught when the bankers see this thing tomorrow?”

“I think so,” said Victor. “We still have some of the ancillary documents to prepare– and the bank needs to be formally served with the papers– but the core pleadings are out the door, and we won’t be changing them again. Nobody has ever done anything like this before, and I have the distinct feeling that our friends at Turn of the Century Bank and LawbridgeTrimble aren’t going to like it one bit.”

“Fuck ‘em.” Scott Langsden spoke for all of us. “Who do these criminals think they are?”

“Actually, they think they run the world,” said Victor with his first real smile in a long time. “So maybe it was up to us to tell them that they don’t.”

Caroline came into the conference room, carrying a thick document which she handed to Victor. “This just came in,” she said. “By email, from David Kincaid in Des Moines. I thought you’d want to see it right away.”

Victor looked at the face page. It was Kincaid’s report on the death of Harlan Bloom.

REPORT ON THE EVENTS OF DECEMBER 31, 2020 AND PRIOR WHICH CAUSED THE DEATH OF HARLAN BLOOM

BY DAVID KINCAID

I. BACKGROUND FACTS AND CIRCUMSTANCES

Decedent Harlan Bloom was an American actor, age twenty six, single, who lived in North Hollywood, California. He died on the night of December 31, 2020 when his Porsche Carrera automobile struck a freeway abutment in Cahuenga Pass at a speed of approximately 100 miles an hour. No one else was injured in the incident.

Over a period of several years leading up to his death, Harlan Bloom had been an outspoken critic of the Federal Reserve System, the central banking apparatus in the United States. Mr. Bloom frequently described the Federal Reserve as a fraudulent organization, as a counterfeiter that printed phony money out of thin air, and as an immoral entity which sought to enslave the American people through a web of debt. Mr. Bloom on multiple occasions called for ending the Fed, and advocated that leaders of the Federal Reserve and the American banking community be prosecuted as criminals. In his speeches, Mr. Bloom called for the return of the guillotine, although he did not at any time specifically advocate violence against the bankers or anyone else. Mr. Bloom's public criticism of the Fed fell within the ambit of protected speech under the First Amendment, but his provocative words created an active response from the banking community. Mr. Bloom stated on multiple occasions to friends and family members that he feared the bankers, and believed they were following him and harassing him.

Theresia Anjau reported that Harlan Bloom owed money to Turn of the Century Bank in Century City, and this factor was causing unpleasant interaction between Mr. Bloom and his bankers. Ms. Anjau described an incident which Mr. Bloom said occurred while he was driving home after a dinner engagement with her on the night of December 22nd. Mr. Bloom told Ms. Anjau that he was pulled over by two plainclothes police officers who were driving an unmarked car. Mr. Bloom said they used a flashing red light to signal him to stop his own car and pull over, and that he was then instructed to get out of his vehicle and undergo a field sobriety test. While he was involved in the field test, one of the officers searched the interior of his car. The two plainclothes officers displayed badges to Mr. Bloom bearing an insignia with the title "Federal Reserve Police: New York."

A bit of history about Federal Reserve police is necessary for an understanding of what occurred to cause Mr. Bloom's death. Federal Reserve Law Enforcement Units derive their authority from the Federal Reserve Act itself. For most of their history, such officers operated as protective personnel for the various Federal Reserve buildings and facilities located throughout the United States. Their task was in the nature of low level security, but a change in the law occurred in 2001 following the September 11th events, a change which granted broad ranging domestic policing power to the Federal Reserve. The USA Patriot Act provided that Federal Reserve police would thereafter be designated as law enforcement officers authorized to carry firearms and make arrests without warrants. The Federal Reserve police were empowered by the Patriot Act to operate in plainclothes or uniform, to organize specialized units known as "Special Response Teams," to operate 24/7 command and communications centers, and to utilize both marked and unmarked police vehicles as part of the Federal Reserve fleet. Under the authority granted by the Patriot Act, Federal Reserve police are certified to carry a variety of weapons, including semi–automatic pistols, assault rifles, submachine guns, shotguns, pepper spray, batons and tasers. Officers are authorized to wear bullet resistant vests and body armor.

Federal Reserve police have authority to enforce state and local laws, in addition to federal statutes. There are presently more than 20,000 such officers operating out of 37 stations within the 12 Federal Reserve districts. The Los Angeles Branch of the Federal Reserve operates its own Special Response Team and maintains a state of the art command center in its downtown office location.

II. EVENTS ON THE NIGHT OF DECEMBER 31, 2020

Harlan Bloom took Theresia Anjau to dinner at the Carousel Restaurant in West Hollywood on New Year's Eve. Mr. Bloom and Ms. Anjau had a friendly dinner, and left the restaurant at approximately 11:00 p.m. Ms. Anjau went home to her residence on Stanley Avenue in her own car, and Mr. Bloom left in his Porsche. Mr. Bloom and Ms. Anjau each had a single glass of wine at Carousel with dinner. The police report states that Mr. Bloom showed a blood alcohol content of 0.05– below the drunk driver limit of 0.08.

Several eye witnesses identified in the police report tell of observing Mr. Bloom's car going at high speed northward in Cahuenga Pass, and one witness driving a car behind Mr. Bloom saw the Porsche suddenly turn sharply to the right, leave the roadway, and hit the freeway abutment. It happened in a matter of seconds. Three witnesses saw a second car some distance behind the Porsche, also moving at high speed. These witnesses identify the second car as a dark gray sedan with no police markings or law enforcement identifiers. The identity of the second car is a mystery, and the written police report gives minimal credence to the involvement of a second vehicle. The conclusion stated in the police report is that Mr. Bloom, for whatever reason, was driving at high speed and lost control of his vehicle, causing his own accidental death.

III. ANALYSIS AND OPINION RE CAUSE OF DEATH OF HARLAN BLOOM

This incident has been treated as a single vehicle fatality accident by law enforcement authorities. I disagree with that conclusion, based on the results of my findings and interpretations of the Electronic Control Unit readings downloaded from the Porsche. My conclusion is that Mr. Bloom's vehicle was tampered with on December 22nd, and that a malware attack software code was uploaded that night into the vehicle's telematics module which thereafter enabled offsite control of Mr. Bloom's vehicle by remote communication. In my opinion, an offsite controller at the Federal Reserve command center in downtown Los Angeles took control of Bloom's vehicle on December 31st at the critical moment, and caused the crash.

The malware code installed in the Bloom vehicle is the most sophisticated I've ever seen, and represents a significant step forward in law enforcement capability. The code impacted the telematics environment itself, and installation of an attack code allowed the malicious code to co–exist with the legitimate telematics software, such that the malware code could displace the legitimate software and override driver inputs which would otherwise control the vehicle. The sophisticated attack code which I identified in Mr. Bloom's vehicle was capable of directly manipulating safety–critical ECUs of the vehicle and fundamentally compromising the operating environment. In my opinion, the malware identified in my investigation was installed on the night of December 22nd by way of the same OBD–II port that I utilized to download the ECU readout data during the course of my inspection of the vehicle.

My diagnostics readout generated two types of information useful in the investigation. First, the readout tells us that someone accessed the OBD–II port on the night of December 22nd at 10:38 p.m., which would place that access in the time frame when Federal Reserve police from New York were executing their field sobriety test on Mr. Bloom. Second, the readout tells us the actual operating history of the vehicle– specifically the utilization of malware attack code to remotely control the vehicle on the night of December 31, 2020.

The task of analyzing the data readouts presented significantly more difficulty than the initial function of identifying the time and place of OBD–II access. The highly sophisticated malware attack code in the Bloom vehicle had the capability of operating in such a manner as to erase any evidence of its existence on the ECU devices. With an attack code of this level of sophistication, a simple rebooting of the system will result in the masking of any evidence which might indicate that anything was amiss. Indeed, the erasing software goes so far as to eliminate evidence of the attack code's existence, such that a printed readout of the telematics data will show no trace of any intrusion.

The malware attack software installed in Mr. Bloom's vehicle constitutes a state of the art installation which has been developed only in very recent times. The leading group in the country that develops and manufactures software of this sort is a specialized unit known as Periscope which operates within an investigative firm called Mirrorprobe. The Periscope unit recently introduced a product in the military marketplace that has the same capabilities and features as the software I identified in Mr. Bloom's vehicle, and I conclude that the Bloom installation is a domestic law enforcement version of the military product. The two identifying components of the product are the malware attack software itself, and the erase software package which masks the existence and operation of the malware code.

Even the most sophisticated software erase mechanisms are not entirely foolproof. The Periscope erase product does not actually eliminate the data contained in the telematics module– instead it shields the data under a secondary system that redirects the analyst to revised data sets which appear to reflect normal operation of the vehicle. Breaking through this "shield" has been the work of the last several months for my office, as the breakthrough could only be accomplished by a complex environment of trial and error testing which ran millions of tests until the shielding effect was finally penetrated to allow access to the genuine data which existed below the shield. My analytic software was able to achieve this breakthrough only after considerable difficulty and rewriting of the testing code, but the bottom line is that I am now able to state with a high degree of confidence that the telematics module readouts for the time of the incident on the night of December 31st are available and complete. I'll attach the actual data readouts to the hard copy of this report. For analytical purposes, however, here are my conclusions:

(1) The malware attack software was initiated in Mr. Bloom's vehicle at 11:32 p.m., six minutes prior to the crash.

(2) The malware attack software caused the vehicle to speed up to 100 miles per hour as it proceeded in a northerly direction through Cahuenga Pass.

(3) At the critical moment, the malware attack software caused the vehicle to execute a sharp right turn into the freeway abutment.

(4) The malware attack software was manipulated out of the Federal Reserve command and communications center in downtown Los Angeles. I reach this conclusion on the basis that Federal Reserve police were the ones who installed the software in Mr. Bloom's vehicle, and no other person or party had access to the vehicle for such purpose.

(5) Once the event occurred, the malware attack software was disengaged by the remote control operator, and the erase mechanism was automatically implemented.

Based on the foregoing, I conclude that Federal Reserve police are responsible for the death of Harlan Bloom, likely New York and Los Angeles officers operating in tandem.

Respectfully submitted,
David Kincaid

PART TWO

The Night of the Bankers' Ball

I.

The crowd at Millford International Airport wasn't there to see the lawyers– except for Victor's mother and stepfather, of course. No, this unruly gathering of photographers and young girls dressed up like witches and vixens was a welcoming committee for the pop music icon of the moment. The Academy Awards performance had launched Katy Hooper into the top tier of celebrity, and a paparazzi event on her arrival in Millford was the result. I don't know how these fans and photographers had found out that Katy would be on the flight, but word traveled fast in that 2020s era of social media and celebrity worship– so here they were.

Victor and I were greeted by Walter Kollett and Victor's mother in the waiting area while Katy went over to be swallowed up by her fans. Joanne Kollett was crying– she hadn't seen her son for more than two years. It was a mother thing.

"Oh, Victor . . . Victor. I'm so happy to have you back in Millford, even if it's only for a few days. We have rooms all ready for you– Jerry can't wait to see you, he's handling the front desk today, otherwise he would have been here. And we have a reservation for dinner tonight– I made it at the Caravan Inn, of course; I know that's what you would have wanted. So introduce me to your friend, and of course I want to meet your young lady once she gets free of all this commotion." Victor's mother gestured dismissively toward the crowd of people surrounding Katy Hooper.

"Mother, I'd like you to meet Randolph Blaine. He's a senior partner in the law firm, and he's come up to take a look with me at Paul's property on Silver Bay." Joanne Kollett greeted me with a warm smile. She was a vibrant woman about 50 years of age, and highly engaging in a way that I'm quite sure was reminiscent of her acting days in Hollywood many years in the past. Once you have the actor training it never leaves you. I shook hands briefly with her husband, and we started on our walk to the baggage claim area.

Victor went over to the milling crowd of young witches to gather up his celebrity consort, but it soon became obvious that the throng of fans wasn't going to break up anytime soon. Millford isn't visited by the likes of Katy Hooper very often, and Katy was enjoying the attention. She'd only been a big star for a few weeks, and this sort of welcome was still a novelty. Victor left her alone and joined our group on the walk to pick up the luggage.

"So Victor, you're here to take a look at the Cutter property, I understand." Walter Kollett had a formal speaking style that was befitting of his former role as an air force commander. Talon Air Force Base in eastern Washington was a busy place. B–52 bombers had been flying out of there on missions to the perimeter of Russian airspace since the 1950s, and even in the 2020s– years after the end of the Cold War– a base like Talon that had long since outlived its usefulness as a first strike bombing platform still found ways and means to continue to exist in the US arsenal.

The base was one of the largest employers in Millford County, and woe be to any Congressman who might have had the temerity to suggest that the aging facility should be shut down. Walter Kollett had been the commander at Talon for ten years, and he carried himself like a man who was used to getting his way. He and Joanne Desert had been married for more than two decades, and they had a son, Jerry, who was Victor's younger half–brother.

"Yes, Paul asked me to come up, and it's a nice opportunity to get back home again and see the family. I wasn't expecting we'd cause such a stir though."

Walter Kollett was watching with interest as Katy Hooper made her way toward the baggage claim area with a train of photographers and witch fans in tow. "I wouldn't have known we even had paparazzi in Millford," said Kollett. "But I suppose they're going to be popping up wherever she goes after that big performance at the Oscars. Were you ready for all that?" Walter was looking at his stepson with amusement.

Victor was noncommittal. "Not your typical lawyer stuff, that's for sure. But I'll manage."

Katy caught up with the Desert family group as our baggage was arriving. Victor made the introductions, and Joanne insisted that Katy ride with Walter and her on the short trip to the hotel where we'd be staying. Victor and I went on alone to the rental car area, while some of the lingering paparazzi took shots of Joanne with Katy. The older woman's actor training was on full display.

"Your mother seems to be enjoying the visit so far," I said. Victor and I were watching the photographers and fans interacting with the two women.

"My mom has always looked on her Hollywood years as the best years of her life, and that's never going to change. So whenever she gets an opportunity to relive those days . . . well . . . that's exactly what she's going to do." Victor was smiling as his mother worked the crowd.

Victor continued to reminisce on the drive to the hotel. "It's been a good life for her in Millford, but there's no doubt in my mind that it bothered her a lot to leave LA. She gave up her acting career just at the moment when she had the chance to start getting some genuinely good roles. Joanne had paid her dues, and a couple of times she told me in a wistful sort of way how much she enjoyed the acting game back in the day."

We came over a rise, and a broad river valley opened up below us. There was Millford, spreading out on both sides of the Pine River, and rising up on a promontory to our right was the Desert Caravan Inn, a five story roadside hotel with a commanding view of the city below. It was the only remaining hotel property in the family– eleven others built by the first Victor Desserte in the early days of Millford had been sold off over the years.

Katy Hooper arrived a few minutes after us in Walter Kollett's car. There were still a few fans in tow, but the paparazzi seemed to have had enough and hadn't followed along to the hotel. I helped Katy with her bags while Victor went to greet his brother and check us in at the front desk. Within a few minutes we were relaxing in comfortable rooms overlooking the city.

The gathering that night at dinner had a certain symmetry– Victor, Katy and me on one side of the table; Walter, Joanne and Jerry on the other. And of course the Millford contingent wanted to hear from Katy all about the driving tour Victor took her on that afternoon while I was enjoying a nap.

"Oh, it was so much fun to see the houses Victor grew up in, and his schools, and things," said Katy with a winning smile. "The South Hill is so pretty– and I'm from a small town too. Bakersfield, in the dusty part of

California . . . it makes Millford look like heaven. So I really enjoyed the tour."

Jerry loved Hollywood stories, and he wanted to hear all about the fans at the airport. "Actually, I'm getting used to it," said Katy. "I guess you could say it's what every performer wants. I'm a singer, and I like it when people enjoy my singing."

"But what about how they're all dolled up with that Satan stuff? Does it bother you that maybe these young girls aren't getting the right message from your music?" Jerry Kollett had asked a question that was probably better left unspoken, but Katy didn't seem to mind.

"Oh, that's all just good fun. Like playing dress–up when we were kids. And besides, if you really want to hear about the old gods and their mysteries, you should talk to your brother. He's representing a movie production company with a movie in the works about the ancient gods that's going to shake things up all over the place. Victor's clients are the ones who are really into the occult, not me."

Jerry looked at Victor, obviously wanting to hear more.

"Well, I may have written you about it– but *Blood Children*, this movie I'm working with, is about ancient Genesis from a different perspective than we get in the Biblical Old Testament. The Bible tells us God is our friend and protector– but *Blood Children*, when it comes out, is going to carry the message that there were multiple gods in the days of the ancients, and the god Enlil created the human race to be slaves. Meanwhile, his half–brother Enki created a high blood race to lift up the ordinary people so that mankind wouldn't be destined to serve as slaves forever. Their rivalry is the heart of the *Blood Children* story– Enki trying to lift humans up, with Enlil wanting to keep them down."

"How does it all work out?" asked Walter, with a twinkle in his eye.

"Well, since most people are still slaves today, I suppose it isn't going very well so far. But there's hope– we'll just have to wait awhile for the final returns to kick in. The battle between Enki and Enlil is still going on."

"I'll say it's still going on," said Katy. "I keep hearing about how the young stars of the movie have actually become the gods and goddesses they're playing in the film. Isn't that so, Victor? Doesn't Theresia Anjau go around telling you she's Ninhursag? And Sarah– doesn't she think she's Naamah?" There was a noticeable edge to Katy's questions about the two actresses. Victor took a moment to carefully frame his response.

"Well, they might say things like that, but they don't really mean it. They're actors– and they're living their roles. It's like me with my lawyering. People call me the Facade, and say I don't actually exist outside my front as a lawyer. But you know, of course, that it's totally untrue." Victor had smilingly addressed his last comment to Katy Hooper, but if he expected something warm in return he was destined to be disappointed.

"Actually, I agree with them. You are a Facade."

Walter Kollett sensed the unpleasantry, and came in quickly to change the subject. "Tell me, Victor, what did you think of Millford from your little tour today? Does it look the same as when you left?"

"Pretty much, and that's one of the great things about Millford. It never changes, and of course springtime is the right time for a visit, with all the trees and flowers coming into bloom. Not like LA at all– the land of movie set streets where everything can change overnight."

Walter looked around the nearly empty dining room, "One thing that's changing in Millford for sure is that people aren't going out to dinner anymore. We've been losing money in this dining room ever since the real estate crash, and I don't see it turning around anytime soon. And the hotel is running way below normal occupancy too. Business is down in Millford across the board– and I mean way down."

"More than just the hotels and restaurants?" asked Victor.

"Everything. Prices going up, and business activity dropping through the floor. It's as if there isn't any private enterprise anymore. Back when I was at the air base, there were a dozen or so private companies in Millford that employed more people than the base. Not anymore– the base is the biggest employer in town. Millford businesses have been dying out– and that's why things are so tough. All the private employers are disappearing, and it seems more and more like the only jobs left these days that are worth anything are school teachers and postal workers– government work. I'm a military guy, but I've got to tell you that I don't see any way this economy can hold together much longer without private sector businesses. So here at the Caravan Inn, we're in the same boat as everyone else– just trying to make ends meet. And I have to tell you, either we start seeing a turnaround, or we're going to close it down."

Not exactly what Victor and I wanted to hear as prospective investors on nearby Lake Ponderosa, but there was nothing to say in response. We finished out the dinner with small talk in the nearly empty restaurant, and soon were in bed. Tomorrow would be a new day, and I held onto the hope that the lake environment would show more signs of economic life than what Walter had described for Millford. I slept fitfully, not sure what the new day would bring.

Paul Cutter met us for breakfast in the Prospect Hotel. The town of Prospect was about five miles up the lake from Silver Bay, and Paul would be taking us out to the property by boat. His wooden Chris Craft was docked right below the restaurant, and it was a thing of beauty– a 1940s vintage red and white express cruiser, 25 feet in length. Just looking at Paul's boat made me want to be out on the water. There was still a hint of a chill in the air, but the day was sunny and the winds were calm. It would be a beautiful ride to Silver Bay.

I'd seen the photos and layout map that Paul had sent down to Victor when the two men first started talking about trying to do an equity deal. It was beautiful to look at, but the core question in my mind was whether the lodge and cabins could produce an occupancy rate that would actually make a profit. Walter Kollett's discouraging words about the economy the night before had stuck with me. Where were the paying customers going to come from to fill the place?

Paul handed out a fresh set of pro forma financials to answer that question. "Obviously the summer months are the key," he explained. "If we can run at 90% occupancy or more during the summer, the numbers will work." Cutter pointed to the line items on his spreadsheet that illustrated his point. "We'll keep the lodge and restaurant open year round, but obviously the cabins and the marina operation will be seasonal. We can expect some pretty good cabin usage in the spring from fishermen, and boat slip rentals as well. But our key is the summer– and there's no reason to believe we can't do it. Lake Ponderosa is the biggest attraction in this part of the country, and that's not going to change. Once we get into full operation again, Silver Bay will draw its share of people."

After breakfast we made our way down to the boat dock and climbed aboard Paul's Chris Craft. Within a few minutes we had pulled away from the marina area and were in the main channel of the lake on the way to Silver Bay. Paul entered the bay with a broad sweeping turn, and slowed as he approached a long dock in a private cove that jutted off the main body of the bay. The place was deserted. We had arrived at the Silver Bay Lodge– and no one was there to greet us. I could see the five story wooden lodge building set back from the docks and partly shielded by tall ponderosa pines. Cutter pulled expertly into one of the empty boat slips and we made our way up the path to the grand old building.

"We have over a thousand feet of frontage," Paul said, pointing both to the left and the right. "Our beachfront curves around onto the main body of the bay and connects up with the boat launch area for the Spinnaker Retreat property that sits across the way on the other side." Paul pointed out the area he was talking about– the bay was about a mile across. "The Spinnaker boat launch is just to the east of our property line. We have road access on this side of the bay– but Spinnaker is water access only."

We walked up the heavy wooden stairs to the main lodge entrance. The stairs were protected by an overhang which probably served quite a useful purpose in the wintertime when the snows came. Paul Cutter produced a set of keys, and in a moment we were inside the lodge building itself. It was all done in rustic wood– a classic design that showed its 1920s heritage. "My great grandfather built this building," Paul said with a distinct note of pride, "and he built it to last."

I could see Cutter's point– everything about the lodge showed attention to detail and the sort of robust use of wood decoration that makes a structure timeless when done right. The lodge obviously hadn't been used for awhile, but it seemed apparent to me that it could be up and running pretty quickly with some elbow grease and cleanup. We spent a few minutes walking around the lodge interior and exploring the dining room and bar, and we visited some of the guest rooms on the upper floors. No question about it– this building was structurally sound and only needed to be brought back to life with some loving hands and hard work.

We came out of the lodge through the large doors which faced away from the lake. The building opened onto a play area for visitors and guests. Tennis courts, a full sized basketball court, areas for ring tossing, and even a lawn bowling setup were all in place. But the courtyard area was overgrown with weeds and encroaching brush– nature wasn't wasting any time in taking back her own. A gently sloping hillside led to the upper areas of the property where individual family cabins were scattered in the trees. Seventy eight cabins in all– mostly invisible in the thick forest unless you were right on top of them. Much like the lodge building, the cabins were in quite good condition– they had been built to last.

We spent about four hours at the property that day. I enjoyed every minute of it, as did Victor. I could see his enthusiasm as he revisited this place that had such good memories for him, but not so with Katy Hooper. The young singer was ready to leave after the first half hour or so, and she made her unhappiness apparent to all. I later learned from Victor that her negative reaction was to be expected– Katy liked city life, and wanted nothing to do with the out of doors. She had been raised in a small town, and Katy Hooper showed no desire to ever go back.

We took a cruise around Silver Bay itself before turning back toward the town of Prospect. Paul showed us the million dollar mansions– once glorious, but now in disrepair. There were a few newer homes along the lakefront, but all in all the tour was discouraging. I had the distinct feeling that Silver Bay was a place where the faded glory of the past wasn't going to be recaptured any time soon. Even to my untrained eye, it seemed obvious that an investment in the Silver Bay Lodge was not likely to turn out well. The area was in the doldrums– and it showed.

Dinner that night was at the Ponderosa Floating Restaurant in the marina area. Paul explained the geography to me– the Pine River flowed west to Millford, and ran through the center of the city before eventually joining with the Columbia for the trip to the Pacific Ocean.

Nathan Handler from Idaho Neighbor Bank joined our party for dinner. While the banker seemed a bit star struck by Katy's presence, he was still able to maintain sufficient focus on business to get out the obvious question: "So what did you think?"

Victor gave his reaction, which was very close to mine. "I think it's a sensational piece of property . . . as good as one could find anywhere on Lake Ponderosa. Great frontage, a beautiful and spacious parcel of land, and a set of structures that are in quite good condition and ready to be reopened. So it's strictly a question of money– does it make economic sense to invest in the project and reopen the lodge in the kind of uncertain economic times we're living in? I don't know the answer to that any more than anyone else. But that's the question . . . and it would be a travesty if Paul were to lose the property for an unpaid mortgage after all the time and effort his family has put in."

"I quite agree," Handler said smoothly. Just as Victor Desert knew how to talk like a lawyer, Nathan Handler knew how to talk like a banker. Lot's of pleasant words . . . but no commitments unless he wanted to make them. "We're talking about one of the premier parcels on the lake. If one believes in the future of Prospect and Lake Ponderosa– then one can believe in the Silver Bay Lodge . . . that property is as good as it gets."

"So what do you see for the local economy?" asked Victor.

Handler paused for a moment before answering. "I think we're in a recovery. Like all resort communities, Prospect suffered during the last downturn. I can't tell you we've fully recovered yet, so to that extent there are still some real estate bargains out there. And one has to say that a long and slow recovery like we're living creates a lot of uncertainty about how to deploy resources. So is Silver Bay the right spot . . . that's for you to decide, isn't it?"

Victor looked at the banker with a coldness in his eyes, and made what I considered to be a surprising change of subject in the conversation. "May I assume you've read about the anti–foreclosure lawsuits I filed a couple of weeks ago?"

Handler tried to hide his discomfort, but was only partially successful. "Yes . . . I saw some commentary about them. You caused quite a stir in the banking community, I think I can say with confidence."

"How much of a stir?"

"Well, of course, some of the theories about fraud and lack of valid consideration that you raise in your court filings involve matters where most bankers would disagree with you. I expect that Turn of the Century Bank will assert the appropriate counter–arguments in your litigation, so it will be a matter for the courts to decide. My initial reaction is that your cases are a matter of wait and see. Let's see how the courts handle it."

But Victor was determined to press the point, irrespective of Nathan Handler's discomfort. "So what I don't understand is why Idaho Neighbor Bank doesn't simply offer Paul Cutter a restructured loan for the amount of money he needs to clear the taxes off the property and get it operating again. Why are you asking for equity . . . whether from me, or anyone else? Your bank has been doing business with the Cutter family for generations– why aren't you standing with them now? You wouldn't be risking much of anything if you granted a renewal on Paul's loan– I don't understand why new equity is needed at all."

"I tried to explain it to you on the phone awhile back. Our bank simply can't make loans against land where there's a defunct business in place. It's against our rules. No matter how long we've done business with the Cutter family, if I tried to put through a loan of the sort you suggest I'd be fired. Frankly, Victor, I thought you understood that when we discussed this before."

Victor had no intention of being put off, "Actually, I don't believe for a minute that what you just said is accurate. I've done a lot of studying since we last spoke by phone– and I understand today what I didn't understand as recently as a few weeks ago. You create your loan money out of thin air– from nothing. That's what I've learned as a result of representing my group of homeowner clients, and it's been something of a revelation to me. If you can't make one of your fractional reserve loans to a multi–generational client like the Cutter family when they need it, what good are you? What service do you perform? Basically, you're useless."

Handler sat silently for a long moment. Then he stood up and said to Paul Cutter, "Paul, I'm sorry your cousin feels the way he does. You can be sure that Idaho Neighbor still has faith in you, and we'll do everything in our power to help you solve your problem with the property. But your cousin, I'm afraid, has spent a bit too much time down in Hollywood . . . the arrogance of the big city has gone to his head. And I'm not going to sit here and be insulted by some second rate lawyer. Thank you for the dinner invitation . . . but I think I'd best be on my way." Nathan Handler left the restaurant, and the rest of us finished our dinner in silence.

We had one more stop to make before catching our plane to Los Angeles the following day. Victor and Jerry Kollett wanted to visit the Desserte family mausoleum at Greenleaf Cemetery, and Katy and I were invited to join them. I figured it couldn't get much worse than what I'd seen the night before, so I decided to go along.

We pulled into the cemetery entrance, and Jerry stopped his car at the office to pick up the key to the mausoleum. Then he drove up to the second terrace, and parked in front of a prominent marble structure flanked by towering birch trees. The mausoleum had wide pillars in front, with the name DESSERTE prominently displayed in large stone letters above the doorway. Jerry opened the heavy metal entry door, and inside was a burial vault along the back wall, five rows across and four rows high. They were all here– the entire Desserte family in America beginning with the first Victor Desserte from Alsace. The vault was nearly full– only six drawers remained for the living. But that would be enough. Victor and Jerry would both be buried here, and their wives, along with their mother and probably Walter Kollett as well.

It was the last Desert Hotel.

II.

Frank Paladin wasn't the sort of man who gives up easily. So there was no reason for surprise when Victor received his call.

"Hey, buddy . . . how ya doin'?"

Paladin was in a very good mood, but Victor was not. "I'm hanging in there, but bone crushed with work. My anti–foreclosure cases are killing me."

"Well, those bankers . . . you know how they are. Hard to imagine that they don't like it when you say in 123 lawsuits that their entire worldwide business model is a fraud and a scam. And here they've been telling us all along how they were doing God's Work. Upstanding members of the community, and all that sort of thing. How could you possibly criticize?"

"Yeah. Upstanding– just the right word."

"So are you ready to hear some good news?" The investigator was enjoying the moment.

"I'm so ready for some good news that you couldn't even begin to imagine. What have you got?"

But Paladin wouldn't be rushed. "Well, here's the thing. I've been running into nothing but a bunch of dead ends where Mark Greenlee is concerned. The guy just dropped off the face of the earth a couple of years ago, and I couldn't find even a trace. So I'm looking at this thing closely, all over the place, and there's nothing turning up."

"This is your idea of good news?" said Victor. "You're calling to tell me you can't find Mark Greenlee, and that's supposed to brighten things up?"

Paladin ignored the sarcasm. "So I figured that Greenlee is using an assumed identity. It's the only explanation. Even if he were dead, I would have found him if he was still going by the name Mark Greenlee. So he's using a different name."

"OK. I'll bite– he's using a different name. And your point is . . .?"

"My point is that I went over Greenlee's history, and I found way back in his undergraduate days at Yale that he used an assumed name for awhile to publish a journal that was filled with all kinds of provocative writings. It was Greenlee all right, but he was publishing under the name Lloyd

Somers. Twenty years ago– Greenlee must have figured that he'd get into trouble if he published under his own name. His stuff was all about how religions based on one god lead to holy wars and centralized government tyranny . . . that kind of thing. The sort of writing that makes people uncomfortable. Anyway, his journal went out of business in less than a year, and Lloyd Somers disappeared into the mists."

"Lloyd Somers . . . OK, I'm with you." Victor was waiting patiently for the punch line that he already knew was coming.

"Well . . . here's the thing," said Paladin with a distinct note of pride in his voice. "Lloyd Somers has come back to life! He has a new blog out there called onegodmeansslavery.com. Same sort of edgy content as Somers was putting out twenty years ago. Mankind has been tricked and enslaved by their willingness to worship one god, revolutionary stuff. This guy doesn't think much of authority figures, I can tell you that for sure. So I trace back the domain registry on the new blog, and what do I find?" Paladin paused one final time for effect . . . "I find the blog domain is owned by someone named Akeel Gutierrez in Rio de Janiero."

"That's helpful."

Paladin was on a roll, and he wasn't about to be knocked off stride. "Actually, it's very helpful. So what I do is, I call my contact in Rio, and have him check out the address listed for Gutierrez. He goes out to the house, and he takes some pictures. It's a small house in kind of a run down area in the suburbs, and there's two guys living there. Like a gay couple– that kind of thing. One of them is our friend Akeel . . . and the other one– well I took a look at the pictures my buddy sent back, and it's Mark Greenlee, for sure. Same guy as we saw in the pictures Ashley showed us in Philadelphia. He's living on a temporary visa in Rio under the name of Lloyd Somers and publishing his blog from there. Gutierrez is a waiter at one of the high end restaurants in the city. A pretty decent job in that bad economy they've got down there, so Akeel brings home the money and Somers– actually Mark Greenlee– spends his days writing on the blog."

"Great news, Frank. You're really onto something, so what's the plan?" asked Victor.

"Hang on a minute . . . don't get ahead of me. I'm not finished." Paladin was having fun. "My guy in Rio checks out Akeel Gutierrez, and it turns out he has a younger sister. Her name is Raffi Gutierrez. So I did some quick follow–up on our young friend Raffi, and what do you suppose I find?" Paladin waited expectantly for Victor to rise to the bait.

"OK . . . tell me . . . what did you find?" Right on schedule– Victor hadn't been able to resist.

"What I found is that Raffi Gutierrez lives right here in beautiful Hollywood, California. And she's a writer. She works on *Earle and Harry* . . . you know, that new TV sitcom everybody is watching– it's actually pretty funny." Victor wasn't much interested in *Earle and Harry*; he was waiting for Paladin to get to the point. "Anyway, as a sideline, Raffi Gutierrez also writes screenplays. She's sold one so far– a small deal that probably isn't going anywhere, but she has a couple of other scripts that people in the industry are looking at. Raffi Gutierrez, my sources tell me, actually has some genuine talent . . . undiscovered, of course. The kind of talent that can show up as a knockout script for a film by the name of *Blood Children* if you want my humble opinion."

"What's the next move?" asked Victor.

Paladin didn't hesitate "We pay a visit to Raffi Gutierrez, of course."

III.

The short stretch of Fuller Avenue lying north of Hollywood Boulevard is lined with apartment buildings that house young wannabe actors and writers crammed together four or more to a unit. Victor and Frank Paladin found a parking spot on the crowded street and walked to the building where Raffi Gutierrez lived. A knock on the door brought a gruff response from a woman's voice inside.

"Yeah . . . who is it?"

"We're here to see Raffi Gutierrez," shouted Paladin through the closed door.

"OK. Just a minute. . . . Raffi– there's someone at the door to see you."

Victor and Paladin waited, and after a few moments the door opened. A woman looked at the two strangers with suspicion. "I'm Raffi Gutierrez. What can I do for you?"

Raffi Gutierrez was a tall young woman of about twenty two. She had long black hair, and the sort of unique eyes that told of a Brazilian background. Gutierrez may not have been a beauty in the classical sense, but she had a look about her that seemed to exude a sort of quiet and easy confidence. She has a lot of talent and knows it, thought Victor to himself.

"We're here to talk about *Blood Children*." Paladin spoke to her in Spanish, and wasted no time. His well developed instincts told him Raffi Gutierrez was the one he'd been looking for.

Victor watched with interest as the young woman tried to compose a response to Paladin's blunt point. "Uh . . . who are you? . . . and what are you talking about . . .? I mean, are you sure you have the right apartment?" She had answered in Spanish, but even Victor, who didn't speak the language, could tell that her words were uncertain and fumbling. Paladin had caught her by surprise.

Paladin said, "I'm going to speak to you in English now. Please don't be alarmed–we're not here to hurt you or anything like that. This is Victor Desert, he's the attorney for Eanna Pictures. You've heard of them, I'm sure– they're filming the movie from your screenplay. And I'm Frank Paladin, private investigator. We've been trying to find you for awhile now, and it's a pleasure to meet you at last. We enjoyed your work.

Callien, isn't it? Excellent piece of writing on *Blood Children*– I think you're going to have a hit on your hands."

"I'm afraid you've made a mistake. I'm a writer for a television sitcom, and I don't know anything about any movie, or a screenplay for a project called *Blood Children*. You have the wrong person– sorry I can't help you, but . . .". Raffi Gutierrez was moving to close the door, but Paladin stood in the doorway and blocked the effort.

"There's no reason for you to hide, Raffi. We've found you, and we know all about your brother and Mark Greenlee down in Rio. It's out in the open now– and this isn't some random visit out of the blue. We're here because we need your cooperation in establishing Eanna's right to use your screenplay– which is exactly what you wanted when you sent it over to Theresia and Sarah to begin with. Now please stop insulting our intelligence, and let's start hearing where your script came from, and how it was that you came to write it."

Victor hadn't said anything yet, but he added his comment now. "Like Frank says, I'm the attorney for Eanna. Sydney Anjau's company." Victor handed Raffi Gutierrez his business card. "My clients have a lot of money invested in this project, and they're making the movie that you gave them. It's the movie that you wanted to be made. The *Blood Children* project is likely headed into litigation, and we simply must hear from you– and Mark Greenlee, of course– about how you came to write the script for this property. We're here on a friendly basis– we're asking for your help– but you should understand that this will all come out anyway in litigation, so you might as well cooperate now and save a lot of wasted time and effort."

"Listen, I'd like to help you," said Gutierrez, sticking to her story, "but I really don't know what you're talking about. Now, if you'll excuse me . . ." She pushed the door closed with a burst of energy strong enough to force Paladin to move out of his blocking position. Victor and Paladin were alone in the hallway– there was nothing to be done except return to the office and plan the next step.

* * *

It was around noon on the following day when Victor and Frank Paladin pulled into the driveway at the Sydney Anjau estate. Arthur answered the bell, and showed them into the library. Victor and the investigator took seats at the conference table, and waited for Sydney Anjau to join them.

"Gentlemen, gentlemen," said Anjau as he entered the library, closing the double doors behind him. "Thank you for coming. I understand you've had some success– I'm looking forward to your report."

Victor took the lead. He briefed their host on the events of the past few weeks, concluding with a report on their visit to Raffi Gutierrez in Hollywood the day before. Anjau listened with interest, then spoke.

"Yes, Raffi came by last night and told me you'd been there to see her. A nice piece of detective work, Mr. Paladin– you should be pleased with your effort." Sydney Anjau was smiling in an unconcerned way as he spoke.

"You mean . . . you're saying . . . that you know Raffi Gutierrez?" Victor was struggling to find the right words in his state of confusion.

"Of course I know her," said Anjau. "She's the screenwriter for my movie. I have quite an investment tied up in the work of that young woman." Anjau was looking at Victor and Paladin as if there was nothing out of the ordinary about what he was saying.

"Well perhaps there's been a misunderstanding on my part," said Victor in a mystified way. "I thought the assignment given to my firm by Eanna was to locate the writer of the screenplay and make certain there was no defect in your legal rights to produce the movie. Now you're telling us that you've known all along who wrote the script . . . and that you've been working with Gutierrez on the project for awhile. I'm a bit lost . . .

what was the purpose of the Callien letters, and the anonymous script delivery to your daughters? Why keep it a secret?" And particularly, why keep it a secret from me as your lawyer?"

Anjau looked at Victor Desert with amusement. "I suppose you're right– perhaps we were being a bit overly dramatic. And obviously everything changed when Harlan Bloom was killed." Victor noticed Anjau's choice of words about Harlan. Apparently he'd been kept informed by Theresia and Sarah about Kincaid's findings. "But Raffi wanted to keep it private. She and her brother didn't want Mark Greenlee's name tied to the project, and I tried as best I could to come up with a way to accommodate their wishes."

Frank Paladin had a question. "So if you don't mind my asking, what actually happened with the screenplay?"

"Raffi brought the *Blood Children* script to me about a year ago. She had done her homework– she knew from some of my prior pictures that I was sure to like the subject matter . . . which of course I did. I realized right away that *Blood Children* was going to be a terrific film, so I did a deal with Gutierrez where I would produce it. She was using Callien as a *nom de plume* on the work, which was fine with me, and I got the story from her about Greenlee being fired at the Mezo Institute, and saving the Callien tablets from destruction back in New York. Mezo has no claim to those tablets– they were trying to destroy them. Greenlee stepped in and put a stop to it. Raffi's brother Akeel sent her the translation of the tablets that Greenlee prepared, and Raffi then wrote the script based on the tablets. All legal and aboveboard– Eanna has the rights as a result of my contract with Raffi. Mezo, of course, is clueless. I saw the letter they sent demanding that we cease and desist. Apparently they don't even know back in New York that the tablets are still in existence. But I suppose you'll explain it all to them one day."

Frank Paladin was quicker on the uptake than Victor. “So you had Raffi send the script to your daughters anonymously to protect the secret, is that it? And of course you knew Theresia and Sarah would bring the script to you.”

“Pretty much that’s right. But I had another motive as well. I saw right away that Sarah and Theresia would be perfect for the leads as Naamah and Ninhursag, and I figured if I went to them with the script they might not look at the project in the same way as if the author of the screenplay sent it directly to them. It added some intrigue to the process, and I was hoping would cause them to take a more proprietary view of the screenplay. I thought it would work better if the script came to them from Callien rather than me.”

Victor was dumbfounded– Sydney Anjau had figured the whole thing out a year before, and had known all along that he had the rights to Raffi’s script. But one thing Anjau had said was bothering Desert “Why do you think Mezo would destroy the Callien tablets, and fire Mark Greenlee? I don’t understand the logic of that.”

“Mezo has been destroying Mesopotamian tablets for decades. Anything that doesn’t fit comfortably into their modern day world view they throw away. You have to understand . . . Mezo, and Amerosa, and Eurosa, all of those bogus archaeological foundations . . . are owned by LawbridgeTrimble. That’s why they have their corporate offices in the LawbridgeTrimble tower. So the Lawbridge people can keep an eye on them.

“Knowledge is the single most important thing in the world we live in, and it’s the very thing that will one day cause the overthrow of Enlil and his Igigi. They know that, so LawbridgeTrimble destroys knowledge. They try to control the past, because he who controls the past controls the future. And our banker friends on Maiden Lane, I can assure you, are all about control.”

IV.

The long airplane flight gave Victor plenty of time to think about what Sydney Anjau had told him at the Anjau mansion. The man who called himself Enki had explained it all when he said that he who controls the past controls the future. But Victor was on his way to see Mark Greenlee– and Greenlee was the man who had taken control of the past away from the people at LawbridgeTrimble.

It's difficult to comprehend from the ground how truly big and bustling Rio de Janiero actually is. Victor's view from the airplane put it in perspective– more than six million people lived there, and it's home to the grandest carnival in the world. People go there for fun, but on this visit, Victor Desert and Frank Paladin had a different purpose. At long last, they would be seeing Mark Greenlee face to face.

Akeel Gutierrez met the two visitors at the airport in a beat up Chevrolet Impala. The car was a mess, but it still ran and that was good enough for Akeel. He explained that he didn't need a car to get to work– mostly he and Greenlee spent their time at home. They were both writers, Akeel explained, although he was quick to point out that his younger sister Raffi was the real talent in the Gutierrez family.

As with so many people in Rio, Raffi and Akeel Gutierrez had an exotic family heritage. Their father was a policeman from Bolivia– their mother an Egyptian raised in Cairo. The two had met at the carnival in Rio and it was love at first sight. Blood Children, Victor thought to himself. They must have been– after all, Raffi Gutierrez was Callien . . . . Victor shook his head to clear away this unwelcomed notion that people around him were becoming ancient gods and poets. I'm getting to be as bad as the rest of them, the lawyer thought to himself with annoyance.

Akeel drove expertly through the crowded streets, avoiding pedestrians who apparently felt no concern about walking in narrow roadways with speeding cars on all sides. After a few minutes the Impala began to make its way into the outskirts of the city, the places where people didn't live so well. There were tin shacks here, and houses made of cardboard, or anything else that could be picked up to provide some shelter. The small residence that Akeel and Mark Greenlee called home was at the end of a cul de sac street, and backed onto what appeared to Victor to be open jungle. The house was run down and in ill repair, but it actually was set in quite an exotic and spectacular location. Dogs, and cats, and other lesser known animals, walked in and out of the house with impunity. Victor couldn't help but wonder if they were actually domesticated.

Mark Greenlee had heard the approaching car, and he met the visitors in the doorway with a booming welcome. Greenlee was wearing baggy shorts and sandals, and a faded t-shirt with a logo for Miller Lite beer on the front. He was a big man with a barrel chest and looming stomach, and it was immediately obvious to anyone who spoke with him for more than a few moments that Mark Greenlee was a genius.

He had done his undergraduate and doctorate work at Yale, and over the years had emerged as the leading expert in the world on the subject of ancient middle eastern cultures. No one knew more than he about the ancient civilizations of Sumer, Assyria, and Babylon. Greenlee knew the stories of Enki, and Enlil, and he understood better than anyone the early times of the Blood Children.

Mark Greenlee settled into the role of gracious host while Akeel went off to get cold drinks for the visitors. A tour of the house took only a few moments, and the centerpiece was obviously Greenlee's amazingly cluttered desk in the rear room which fronted onto the encroaching jungle. Here he produced his daily blog at onegodmeansslavery.com.

"I began studying monotheism twenty years ago, at Yale," Greenlee explained. "I had a journal there for awhile where I wrote about how the monotheist religions all say they worship the same god, but then they go around starting up holy wars and claiming special status for themselves with their god of choice. Such nonsense! Such foolery! The whole idea of one god has an entirely ridiculous history when you look at it closely.

"Even the Romans, with all their authoritarian ways, were smarter than we are– they allowed conquered barbarians to maintain their own gods and laws even as they became a part of the Empire. Is there any reason we can't do the same today? Of course not– but try telling that to 99% of the people and they'll call you a fool, or a traitor, or worse. It's as if we can't live without our dream of special favor in god's eyes– we revel in it."

Paladin told Greenlee how he had tracked him down through the old journals.

"Good job of finding me, I suppose," said Greenlee with a rueful smile. "I actually thought I'd made a pretty good effort in not leaving any kind of paper trail behind. Not good enough apparently."

"But why did you want to go undercover at all?" Victor asked.

Greenlee looked at Victor with amusement. "Apparently you haven't had a lot of dealings with LawbridgeTrimble. You don't just leave those people and go on with your life as if nothing had happened. They're like the gangsters . . . they never let go. And I mean never. So in my case I chose to drop out of sight. And of course I found Akeel here– which made the whole process both easy and enjoyable." Akeel Gutierrez smiled at the compliment from his partner.

"Tell us about the Callien tablets," said Victor, getting down to business.

"It's not very complicated, actually. I found the tablets in inventory and recognized that Callien was the author. Callien was familiar to me– I'd translated other works of his over the years, and I knew he was one of the poets of his time who actually had something interesting to say.

"We have all these hundreds of thousands of Sumerian clay tablets, but the problem we're facing is terminal boredom. Most of the writings are mundane. There were only a handful of writers in ancient Sumer who had any sense of artistry in their work, and Callien was one of them. The rest of the Sumerians were a bunch of conformists who reveled in higher authority and obedience. A culture of slaves, sorry to say. Civilized in many ways . . . but slaves nonetheless. And that's what we see in their writings . . . except for Callien. He was nobody's slave, and his poem about the Blood Children was the single most radical and revolutionary Sumerian writing I'd seen in twenty years of translation work. That's why his tablets resonate so strongly.

"When I discovered that Callien had written a comprehensive poem about the battle between Enki and Enlil I was genuinely excited. Particularly the part about Enki's creation of Cain, and then the gift of Luluwa after Cain failed so miserably to measure up on his own. The twelve tablets had been in inventory for decades gathering dust in the warehouse, until I found them by accident. Magnificent treasures– just sitting there, waiting to be discovered. So I picked them up and started a transcription."

"When in the process did you do your interview with Karen Ashley?" asked Victor.

"I was most of the way through the translation when she talked to me. We had worked together quite a bit, so she knew what I was doing. I think she realized– just like I did– how extraordinary these tablets actually were. I tried to give her a feel in the interview for Callien's revolutionary views, but I'm not sure if it came across as well as I might have liked."

"It apparently came across too well," said Victor. "You seem to have made some people upset."

"Well that's certainly true. Once Peter Takhar and the other senior management people at Mezo began to realize what Callien was saying in the tablets, they didn't want anything to do with them. They weren't interested in hearing about any sort of redemption for Cain, or the birth of a high blood goddess like Luluwa, so they put a freeze on my transcription work– which had never happened to me before at Mezo. I was a senior fellow by that time, and I had the freedom to work on projects of my own choice . . . or so I thought at the time. Turns out I was wrong about that, along with a lot of other things."

"Seems so," said Victor. "And of course Takhar told us a pack of lies when we went out to meet with them."

"No surprise there. So anyway, they physically took the tablets away from me. That was when I realized they were going to destroy them. I'd seen it happen before, but never on a project that I was so closely involved with. Mezo has destroyed thousands of tablets. And after I did some research, I began to realize that the tablets they destroyed all fit into a common pattern. If the tablets discussed multiple gods– and particularly Enki and Enlil– they would be destroyed. If the tablets talked about the human race as a slave race– they would be destroyed. If the tablets talked about Enki's creation of Cain and Luluwa, or anything else that challenged a monotheistic view of Biblical Genesis– they would be destroyed. Once I started looking into it, I began to realize that Mezo– actually LawbridgeTrimble, since they were the ones calling the shots– was engaged in a systematic worldwide effort to wipe out any traces of early historical writings that would support the idea of human freedom. They want mankind to believe in their masters– and stories about Enki and the Blood Children don't fit the mold."

"I take it you didn't think much of the idea that the Callien tablets were going to be destroyed?" Victor asked.

"I was furious, but I kept my mouth shut. What I did was arrange things so that I became the person at Mezo responsible for the destruction of that particular collection of tablets– about a thousand tablets all together. Once I had the access, I substituted a collection of meaningless accounting tablets for the Callien tablets, and nobody knew the difference except me. Off they went to destruction– except the twelve Callien tablets came home to my apartment in Manhattan. I didn't view it as stealing– Mezo had sent them out to be destroyed, so as far as I was concerned they could hardly claim any sort of ongoing ownership interest."

"They might try to argue otherwise, but I agree with you. Anyway, go ahead with your story. I don't mean to interrupt."

"It was obvious by this time that Mezo wanted me gone. I was saying things they didn't like, and let's face it, I wasn't much of a team player anymore. So we worked out a severance agreement, and I was very careful to draft it in a way that said anything I did after leaving Mezo belonged to me. I didn't take any of my work product with me when I left Mezo– the transcription that Raffi used to draft her screenplay was something I wrote from here. As far as I'm concerned, they have nothing to complain about."

"When did you decide to turn the transcription over to Raffi?"

"Actually, never. Akeel gave the transcription to her without telling me about it. I was really upset at first, but then when I thought about it, I realized he was right. What's the point in having this great story if it isn't going to be told? The Blood Children story needed to get out there as modern day entertainment– and that means a feature motion picture. Sydney Anjau was the right person to do it, so Raffi figured out a way to get the script into his hands. Anjau saw right away that Raffi's workup was a major piece of artistry– so that's where we are today."

Greenlee and his visitors talked late into the night that evening, and again the following day. Mark Greenlee explained so many things to Victor Desert, and when Victor left Rio that evening, he knew about the important things in ways that he had never considered before. The young Victor Desert, for the first time, was beginning to understand. And Mark Greenlee was his great teacher.

V.

When Victor took the time to think about it, he realized that the lawyers at Kessler & Abramowitz couldn't have picked a better day to serve their intellectual property infringement lawsuit. Victor received his copy of the complaint on the day he got back in the office from Rio. Mezo had sued in the Median Division Court, with all the bells and whistles demanding that production of the movie be stopped, and all sorts of damages and attorneys' fees be paid for infringement, blah, blah, blah. Victor was smiling as he looked through the 114 pages of pleading. Mezo still believed the tablets had been destroyed– but Victor had his witness to prove the true facts and blow the Institute case out of the water. Mark Greenlee had agreed to come out of hiding and testify.

The new litigation was going to be a lot of additional work piled on top of the already busy collection of matters that Victor was trying to keep up in the air. The stress was affecting him, and from his dinner with Katy the night before, it was pretty obvious she was feeling it too. Victor had tried his best to make the evening festive. Several very feminine gifts from Rio were unveiled, but Katy was having none of it. She was bored to tears with Victor, and his lawyering, and with being left alone. Leaving Katy Hooper to her own devices might not have been the smartest thing for Victor to do, but actually there was no choice. The client work had to come first, and Victor expected that Katy would understand . . . and wait. But absence, it turned out, didn't make the heart of a young celebrity grow fonder. Katy was sullen and uncommunicative all during Victor's romantic dinner.

Victor called Sydney Anjau to arrange a time to meet and go over his trip to Rio and the new legal filing by Mezo. Anjau seemed pleased to hear from the lawyer, and they set up an appointment to get together that afternoon. When Victor pulled into the driveway of the mansion he noticed two cars already there. Theresia's Mercedes was parked next to the garage, and a late model BMW that Victor didn't recognize was in front of the entry steps. The lawyer had to walk around the BMW to get to the front door.

Arthur answered the bell, and he took Victor into the living room where Theresia and a stranger were waiting with Sydney Anjau.

"Victor, come in," said Anjau, rising from his chair to shake the lawyer's hand. Theresia and the other man rose too. "Let me introduce Robert Rossignal."

Victor's hand was grasped in a vigorous handshake. Rossignal was a big man, about six foot five, and obviously an athlete. Rossignal had played some basketball at Fresno State, and he had the look of a man who spent a lot of his time outdoors. The big man was well tanned, and wore an open shirt over a muscular chest. Robert Rossignal had close trimmed black hair, and alligator cowboy boots to complete the look. He would be comfortable on a horse, Victor thought to himself.

"Pleased to meet you, Victor," said Rossignal. "Sydney and Theresia have been telling me all about the litigation disputes. Pretty exciting stuff, being a lawyer and all. I'm looking forward to working with you."

"Working with me?"

Sydney Anjau jumped in. "I've decided to do the Silver Bay deal with Paul Cutter. Spent the morning on the phone with him up in Prospect talking about the logistics and what all needs to be done to get the property in shape. Smart guy, your cousin. He really knows that neck of the woods. Anyway, I've decided to put Bob here on the project to oversee the construction and repairs for me. So the two of you are probably going to be spending some time together."

Victor was taken aback by the news. Something about Robert Rossignal sparked a visceral reaction in Victor Desert, although he wouldn't have been able to tell you why. But there was nothing to be said– if Sydney was going to put up money to save the Cutter property, more power to him. Anjau would be calling the shots, and Victor had the good sense to say the right thing: "That's great. I think it will be a good investment for you, and I'm pleased that you and Paul were able to work a deal."

"Actually. Victor, I'm not looking at this project as an investment at all. Or at least not an investment in any kind of traditional sense. I think the bottom is going to drop out of this economy . . . soon . . . and when it does, we're going to see turmoil like nothing we've ever experienced before. That's why I've brought Bob in on this deal. He'll be in charge of getting the plan together for a move to the property. And he'll be working with Paul to get things ready."

"Ready for what?" asked Victor, still not grasping Sydney's meaning.

"Bob, why don't you bring Victor up to date," said Anjau.

The big man launched into his report. "Ready to serve as a compound for a group of people who want to survive what's coming. I figure the property can support about 3000 people on the existing grounds if we build it out with some additional living quarters and the other facilities people are going to need. And we'll be securing the perimeter, and putting up some observation towers and early warning devices."

Victor couldn't hide his surprise. "You're doing a survivalist location? And getting ready for attacks against the property . . . is that what you're saying?"

"Attacks are a very distinct possibility if Sydney turns out to be right about what he sees coming. Once things go bad, there are going to be a lot of desperate people around, and they're going to be looking for food and shelter. My job is to make sure we're ready for it."

Victor had a bad feeling when he drove home to the Curson house that night. Sydney and Theresia were obviously taken with this idea of turning the Cutter property into a hideaway for survivalists, but Victor didn't believe in that sort of thing. An armed camp was nothing Victor had in mind when he had approached Sydney Anjau about the prospect of investing, and he wondered what Paul Cutter thought about all this. Maybe Paul didn't care– at least he wouldn't be getting foreclosed by Idaho Neighbor Bank. Rossignal and Anjau were planning to expand– they were already in the process of acquiring several thousand acres of farmland in the surrounding area, so maybe Paul was on board. In any event, there was one thing for sure . . . Sydney Anjau had a plan, and Robert Rossignal was the man who was going to bring it all about. Whether Victor Desert liked it or not.

Katy's car wasn't in the garage when Victor pulled in. He walked into the empty house and made himself a grilled cheese sandwich for dinner. Then he went to bed . . . alone.

VI.

Sarah Anjau put down David Kincaid's report after reading it yet another time. She understood what had happened to Harlan Bloom– he'd been murdered. And his murderers were working for the father of Winston Bartell– the very man she had been meeting for dinner over the past couple of months. The killers didn't work directly for Winston– he was still just a young lawyer, not important enough for things like killing. But his father, Wellington Bartell, was the President of the Federal Reserve Bank of New York, and that's where David Kincaid had placed the blame.

Winston Bartell was constantly after Sarah these days to sleep with him, but she was only casting shadows his way. It was all a ruse– Sarah had made up her mind to do something about Harlan Bloom's death, and she was setting the trap. Winston Bartell's assigned role was to fall in.

Sarah had first met Winston when he came onto the set of *Blood Children* during one of his visits from New York. It had been flowers, emails and dinner invitations ever since– Winston was trying everything to get her into bed. And finally, this weekend, he was convinced his time had come. The two were driving to Jeu Blanc Resort in Palm Springs for a getaway weekend, and Bartell believed Sarah was ready to say yes even though she had insisted on separate rooms. This would be his chance.

"So what brings you to Los Angeles again so soon?" Sarah and Winston were in his rented Ferrari en route to Palm Springs.

"Business, actually . . . although after our dinner last time I was in town I mostly wanted to see you again. Anyway, I'm out here again on that case involving Harlan Bloom."

"Case? What case? I didn't know there was any kind of lawsuit filed." Sarah favored Winston with a look of genuine interest.

"Well, I'm actually following up on my earlier visits. You know I came out when Bloom was still alive and making threats against the Federal Reserve. My father takes that kind of thing very seriously, as I'm sure you can imagine, so he asked me to fly out to LA again and take a fresh look at the situation now that Harlan is dead. We're trying to pin down whether Harlan's threats were something to be taken seriously or not. After all, he was only an actor; maybe he was just talking off the top of his head, or trying to generate publicity for the film. We had no way of knowing for sure whether it was a genuine threat or not."

"I can understand that. Knowing how actors are, and all."

Winston missed the irony in Sarah's voice. He was busy passing cars at a high rate of speed. "Exactly. So I've been checking it all out. And it certainly seems to me that this was more than some sort of publicity talk to promote a movie. For whatever reason, Harlan Bloom actually had it in his mind that the Federal Reserve and LawbridgeTrimble, and his own bank, Turn of the Century– that he owed a lot of money to, by the way– were all acting together to get people enslaved in debt and financial misery. Real tin foil hat conspiracy stuff, but Harlan apparently believed it. That's my conclusion anyway."

"I think you're right," said Sarah. "Every time he talked to me about it he made it very clear that this was something that was entirely real to him. He believed in everything he was saying."

"And that's what I'm reporting back to my father and the people in New York. They all feel bad about Harlan's tragic death, of course."

"Of course," said Sarah Anjau.

Winston decided the time was right to start laying some groundwork for his planned evening at Jeu Blanc.

"I hope you understand, Sarah, that it's not my goal to try to interfere in your life in any way. You're a big girl– and you'll make your own decisions where men are concerned. So you won't receive any unwelcome pressure or advances from me this weekend." Winston Bartell flashed a winning smile as he dished out his line of crap.

"I appreciate that," said Sarah, returning his smile, but not fooled. "I didn't want there to be any false impressions or expectations, that's for sure."

"Understood." Bartell was quiet for a few moments while he enjoyed the exhilarating feel of the Ferrari.

"But I hope we're going to at least have a chance to get to know each other . . . that way maybe you won't be so scared of me . . . or whatever it is that's holding you back."

Sarah was trying to offer just enough to encourage Winston to talk freely. She smiled at him, "We are getting to know each other, Winston. And I'm not scared of you at all."

"Well that's good. And I hope you won't take this the wrong way, but another reason I'm back in LA has to do with that movie you're making, and all the legal issues that seem to be popping up around it."

"How so?" Sarah asked, trying not to show any particular interest in his lawyer talk.

"Well for one thing, a couple of my law partners are looking into whether your father actually has the rights to make the movie. My firm represents the Mezo Institute, and they were the owners of the Callien tablets that apparently were used to create your screenplay. They're talking to some lawyer out here about it."

"Yes. Victor Desert, I know him."

"Right, Desert . . . that's his name. And he just filed a whole big wave of lawsuits against another client of ours on some bogus theory that banks shouldn't be allowed to foreclose on mortgages when a borrower defaults and can't pay his debts. Now we find out that this same guy has sent the Federal Reserve a letter and an expert report claiming that Harlan Bloom's death was somehow caused by my clients. Your sister is mentioned in the report, by the way. This Victor Desert seems to be showing up all over the place."

"So is that why you're here? To meet with Victor Desert?"

"No . . . we don't put credence in any of the stuff he's coming up with. I'm here to talk to the local Fed people and just try to help them understand the nature of the claims that are being made in the expert report. I'm not planning to talk to Desert– no reason to."

"Well, I'm sure you've analyzed it carefully. But just in case you do want to talk to Victor while you're in town, I'm sure he would be willing to sit down with you and tell you what he knows. I'd be happy to arrange a meeting for you– it might make your job a bit easier." Sarah was speaking in a sincere tone, even though she knew very well there was no possibility Winston Bartell would take her up on the offer.

"Thanks anyway, but I don't think any of that is necessary. I'll just take care of the things I need to do, and then head back to New York." Winston sensed a hint of annoyance on Sarah's part, and he tried to explain his thinking.

"I hope you understand, Sarah, that my father is President of the New York Fed. And my grandfather is Lawrence Yasgar's number two man at LawbridgeTrimble. These are highly visible positions, and they generate a lot of haters and cranks who blame the Fed and LawbridgeTrimble for all the economic problems our country faces. When people go broke, or suffer a financial reversal, they look around for someone to blame . . . a scapegoat if you will. The Fed, and LawbridgeTrimble, because of their highly visible roles, are the ones that people begin to fixate about."

"And your point is?" Sarah had allowed a bit of an edge to appear in her tone.

"My point, Sarah, is simply this. And I'm sure you already know that what I'm about to say is true. Harlan Bloom, we learned, had become an outspoken critic of the Federal Reserve System. Now we're all entitled to our opinions, of course, it's a free country and all, but Harlan Bloom went too far. He was spewing hate, Sarah, and inciting people to take action on their own without going through the proper authorities. Harlan was advocating violence . . . talking about bringing down the banking structure and throwing people in prison. This was my father and grandfather he was talking about, and Lawrence Yasgar, and frankly Bloom had no business talking like that– free speech or no free speech. He was trying to undercut peoples' confidence in the legitimacy and good faith of the Fed, and as you can probably imagine, my father and grandfather found those sorts of antics to be most unsettling. It was like yelling ‘fire’ in a crowded theater– that’s against the law in this country.”

“So what are you here to do? Just blow things off? A cover–up perhaps?” Sarah tried to keep the annoyance from showing in her voice, but with difficulty. Winston Bartell’s hubris was disgusting to her.

“No, no, nothing like that at all. The first time I was out here I had the bank arrange a meeting and I actually spoke to Bloom. I tried as politely as possible to make the point that he would be better off leaving well enough alone.”

“So what did he say?”

“He wouldn’t listen. The guys at Turn of the Century were trying to put a deal together to give him an extension on his loan . . . we were trying to work with him. But he just wouldn’t listen. There was a lot of discomfort– and he wouldn’t listen.”

The two had arrived at Jeu Blanc.

* * *

Sarah had put her plan in place for Winston Bartell this weekend. Bartell knew the true story from the banker side about Harlan Bloom’s death, and Sarah had made up her mind that she was going to get it out of him. If it took the use of some feminine wiles along the way, so be it.

The actress wasn’t sure what particular strategy was going to work, so she was ready to do some trial and error. But she knew for certain that the ever–arrogant Winston Bartell would want to impress her– so ego massage was the logical place to start. The drive to the desert had been her starting point, and when the two met for dinner in the restaurant, Sarah picked up her effort.

“It’s interesting to me, Winston, that you know what happened to Harlan Bloom, and I don’t. I’ve read Kincaid’s report, but does he actually know what he’s talking about? Kincaid says that the very people you know at the Federal Reserve in LA are the ones who killed Harlan, and I have to admit that I'm a bit uncomfortable having dinner with you, knowing that you're the lawyer representing those killers."

"Killers? You're wrong about that, I can tell you for sure. Harlan Bloom's death was an accident– that I know for a fact."

"Really?" Sarah looked at Winston with searching eyes. "Why should I believe you? David Kincaid says something very different from what you're telling me."

"Kincaid, eh," Bartell was dismissive. "I've seen his report. Just a bunch of speculation, I'm afraid. His unproven theories hardly rise to the level of proof needed in a court of law."

"But is Kincaid actually right? And are you just giving me a bunch of lawyer talk about how he won't be able to prove a case in court?"

The secluded restaurant at Jeu Blanc had only a handful of tables, and Winston and Theresia were seated in a quiet corner near the front window. Everything was so . . . romantic. Winston Bartell was nursing his third gin and tonic of the evening, and he wanted Sarah to understand how things truly were.

Winston's words were ever so slightly slurring in the special mood of the moment. "You know, Sarah, I really care about you very much. More than you seem to know. But I'm frustrated. You seem to disapprove of me, and I can't understand why."

Sarah spoke sharply: "Have you thought about the idea that Harlan Bloom is dead because of your clients? And for all I know, because of your father personally? Those things bother me, Winston. I can't get them out of my mind."

When Winston responded, his voice was low, and entirely serious.

"I wish I could make you understand, Sarah, that Harlan Bloom was involved in some very bad activities. Criticizing the Federal Reserve, and LawbridgeTrimble, and calling for bankers to be put in prison. We can't allow that sort of talk– particularly from someone like Harlan who was going to be in the public eye once your movie caught on. People like my father and grandfather are in danger from that sort of talk, and quite frankly, they have every reason to nip it in the bud."

Sarah knew this was her time to push. "Nip it in the bud by killing him for speaking out?"

Winston was defensive. "Nobody at the Federal Reserve or LawbridgeTrimble wants to kill anyone, Sarah, and I can tell you for sure that my father and the people over at Lawbridge were as upset as you were when they heard Harlan was dead. That wasn't something that anyone wanted to happen. But you have to understand how the world works, Sarah. It's not the nice little place that you or I might think it should be. We don't live in a perfect world . . . and we never will. So we have to accept things as they truly are."

Sarah allowed some sarcasm to come into her voice, egging him on. "And how is it, Winston, that things truly are?"

"Well, for one thing, no one is going to interfere with the free flow of money around the US and the world– and I mean nobody. The free flow of money is the single most important thing that keeps our economy going, and it's too important for any interruption from Harlan Bloom or anyone else. People like my father, and my grandfather at LawbridgeTrimble, run the world, Sarah– they control the money, and they control the politicians, and they control the media. So when someone like Bloom stands up and starts talking a lot of trash about bankers, and slaves, and Enki and Enlil– well, I can tell you it's going to be noticed. And something's going to be done about it. I'm not saying anyone's going to be killed, but I will tell you this: if the Federal Reserve Bank of New York– headed by my father– wanted to have someone killed, well, that someone would be killed. No questions asked. The heads of finance in this country can kill anyone they want, and nothing would be done about it. Nothing. They'll kill because it's necessary, and because they can, and you're being incredibly naive if you don't accept that as a simple fact of life."

"So it's true then," said Sarah in a resigned voice. "Your father, or some of his henchmen, had Harlan Bloom killed. Isn't that what you're saying?"

"No, that's not what I'm saying. I'd like you to accept that there was an accident, and leave it at that. I can tell you that much– but anything beyond that I can't share with you. I hope you understand."

"Of course, I understand," said Sarah with a warm smile. It was the first time she'd favored Winston Bartell with her smile all evening. "You have obligations and commitments, and I would never expect you to step over the line just to satisfy me."

Winston had been feeling an enormous attraction for this woman all evening. He wanted her to understand what happened; and he wanted her to know that his father, and his clients, weren't criminals and hadn't actually done anything wrong. There'd been a screw– up, but it wasn't planned, or premeditated. So finally the moment of truth was here, and Winston couldn't help himself. Sarah's pull was too strong . . . the words came out.

"Your expert is right about one thing . . . the Fed cops did put a software package in Harlan Bloom's car. These are the newest things out there– they're still in prototype right now, but in a couple of years they're going to be standard in every new car sold in the world. Think about it . . . if there's a drunk somewhere driving around, you can simply take control of the car and bring him to a safe stop. Or a terrorist team heading out on an assignment, you can pull them over before they get anywhere, and quite literally drive them to a police location. This technology is going to keep us safe . . . and change law enforcement forever."

"So why didn't things work in Harlan's case?" Sarah was having difficulty containing her excitement.

"There were two Fed units working that night. One group was out of New York– they were in the chase car. The New York guys were experts, and when Harlan started trying to shake them off, they called the LA command center for assistance. They told the guys working the command post to take control of Harlan's car and pull him over so they could talk to him. I've listened to the radio call tapes– the New York team wasn't trying to hurt him or anything like that. The opposite was true. They just wanted to get a stop in place. Harlan was driving too fast for the conditions, and he was a danger to himself and others.

"So the chase team asked for a stop, and the command center tried to comply. That was where things went wrong."

Sarah gave him a look of sympathetic interest. "Went wrong . . . how?"

"Pretty much in the worst way possible. The system was brand new– Harlan's car was the first installation, and no one had ever operated the thing in a real world setting before. There were some experienced operators from Periscope visiting in LA to train the local Federal Reserve cops on how use the equipment, but it was New Year's Eve and they had already left for the evening. The only people in the command center were a couple of LA Fed cops who didn't know what to do. Sure enough, they screwed it up. Instead of slowing Harlan down they actually speeded him up. The people in the command center were misreading their instruments. They thought the vehicle had been slowed down and was ready to be brought to a gentle stop. Instead, it was going over a hundred miles an hour– and when they pulled it over to the side of the road it hit the freeway abutment. We know what happened then."

"Are the people at the Fed planning to go public and tell the truth about all this?" Sarah was trying– with considerable difficulty– to maintain a supportive tone in her voice.

Winston shook his head. "What I'm saying to you is all in the strictest confidence. I would deny ever saying it if you tried to repeat what I just told you. I understand you were a friend and colleague of Harlan Bloom, so I wanted you to know what happened, but as far as going public with what happened, I don't think that's an outcome the Fed is interested in. Better to let sleeping dogs lie."

Once the dinner was over, Winston was ready for his payoff. He walked Sarah up to the door of her room, fully expecting to be invited inside for a pleasurable conclusion to the evening. Winston felt he had shown her his best side, and he had shared with her an inside story about events that were occurring at the highest levels of leadership in the country. Now it was her turn to share with him.

But unfortunately for Winston, that wasn't the way things would turn out. Sarah opened the front door and closed it in his face before he even knew what had happened. Winston Bartell found himself standing alone on the front entry porch, and there was nothing to do except walk to his room down the hall. The next day, when he called her room to see about breakfast, the people at the desk gave him the bad news. Sarah Anjau had checked out earlier that morning.

VII.

Sarah Anjau had thoroughly enjoyed the group meeting at Hazeltine Phillips & Blaine. This had been her opportunity to explain to the lawyers and the Blooms all that she had learned during her visit to Jeu Blanc with Winston Bartell. What an extraordinary thing this girl had done! Bartell, the young fool, had implicated the Federal Reserve System and his own father in the death of Harlan Bloom. And LawbridgeTrimble, for covering things up. And Periscope, for turning their software system over to a bunch of untrained goons to operate in a real world setting. Sarah was handing Victor and Adrian their wrongful death lawsuit on a silver platter, and the parents of Harlan Bloom could now believe that the people who killed their son would soon be brought to justice.

Harlan Bloom's wrongful death case was a blockbuster lawsuit– good for the firm, and good for our clients. But not so good for an unhappy Winston Bartell, who had waived attorney–client privilege by talking to Sarah. All of us at HP&B were confident the truth would come out . . . that was what we thought at the time anyway.

* * *

For Victor Desert the days after his filing of the Bloom case were the busiest of his life. He had three major and multi–faceted litigation matters under his direction and control, and they were all going on at the same time. Hazeltine Phillips & Blaine had been around for nearly a hundred years, and the firm had never seen anything quite like it. Money was flowing in and work moving out the door– all because of Victor Desert and his cases. He should have been on top of the world, but as so often seems to happen at a moment like this, there was a heavy price about to be paid for what we so flippantly call "success."

The price Victor paid was the loss of Katy Hooper. Should she have been more understanding about the burdens he was operating under? Of course she should have. Should she have stood by her man? Absolutely. But the bottom line was that Katy was twenty one years old and living in the world of rap music. Victor's legal work bored her, and he was never around anymore. So Katy Hooper had left the Curson home, and Victor.

It came as a complete surprise to Victor Desert. He arrived home one evening and found no trace of Katy Hooper left behind. No note; no sad farewells– nothing. After that night, Victor never saw the need to talk about it. It wouldn't have been his style to share the heartache– but those of us who knew him could tell. All of a sudden, Victor Desert was a sad and lonely man.

* * *

"Won't it be strange when there are no more courts?"

Victor didn't understand what Theresia was saying at first, but then he grasped her point. "You've been listening to your father too much," he said.

Theresia smiled at her visitor. "I'm surprised you don't see what he sees. Aren't these things real to you even now? With all that we've been learning every day?"

Victor and Theresia were walking in the rear garden of the Anjau estate. Victor had come to celebrate a major success– the Mezo intellectual property lawsuit against Sydney Anjau and Eanna Pictures had been dismissed in court. He had hoped that Sydney might show interest, and give at least some minimal sign of appreciation for the hard work Victor had been doing. Instead, all Sydney wanted to hear was how the construction was coming at Silver Bay. And Robert Rossignal was the one who would talk about that tonight.

"No," said Victor gruffly, "what your father says isn't real. He's an old man, Theresia, and he believes what he chooses to believe. But that doesn't mean you should accept everything he says as true."

"Not accept what he says, Victor? I'd say it's just the opposite. How about the murder of Harlan Bloom and the cover–up those criminals are trying to engage in? Or how about your 123 families who are losing their houses to some bank that creates its phony money out of thin air? Are those things true? The lies are swirling around you every day, Victor, just like my father has tried to tell you. You're the one who isn't seeing what's real, Victor . . . my father is far, far ahead of you." Theresia was close to tears. "But one of these days you'll understand . . . I know you will."

Victor wasn't sure what to say, so the two sat in silence for a long moment in the gazebo that faced onto the lower grounds in the rear of the estate.

"I'm leaving, Victor." Theresia took his hand as she spoke. "I'm moving up to the compound this week, and I won't be coming back. I wanted to tell you myself– so it wouldn't come as a surprise."

"This week?" Victor turned away so Theresia wouldn't see the hurt in his eyes. "With Rossignal? Is that what you're doing?"

Theresia held his hand tightly. "We're flying up together to Millford on Tuesday, but it's not what you're thinking." She was quiet for a long moment. "I'll be working– helping to decide who we want to accept at the camp, and who we should turn away. Lots of people have heard about what we're doing, and we're getting all sorts of emails and phone calls from people who want to join us. No one knows how to handle it, so my father asked me to go up and take charge. That's all, Victor– it's nothing more than that."

"Nothing more, Theresia? You're leaving Los Angeles to go live in some faraway survivalist camp in Idaho, and you say it's nothing more than that? I . . . I don't understand. Especially when there's so much to be done down here, with all the litigation and everything else that's going on." Victor was having difficulty hiding his pain.

"No more courts, Victor– don't you see? My sister actually spent time with Winston Bartell to get him to talk about Harlan's death, but your case isn't going to make the slightest bit of difference. The litigation doesn't mean a thing when the collapse comes. . . I wish you could see that."

"Well I can't. You're telling me my work has no meaning, and I don't agree with you in the slightest." Victor stood up and let go of Theresia's hand. "I'm staying here, Theresia– this is where I'm needed. You and Robert will have the compound all to yourselves."

They walked in silence for a time, and Victor was furious with himself for behaving like such a fool. His jealousy of Robert Rossignal had taken over, and he knew it. So he said the only thing that could be said: "I'm sorry."

Theresia smiled. " It's OK– I understand what you're going through." Theresia touched Victor lightly on the arm, and leaned close to him. "You'll be ready one of these days soon, and when you are, Silver Bay will be waiting." She gave his arm the slightest squeeze. "And so will I."

* * *

Sydney was deep in conversation with Robert Rossignal when Victor and Theresia returned from their walk.

"I'm telling you, Robert, we're trying to support a population of seven billion people on counterfeit dollars– and it can't be done. Not now, and not ever. We're living on borrowed time and borrowed money, and our leaders in Washington DC and on Wall Street are going around trying to pretend they can solve things. They're fools . . . fools! When it falls apart, there's going to be a kind of animal behavior breaking loose from the Eljo that none of us would ever have dreamed was possible."

Robert Rossignal nodded his head in agreement. He was a believer.

Sydney continued with the prophesy. "They can't lie their way around reality, Robert, no matter how hard they try. Eventually it catches up with them, and when it does, their heads are going to roll. So then we'll see another Bankers' War to deflect attention away from what they've been doing. They'll start a war, just like they always do when things get out of control. It's their only way out once things really fall apart."

Rossignal had nothing to add. He nodded his head again.

"Enlil and his Igigi can't keep it together any more," said Anjau. "Their phony money has lost its power, and without that they have nothing to offer. As soon as enough people lose hope, Enlil will be finished . . . and that's when the wars will start. Wars against us, Robert– against their own people. Enlil knows the Eljo. He knows they'll turn against him in an instant once the money dries up. That's why people are pouring into Shanidar– because very soon there'll be no place else to go."

"Shanidar?" asked Victor.

"Our new name for the camp. We chose it because of what Mark Greenlee said. The Shem iti of Enki and Ninhursag was in the area of Shanidar Cave, and I thought it was a fitting connection to the compound."

Victor looked at Theresia. She was listening calmly to Sydney Anjau, giving every appearance of complete agreement.

But Victor said what was on his mind. "I don't like to be a doubter, Sydney, but are you really so certain that this move to the compound is actually needed right now? Aren't you leaving too soon? I'm all in favor of developing the Silver Bay property– but not as some kind of hideout from an economic collapse that might never happen. You'll be seen as a fool if the prophesy doesn't come true, and in the meantime, look at the impact you could be having here! Look at your movie that's about to come out. You're going to have a huge impact with the film. And our big litigation win over Mezo. We're doing so well . . . you're doing so well! And Theresia, and Sarah– they're going to be at the top of the profession once *Blood Children* is released. Don't you see what it is that you're giving up? And it could all be on the basis of a false alarm."

Sydney only smiled; he was patient with the younger man. "I understand your point, Victor– we could stay, and perhaps things will remain just as they are. Nothing bad is going to happen, you say, and can I really tell you you're wrong? Of course not! I see the possibility you raise, but I also see something else, Victor. Use your imagination! Think about what it will mean if you're the one who's wrong.

"Is any of your world actually grounded in reality? Right now you're pursuing a lawsuit where you're claiming that banker loan money isn't real– what do you think is going to happen when people actually come around and agree with your view? How can Enlil maintain any sort of legitimacy in the face of a court case like yours?

"We're living in Noah's time, Victor . . . and the great flood is coming. People laughed at Noah when he was building his Ark, and while I appreciate your concern that people might end up laughing at me if I'm wrong, that's a risk I'm quite willing to take. So Robert– you're the builder– tell us how our Ark is coming along."

Robert Rossignal wasn't much of a group speaker– his work did the talking for him. But he took out a collection of drawings and maps and prepared to give a report on his progress. While he was setting up, Theresia said quietly to Victor in a manner that couldn't be heard by the others, "I know you'll be with us. I know it!" She gave his hand a momentary squeeze, and the lawyer had the rush of confused thoughts and emotions that he so often felt in the company of this woman.

Sydney and Theresia gathered around the library table as Rossignal spread out his maps. Victor looked on from a distance.

"The first step has been to acquire the necessary property. Paul Cutter's parcel is the starting point, the anchor if you will, but it's only the beginning of what we have in mind. The Cutter property will serve as the core compound where the initial group of people will live. We call them our pilgrims, by the way. Modern day pilgrims– on a spiritual journey.

"We're building an entire new dormitory building near the existing lodge with separate wings for men and women and a large kitchen and dining area capable of providing food service to the entire group. By the time the dormitory building is completed I estimate that we'll have accommodations for 2000 people on the Cutter property alone, and we'll have room to expand it further if needed. Paul estimates that we could ultimately support as many as 3000 people on his existing property, and I think he's about right. There are seven good water wells on the property, and plenty of space for septic and waste disposal. We'll have energy issues of course, once the electrical grid goes down, but Paul is installing several large fields of solar panels to take up at least some of the slack where electrical power is concerned. Wood burning stoves will be our primary source of heat in the wintertime– fortunately we have a lot of forest resources available on site. That leaves food and security as our two primary concerns."

"So how do we feed all these people?" asked Theresia.

"Paul has acquired three nearby ranches so far, and is looking at two more. We have about 3000 acres under contract in the three ranches– two of them are primarily agricultural and wheat field properties, and the third is a very well outfitted cattle ranch. Once we have our entire group of five ranches in place, we'll be self sufficient for the size of population we're looking at."

"And security– what are we doing about that?" Again it was Theresia who was asking the question.

"I'm not really prepared to talk about the security arrangements in any detail, but obviously they're going to be a high priority. Walter Kollett is taking the lead on the security issues . . . he really knows what he's doing after all his years at the air force base." It was news to Victor that his stepfather was involved in camp preparations.

"Walter thinks there are going to be a lot of desperate people out there when things start going bad. He says remnants of functioning civilization like ours will surely come under attack, and I believe him. Can we defend the property? Walter and Paul think so. A significant portion of the property fronts onto the lake, but the total perimeter that will need to be defended is still very large, so that's the primary area of concern." Rossignal was using a pointer with the map to illustrate his points.

"There's only one road entrance into the property, here, and that can be gated with some field of fire gun placements directed toward the road. We'll be seeking to funnel any attack onto the road through the use of natural and manmade blockades at several points around the perimeter, here, here, and here. This area to the west of the compound is difficult to access for any kind of attacking force– they would have to work their way through forest terrain to mount an attack from that side. Walter is looking into the kinds of weapons we're going to need– it's a considerable task to get a defensive plan in place. Walter still has a lot of work to do before we're going to be defense ready, but at least we have someone who knows what he's doing." Grudgingly, Victor had to acknowledge that Rossignal was well prepared and knew what he was talking about. Obviously, he had been taking Sydney Anjau's prophesy with complete seriousness.

Theresia and Rossignal were flying up this week, and of the people in this room, only Victor was not yet committed. He asked Sydney Anjau when he would be moving.

"*Blood Children* will open in July. By the end of August I expect that all of us will be gone."

The planned move was only four months away.

VIII.

Several weeks had passed since Victor Desert's big win in the Mezo case. The lawyers at Kessler & Abramowitz has appealed, of course, but Victor was confident. Mark Greenlee had structured his severance agreement with Mezo to allow him to develop the Callien tablets however he chose. Mezo's lawyers never knew what hit them– they had believed the tablets wouldn't see the light of day.

It was a lonely period for Victor. Katy Hooper had dropped out of his life entirely. He saw her on TV from time to time, or in a music video for one of her satanic songs, but he hadn't heard a word from her since the day she disappeared. The tabloids had some blurbs– she was seen around town in the company of a singer named Buster Reeves. It looked as though Buster had been showing Katy some of his new things even while she was still living with Victor. The busy lawyer never had a clue.

Victor was in touch with Paul Cutter up at Shanidar. The new dormitory and dining facilities were coming along well, Paul said, and they'd installed a waste treatment facility onsite large enough to handle 3000 people. Robert Rossignal was living full time at Shanidar now– overseeing the construction. And Theresia . . . Paul said she was living there too. She and Rossignal were working closely together, Paul explained. Victor should come up for a visit, he said, and the sooner the better.

* * *

Victor's mother and stepfather met him at the airport, and they drove to the Kollett house on the South Hill. There was a For Sale sign in the front yard.

"You're selling the house?" Victor had been taken by surprise. "I hadn't heard anything about that. Why on earth are you moving? And where? You've lived on the South Hill all your life . . . I don't understand."

"Well," said Joanne Kollett, choosing her words carefully, "we've been planning to make a change for awhile now, and Sydney Anjau was in town a couple of months ago. We talked to Mr. Anjau over dinner one night out at the lodge and he told us about his plans. Anyway, to make a long story short, we decided to move to Shanidar. We're taking one of the cabins up on the hill, and that's where we'll be living from now on."

Victor was dumbfounded. "You mean you're giving up your home to go live at the compound? Is that what you're telling me? And what about the Caravan Inn– how can you run the hotel from that far away?"

"Actually, we won't be owning the Caravan any more," said Joanne. "It's in escrow– the Hayworth family is buying it. They want to try to fix the place up, and Walter and I pretty much felt this would be a good time to let it go. With the Banker Wars coming and all, it seemed like the right thing to do."

Sydney Anjau had found some new believers in Walter and Joanne Kollett.

That evening over dinner, Walter Kollett told Victor that he had agreed to take charge of security at Shanidar. He had been spending most of his time at the compound, and he explained that he'd only come into Millford to pick Victor up at the airport. He and Joanne would be going back out to Shanidar in the morning, and they invited Victor to join them. There would be no reason to stay in town, Walter explained– Jerry Kollett was living at the compound too.

"Yes, he's quite taken with what's going on out there," said Joanne. "And of course you probably know that Theresia Anjau is living there at the lodge? Jerry has a massive crush on her, like pretty much every other man in the camp. Stunning young woman, Victor . . . stunning." Joanne Kollett was looking closely at her son as she spoke, but Victor showed no sign that he had grasped what she was saying.

"Theresia does have that effect on people," said Victor. "Her actor training, I suppose."

Joanne and Walter shared a quizzical look with each other at Victor's clueless words.

So the plans were made– Victor would go with Walter and Joanne to the compound in the morning. Everything seemed a bit different from what he'd expected to find, but it was quite apparent that anything Victor might wish to see would be at Shanidar, not in Millford.

The compound had a freshly installed perimeter gate– the first of many changes that Victor was soon to learn about. As they made their way toward the center of camp, Walter pointed out the wastewater treatment facility along the road. It was impressive if one was an engineer, but not nearly as interesting to Victor as the new dormitory and dining facility. The structure was huge, and it was being swarmed over by a crew of at least thirty busy workmen. Leading the effort was Robert Rossignal, and he joined the new arrivals when Walter parked his car in front of the building.

"Hello Victor. Nice to have you here. A few changes since your last visit, I suspect."

"Robert," said Victor, acknowledging his handshake. The man seemed friendly enough, but Victor somehow couldn't help thinking of him as a rival. But rival for what? Leadership of the group? A close association with Sydney Anjau? Theresia? Victor didn't know, and he tried to put these thoughts out of his mind. "Looks like you've been busy."

"Yep. Has Walter shown you around yet?" asked Rossignal with a smile. "The grand tour?"

"Not so far– we just got here." said Victor. "I'm going to check in at the lodge, and then hopefully get a chance to take a look around."

"Fair enough," said Rossignal. "I'll be here for awhile. Pick me up when you're ready and I'll join you."

Victor entered the lodge through the main doors on the inland side, and was amazed at the transformation. On his last visit, everything had been dusty and unused– but now the antique woodwork was polished to a high gloss. It was the original rustic style that Paul Cutter's great grandfather had put in place a hundred years before.

There was no one attending the front desk– the lodge wasn't being used for paying guests. Walter went behind the desk and selected a key to a room on the second floor, and just then Theresia Anjau appeared at the top of the staircase.

"Victor! You're here!" She spoke with a sweep of her hand. "So what do you think? Quite an improvement over your last visit, I suspect."

"Like a completely different place," Victor agreed. And of course the biggest difference of all was that he was standing with Theresia Anjau, not Katy Hooper. Victor remembered Katy's negative reaction on seeing the lodge– better that she isn't here, he thought to himself.

"And how are you enjoying the new life?" asked Victor. "A bit of a change from your Stanley Avenue house, I take it?"

“I’ve never enjoyed anything so much,” Theresia said, “and of course there’s always something more to do. We have 1000 people living here now, and more joining us every day. Some of them you already know– and I think one of our new arrivals in particular is looking forward to seeing you.”

Victor didn’t know who Theresia was talking about, but she put him off when he asked who it was. Didn’t want to give away the surprise, she said.

Victor went up to his room, and found it to be impeccably clean and fully outfitted with linens, towels, pillowcases and blankets. It looked like the sort of room you’d find at an upscale mountain resort. Victor’s room had a view of the lake– and the deep blue water of Silver Bay was inviting. Across the bay Victor could see Spinnaker Retreat in the distance.

Theresia and Robert Rossignal joined Victor and Walter Kollett for the arrival tour. Their first stop was a helicopter pad on a rocky promontory to the west of the main buildings. Victor was surprised to find a Bell JetRanger awaiting the group.

“We bought it from a heli–ski group that was operating in the Monashee Mountains,” explained Walter. “The price was cheap enough that we just couldn’t say no– and besides, it’s one of the models I’m actually certified to fly.”

Victor watched with interest as Walter slipped comfortably into the pilot’s seat and began his preflight routine. Victor was seated beside the pilot, with Theresia and Rossignal taking seats in the rear. After only a few moments, the JetRanger was airborne, and Walter was banking in the direction of the main highway to the west of the compound.

“I figured a view from the air would get you oriented most quickly,” said Walter through the helicopter radio intercom. The four occupants were wearing earphones and mics. “Particularly where the security issues are concerned. Looking at it from up here can give you the layout, and what our opportunities and problems are."

"Take a look down there." Walter was gesturing to the junction of Silver Bay Road and US 345, the main north/south highway in the area. "That's the natural security choke point. If anyone wants to approach the compound, they have to make this turn from the highway onto Silver Bay Road and cover about five miles to our entry gate– it's the only way in."

"So what are you picturing– some sort of checkpoint at the turnoff?" Victor was not a security expert by any means, and his frivolous question brought smiles to the faces of the pilot and other passengers.

"Well, sort of," said Walter. "But what I actually had in mind was a collection of machine gun locations on both sides of the road. Stop them here, before they ever get close to the compound."

It wasn't what Victor had expected to hear, "What about the other families who use the road?"

"That's the problem– those people don't see what's coming."

Walter swung the JetRanger around and was soon back over the compound. The next segment of the tour took them over the camp next door to the Shanidar property.

"That's Camp Eagle Nest– owned by United Scouts International, but they've been closed up for the last five years. Scoutmaster issues– the controversies killed this camp. I suspect they'll never get the thing reopened. Take a look– Paul's been working to acquire the property. All that open ground, and the structures are in good condition. It would be a great expansion facility for us because it's so well built out." Victor was looking down on a large expanse of mostly unforested land that had multiple large structures which Victor took to be dormitories or lodges, combined with a collection of smaller cabins widely spaced through the remainder of the property.

Victor saw what appeared to be a baseball field on the opposite side of Silver Bay Road near the boundary with the Cutter property. The Eagle Nest location wasn't as large as Shanidar, but the extensive development would mean a lot more pilgrims could be accommodated quickly.

Walter turned the JetRanger out over the water, and within a few moments they were above the Spinnaker Retreat on the opposite side of the bay.

"If we want security, this is the property that really matters," said Walter through the intercom. "It can only be reached by boat– and the boat landing on our side is right on the property line between Paul Cutter's property and Eagle Nest." Walter was swinging low for a closer look at the rambling Spinnaker Retreat facility. "The Spinnaker owners have a big touring boat, the old Seawelanna, stored away in town. It's large enough to carry seven hundred people across the bay in one swoop. If we needed to retreat, this Spinnaker property would be a security man's dream."

"Why would that ever happen?" asked Victor.

"We're never going to have a fully effective defensive perimeter at Shanidar," explained Kollett. "The property is too big, and we won't have enough skilled people with the kind of high end firepower it would take to hold off trained gunmen carrying assault weapons. The compound has so much perimeter that an organized attack by enough desperate people could probably get in somewhere along the wire. Our pilgrims aren't soldiers– only a handful have any military training– but if we had Spinnaker for a fallback, we could survive pretty much anything. I'm exploring some new ideas for a defense strategy that I don't want to talk about yet– let's just say we'll need Spinnaker if we're going to make it work. So I've been talking to Paul about buying the Retreat property– he's on top of it."

Walter expertly landed the JetRanger on its pad; he was obviously a skilled pilot. The passengers were on their walk back to the lodge when Paul Cutter met them halfway and welcomed Victor with enthusiasm.

The two men went into the lounge area of the lodge to bring each other up to date. Paul was interested in Victor's litigation stories from Los Angeles, but the visitor hadn't come to talk about that. Victor Desert wanted to know what had been going on here at the compound– everything was so much different from when he had been here before.

"At first I didn't like the idea of doing a conversion to this compound idea," Paul explained. "I didn't believe all the talk about the collapse, and the Banker Wars . . . you know the stuff I mean . . . but after awhile I began to catch on. Sydney Anjau may sound a little crazy going around telling everybody he's Enki and all, but the things he has to say about the economy and the bankers make a lot of sense. Transcendent perception, the believers say– and I have to admit I agree with them. Sydney Anjau told me the highest and best use for this property– its destiny he calls it– is to be the safe haven in the Banker Wars, and I've come around to his point of view. So that's the way things are. There are a lot of believers here now– and new people joining us every day. The word is getting out– pretty soon we're going to be flooded with pilgrims. Kind of a scary thought when you think about it."

"And Theresia is deciding which people get accepted?" asked Victor.

"Yes. She does the screening, and there are a lot of people she's had to turn away already. Some of them were pretty unhappy, but Theresia has her own criteria in mind, and she's been putting together quite an intriguing group. We have all kinds here– everything from PhDs to ordinary workmen and their families. Theresia decides who she wants, and that's who comes."

"Is it Anjau money paying for this?"

"Not at all," said Cutter. "Our investor group is from Silicon Valley. Scientists and venture capitalists– they call themselves the Singularity. They're all young people, leaders in new science areas that focus on the human brain, and DNA, and the use of computerized digital technologies to create the singularity. I don't understand it myself, but their group is excited about it.

"There are nine of them so far– six men and three women. They spend all their time working on their theories and doing modeling about whatever it is they're trying to do with the new science. The group has their own laboratory structure in the back area of the property– and they're building a dormitory and dining area. Sort of a compound within the compound, you might say. And all because of Sydney Anjau and his prophesy . . . they're believers."

"Are you happy with the way this is all turning out?"

"I don't know if anyone can be happy about the end of the world as we know it, so that's probably not the term I would choose. It would be more accurate to say . . . I'm ready."

At just that moment an attractive woman in her mid-thirties walked into the lounge. She was looking for someone, and when she saw Victor, her search was over. Karen Ashley approached Paul Cutter and Victor Desert with a broad smile on her face, and Victor had difficulty believing his eyes.

"Karen! I'd ask a silly question like what are you doing here, but it's pretty obvious what the answer would be. Are you here to stay? And how on earth did you find out about this place in far off Philadelphia?"

Karen Ashley was pleased with Victor's obvious befuddlement at her surprise entrance. She gave the lawyer a big hug as she began her explanation. "I'm definitely here to stay. I quit my job at Talmadge– poof– and moved out here as soon as I heard what you and the Anjaus were up to. This is the place to be– and it's all because of Mark Greenlee that I'm here. When he came back from Brazil for your Mezo litigation, I got in touch with him. He told me the whole story, about saving the Callien writings, and how Mezo had been destroying tablets over the years, and I realized right away that I couldn't be part of that anymore. Mark will be joining us soon, and he was the one who put me in touch with Theresia. No more complicated than that– so here I am."

It was becoming obvious to Victor that major things had been happening while he had been grinding away in Los Angeles. Karen Ashley would be a huge addition to any community.

"Sylvia . . . over here . . . come and join us." Karen was waving to a plump woman in her early 40s who was standing uncomfortably at the lounge entrance looking around as if she was in the wrong place. But she recognized Karen Ashley in the dimly lit lounge and made her way to the table.

"Victor, meet Sylvia Burstein. My best friend for . . . I don't know how long. From New York. Sylvia– this is Victor Desert."

"Ah," said Sylvia with a knowing smile. "The famous Mr. Desert who I've heard so much about. A pleasure to meet you counselor."

"And you," said Victor. "May I assume from the fact you're here that you are joining Karen in this new life? You're a long way from home if you're not."

"New life indeed. And I'm happy to say as far removed from my life in New York as I could ever hope to find. Did Karen tell you that we were classmates at NYU?"

"No," said Victor, "we hadn't gotten that far. Are you another middle eastern archaeology expert like our Miss Ashley here?"

"Me . . . archaeology? I don't think so. I wouldn't know one of her skeletons if it jumped up out of the ground and bit me."

"Sylvia's a psychiatrist," said Karen. "She was in private practice; in New York. Or at least that's what she used to be. Now? Well I suppose we'll soon find out."

Victor was smiling at the thought of a psychiatrist in the community of pilgrims. "From what I can gather, there's going to be a pretty diverse group finding their way to the compound in the not too distant future. So maybe you'll pick up a whole new practice right here." A psychiatrist from New York . . . Theresia pretty clearly had a wide ranging view about the kinds of skills that were going to be useful at Shanidar.

"Perhaps there will be a need, but maybe not at all. The Anjaus are gathering their Blood Children in this glorious place, and do you even begin to realize how special it's all going to be? The delicious irony when the collapse comes, and the Blood Children are together here when the structure of Enlil and the Igigi falls to pieces! Special is barely an adequate word for the magnificent events we're soon to see. A change for the ages."

IX.

Victor was surprised to find Karen Ashley at the *maitre 'd* station in the dining room that evening. She explained as she showed him to a table. "Well," she said breezily, "there's not a lot of demand here for a PhD in middle eastern studies. So I decided to make myself useful doing something else. I'm the head of food service here at the compound. We're running two operations– this dining room in the lodge, and our cafeteria facility in the new dormitory building. We'll be doing several thousand meals a day by the time the rest of our people get here– so there's more than enough to keep me busy." She seated Victor at his table overlooking the lake and produced two menus. "And I enjoy it– turns out I was actually a closet chef all along."

Theresia joined Victor at the table a few minutes later. She looked particularly lovely that night– no makeup, a simple country styled dress, and Indian moccasin shoes. Her long red hair fell loosely to her shoulders, and her face and arms were deeply tanned. Such beauty . . . without even trying.

"So I suppose you're pleased about the film?" said Victor.

Theresia had a look of no particular interest. "Yes, I suppose so. My father and Sarah have certainly been busy on the editing over these last couple of months, and I think they're enjoying it even though it's meant they haven't been able to spend much time up here. Actually, the movie has become a burden for my father, and I'll be glad when it's finished and he can be with us on a full time basis."

"Who's been running things here while your father is tied up in LA?"

"We have a group. Paul Cutter, of course. He kind of informally heads things up. And Robert– he's in charge of all the construction projects. Your stepfather Walter Kollett has become a leader too, and Karen Ashley in food service. I'd say that's the core group, but of course it's my father who sets the tone and makes the hard decisions."

Sylvia Burstein entered the dining room and walked over to the table. "Aha, our two Hollywood stars out on the town I see. Brightening up the dining room to help attract a crowd– smart business, Theresia. I'll tell Karen to factor that in for future planning."

Victor invited the New Yorker to join them, and she pulled up a chair and sat down. "I won't stay– I'm sure the two of you have a lot to talk about. But did you hear? Paul Cutter told me this afternoon that he's put the deals together to acquire Eagle Nest and Spinnaker. I can't wait to get out and take a look. Quite a pair of properties from what Paul says."

Theresia had already heard the news. "Yes, he's been working on those deals for months. It means a lot to us– we can double the size of our population with the extra facilities, and really have a center of gravity in terms of numbers that we'll need if we're going to make it here for the long term. I'm excited. And it's so like Paul to keep his mouth shut until the deals actually happened."

"So how many people can settle here in the combined properties?" asked Victor.

"About five thousand. Maybe more when we get some more dormitories up."

"Like running a small city," said Victor. "Are you going to find enough good candidates who actually want to come here?"

Sylvia and Theresia looked at Victor with amusement. He still didn't get it, so the psychiatrist took the lead in trying to explain. "Victor, don't you know we're being flooded with applicants? Thousand and thousands of people are asking to come live here, and Theresia gets a wave of new inquiries every day. Just going through the correspondence and emails from strangers who hear about what we're doing is a full time task. I know– because I'm the one doing it." Sylvia added a pointed comment. "Everyone seems to understand . . . except you."

Victor felt a bit embarrassed, "I'm sorry; I really am behind the curve. I've been so busy with the litigation in Los Angeles that I haven't had time to think about anything else. I didn't mean to be a negativist about what you're doing– the opposite is true, I'm hugely impressed with what I'm seeing, and it's pretty obvious that I don't really have a good feel for how many people there are out there who understand this place."

"The hatred of Enlil and his Igigi runs deep," said Theresia. "Sylvia can tell you– she's seen it with her own eyes."

Sylvia was staring intently at Victor Desert as Theresia was speaking. "I saw it all right. It's a way of life for the bankers in New York, but Enlil can't keep up anymore. Not when he's faced with transcendent perception, like we have here at Shanidar. And it's spreading."

Sylvia Berstein talked to the young couple for awhile longer, then she wandered away and Victor was alone with Theresia. They took a walk around the compound after dinner. It was a warm summer night, and Victor took Theresia's hand while they walked. She didn't pull away.

"I wonder what it will be like when the cold weather comes," said Victor. "If the grid goes down like Sydney says it's going to, you'll be toughing it out in an environment that's not much like what you grew up with."

"I'm looking forward to it," said Theresia. "We have wood burning stoves, and a huge stockpile of cut timber. We'll be fine."

"Spoken like a true Californian," said Victor with a smile. But he didn't argue the point.

Then the two of them were back at the lodge. Victor went up the stairs to his room on the second floor while Theresia busied herself behind the front desk on an imaginary errand. It was easier that way– no need to make decisions about things like a good night kiss, or more. Decisions that neither Victor nor Theresia were ready to make.

X.

The next day, Victor found himself seeking out Sylvia Burstein. He found her helping out in the lodge kitchen.

"Got a few minutes?" asked Victor.

"Of course," answered the New Yorker, drying her hands on a dish towel. "Come into my office." Sylvia led Victor into a small anteroom off the kitchen which appeared to have been initially used as a chef's office. There was no desk in the room, but several chairs were haphazardly spread around. Sylvia and Victor took seats, and both laughed at the circumstance. "I suppose I'm coming to you as one of your patients," said Victor.

"Just be yourself," advised Sylvia, "you'll be fine."

"I'll try. But that means I get to ask you some questions first. Because that's what a lawyer does."

"Shoot."

"First question. Do you believe that Sydney Anjau is Enki?"

Sylvia had no trouble with that one. "I believe he believes he's Enki. And that's good enough for me."

“OK– try this one. If Sydney Anjau believes he’s Enki, doesn’t that mean he’s crazy?”

“Well crazy is a word that we psychiatrists shy away from, but if I were to address the thrust of your question, the answer is clearly no. Sydney Anjau is one of the least–crazy people I’ve ever met in my life. He knows exactly what he’s doing at all times, and exactly why he’s doing it. Including telling people he’s Enki . . . and causing them to believe him. Crazy like a fox perhaps, but not in any other way.”

All right, here’s another one. Why is Theresia here instead of in Hollywood making movies where she belongs?”

“Ah, now that’s one you need to ask Theresia, not me. Nobody ever wanted me to come to Hollywood and be a movie star, so I’m not really much of a person to answer. But maybe this would do it . . . a psychiatrist’s answer. And my psychiatrist’s answer is that Theresia is here because she has chosen to be here. Is there any reason to think the answer need be any more complicated than that? Only one more, by the way– and then it’s my turn.”

“OK– last question. Do you think this compound idea is actually going to work?”

Sylvia Burstein looked at Victor with a smile. “Oh what a doubter you are! Of course it’s going to work . . . Sydney Anjau has told us what’s coming, and when the moment of collapse is here we’re the ones who’ll be ready. When everyone else is just looking around for shelter, we’ll be safe and warm. It’s going to work because the Blood Children who’ll be living here will make it work. It’s our moment, and we’re ready.”

“So now it’s my turn.”

Sylvia obviously knew what she doing– her first question made Victor Desert enormously uncomfortable. “Are you a Blood Child? And as you lawyers like to say, that’s a question that can be answered yes or no.”

"If it has to be yes or no, then I suppose the only answer can be yes. I don't really believe it though."

"Aha, first answer gets an A minus. Now let's try one a little harder. Do you think the collapse is coming soon, like Sydney Anjau says?"

"He's Enki, not me. With the transcendent perception everyone up here keeps talking about. So I guess the best I can say is that Sydney Anjau says it's coming, but I don't have the faintest idea what's going to happen."

"Hmmm, that one only gets a C minus. I think you ducked the question . . . but I'll let it go. Here's one more, and something a bit more personal: who is Theresia Anjau going to marry?" Sylvia was smiling again with her final question.

"Robert Rossignal, it appears. He's obviously in love with her."

"An F. And after an answer that hopelessly bad, I don't even want to talk to you anymore." Sylvia gave Victor Desert a warm kiss on the cheek . . . then she was back to her work, and Victor was alone.

XI.

The offices of Eanna Pictures on Wilcox had that cluttered and busy look that was entirely suited for a company in final stage post production on a major motion picture. The *Blood Children* project was still tied up in editing, but completion of the final cut was only a couple of weeks away. Sydney Anjau didn't even remotely look like a man of 76 years– he was living this project day by day now, and growing younger and more vibrant in the process.

"Victor!" Anjau's voice boomed out when Desert entered the office. "Come in, come in. What do you think of our new poster?"

Victor looked at a wall poster featuring the faces of Harlan Bloom, Theresia and Sarah set against a background that appeared to depict a fiery world in the making. Ample cleavage was displayed by each of the Anjau daughters– *Blood Children*, it seemed, wouldn't be presented as a dry and lifeless tale. Victor made approving noises about the poster and waited while Anjau completed his tasks.

"Have a seat here," said Anjau gesturing to a chair to the side of his large desk. "And tell me all about the progress up north. Did you see Theresia? And the Singularity people– have they moved in yet? I've wanted to go up, but the movie just hasn't allowed it to happen."

Victor brought Sydney Anjau up to date about all that he had seen during his visit to the compound, and as he looked around the crowded Hollywood office, he felt a definite sense of the end of an era. Eanna was a bustling and prosperous company, but Victor realized that when this picture was completed, all these people would be out of a job. There were no follow–up projects in the Eanna pipeline– *Blood Children* was the end of the line. Victor wondered out loud how many of the Eanna team would be making the exodus up north, and Anjau answered quite a few. But for the others, there would soon be no place to go.

When he got back to the office that evening, Victor found an email from Theresia on his screen. Here's what it said:

> To: vdesert@hpb.com
> From: Theresia@shanidar.com
> Re: Your Visit
>
> Victor– You were wrong about what you said to Sylvia; I'm not going to marry Robert Rossignal. When will I see you again?
>
> Love T

XII.

Colin O'Neil enjoyed his job. Being an Assistant United America Attorney in the Median Division was high prestige, and particularly so when you stacked it up against his old neighborhood in the Bronx. O'Neil had come a long way, and he'd done it by always being a friendly and jovial voice along the road.

Except when he was going about his business as a prosecutor, that is. In his United America Attorney role, Colin O'Neil had carefully nurtured a reputation as tough on crime. His approach lent itself well to publicity, and Colin O'Neil had a particular affinity for the high profile case.

The court action he had filed that day against Eanna Pictures and its founder Sydney Anjau certainly fell in that category. O'Neil was suing Eanna and Anjau in the name of the United States of America for hate speech– because of the impending release of *Blood Children*. Colin O'Neil and two junior colleagues stood before the microphones outside the Broadway Avenue courthouse and explained the new filing.

"We've looked at a print of the film," said O'Neil, "and it's filled with hate, racism, xenophobia and discrimination, all wrapped up in a call for revolution. We in the United America Attorney's office believe in free speech– it's one of the cornerstones of our great country. People have a right to their own opinions, even hateful opinions, but not if they're going to incite others to violence. And that's exactly what this *Blood Children* movie does– it advocates views that are intolerant and disrespectful, and it's clearly designed to create divisiveness toward our common heritage and the religious roots and racial pluralism on which our nation is based.

"The story of the so–called Blood Children that we see depicted in the movie is racist and anti–religious to the core, and such discourse in a public forum– particularly in the commercial setting of a feature motion picture– cannot be tolerated in a civilized nation. *Blood Children* constitutes a clear and direct assault on our shared human values, and tramples on the fundamental right of equal dignity. Any hateful and exclusionary expression of separatist and anti–religious views such as we see in *Blood Children* creates an environment in which equality and freedom from discrimination simply isn't possible, and as a result we've filed an action in the Median Division Court today seeking a temporary restraining order and injunction against distribution of the picture. So with that introduction, I'll open it up to take your questions."

A man in the back asked: "I'm a bit troubled by what you're saying: aren't you describing censorship, and a violation of the right of artistic expression?"

"Absolutely not," said O'Neil emphatically. A lock of black hair fell down over his eye as if to emphasize the sincerity of his response. "We reject the concept of prior restraint in 99.9% of these sorts of hate speech cases. But *Blood Children* falls in a special category all its own. The entire purpose of the movie is incitement of people to engage in racial exclusion and civil disobedience. Incitement is a criminal offense when it's coupled with a likelihood of imminent violence, and that's exactly what we find in *Blood Children*. Dangerous words that are meant to produce violence may properly be excluded from a public showing."

Another skeptical news reporter in the audience on the sidewalk asked: "What is it specifically about this film that you found so distasteful? Can you give us a flavor of what actually creates a danger of violence?"

"Well, without going into detail, I think the most obvious incitement comes from the fact that the premise of the movie is that human beings are slaves, and they should throw off their shackles and overthrow legitimate authorities. We've concluded that the entire movie is a call for overthrow of the public order in civilized society."

To O'Neil's obvious annoyance, the questioner persisted: "But aren't you really seeking to regulate opinion here? And criminalize speech? I recognize the need to stand up to hate– after all, who isn't against hate– but what you're talking about here seems to be punishing disfavored speech where there's no crime."

"Well, I appreciate your concerns, and as I said before, there are clear constitutional rights to free speech that we deeply respect. The problem comes when speech is used to incite violence and advocate overthrow of legitimate authorities. When we see that kind of hate speech, we're going to prosecute . . . and that's exactly what we find in this movie. So thank you all for coming, and for a look at the specifics of our complaint that we filed this morning go to our website at uaa.gov and you can find it posted online. Again, we appreciate your being here today."

* * *

Victor's phone was ringing off the hook. Hate speech laws– being used to censor a movie? It wasn't anything Victor had ever seen before, and that's what he said to Silverstein and Sydney Anjau in a conference call held soon after the O'Neil press conference. There was a TRO court hearing scheduled for the following morning– Victor would be spending a long night in the office preparing his papers. Caroline looked at him with genuine concern– she knew how hard he had been working. She offered to stay with him at the office that night: Caroline, of all people, knew he was going to need a lot of help getting his response together.

* * *

Victor Desert lost . . . big. Judge Miriam Westerley of the Median Division Court had no difficulty accepting Colin O'Neil's characterization of *Blood Children* as a movie that incited unsuspecting patrons to racism and violence. Victor tried to argue the First Amendment, and the laws about prior restraint and judicially imposed censorship, but Judge Westerley was having none of it. She pointed out that the very title of the film conjured up a threat of violence– not to mention the discriminatory overtones she found in the premise that some people might qualify as Blood Children while others were excluded. Judge Westerley found such racist thoughts to be repugnant– that was the very word she used in granting the TRO banning distribution of the film for a three week period until such time as a preliminary injunction hearing could be held. Judge Westerley pretty much agreed with everything Colin O'Neil had to say– so the movie had been branded with the badge of hate. Judge Westerley went so far as to suggest that *Blood Children* was an attack against our democratic political process itself. In a free society, she explained, this sort of threat couldn't be allowed to stand.

Victor tried to do an emergency appeal of course, but the higher court declined to hear the matter. The name of the film– *Blood Children*– stood out, and the appellate court saw no reason to search below the surface. Victor tried to explain that the name was drawn from historical tablets . . . to no avail. He pointed out that a multitude of earlier films had used provocative names . . . *Kill Bill, The Texas Chainsaw Massacre, Bullet In the Head, Shoot To Kill*– the list went on and on. But nobody cared. Judge Westerley's ruling stood, and there would be no distribution of *Blood Children* until after the preliminary injunction hearing . . . if ever.

Victor Desert took it hard. And when Colin O'Neil called to ask whether they could reach some agreement to avoid further court action by changing the name of the film and editing out some of the offending content about slaves turning on their masters, Victor began to understand the true face of the world he was living in. Don't rock the boat; don't upset the powers that be– these were the things that were paramount to a government prosecutor like Colin O'Neil. Follow orders; do what you're told; comply with authority– this was what O'Neil was saying to Sydney Anjau and Eanna Pictures. He was saying it under full force of law, and there was nothing Victor Desert could do about it.

XIII.

The firm received a written ruling from the Northern Magisterial Court on the Harlan Bloom wrongful death case in the mail:

Minute Order of the Northern Magisterial Court Department 235: Court Ruling on Defendants' Summary Judgment Motion

To: All Counsel
From: Honorable Judge Jeffrey Tucker
Matter: Northern Magisterial Court Case No. 30– CV2011879 Samuel Bloom and Bella Bloom v. The Federal Reserve Bank of San Francisco (Los Angeles Branch), et. al. (Harlan Bloom Wrongful Death)

A. The Activities of Harlan Bloom Which Led To His Death

In order to place Mr. Bloom's death in proper context it is necessary to review the activities of Mr. Bloom which led up to the evening of December 31st.

The Federal Reserve had looked upon Harlan Bloom as a person of law enforcement interest for a period of approximately three months prior to his death. Mr. Bloom had a fixation on what he referred to as the "Overlords" in our American banking and political system, and he was convinced that our Federal Reserve System and a cabal of banks were engaged in an illegal practice of creating money out of thin air through counterfeiting, and then using those counterfeit dollars to maintain control over the American people through debt and economic power. Mr. Bloom used his status as an actor to serve as a soapbox from which to promote conspiracy theories about how the Federal Reserve was privately owned by bankers and was not acting in the public interest.

The Federal Reserve learned about Mr. Bloom's threats and undertook to investigate by way of the law enforcement powers entrusted to them. Mr. Bloom was saying in the last few months of his life that he was a Mesopotamian god named Enki (the role he played in a movie), and this delusional state of mind apparently reinforced his theories about our supposed condition as slaves to the bankers. Mr. Bloom had no scholarly grounding for his views– the Internet sites that he relied upon for information (most notably a site called "EndtheBailouts") were all considered to be extremist by reputable investigators and law enforcement personnel who track such activities. Very simply, Mr. Bloom had the outward appearance of a successful entertainer, but in fact he was a disappointed romantic suitor, an unknowledgeable political extremist, and a man who was himself in debt to a prominent

Southern California bank in an amount in excess of $100,000 at the time of his death. These facts support the evidentiary inference that Mr. Bloom made his own bad decision to try to speed away from FRP officers who sought to pull him over due to erratic driving.

B. The Interactions of Federal Reserve Officers and Related Persons With Mr. Bloom Prior to his Death

The Los Angeles Branch maintains a communications center at its facility on Olive Street in downtown Los Angeles. The specific components and operating capabilities of the communications center are classified as top secret, and plaintiffs seek to draw negative inferences from the fact that the Federal Reserve maintains specialized police units and sophisticated law enforcement capabilities. The Court declines to adopt any such conclusion– indeed, the Court finds sufficient and proper ground for the existence of a Federal Reserve police force and the use of sophisticated tools and weaponry by its officers. The Federal Reserve performs important work for the benefit of our nation, and this Court will not second guess the Congressional judgment which authorized police power at the federal level. Nor will this Court second guess the need for secrecy in Federal Reserve activities, and the requirements for confidentiality that clearly exist in its structure. The maintenance and safety of our nation's monetary system necessarily requires public confidence and trust, and it is quite apparent to this Court that any breach of such confidence would negatively impact our national security on the world stage. Accordingly, the Court declined to allow plaintiffs to conduct discovery with respect to the components and operating capabilities of the Los Angeles communications center. The Court does not perceive that a sufficient evidentiary showing has been made by plaintiffs to justify an intrusive discovery exercise that would compromise the Federal Reserve's ability to operate effectively in the future. If wrongdoers know the precise parameters of Federal Reserve law enforcement capabilities, the task of breaching security would be made easier in future cases.

An expert report submitted by David Kincaid contains a recitation of Mr. Kincaid's experiments and opinions about the cause of Mr. Bloom's death. Expert witness Kincaid claims to have extracted computerized data evidence from the wreckage of Mr. Bloom's Porsche automobile which Mr. Kincaid believes establishes that Officers A and B inserted some form of attack software into the electronics components of Mr. Bloom's automobile during the course of a December 22nd traffic stop. Mr. Kincaid concludes that the malware installation was for the purpose of overriding Mr. Bloom's driver inputs to the car such that the car could be controlled by way of remote operation from a distant location. The Court has reviewed this evidence, but finds no indication that such malware was ever installed, or that remote control of Mr. Bloom's car occurred on the night of December 31st. The Federal Reserve submitted a competing expert report on this same issue which concluded that no such malware software existed in Mr. Bloom's vehicle, and there is no evidence whatever to support the farfetched notion that remote control operation of Mr. Bloom's vehicle took place on the night of December 31st. Counsel for plaintiffs took the depositions of all Federal Reserve officers on duty on the night of Mr. Bloom's death, and all officers denied such activity, or even that the Federal Reserve had the capability to implement such a remote control regimen if they had wanted to. Nor is there any inkling of a motive as to why the Federal Reserve might wish to interfere in Mr. Bloom's life in such an intrusive manner. The Court rejects the notion that the Federal Reserve was seeking to silence Mr. Bloom because of his outspoken opposition to the Fed and our private bankers, and there was no evidence submitted in opposition to the present motion which would show some sort of system–wide effort on the part of the Federal Reserve to silence critics.

Expert witness Kincaid tells us about a complicated computer software program he developed for the purpose of reading messages in the electronics of Mr. Bloom's vehicle which supposedly showed remote operation of the vehicle at the time of the accident. Suffice it to say that Mr. Kincaid's evidence is not evidence at all. Rather it constitutes speculation and conjecture made up to look like evidence. There has been no scientific peer review of Mr. Kincaid's methodology, and expert Kincaid admits that he developed his magic software for the express purpose of reading the telematics of Mr. Bloom's vehicle. The expert witness for the Federal Reserve found no corroboration of Mr. Kincaid's theory during his inspection of the same telematics systems, and the Court rejects Mr. Kincaid's conclusions as entirely lacking in evidentiary support.

Finally, plaintiffs offer the testimony of Sarah Anjau. She testifies that Winston Bartell, a lawyer for the Federal Reserve and the son of the President of the Federal Reserve Bank of New York, admitted the Fed wrongdoing to her during the course of a dinner engagement at Jeu Blanc Resort in Palm Springs. With all due respect to Ms. Anjau, the Court rejects such testimony. The Court finds Ms. Anjau's testimony to be not credible– the occasion at Jeu Blanc was a romantic endeavor, and was hardly the sort of setting where one would expect to find serious matters of Federal Reserve business discussed. Mr. Bartell has denied making the statements attributed to him by Ms. Anjau, and the Court accepts his testimony.

For all the foregoing reasons, the Motion for Summary Judgment is GRANTED. Counsel for defendants to prepare the written order.

Jeffrey Tucker
Judge of the Northern Magisterial Court

XIV.

Every once in awhile a busy trial lawyer gets a much needed laugh. It came for Victor Desert when an invitation to the Bankers' Ball appeared on his desk with the regular law firm mail. The bankers, it seemed were gathering in Los Angeles to congratulate one another . . . and Victor Desert had been invited to the gala.

The invitation at first seemed to be a mystery, but then Victor saw that Colin O'Neil was one of the honored guests. Victor had found his way onto the mailing list of an ambitious United America Attorney on his way up the political ladder. O'Neil was apparently ready to let bygones be bygones where the hate speech case was concerned– after all, Desert was a successful lawyer and he might be a campaign contributor down the road. Victor knew right away that he was going to attend– the guest of honor that night was none other than Lawrence Yasgar, Chairman and CEO of LawbridgeTrimble, Ltd. This was an occasion not to be missed.

The invitation brightened Victor up so much that he sent an email inviting me to join him at the Ball. Here's what he sent:

To: rblaine@hpb.com
From: vdesert@hpb.com
Re: Invitation to the Bankers' Ball

Randolph– Check this out. I've been invited to the Bankers' Ball . . . and apparently I'm even being encouraged to bring a guest! Would you care to join me? Should be interesting to watch these people patting each other on the back, and with Lawrence Yasgar as the guest of honor, no less. Our bankers . . . busy at work, busy at play . . . and it doesn't get much better than that. Let me know if you're interested. Regards.
Victor
Attachment (Invitation to the Bankers' Ball)

YOU ARE INVITED
TO A GALA EVENING WITH BUSINESS AND FINANCE LEADERS
FROM AROUND THE UNITED STATES

HONORING THE LOS ANGELES BRANCH
OF THE FEDERAL RESERVE BANK

Date: June 15th
Dress: Black Tie
Place: LA Fire! Grand Ballroom
Music by the Fred Klein Orchestra
Cocktails @ 6:00 p.m.
Dinner Starts Promptly at 7:00 p.m.

Please join us with a guest of your choosing
as we celebrate the grand opening of our new expansion wing
at the Los Angeles Branch of the Federal Reserve Bank

GUEST OF HONOR AND FEATURED SPEAKER:
LAWRENCE YASGAR
CHAIRMAN AND CEO OF LAWBRIDGETRIMBLE, LTD.

MASTER OF CEREMONIES:
Colin O'Neil
United America Attorney for the Median Division

I wasn't sure what to make of it at first. Did Victor really want to go, or was it just a joke? We would be the only ones there from outside the banker orbit, that's for sure. But wasn't that the very thing that would make it a lot of fun?

My response to Victor's email was simple and to the point:

To: vdesert@hpb.com
From: rblaine@hpb.com
Re: Invitation to the Bankers' Ball

Victor– I happily accept your invitation. Randolph

XV.

Mark Greenlee had brought the tablets with him, and they were spread out on the conference room table. It was the first time I'd ever seen them– the collection which had impacted all of our lives so greatly. The priceless collection that Mezo had been willing to throw away, and now it was here.

"I want these to go to Shanidar," said Greenlee. "I'll be coming up later, but I'd like to get the tablets up there now, just in case things start going wrong quickly. Can we do it?"

Adrian explained that he would be driving to Shanidar that week, and he was willing to take the writings on their journey. Greenlee handed the younger man his transcription to accompany the tablets.

"Keep this with them. Sydney and the team up there will know what to do. Once the movie comes out, I want him to be able to use the tablets and the poem however he sees fit in his publicity campaign."

I read the transcription with Victor looking over my shoulder. As Greenlee had said, it was a poem, but not like anything I had ever seen before. The unusual Sumerian phrasing added an element of otherworldly flavor to the writing, and increased the sense of timelessness that stood out so strongly in the epic tale. Greenlee explained that his translation approach was to capture the phrasing in the manner that it had actually been written, and the result was a poem that seemed far removed from the sort of traditional literature that I was used to. It was more direct, almost simplistic, but the very sparseness of the text added to its power. I could see what an enormous task it must have been for Raffi to capture Callien's essence in her screenplay without losing the undercurrent that all of this came from a time almost 5000 years ago.

I told the girl what I thought. "You should be so proud, Raffi. I don't think there's been anything like your screenplay ever written before."

Raffi Gutierrez smiled.

"So what can we do to get Akeel into this country?" asked Greenlee.

Adrian had been handling the matter at the firm. "I've been in touch with the Brazilian emigration authorities for more than a month now, and I'm having no success at all. They were willing to let you come back to the US, but someone has gotten to them. They're not going to let Akeel leave the country. It's payback . . . I'm certain of that. For what you did in standing up to LawbridgeTrimble and Mezo."

"Is there anything the US embassy can do?" asked Raffi.

"I actually think they're willing to help," said Adrian, "since Mark is an American citizen. But Akeel is a Brazilian national, and Brazil makes the decision. So far the answer is no."

I could see the disappointment on the faces of Greenlee and Raffi Gutierrez, but there was nothing more we could do. They would be going to Shanidar on their own, and Akeel wouldn't be joining them for the foreseeable future.

Adrian Garfinkle found the following ruling posted on the website of the Southern Magisterial Court when he returned to his office after the meeting with Greenlee.

Minute Order of the Southern Magisterial Court, Department CS– 142: Court Ruling on Defendants' Demurrer to Fourth Amended Complaint

To: All Counsel
From: Honorable Judge Angela Bridgestone

Matter: SMC Case No. CV155392 Scott and Barbara Langsden v. Turn of the Century Bank, et al, (the anti–foreclosure lead case). This ruling will also apply to 122 follow–on cases which involve the same issues but different plaintiffs represented by the same counsel as the Langsden lead plaintiffs.

This demurrer comes before the Court in response to plaintiffs' Fourth Amended Complaint. Four prior demurrers have been sustained with leave to amend, and plaintiffs have attempted each time to amend their pleading to state a valid cause of action on the theories alleged. Having now had four tries, plaintiffs' complaint can be viewed as fatally flawed, and the Court concludes that the present demurrer will be sustained without leave to amend.

A. The Applicable Legal Standard As Applied to the Present Fourth Amended Complaint

In deciding a demurrer, the Court considers all properly pleaded allegations of the complaint as true, and then determines whether, based on those allegations, a legally cognizable cause of action has been stated. Here, the Langsden Fourth Amended Complaint (as with the earlier complaints) is fundamentally grounded in the allegation that Turn of the Century Bank created its loan funds out of thin air by computer journal entry at the time the mortgage loan was made. The Langsdens allege that this act of creating money our of thin air is akin to counterfeiting, and is not an act which should find support or affirmation in our legal system.

The Court finds that such allegations are without merit. Moreover, even if we were to give full credence to the Langsden allegations about bank practices, their pleading still fails to state a cause of action on which relief may be granted, and the Court sustains the present demurrer without leave to amend.

B. The Fourth Amended Complaint Fails to State a Legally Cognizable Cause of Action Against Turn of the Century Bank

Plaintiffs appear not to like fractional reserve banking– they call the practice a fraud and an act of counterfeiting whereby the bank creates money in much the same way that a second rate counterfeiter running a printing press in his kitchen would do. Plaintiffs argue that they have no more obligation to pay back the bank than an unsuspecting recipient of the kitchen counterfeiter's phony money would have to pay back a counterfeiter in the event that the counterfeiter loaned him some printing press money. The Court declines to consider such arguments– they are a matter for political determination, not a court of law. Plaintiffs should take their arguments to their Congressional representatives or bank regulators– not to this Court.

But in any event, the Court finds plaintiffs' arguments to be unpersuasive. As plaintiffs themselves acknowledge, fractional reserve lending has been around in this country at least from the founding of the Federal Reserve System in 1913. One of the core purposes of the Federal Reserve is to serve as a lender of last resort to banks by backstopping bank loans that go into default and by providing needed liquidity to banks to prevent the evils of runs on a bank. Fractional reserve lending serves a useful purpose– it creates liquidity and encourages growth in our economy. The Court finds that the practice is justified by the age old principle that not every bank depositor will seek to withdraw his or her funds from the bank at the same time– so the bank can safely lend out money in an expansionary way while at the same time maintaining a modest reserve amount on hand to cover bank overhead and pay depositors who do come forward to withdraw their money on a current basis. This lending practice is one of the strengths of our national monetary system– our leaders in the fields of finance and banking have decided that the practice of liberating capital is beneficial to the economy, as opposed to allowing money to simply languish unproductively as depositor savings in a bank. Very simply, fractional reserve lending has been the monetary system of choice in the United States and around the world because it works for the benefit of all. Plaintiffs' concerns about fraud and counterfeiting are unfounded, and have been proven to be irrelevant and insignificant in actual practice over an extended period of time. The Court declines plaintiffs' invitation to upset the monetary apple cart.

C. Plaintiffs Would be Unjustly Enriched If the Court Were to Adopt Their Radical Anti–Foreclosure Scheme

Plaintiffs complain that Turn of the Century Bank would be unjustly enriched if it was allowed to foreclose on a loan where it never put up any money of its own to begin with. But plaintiffs overlook the obvious: they actually received the loan proceeds they complain about. They used the loan proceeds to refinance the house they're now living in. They took full advantage of the bank's willingness to lend– and only now do they complain that they shouldn't be responsible to repay their debt. Plaintiffs' argument is hypocritical– it is they who seek unjust enrichment, not Turn of the Century Bank. The bank is simply protecting its collateral on a loan it made to the Langsdens in good faith. Plaintiffs are losing nothing if their home is foreclosed upon– they didn't pay for the house to begin with: Turn of the Century Bank did.

The present case is a call for widespread disruption and disorder– if the Court were to grant relief to the Langsdens it would be opening a Pandora's box where every defaulting homeowner in the country would be seeking the same remedy. This Court declines to participate in such far reaching change– the Langsdens must look elsewhere for relief.

Demurrer **SUSTAINED WITHOUT LEAVE TO AMEND.**
Defendant to prepare the proposed order.
Hon. Angela Bridgestone
Judge of the Southern Magisterial Court

XVI.

This sort of meeting wasn't the norm at Hazeltine Phillips & Blaine. There were nine partners in the firm, but among that group only the three name partners actually had a say in the operation of the firm. The rest were like Victor– junior partners who were supposed to bring in business and otherwise keep their mouths shut about firm affairs. So today would be a new experience for HP&B, and the meeting, unbeknownst to Victor Desert, was all about him.

The partners began to gather in the conference room a few minutes ahead of the 5:00 p.m. start time. Some of the younger partners arrived first, including Victor, then promptly at five o'clock Jack Hazeltine came in, accompanied by Roland Phillips.

Hazeltine, as was his due, took the seat at the head of the table. "It appears that everyone is here, so I suppose we can get started. Randolph Blaine had another engagement and couldn't join us, but we've briefed him about what we have to talk about today and he understands the issues. Let me begin by thanking all of you for coming. I don't think we'll need a lot of time– so I'll turn things over to Roland who has agreed to act as chair tonight."

Roland Phillips was seated about halfway down the conference table on the window side of the room. Victor Desert was on the interior side, seated at the end of the group of partners furthest away from Jack Hazeltine. Phillips began with some introductory remarks, then said, "So let me turn to the business at hand for tonight's meeting." Directing his words to Victor, he said "Victor, it has to do with you, and the group of cases you've been handling over the past several months. Perhaps you can bring us up to date on current status."

Victor almost groaned out loud. He had spent most of his waking hours over the past several days explaining in detail the negative outcomes of his cases to unhappy clients and colleagues. When Samuel and Bella Bloom read the wrongful death decision from Judge Tucker, Victor had genuinely feared for their lives. The opinion had crushed the two older people, and Judge Tucker's whitewash of the men who had killed their son was a blow they would never accept. The Blooms asked Victor and Adrian over and over again how Judge Tucker could reach the findings and conclusions that he did– but the lawyers had no answers.

The Langsdens had been a bit easier to deal with. Victor and Adrian had driven to San Lomas for a group meeting with the 123 families, and the conference room at the church was crowded. Barbara Langsden, always the trooper, had made Victor's job much easier by explaining to the group that Victor and Adrian had done their very best, and had submitted excellent papers. The group was disappointed with the demurrer ruling, of course . . . but in their hearts the families had known that the anti–foreclosure arguments were an uphill battle. Victor had explained the challenges to the 123 families on multiple occasions prior to filing the action in the first place. Nevertheless, the ruling stung. Where were these families to go?

Victor talked to Theresia about the rulings several times by phone. She understood what had happened, of course, and hadn't been expecting anything different. Her only concern was with Victor himself.

"Are you OK?" Those were Theresia's first words when Victor called her at Shanidar after emailing the decisions to her.

"Well . . . I suppose it would be fair to say that I've been better," said Victor. "It always hurts to lose– and I've now been hit with three massive losses all in a row. On cases that I thought I should have won. It hurts . . . but I'm OK."

"How did my father take it? The hate speech ruling, I mean?"

"Exactly the way you would expect– like it was nothing. A matter of no importance."

"Of course . . . that sounds exactly like my father. He sees what's coming, and if he's right the court decisions won't matter at all. Sometimes I wish I had his confidence."

"Me too," said Victor. "But maybe that's why he's Enki and you and I aren't." Victor spoke in a joking way, but there was actually a serious undercurrent to what he said.

Theresia wanted to know when Victor would be moving to the compound. He told her he didn't know, but that it probably wouldn't be anytime soon. His legal obligations were still overwhelming– there were multiple appellate proceedings to file. Theresia had a word of warning.

"Come soon, Victor. Get out of there– now. Father is right– and you don't want to get caught up in what's coming. There's no way to know how bad it's going to be."

"I'm thinking about it," Victor said with some evasiveness. Actually he hadn't made any plans at all. It hadn't entered his mind as a realistic option while he'd been so buried with the multiple litigations, and now that the cases were all lost he still needed to be there to prosecute appeals and help the clients deal with the consequences.

"And I'm thinking about you," said Theresia.

At the partner meeting, Victor launched into his now well practiced explanations about the three losses. There was no emotion in Victor's presentation– he was a lawyer reporting about adverse legal rulings, and nothing more than that. Nevertheless, it was an ordeal, and Victor was glad when the unpleasant task was completed.

"Victor, thank you for that report. All of us here in this room have lost cases in the past, and every one of us knows how it feels. We admire the efforts you've been making on these cases, and there's no doubt that you gave your very best for the benefit of your clients. To try a tough case to the best of your abilities and lose is not something to be depressed about. It's a regular part of our business and we all recognize that you now simply need to put these setbacks behind you and move on to a better frame of mind for the next group of matters that come your way."

Victor mumbled some words of appreciation in response to Phillips's words. But to his surprise, there was more to follow from his senior partner. "Despite that, Victor, the partners have some genuine points of concern about the events that have happened here."

"Concerns about what?" Victor wasn't grasping the point.

"Concerns about the nature of the litigation matters, and perhaps more importantly about your decision making with regard to choice of adversaries." Phillips obviously had something in mind, so Victor remained silent. “In particular, we’re troubled by the fact that Turn of the Century Bank was targeted by your 123 anti–foreclosure filings and that LawbridgeTrimble and the Federal Reserve System were sued in the wrongful death case. The appearance has been created that you and the law firm are attacking our bankers and the monetary system itself, and that’s a dangerous road for the firm to follow. You’re making enemies among people who we want to regard as friends.”

Victor sensed a very negative undercurrent to what his senior partner was saying. “Enemies . . . among friends?” said Victor. “I’ll tell you, Roland, that I personally investigated the Harlan Bloom wrongful death facts in detail, and I have no doubt in my mind that a bunch of runaway rogue cops from the Federal Reserve killed that young man. With the acquiescence and active support of LawbridgeTrimble. And as far as the anti–foreclosure cases are concerned, I’ve studied what our bankers have been doing with their fractional reserve banking system, and I can tell you to a high degree of certainty that their system is exactly what we alleged it to be– a fraud and a counterfeiting scam. These people that you say you want to regard as friends are a bunch of crooks, Roland, and they’ve been destroying the lives of ordinary Americans for decades. Not just the 123 families I represented in the anti–foreclosure cases, but millions of families . . . all around the country. Do a bit of research, Roland– I’m confident you’ll agree with me if you study up a bit.”

The room was deathly silent. A young partner like Victor Desert simply didn’t speak to Roland Phillips that way.

Phillips responded in a carefully measured voice. “You may well be right Victor, and I certainly don’t claim to be any sort of expert where fractional reserve banking is concerned. That’s one of those topics that falls above my pay grade. But what I do know is that the firm has been receiving calls from clients and colleagues in the community asking what we’re doing taking on the monetary system in a way that could literally destabilize the economy and send the whole structure crashing down. Worried people, Victor. People that have a lot to lose if some of the allegations you've been making were to find their way into the public eye. It's not our place as lawyers to run off and lead vendettas against one of the most important and sensitive sectors in our community, and we simply can't be put in a position where we're asserting arguments and positions in litigation that are inconsistent with the values and views of the partners in the firm."

"So what is it you're telling me, Roland? That the bankers got to you? Is that it? Are they the friends and colleagues you're talking about?" Victor knew he shouldn't be saying such things . . . but he said them anyway. All of a sudden, Victor was feeling quite a level of contempt for the group of men seated in this room with him. The word cowards came to his mind.

Phillips waited a long moment before answering. His face was red and blotchy with emotion, and his voice was shaky when he finally broke the silence. "You're a young man, Victor, and I'm going to forgive and forget what you just said to me. But this firm hasn't stayed in business for three generations by taking on crusades for issues and ideas that will destroy our client relationships and put the firm out of business. We simply can't do that, Victor– not if we want the firm to survive. I've received a number of calls recently from people whose opinions I respect, and all of them are telling me that these lawsuits you've been filing are not the sort of thing they can be associated with. Jack Hazeltine has had the same experience. We've been warned, Victor . . . in no uncertain terms. So the only issue now is what we're going to do about it." Victor looked at Hazeltine, and saw that the senior partner was in agreement with Roland Phillips's comments. Hazeltine wasn't the sort of man who rocked the boat.

"So what do you have in mind?" asked Victor. The little drama needed to play itself out to its conclusion, and Victor already knew what that conclusion would inevitably be.

"Well, as I said before, we're all appreciative of your work, and the success you've had in the past. You've been a contributor in the firm, and that means something to us. But we can't continue to assert the sorts of arguments you're making. Not in the hate speech case, not in the wrongful death case about that young actor, and most of all not in the anti–foreclosure cases where you are asserting that our bankers create counterfeit money. We can't go around alleging those sorts of things– it simply can't be done."

"So what is it you suggest?" asked Victor, in a surprisingly calm tone of voice.

"What we're thinking is that all three of the troubling cases have now been fully resolved at the trial court level, so this is a perfectly legitimate time for you and the firm to withdraw as counsel. We can make arrangements to get competent appellate counsel for the clients so they won't suffer any detriment from the transition. In that way, you can end our firm involvement in the cases in a way that will work to the benefit of all concerned." Roland Phillips had said those words smoothly, without apparent difficulty of any kind, and Victor marveled at the slave mentality of the man. A few words from the Overlords, and Roland Phillips was ready to abandon clients and run for cover. But Victor Desert was not.

"What you're suggesting is quite impossible, Roland. Under no circumstances would I abandon these clients mid–case in the manner that you suggest. If I were to leave the cases it would send the worst possible message– not just to the clients, but also to the court. The wrong message about our professionalism, and the wrong message about our commitment to the clients' causes. I can't do what you suggest, Roland, and I won't. Frankly, my view is that this isn't something you should even be asking. The firm took these clients and cases with full knowledge about who the clients were, and what the cases were about. You have no legitimate right to tell me or anyone else that we're going to bail out midway through the process."

This was not a conflict that was going to be amicably resolved, and of course it wasn't. Roland Phillips and Jack Hazeltine put the issue to a vote of the partners, and every partner in the room raised his hand in agreement with the senior partners. Victor was given a choice– he could either withdraw from the client representations in his three troubling cases, or he would be asked to leave the firm. Roland Phillips suggested that Victor sleep on it and advise the partners the following day as to what his decision would be.

The meeting was over . . . and the partners left quickly. It had been one of those defining experiences that none of them would want to remember– the partners of Hazeltine Phillips & Blaine had stepped out of the shadows and identified themselves as what they truly were. And somewhere deep inside, they all knew they had done something very wrong.

XVII.

Victor Desert was actually taking a Saturday off. After working every weekend, and moving out of the old firm to form Desert & Blaine, the busy lawyer was looking forward to a quiet Saturday in the Curson house. Nothing to do, and no one to see– that's what Victor wanted. But it wasn't to turn out that way.

When Victor had announced that he was leaving the firm, I was the first to leave with him. Jack Hazeltine and Roland Phillips had come to me in advance of the meeting of partners and asked if I would go along with the plan to give Victor an ultimatum. They were getting calls, they said. Calls from their banker friends, and friends of their banker friends. Calls from people who were upset– to put it mildly– that Victor Desert of Hazeltine Phillips & Blaine LLP was out there in the legal arena spouting radical ideas. It was bad enough that he was representing Eanna Pictures in connection with a movie about slaves rising up and throwing off their shackles. That kind of film was troubling, but much more serious were the allegations in the Harlan Bloom wrongful death lawsuit. These sorts of charges put the bankers in a bad light, and ridicule was something they could not abide. It was a confidence game, and the confidence of the Eljo couldn't possibly be maintained if the Federal Reserve was made to look like bumblers. That's why the Harlan Bloom wrongful death case was a threat.

But the biggest threat of all came from the 123 families who filed the anti–foreclosure cases. If ordinary people were to figure out the allegations in the anti–foreclosure cases, the process of creating money out of thin air would quickly come to an end. Defeat and ridicule of the counterfeiting allegations was essential– there was no room for another Justice Mahoney in the modern world. That meant there was no room for a Victor Desert– so the bankers went to Hazeltine and Phillips. That was the end for Victor at the firm . . . and for me.

Adrian Garfinkle came with us to Desert & Blaine, and so did Minnie Larren and Caroline Sikes. We had plenty of paying business, and I could picture the new firm taking off and surpassing the tired rabbits at Hazeltine & Phillips in a short period of time. We were hot . . . they weren't.

It was a frenzied process to get the new firm up and running, but somehow it all seemed to come together. Victor was ready to spend some time alone at his Curson house that Saturday night, but the doorbell rang. Victor was sitting in front of the TV, and he groaned at the thought that someone would be bothering him this late at night. Victor opened the door in an unpleasant state of mind, and there stood Katy Hooper holding a bottle of wine.

"May I come in?" she asked innocently, as she maneuvered past her host into the entry hall. Katy had answered her own question– she was already in, and there was nothing Victor Desert could do about it even if he had wanted to.

Katy took a seat on the couch while Victor opened the wine. He could see that she had prepared for this event– her makeup looked good and she was dressed to kill. But beneath the surface, Victor sensed there was something missing. She had a haggard look, and she was too skinny . . . like she wasn't eating enough. Victor poured each of them a glass of wine and sat down to listen. It didn't take long for the story to come out.

"I've been doing OK . . . got my new CD out and I've had some tour dates. But the sales just haven't been there. I don't like the songs I've been getting. When I first started with Camelhump, I thought he was bringing me the right kind of material, but now he's out of the picture with me and I'm not so sure what to do anymore."

"So where have you been living?" Victor asked.

"Well, I'm a bit embarrassed to say it, but I was living with Buster Reeves out in Malibu."

"The rap singer?" Victor had seen stories in the tabloids, but it hurt to hear Katy say it to his face.

"Yes, that's him. He's been kind of guiding me along, giving me the new songs and all. Buster sort of took over for Camelhump, forcing him out of the way, and it all turned out to be a huge mistake. I never should have gotten mixed up with him and his crowd, but I did. And now I need to make a change."

"Do you have a place to stay?"

"Well, I have a lot of friends. So I've been kind of moving around for the last couple of weeks. I haven't really wanted to settle down in anything permanent, so I don't have a place of my own."

Victor had figured out by this time that Katy Hooper was broke.

"Actually," said Katy, with her best attempt at a winning smile, "what I want is for us to get back together." The wine was kicking in, and even though Katy's words were a bit sluggish, she was able to project a very sexy look. Katy knew what worked.

"Well that's a surprise," said Victor. He felt the attraction– it would never go away.

"Oh, I know I didn't handle things very well when we split up," she said in a rasping voice. "Not talking to you about it, or leaving a note or anything. But I just had the feeling that I was being treated like a second class priority to all your law cases– and I thought I should have come first. I was wrong . . . I see that now. And I want us to try again."

Katy was looking at Victor closely, trying to judge his reaction. Katy saw a hint of indecision on his part, and said, "You know, there's nothing stopping us. We could start again right now."

Katy got up from the couch and walked over to sit on the arm of Victor's chair. She bent down and kissed him.

"Katy, we can't do this . . ." But she ignored him and slipped onto his lap, kissing him again– harder this time. And Victor felt the irresistible pull of this woman.

The two of them got out of the chair and walked up the stairs and into the bedroom holding hands. Katy unbuttoned Victor's shirt, and within a matter of only a few moments was out of her clothes and into the bed with Victor. He was lying on top of her, and she was a woman ready. But suddenly, in the heat of the moment, Victor knew better.

"Katy, this isn't going to work."

Her eyes were closed and she had a seductive smile on her face. "I want you," she said. "I want to have your baby."

This was the moment when Victor Desert knew that he wouldn't be taking Katy Hooper back. And he realized something else as well. This was the moment when Victor Desert truly grasped for the first time that he was in love with Theresia Anjau, and that he was going to marry her.

Victor rolled off, and lay on his back, naked beside this infinitely desirable woman who was in bed with him. After a few minutes, Katy realized that she wasn't going to get what she wanted– so the truth came out.

The two former lovers talked for a long time that night. Katy Hooper had no money– Buster Reeves had been feeding her drugs, and she had entrusted him with her cash. So now it was gone. Her latest disk wasn't selling, and the music company was starting to say that *Serpent's Seed* was a one–time wonder. Katy Hooper had made a momentary splash, but there was a lot of competition out there in the pop tart marketplace, and she had already slipped behind.

"Camelhead tried– he really did," she said through her tears. "He wanted me to succeed, and he wanted to help me. But Buster Reeves started running things for me, and once that happened it all just went downhill. His music wasn't right for me, and neither was he. Actually he's just a con man, and I've been struggling ever since I've known him. I never should have had anything to do with that guy– I'm so sorry about what I've done. That's why I came to you, Victor . . . you always know what to do."

"I understand," said Victor. "Why don't you get some sleep now. You can stay here tonight, and then we'll talk some more in the morning." Katy gratefully slept in Victor's arms that night, and as he looked at her strikingly beautiful face in the moonlight flowing through the bedroom window, he remembered how much he had cared when they were first together. It hurt for him to realize that he couldn't help her with what she was going through.

The next morning Victor made coffee and a simple breakfast of fruit and toast. They both knew it was over. After they had talked for awhile Victor gave her some money, and she got in her car and left. Katy didn't say where she was going, and Victor Desert didn't ask.

XVIII.

The evening promised to be everything we had imagined. The ballroom of LA Fire! was filled to overflowing– bankers dressed in black tie, and out for a good time. They were dancing to the tunes of the Fred Klein orchestra, with laughing wives along for the ride. These were the Overlords, and they were gathered this night to honor Los Angeles with an official welcome into the inner circle of global finance. The Federal Reserve branch in LA had been designated as the counterparty currency exchange trader with the Bank of Pailiang, and visions of sugar plums were everywhere to be found. I wondered if I was the only one who sensed the absurdity: a Bankers' Ball– at a time when all around us the signs of decay and decline were multiplying with astonishing speed.

Someone needs to explain to the celebrants what was coming, I thought to myself. But then I realized that anyone who tried would be wasting his breath. Nothing bad had happened yet . . . to them. Nothing had changed yet . . . for them. There was no reason for any of the assembled Overlords to be concerned, or even aware . . . financial collapse was out of sight and out of mind. On this night of the gala, Enlil and his Igigi had no reason to suspect that their carefully executed schemes of a lifetime were about to go terribly wrong.

Victor and I arrived at LA Fire! in a limo– nothing less would have been appropriate. For a fleeting moment I wondered if the iconic hotel name might prove to be prophetic, but then we were swept up in the bustling crowd and the thought was forgotten. A red carpet was out– much like a night of the Oscars– and there was even a grandstand set up for onlookers seeking a glimpse of the glittering Overlords. It was a bizarre display of wealth and arrogance– a Hollywoodesque movie premier for ugly people. I made my way up the red carpet as quickly as possible.

There were a few straggling protesters outside the wooden barriers, but nothing that suggested any serious potential for disruption. A cordon of police in riot gear walled off the young people, and their chants could barely be heard. "Level Z, Level Z," it sounded like to me, but the protesters were too far away and too few in number to make their voices heard with any force and power. This was an evening for the rich and powerful . . . the cries of the left–behinds had nothing of interest to offer.

It turned out to be no accident that Victor had been invited to the gala. Colin O'Neil greeted us warmly in the hallway outside the entrance to the ballroom.

"Victor! I'm so glad you could make it." Victor's hand was being pumped in a forceful– to put it mildly– handshake. The candidate turned to me. "We haven't met. I'm Colin O'Neil– pleased that you could join us."

"Nice to be here. Randolph Blaine."

"Ah, Hazeltine Phillips & Blaine. Honored to meet you. I'm quite familiar with your firm– and not just from my recent experience with Victor on the movie case. Actually, I've been reaching out to Jack Hazeltine to see if he would help in my campaign. Haven't been able to connect with him yet– maybe you could help. In case you haven't heard, I'm seeking to be appointed as Chief United America Attorney for the Median Division now that Kevin Jarrett is going on the bench."

"Yes . . . I've heard. But perhaps you weren't aware– I'm not with the Hazeltine Phillips firm anymore. Victor and I left about a month ago."

The candidate was obviously taken by surprise– but he righted himself after only a brief moment. "OK then . . . I'd like to have your support as well. And Victor's of course. I think I'm the right man for the job." O'Neil handed me one of his campaign cards.

"Check out my website. I'd be appreciative if you would sign up with my list of supporters." O'Neil was looking deeply into my eyes, with sincerity, just as political candidates are taught to do. "I'll give you a call.

Perhaps we might have lunch one day soon." Then, in an instant, Colin O'Neil had left us for the next group of potential supporters.

I turned to Victor, who was examining the crowd in the hallway with a look of wry amusement.

"Now I know why you were invited, anyway," I said with a smile. "Our political process at work."

"Yes– Colin has been after me to support him ever since we had that case together in front of Judge Westerley. Let bygones be bygones– that's what he's saying anyway. We're big buddies now, it seems."

"I can tell. And speaking of your favorite Median Division judge, isn't that her in the flesh?" I pointed toward an attractive woman in her mid–forties who was wearing a strapless evening gown appropriate for the gala.

"In the flesh indeed," said Victor. "Miriam Westerley, friend of the little people. Shall we wander over? I can introduce you . . . she's another of the new friends I've found since O'Neil filed his hate speech lawsuit."

Victor's tone let me know in no uncertain terms that he was still feeling the sting of his recent loss.

"No need for that tonight," I said. "Why don't we just have a good time instead?" Victor was visibly relieved by my response.

It wasn't just bankers on this night of celebration, of course. There were some Hollywood people in the crowd, adding their movie personas to the mix. Worshipers of money and power, I concluded . . . why else would they be here? Movie people aren't really different from the rest of us: if someone has control over a flow of money the stars will come around, just like everyone else.

A sizable group was gathered closely around the guest of honor not far from where Victor and I were standing. One of the men broke away from the crowd and walked over to us.

"Victor Desert, isn't it?" The man asking the question was about Victor's age, with the look of a New Yorker. "Winston Bartell. We met during the Harlan Bloom case, you might recall."

Bartell held out his hand in an accommodating way. His greeting had all the appearances of cordiality, but at the same time I couldn't help but sense that he was taking some pleasure from his recent victory. "No hard feelings about the case, of course. It's just litigation . . . what we do for a living. I hope you feel the same."

Victor didn't feel the same, but he disguised it well. "Of course there are no hard feelings." Victor shook Bartell's hand as if he were a colleague. "Nice to meet you in a non– adversarial setting. So did you fly all the way out here from New York just for this event?"

"No, I'm here on business. You know, of course, that the Federal Reserve is one of my clients, and my father and I are out here for some meetings with the new team in LA. Come over and join our group– I'll introduce you."

Winston Bartell had taken Victor's arm, and he was gently guiding him in the direction of the group of bankers and their wives who were surrounding the guest of honor. At the same time, he turned to me and said, "Please join us, Mr. Blaine. Winston Bartell is my name– and I know who you are." I dutifully followed along as Bartell led Victor toward the banker group.

We were introduced to Wellington Bartell and his wife Ivana. The head of the New York Fed was the man Victor believed was primarily responsible for the death of Harlan Bloom, but we shook his hand as if nothing was amiss. Then we met the elder Bartell– Nelson– the second in command at LawbridgeTrimble. Winston had been steering us toward the center of the group, and now we were standing next to the guest of honor– Lawrence Yasgar himself. The head of LawbridgeTrimble had the appearance of a man who was enjoying his evening, and he looked at

Victor and me with considerable interest when Winston Bartell made the introductions.

"So you're Victor Desert," said Yasgar. "Your reputation precedes you . . . even in far away New York."

"I don't know whether to take that as a compliment or not," said Victor smoothly, "but I certainly can say I have admiration for the success that your firm has achieved. I don't always agree with the things you and your colleagues do– but I would readily acknowledge that you've reached a high station in global finance at a time when all your competitors seem to have fallen by the wayside. That's something worth paying attention to."

Yasgar laughed with genuine amusement. "Carefully chosen words, my young friend. Very well said, with just the right hint of an insult." Yasgar was smiling broadly. He appeared to be taking pleasure in this conversation with his firm's litigation protagonist. Victor Desert wasn't the first lawyer who had tried to cross him, and Yasgar was obviously untroubled by a clash of wills with a courtroom adversary. "You approve of my achievements, but apparently not so much of my methods. So we have a disconnect; we're not on equal footing. My compliment to you was genuine– but yours given in response was conditional, and guarded. You have a momentary advantage, it seems, in this pleasant initial meeting."

"An advantage? I certainly wouldn't describe things that way." Victor was no longer smiling. "I just completed a major case against your firm and several of your colleagues in this room, and lost. I would hardly say we're anywhere close to equal– you and your team have been winning . . . I haven't. You're the one with an advantage, not me."

"Not so at all, Victor, not so at all." Yasgar's tone had turned serious. "Winning or losing any one battle doesn't mean a thing, and no one truly gets ahead on the basis of such transitory things. You and I both live on the edge, and either one of us could come crashing down in an instant of time if some unforeseen event were to break the wrong way. Our successes are ethereal– mine, just like yours. But of course the trick is to rise above the setbacks, and never allow them to take you down, no matter how daunting they seem at the time.

"That's my talent, Victor– I rise above the setbacks. They never hit home, or cause me to lose any sleep at night. Because unlike you, I don't allow myself to care. You care– I can see it. Caring is something that feels warm in the moment, but you'll one day learn that it's a luxury that is actually quite burdensome. What you'll find with experience is that caring is the very thing that drains all the life out of you. It swallows you up, and that's why you'll never turn out to be as successful as you otherwise should be. How's the new firm doing, by the way? And this man, I take it, is one of your partners?"

I shook hands with Lawrence Yasgar, and watched as he took a slight step back from Victor to fully enjoy the effect of his insult. But this was not to be one of Yasgar's triumphs . . . because Victor was ready.

"The new firm is doing fine– thank you for asking. And do you know that one of the people I've spent quite a bit of time with recently is someone who's related to you? Your half–brother . . . here in Hollywood. Isn't it interesting that you and Sydney Anjau share the same mother? What an extraordinary coincidence that you and I would have this chance to talk, and that your half–brother would be one of my clients in the new firm. Sydney asked me to say hello to you, by the way. And to give you his regards. He has enormously fond memories of Errika and his days growing up in New York."

The crowd of people gathered around Lawrence Yasgar looked at Victor with amazement. Half–brother: what was this young upstart from Los Angeles talking about? And for once in his life, even the urbane Lawrence Yasgar found himself at a loss for words. He fumbled: "Half–brother? I . . . I . . . don't know what you're talking about."

"Well, then," said Victor smoothly, "perhaps the person I spoke about is mistaken. Or possibly I didn't understand him correctly when he was talking about your mother. But in any event, congratulations on your award tonight, and I'm looking forward to hearing your comments from the podium." With that, Victor turned and walked away, leaving Yasgar standing alone, flanked by his hangers–on and several burly bodyguards. My young colleague had stuck the knife in . . . and it had found its intended home. I couldn't stop smiling as we walked to our table.

We weren't exactly seated among the guests of honor. Our table was at the rear of the room, along a wall next to some side entry doors. Political invitees of Colin O'Neil who had purchased seats but failed to make the requisite campaign contributions found themselves far down in the pecking order of the evening.

Victor and I took seats and introduced ourselves to the other guests at the table. They were substantial bankers one and all, most accompanied by pleasant looking wives. Solid citizens, by all appearances. But perhaps I'd been in contact with Victor and ETB for too long– because I couldn't shake the feeling that these respectable looking men were engaged in a fraud and a scam every day. Counterfeiting is their business, I was thinking to myself, and the bankers had their antennae out. They sensed my disapproval.

There were police everywhere; not to mention a small army of plainclothes security personnel. Mirrorprobe people were there– the private bodyguards for Lawrence Yasgar had the look that Theresia described so well. Hired killers, she had said.

The police and security guards were mostly just milling around– taking watchful positions up and down the wall areas; gathering in the outer foyer where the cocktails had been served; trying to appear unobtrusive at the back of the raised stage where the honored guests were seated. It was an army, all right– but something of a motley crew. The officers were wearing a variety of different uniforms, and looking at them I wondered how they could know who was who. I recognized the familiar outfits of LA County Sheriff's Deputies, of course, and the Los Angeles city police uniforms were recognizable to me as well. But the new kids on the block wore dark blue uniforms of a sort that I'd never seen before. These were the men and women of the Federal Reserve Law Enforcement Units, and there were a bunch of them in the room.

The Federal Reserve cops seemed to be filling a variety of roles. Some of them stayed close to individual bankers, obviously serving as bodyguards. Others were roving around the room, looking from side to side in a process of threat assessment. Still others were on the sidelines, hanging out with no apparent function at all. The Federal Reserve police outnumbered the LAPD and Sheriff's Deputies by a considerable margin on this night, and they had different uniforms depending on their unit and where they came from. The Fed cops from New York wore sharply creased pants and what appeared to be a suit coat over a dark shirt and tie. The Los Angeles contingent, by contrast, wore a less formal rig– shirt with an open collar, and slacks. Every officer in the room had a gun prominently displayed in a belt holster, with appropriate supporting gear including a nightstick, radio, handcuffs, and probably more that I couldn't spot at first glance.

Victor and I were receiving a cold shoulder from the others at our table, so we entertained ourselves by talking about the people we'd met. I asked about the odd names of the Bartell clan: Nelson, Wellington, Winston . . . it sounded like a gathering of English lords, I said. Victor explained it to me– like so many bankers, the Bartells were Anglophiles through and through. These people loved anything British– and the Bartells had appropriated the names of English heroes as their own.

Lawrence Yasgar was surrounded everywhere he went by four of the Mirrorprobe team. These guards were the best in the world, and it showed in the quality of the men around Yasgar. Athletic, alert, good looking– the Mirrorprobe group that accompanied Lawrence Yasgar looked like they belonged on a college football field. The Chairman was almost invisible when moving in the company of his entourage– the bodyguards knew how to close ranks and stand in such a way as to shield him completely from random onlookers. Lawrence Yasgar on this night in Los Angeles was protected as carefully as any President of the United States.

Colin O'Neil handled the honors as Master of Ceremonies, and I had to admit he did an excellent job in what otherwise might have been a boring lineup of speakers. O'Neil was a natural– one joke after another, and many of them were actually quite funny. Things were off to a good start, but once O'Neil turned over the microphone to the bankers it all flattened out fast. The speakers who followed O'Neil to the podium were singing the praises of this new counterparty relationship between China and the Los Angeles Fed, and I for one found the cheerleading to be a bit tiresome. Los Angeles, we were told, was poised to move out of the shadow of New York and San Francisco and take its rightful place among the top tier of financially elite cities. Los Angeles had arrived . . . blah, blah, blah. I wasn't grasping how this process of international money exchanging was going to create any jobs or otherwise add to the wealth of anyone other than the bankers themselves.

Finally it was Lawrence Yasgar's turn to speak. O'Neil gave an effusive introduction to the evening's honored guest, and the leader of global finance advanced to the podium accompanied by a heartfelt standing ovation. "Thank you, thank you," he said with outstretched arms. "Thank you, thank you . . . please take your seats. Thank you . . .". The crowd was still standing.

At just that moment the side doors next to our table burst open and several ill dressed protesters made their way into the room. They were chanting: "End the Fed! End the Fed! End the Fed!" and they carried handmade signs with words about counterfeiting, and debt slavery.

A swarm of Federal Reserve police fell upon them immediately, and hustled them backwards, out of the ballroom. The interruption was over almost as quickly as it had started, the side doors were closed and secured, and people in the room began to turn their attention back to the man standing alone at the podium.

During the brief turmoil, no one had noticed a single Federal Reserve officer walk to the front of the stage from the wall area on the far side of the room. Just as people were taking their seats, the lone officer reached a point below the podium where he had a clear view of Lawrence Yasgar standing on the raised stage above him. There was a gun in the policeman's hand, and shots rang out. Yasgar grabbed his shattered neck with both hands, just above the Adam's apple. His arms were raised high and splayed out to the sides as he gasped for breath and stared down at the lone officer with a bewildered look on his face. The man continued to fire from nearly point blank range, and after several misses the fifth bullet caught Yasgar just below the left cheekbone. The banker's face and brain were blown to bits in an instant, and the remains of Lawrence Yasgar fell backwards onto the floor of the raised stage. He was dead before hitting the ground.

The Mirrorprobe bodyguards quickly realized that they had massively failed in their one and only task, so they launched an effort to make up for lost ground. Each guard instinctively pulled out his handgun and commenced firing at the lone gunman standing below the stage a few feet away from them. Perhaps not surprisingly, their marksmanship in the fog of the moment was less than it should have been– bullets sprayed wildly, and several of the honored guests seated at the front tables below the podium were hit. Even with all the misses, the Mirrorprobe team succeeded in placing multiple shots in the body of the lone gunman and he staggered backwards against the table closest to the stage. The gunman fell onto a seated woman, and the two of them crashed to the floor in a heap. It was Ivana Bartell who was knocked down by the wounded gunman, and for a brief and unwelcome moment she found herself holding the dying man in her arms.

"Why? Why?" she shouted to the barely conscious killer. "Why have you done this thing?" Ivana Bartell was on the verge of hysteria, but the killer in her arms was calm, and ever so slightly smiling.

"Level Z," he said quietly. Then again, "Level Z." The gunman tried to form words for a third time, but there was nothing left. Ivana was pushing him away with every ounce of strength in her small body, but it didn't matter. The gunman was already gone.

The Mirrorprobe bodyguards had recovered their presence of mind. They surrounded the dead gunman, and one of the guards kicked him hard in the ribs. Ivana Bartell crawled away from the gunman in the direction of her husband, who lay nearby with a Mirrorprobe bullet in his brain. The screams of Ivana Bartell filled a ballroom that was otherwise deathly still.

PART THREE
TEOTWAWKI

I.

The silence in the ballroom didn't last for long. Pandemonium broke out as people looked around for safety and began their mad scramble to the exits. Was the shooting over? No one knew for sure, and most of the guests had no interest in waiting around to find out. From my seat near the back of the room it was difficult to grasp exactly what had happened– the whole event had been a burst of intense activity that ended quickly. My instinct was to leave the ballroom immediately through the open side doors only a few feet away. The ballroom at LA Fire! was a place where angry men were walking around with loaded guns in their hands. Not something I wanted any part of– but Victor Desert had other ideas.

"I'm going to walk up front and get a look at that man," Victor said grimly. He was already out of his seat, and beginning to make his way toward the podium area. I followed, and as we got closer to the scene of the shooting we found ourselves pushing our way forward against a tide of people moving in the other direction. A milling crowd surrounded the dead gunman and the guests at the front row tables who had been caught in the crossfire, but Victor knew what he wanted, and after some considerable shoving we found ourselves standing over the lone gunman lying on his back in a pool of blood. No one had covered the body, and the gunman's face was clearly visible. Victor already knew– he had recognized the man while the shooting was still going on. But to me it came as a complete surprise. The man lying dead on the ground was Scott Langsden.

The killer was dressed in a Federal Reserve police uniform, but it was obviously a fake. Why hadn't anyone noticed, I thought to myself? But then I remembered my earlier impression– there were law enforcement people in a wide variety of outfits all over this event. Scott Langsden was just one more face in the crowd.

Victor looked around for someone in authority, but all the police officers seemed to be busy elsewhere. For the moment, no one was paying any attention to the man lying dead on the floor, but finally, after what seemed like a long wait, Colin O'Neil walked toward us. Victor pulled the politician aside.

"I know this man," said Victor, gesturing toward the killer. "His name is Scott Langsden; he's one of my clients."

O'Neil was stunned. "Are you sure?"

"Positive," said Victor. "He's one of the homeowners I've been representing in that group of anti–foreclosure cases I told you about. He was an out of work architect, and he was focusing on our litigation as his last hope. His case against the bankers was dismissed a few weeks ago, and I have a feeling this is the result. Scott was a quiet man . . . calm . . . not at all the sort that I would expect to do something like this."

"You'd be surprised," said O'Neil, "the quiet ones are sometimes the most likely to snap. You might want to talk to that woman over there; she heard his last words before he died. 'Level Z', he said– or something like that. Like what those protesters were chanting earlier– it seems to be some sort of code for these people. Maybe you can make some sense out of it, but in the meantime, stick around if you would. The LA city police will be taking jurisdiction away from these Federal Reserve cops as soon as they can get control of the situation– you can tell your story to them."

Victor looked in the direction of the woman that O'Neil had pointed to. She was sitting on the floor, legs folded under her, holding a man's head in her lap. Victor recognized her– Ivana Bartell, and the man she was holding was her husband Wellington, the President of the Federal Reserve Bank of New York. His eyes were closed, and he wasn't moving. Ivana was stroking his face as Victor walked toward her. She had overheard his conversation with O'Neil.

"So this killer was a client of yours, Mr. Desert? That must make you feel better. Lawrence Yasgar dead . . . and my husband . . . . This is your chance to gloat, Mr. Desert. Your spoils of war, the bodies of two great men– killed by a nobody, for nothing." Ivana Bartell had spoken softly, but there was a glow of visceral hatred in her eyes.

"I'm sorry about your husband, Mrs. Bartell," said Victor, bending low to be at eye level with the woman who earlier that evening had been Wellington Bartell's wife. "The shooter's name was Scott Langsden, and yes . . . he was a client of mine. I can tell you that he never seemed like the kind of man who would do something like this."

"Save your empty words, Mr. Desert." Ivana Bartell was filled with contempt, "And your phony sympathy. My husband is dead– and the silly court case you filed against him is the reason why. You've been stirring up hate– you and your movie friends– going on and on about Enlil, and the Igigi. Do you think we're fools– that we didn't know what you've been up to? You might show us a bit more respect than that."

Victor was silent for a long moment. He noticed that the woman's dress and legs were covered in blood, and finally he said, "Have you been hit? Shall I get a doctor over here?"

Ivana Bartell looked at him coldly. “There’s no need for that . . . this is the blood of my husband. Killed by Lawrence Yasgar’s bodyguards– ironic, isn’t it?” She stared vacantly, at nothing in particular.

“Colin O’Neil told me you heard Scott Langsden’s last words. Can I ask you what they were?”

“Level Z, he said. A couple of times, and he said it with a smile on his face. Your friend died a happy man, Mr. Desert. He came here to kill Lawrence Yasgar, and that’s exactly what he did. With my husband thrown in for good measure.” Ivana Bartell continued to stroke her dead husband’s face as she talked.

Victor remembered the term from Theresia’s explanation about Harlan Bloom. “Level Z. The last letter in the alphabet. The end of the line.”

“Is that what it means? That he was just another dead–ender? A loser with no place to go and no future to live for . . . and this is the kind of man you choose to represent?”

Victor had no intention of arguing with a woman who was holding her dead husband in her arms. “I can’t know for sure what he meant by his words, Mrs. Bartell. Or why he chose to do what he did.”

“Don’t know, eh.” The woman was looking at Victor coldly again. “Well perhaps you’d best find out, Mr. Bigshot, because this same worthless man who came for Lawrence Yasgar tonight will be coming for you tomorrow. You’re just like us, counselor– you’re no better than we are. The sad people like your client won’t care in the slightest about your high minded posturing once they realize you have something they want. They’ll be coming for you, Mr. Desert, and sooner than you know. We’re the same kind of people, you and me. And Wellington . . . and Lawrence. Now that it’s started, they’ll kill us all.”

Victor reached out his hand and touched Ivana Bartell’s face. He was looking straight into her eyes, and she didn’t push his hand away. For a single brief moment the two were bonded together . . . but then it was over.

Two Los Angeles city police appeared on the scene, with paramedics to take Wellington Bartell's body away. Ivana Bartell was left alone on the ballroom floor . . . Winston and Nelson Bartell were nowhere to be seen.

It took awhile, but Victor was finally released by the police after a lengthy interview session. He called Barbara Langsden from his cell phone and broke the news to her. Barbara and her children had been staying with Samuel and Bella Bloom in Los Feliz since losing their home, and this latest blow was the cruelest cut at all. Victor put her in touch with one of the officers on the scene so she could make arrangements to access her husband's body. By the time he finished talking to Barbara it was nearly midnight, and the ballroom at LA Fire! was deserted.

* * *

The events that night at the Bankers' Ball were only the beginning for the soon to be dying bankers. The killing of Lawrence Yasgar by a simple man like Scott Langsden was front page news, and Barbara Langsden suddenly found herself in the forefront of a worldwide movement of angry protesters. She was besieged by the media, wanting to hear all about Scott, and whether she had known that something like this was coming. They were asking her the mundane questions like where he had gotten the uniform, but most of all they wanted to know about Level Z. The phrase had become a matter of worldwide interest, and people couldn't hear enough about it. Was Scott the leader in a secret society? Was it a code? Speculation was flying, and there seemed to be little comfort in the explanation that Scott Langsden had simply reached the end of the line. Last letter in the alphabet– the Overlords couldn't understand the significance of it all, but the Eljo did. They knew Scott Langsden's meaning . . . there were tens of millions of them living at Level Z in the United States alone.

LA city police tracked down the costume shop on Hollywood Boulevard where Scott had purchased his cheap uniform. The official looking police badge he wore to the Bankers' Ball had come from a local toy store next door to the costume outlet. Scott Langsden, it turned out, had simply showed up wearing a costume. He walked into LA Fire! dressed like a Federal Reserve cop, and nobody had noticed him, or cared. He was invisible, mingling with the crowd of bankers and police officers until finally the moment came when he walked up to Lawrence Yasgar and blew his brains out. The entrance of the protesters through the side doors had been fortuitous– no evidence ever developed that Scott was involved with the protesters or had any idea they would burst into the ballroom at just the right moment to create a diversion. Scott Langsden had apparently believed nobody would challenge a man in a police uniform– and it turned out he was right.

One week after Yasgar was killed, the President of the Bank of Northern Mariana was shot to death in a parking lot in Tysons Corner. It was another lone gunman, but this time the shooter got away. He left a calling card on the body: it read "Level Z."

The chief teller of Monitor Bank of LaDall went for a bike ride on the following Monday morning. He was found dead the next day, at the bottom of a ravine not far from his home. Two shots had been closely spaced in the center of his chest. It had all the appearances of a contract killing, except that the phrase "Level Z" was carved in the banker's forehead.

A senior vice president fell inexplicably from the roof of the 37 story headquarters of Swiss Gentleman's Bank in Boston. Suicide, the media reported, but most of us didn't believe the story. There was no suicide note found, and the man had recently received a promotion. Level Z, the conspiracy theorists said.

Rachel Parks was a senior economist for the Federal Reserve Bank of Kansas City. She drowned to death on a fishing trip at nearby Loon Lake, even though she had been an Olympic swimmer. On the same day, high rolling banker Robert Clark was shot six times in the stomach in the main concourse at Grand Central Station in New York. No one in the crowd tried to stop the killer as he made his way to the street and disappeared.

Robert McGee was the Director of Global Equities for Bankcorp General in Charlotte. McGee was found dead in the garage of his home by his young daughter, with eight nail gun wounds in his torso and head. Suicide, the local authorities said. Level Z, said the rest of us.

When Steven Cale of Blueback Investments was shot twice in the head while on a lobbying visit to Washington DC, the whole thing seemed to be getting too close for comfort where the nervous Overlords were concerned. President Irwin Lester declared a state of emergency, and announced to an attentive nation that the banker killings would stop then and there. The next day, three more bankers were murdered. Two of them were on ordinary errands with their wives . . . and the wives were killed too. The people of Level Z, it seemed, weren't interested in Presidential proclamations.

The following week, three female bank tellers were shot to death in St Louis outside a suburban branch of First National Bank of the Midwest. The killer threw down a collection of leaflets explaining about Level Z. He was soon captured, and he calmly explained to the arresting officers that he was at the end of the line, and was merely executing his final mission. Nothing much mattered anymore, the killer said, so why not go out by shooting some bankers?

There was more of the same. All told, a total of thirty seven bankers and their wives were killed in one way or another during the weeks following the Bankers' Ball. Some of the killers were caught– but none of them seemed to care. They had figured it out, they said, and the only sensible thing to do was decide in a fair minded way who was responsible, and then go shoot them. We're killing the guilty, they explained, and in their eyes that was a good thing.

The start of the collapse was soon to follow. Suddenly there was no money– or at least there was no money with any value anymore. And there was no longer any law . . . because anyone with a gun had learned that he could take the law into his own hands. The rioting came, and the looting. It spread with flash mobs, and after awhile the cities were burning. TEOTWAWKI, as the geeks liked to call it, had arrived with a vengeance. When a roving gang of thugs wandered into Beverly Hills and ransacked my house, I knew the time had come. We made our plans to move to Shanidar . . . before it was too late.

II.

Frank Paladin announced he was leaving LA, and his decision meant that the last of the fence sitters were sure to follow. Frank Paladin, the tough guy, the man who could always make his way in the city, had seen enough. He was heading north to Shanidar, and he wasn't coming back.

I had reached the same decision, and between the two of us, Paladin and I put Desert & Blaine LLP out of business after only a brief existence. The firm ceased to exist when Caroline Sikes announced that she was leaving with Paladin, and Minnie Larren gave notice as well. Adrian Garfinkle had already announced that he was joining up with the Singularity people, so all of a sudden Victor Desert was the only one left. He still wanted to believe– in the legal system, in his life work– but he was living in the past. Legal system . . . what legal system? Los Angeles was tearing itself to pieces with rioting, looting and strife, and the only legal system left was law of the streets. The time had come for Victor to wake up, and Paladin was the one to tell him.

"Take a look around you," Paladin said that morning in the office, "do you see anything worth saving? LA isn't going to recover– not now, and not ever. It's just like Sydney Anjau said it would be. How could he have seen so clearly? Amazing. Bottom line– I'm leaving tomorrow with Caroline and Minnie, and you should too."

Victor hesitated for a long moment; he was deep in thought. "You don't think they can get it together?"

"With what?" said Paladin contemptuously. "A few SWAT teams running around trying to scare people? It's become a joke, Victor– don't you see? From now on it's people fighting over scraps in a world where there isn't enough to go around. Look at the gas prices– $25 a gallon already, and pretty soon there won't be any gas at all. Who's going to drive a gasoline tanker into a burned out city? Same for food, and water, and all the other things people need to survive. Who's going to deliver those things? It's the old warning my father used to give me: the people in power can keep things under control . . . right up until the moment they can't. Then they all just disappear, and that's Los Angeles– the zombie city, with no humans left. So I say get out now, while we still can."

I gave Victor the latest news about our clients. "I spoke to Bella Bloom– she and her husband are leaving today for Shanidar, and Barbara Langsden and her children are going north with them. Jonathan Silverstein– he's already left. Eanna Pictures has shut down completely, and Jonathan is on the road this week with whatever he could take with him from the company. They're all headed off to a new life, the one most of us find out about only when it's too late, and that's exactly what you need to be doing. Stop being such a chump . . . there's nothing left for you here."

I watched Victor struggle as he learned that most difficult lesson of all: TEOTWAWKI, Victor was finding out, didn't care about him and his little lawsuits at all. When the shit hits the fan, it isn't just other people . . . TEOTWAWKI comes for you.

* * *

We were leaving it all behind: Victor's unfinished house on Curson, my wife's collection of antique furniture, the artwork, closets full of clothes, cars, TVs, the stuff of a lifetime. There was no way to get those things up to Shanidar, but somewhat surprisingly I discovered that I didn't care anyway. Once I'd made the decision to leave, I was a free man again. I had Janie, and the boys, and an open road to the new life ahead. It was all I would need– no tears were shed for the life that once was.

Victor Desert left the same day I did. It would be five days on the road for me and the family, and it actually turned out to be quite an enjoyable adventure. Like pioneers, or young kids on our way to summer camp. Once out of Southern California we found that there was still a fair amount of civilized behavior going on– the agricultural communities along Interstate 5 seemed to be getting along fine, and the people weren't concerned at all. The collapse hadn't spread evenly . . . it was hitting the big cities first. But I couldn't help but wonder what would happen to these isolated highway towns once the essential goods and services were no longer flowing in their direction.

I talked to some of the countryside people along the way. They didn't sense any danger; it pretty much seemed to them that the collapse was a piece of entertainment. Something new to watch on TV– a reality show where those obnoxious LA and San Francisco people finally started getting what they had deserved all along. The collapse had no meaning for these people along the highway . . . because it hadn't reached them yet. They were perfectly happy to believe the TV talking heads who told them everything would work out fine, and when I tried explaining what I was doing, and why, they just nodded their heads, and smiled, and went away thinking I was some sort of LA goofball. Sydney Anjau was able to make it all real when he talked about what lay ahead, but for whatever reason I couldn't do the same. The highway people were laughing at my grim warnings about the coming collapse and TEOTWAWKI. I made no converts along the road.

I'd been to the compound only once– on the weekend visit with Victor and Katy Hooper that seemed so long ago. The changes were stunning– starting with an entry area where the aging wooden gate had been replaced with towering steel panels surrounded by barbed wire. There were guards on duty to ask us what our business was, and once inside we found a fair sized city that was buzzing with activity. Construction was going on everywhere– new cabins in the wooded areas, reinforced fences along the perimeter, internal roadways being cleared and paved– a brand new community was taking shape right before our eyes.

I drove to the main lodge to check in and get our assignment for living quarters. The old "Silver Bay Lodge and Cabins" sign over the entry door was gone– replaced by a new one which read simply: "Shanidar." The lobby area was jammed with people– it was almost impossible to believe this was the same deserted facility I had visited a few months before.

"Randolph!" I heard my name called out from the far side of the room. "Over here!" It was Adrian Garfinkle– he was a veteran . . . he'd been here for two weeks already. We shook hands warmly, and I couldn't help but remember that this was the young man who had set it all in motion. But for Adrian and EndtheBailouts, Victor and I would never have met Theresia and become involved in the events that had changed our lives so completely. It had started for us on that New Year's Day weekend when Harlan Bloom was killed, and I pondered for a brief moment what would have happened to me and my family if our lives hadn't taken the turn that they did. Not a pleasant thought– I put it out of my mind and gathered Janie and my sons close to me in the crowded lobby. Adrian took my arm and pushed his way forward to the front desk area. Standing behind the desk with a group of busy assistants was Theresia Anjau.

She was so pleased to see us! I rated a warm kiss and a hug, and she greeted Janie as an old friend. We were treated well where accommodations were concerned– a private cabin had been assigned to us in the Eagle Nest property next door.

"How many people are here?" I asked as I looked around at the throng in the lobby.

"We have about 2000 so far," said Theresia, "and probably another thousand or so coming soon. We're absolutely full up to capacity– so there's a lot of construction going on. We're going to need more housing by the time winter comes."

"Victor– is he here?"

Theresia smiled. "Oh, yes. He came in yesterday. We had a room set aside for him here in the lodge, but he chose to take a bed in one of the dormitories instead. He's over in the Kokanee building at Eagle Nest– not far from your cabin. The two of you can get together after you're situated; I think he's out somewhere in the helicopter with Walter and Paul Cutter right now. They should be back soon– why don't you and your family get settled in, and I'll let him know you're here."

I wandered around the compound with Janie and the boys after we got our things moved in at the cabin. What a beautiful complex it was– or at least it would have been if the place wasn't buzzing in every open space with trucks and construction vehicles. I counted at least ten projects underway just in the segment of the property near to our cabin. There were some very busy tradesmen at Shanidar in those early days.

We came to the waterfront area and walked out on the big dock that serviced the Spinnaker Retreat. A large touring boat with the name Seawelanna on the stern was moored at the breakwater, and several barges that had the look of World War II troop transports were pulled up on the shore. Six speedboats and Paul Cutter's antique Chris Craft completed the armada.

Theresia had invited me to attend a meeting that afternoon with the leadership group, and I arrived at the lodge just as Walter Kollett, Paul Cutter and Victor Desert were returning from their helicopter flight. Victor and I shook hands warmly, and I was re–introduced to the two local men. Victor had only been in camp for a day, but already he had begun to develop a ruddy outdoor look that made him seem very different from the lawyer I'd known in Los Angeles. Within a few moments our group was joined in the lodge conference room by Sydney Anjau, Robert Rossignal, Karen Ashley, Sarah, Theresia, and Frank Paladin. This was the senior management team– Kollett and Cutter took the lead in briefing the group on recent developments.

"The big story last night and today is out of New York," said Walter. "We weren't seeing much on TV, they put a blackout on the story, but we configured our communications setup from the Singularity people to pick up a military radio band from the east coast. The news wasn't good. More than a million people showed up in the Wall Street area last night for a demonstration on Maiden Lane. They were targeting Lawbridge Trimble and the New York Fed, but Maiden Lane is a narrow street, and the demonstrators ended up spreading out over the entire downtown area and Battery Park. The street outside LawbridgeTrimble was so filled with people that the police couldn't get near the place to do crowd control– assuming they even wanted to. In any event, LawbridgeTrimble and the Fed were left to their own devices for security– and you can imagine what that meant. The Mirrorprobe people and Federal Reserve cops started blowing people away. More than 5000 dead or injured, but it didn't make the slightest bit of difference. The people in the streets were fed up, and the protesters got what they wanted. LawbridgeTrimble was completely trashed and burned out, and there were smaller fires burning all over the Wall Street area."

We sat in shocked silence as Walter Kollett continued with his report about the events in New York.

"They broke into the Federal Reserve building, and here's a good laugh. The protesters wanted to get their hands on all that gold in the basement vaults, but once they got down there, the whole place was empty. It was just rows and rows of empty shelves– 4000 tons of gold, completely gone missing. Remember a few years back when Germany demanded that the Fed turn over the gold it was supposedly storing for them? And the Fed told them no– they wouldn't turn it over? Well Germany's gold is long gone, along with all the rest. There were some disappointed protesters at the New York Fed last night, so they burned down the building just so the bankers would know what people actually thought of them."

"Are things back under control today?" asked Sarah.

Walter hesitated for a moment before continuing with his report. "Yes . . . at least to some degree. But except for the missing gold, the protesters got pretty much everything they wanted. They were all yelling 'Level Z, Level Z,' and we know what that means. A group of them found Nelson Bartell, and shot him. He had taken over for Lawrence Yasgar at LawbridgeTrimble, but now he's dead too. Tough time to be a banker, I guess. They killed a bunch of people across the street at the Fed, too. Even with all their firepower, the Federal Reserve police couldn't stop them."

Victor remembered the night of the Bankers' Ball. "So now little Winston is the only Bartell left."

"He's probably hiding out somewhere," said Sarah. "Behind mommy's skirts at their castle in the Hamptons."

"When I talked to Wellington Bartell's wife that night of the Bankers' Ball," said Victor, "she told me the mob would be coming for us too. That we were no different from the bankers. And now Ivana Bartell has lost her father in law, along with her husband. So what do you think, Walter? Are the Eljo going to turn on us like she said they would?"

All of us were interested to hear Kollett's response.

"Are they going to turn? It completely depends on how bad things get out there. If everything falls to pieces, and there's no food, and no water, you bet they'll turn. We'll see lots of people who want to get their hands on what we're putting together here at the compound. Just a simple fact of life."

"So how are we doing on the security issues?" asked Victor.

"We've made a lot of progress with the entry guard station and the perimeter fencing. I've been trying to get a 'no man's land' cleared on the outside of the perimeter fence so that anyone who wants to scale the fence will be visible, and will think twice before coming out into the open. We've got a pretty good start on it– probably 70% of the perimeter has been cleared to open ground– the other 30% still has trees and shrubs. Another month or so and we should have a relatively secure fence line.

"But of course that's only part of the problem. We're relying a lot on barbed wire, and a large enough attacking force can break through that– or any other sort of fencing we might put up. The real issue is firepower. It's a matter of guns and capability– not a lot more complicated than that. If we can meet an attacking group with more guns and more shooters than they have, we're going to keep them out. If they have more guns and people than we do, they're going to get in."

"So what do we have in place so far?" It was Sydney Anjau who asked the question– the first time he had said anything in the meeting.

"Well we're up to about 2000 people now, and Theresia tells me she's expecting to take it up to 3000 or so and then do a cutoff. Right now we have more men that women– maybe 1300 men to 700 women– and a fair number of the men brought their own guns with them and are somewhat trained in the use of firearms. That doesn't tell us our people can actually win a serious firefight– but it's a start. Maybe half the group has some gun training– so we have a lot of work to do getting everyone else comfortable with the idea that they'll be needed in defense if an attack comes. People who've never used a gun before will need to develop a 'life or death' mind set about what we're doing here. Without that, they're just sitting ducks."

"How serious is the threat?" asked Sydney Anjau. "And where does it come from?"

Walter had obviously given the subject of defense a lot of thought– he knew what he was talking about. "The main threat is exactly what we might expect– roving bands of thugs. People who have nothing to lose. Once they see that we're an organized society functioning in a civilized way, they'll want what we have– and they'll be willing to take some risks to get it. If a big enough group gets formed up and starts acting together, the threat could become very real."

"How many people do you think we're likely to see joining up in a group?" asked Theresia.

"Hard to say. There's no big group out there so far– we know that from Paul's contacts in town. I don't see anything that looks like an imminent threat– except maybe the risk of a lone nut. But the issue is the unknown– what happens if things in the cities go downhill even further than they have already? What happens if the electrical grid goes down? That's when the problem will come. So far, people in our area still have power, and food, and shelter. There hasn't been any kind of breakdown in the local area, but if things get worse– if people start migrating here from California in large numbers– we could start seeing an organized group form up. We can handle an attack by a thousand people– probably even two thousand. But if a group of five thousand committed people were to get organized we would be in for a very difficult fight.

"Paul and I will be watching to see if there are new people showing up in town– at this point that's the important thing. And I have some ideas I'm working on for a surprise. We're not defenseless, but it's going to be a numbers game. The worse things get out there, the bigger the threat."

With that, we closed the meeting.

* * *

A week after I arrived, there was an interesting group of twenty or so people that showed up uninvited at our entry gate. Victor Desert was called out to meet the newcomers, and as soon as he appeared, a heavy set older man who was obviously the leader spoke out in a booming voice that was not entirely familiar with the English language. "Victor! My Victor! Our heroic lawyer from Hollywood turned freedom fighter in the wilderness. We are your family . . . and we are here!"

Victor looked at the visitors without comprehension.

"I am Armand . . . Armand Desserte . . . your family from Ramoutier has come to join in your grand adventure! We have traveled all these miles from Alsace, and now we arrive. The Desserte family– together at last!"

Armand Desserte grabbed Victor in a giant bear hug, and for a moment we all feared for his life. The older man was weeping tears of joy as he introduced his son Maurice and the rest of the clan.

"We are workers! From the countryside! We know the land, and how to grow things. We will feed you, and you will like our work– you'll see. The fools in my country, in sad France, are not preparing– they will all die, but not us! The Desserte family is here! With Victor, and the great Sydney Anjau who sees the future. This is where we will live."

Armand was hugging Theresia Anjau by that time, and after she had a chance to catch her breath, she gave a warm welcome to the newcomers. Theresia knew right away that their expertise would be a major plus in a compound population that didn't have nearly enough farming capability.

Three days later, a similar scene played itself out– but with an entirely different cast of characters. Victor, it seemed, had drawn a following to his new life at Shanidar.

Standing at the gate this time was Katy Hooper, and she was not alone. Camelhump was with her, and their group included his family and a collection of music industry colleagues. Theresia's initial reaction was difficult for me to judge. It certainly seemed that Katy might be an unwelcome addition in Theresia's eyes, and perhaps for Victor as well. Why ask for trouble . . . Katy had certainly shown herself to be capable of bad decision making. On the other hand, Camelhump and his people had skills, and would undoubtedly be valuable additions to the compound. Would Katy Hooper's presence create tension? Hard to know, but Theresia laid the issue to rest. She put her arm around Katy's shoulders and the two women walked together through the entry gate. They were talking in an animated way, like two sisters who had been living in the same house for a lifetime.

III.

Diego Garcia is a narrow jungle reef located 1,000 miles off the coast of India. The island was British territory, but since the 1970s it had been mostly populated by the US military. A British colony, colonized by Americans, the lonely reef in 2021 was home to about 2000 military personnel and 1500 civilian contractors. The island was a stationary aircraft carrier . . . sitting in the middle of nowhere.

Diego Garcia was discovered by Portuguese explorers in the early 1500s. It's the largest of fifty– two islands in the heart of the Indian Ocean, and the island's name is believed to be that of a ship's captain who visited on an early voyage of discovery. Diego Garcia's main source of income over the years had been from a profitable copra oil plantation; at one time oil from the Indian Ocean provided fuel to light most of the lanterns in London. The plantation enterprise dwindled away, but with the arrival of the US military a new island business was destined to follow.

Within a few years, American Seabees had transformed the empty speck of land into a massive military base centered around a heavy duty aircraft runway 12,000 feet in length. Endless dredging created a modern ship channel in the lagoon, and the Seabees built an array of taxiways, hangars and support facilities that turned a remote island atoll into a front line attack base. Diego Garcia was the largest peacetime construction effort in Seabee history . . . they called their creation the Footprint of Freedom. The mission of Diego Garcia in the 2020s was simple: deliver massive bomb drops at targets located thousands of miles away. Diego Garcia was home to hundreds of B– 2 bombers, all standing in readiness for immediate mobilization if a preemptive air strike became necessary. And on this moonless night, Diego Garcia was about to find its meaning and purpose in the American military arsenal. Operation Liberty Finder was under way.

The planes left in three waves, and as they reached the Persian Gulf, the units went in separate directions. Tactical Group Implant headed for northern Iran, where they would deliver their payload of bunker busters to rumored underground facilities at Karmuz and Halidar. The US government had been viewing those locations as likely sites for the development of nuclear weapons. After this night Karmuz and Halidar would cease to exist.

Tactical Group Exhale would find its targets in southern Iran at facilities located near the city of Kantel. The suspected underground bunkers in this area were smaller than the facilities to the north, and were believed to be spread out over a larger area. Tactical Group Exhale had seventeen separate targets of opportunity in the Kantel area, and the Exhale bombs were designed to deliver punishing blows in a zone stretching over hundreds of miles.

The Persian Gulf island of Kish was the target for Tactical Group Omerta. Kish is located in the northeast corner of the Persian Gulf, seventeen kilometers from the mainland of Iran. Kish Island is tiny– encompassing an area of only 90 square kilometers– and it is widely regarded as the most beautiful region in the Gulf. The island is flat, and uncultivated, and its coastline is covered with silvery sand. At the time Tactical Group Omerta visited the island, Kish was flourishing as a tourist haven and center of commerce. It was also the home of the Iranian Oil Bourse.

After the night of Operation Liberty Finder, the Oil Bourse would be no more. Any risk of an ongoing Iranian challenge to the dollar power of the bankers died with the Bourse, so the attack was viewed by all concerned as a complete success. Tactical Group Omerta reduced the Bourse and its surrounding area to a flattened pile of rubble, and while an estimated three thousand people were killed in the attack on Kish, the loss of life was explained away as collateral damage in a necessary mission. President Irwin Lester told a worldwide audience that the destruction of nuclear capability in Iran was essential to American national security, and that Operation Liberty Finder had made us all safe. He mentioned his regret about bombing civilians on the island of Kish only in passing.

Irwin Lester had been serving as President of the United States for less than a year at the time he ordered the attack on Iran. The newly elected president had struggled with a difficult term in office– Level Z was creating domestic turmoil, bankers were being murdered all over the place, and something needed to be done. The President had tried the friendly and understanding approach– meeting with Level Z protest leaders in the Oval Office to listen to their demands. He had tried the use of stern words– telling the American people in no uncertain terms that civil insurrection and lawlessness weren't going to be tolerated on his watch. He had used the traditional strategy– unleashing tear gas and military firepower against the disgruntled rabble rousers. But none of these things had worked.

Operation Liberty Finder was the natural next step. The strike was undertaken to rekindle a spirit of unity and patriotism here at home, and Iran's supposed nuclear development threat had been touted for years with just this sort of mission in mind. The President called for a preemptive strike because that's what leaders do when things go badly at home for the regime– a winnable little war is the favored strategy of diversion that works every time. The move had unanimous support from the President's bankers and political advisers.

President Lester and the American people were proud of what they accomplished on the night of Operation Liberty Finder. There was a worldwide uproar about the loss of innocent life, of course, but that was to be expected. Better that there be protests in Madrid, and Rome, and India, than back here at home. Let them complain– the Overlords didn't care, and the American people were with them. Sure enough, civil unrest in the United States seemed to fade away after the bombing of Iran. Patriotic Americans had an overseas victory to celebrate, and the big win abroad for the home team made the killing of more bankers seem unnecessary and superfluous. A revitalized America had sent a powerful message from the Footprint of Freedom . . . the world had listened, and would act accordingly. Civilian casualties on Kish Island were a small price to pay

* * *

Bella Bloom had become our resident educator at Shanidar. She organized all the classes, and we were amazed by the positive reception her effort was receiving. People at the compound were eager to learn, and Bella's courses were not the ordinary schoolyard fare. She was introducing new subjects that none of us had paid attention to before, and tonight would be no exception. Armand Desserte was our speaker, and his topic was the "Big Stack." The grandstands at the baseball field were filled to overflowing as the Frenchman launched his lesson in amusingly fractured English.

"It's a game for fools, I will tell you about today. A game against the Big Stack– a game that can't be won. A game for my sad countrymen in France who still believe their bankers will save them. My countrymen don't prepare, but we know better, *mes amis*. We can learn to never play the bankers' game again, and that is what we do when we change the world, *n'est pas*? So we talk about Big Stack tonight, to be ready when Enlil and the Igigi fall.

"We learn from the fools my friends! So we picture a banker game where two players start out each with a hundred coins of equal value. The players flip a coin over and over again, with the loser on each flip transferring one of his coins to the winner. The game continues until one player runs out of coins. Question– which coin flipper is more likely to win our *petit* game of chance?"

Joanne Kollett called out the answer from her seat along the third base line. "Neither is more likely to win. Each player has an equal chance in the game you describe."

"Ah," said Armand, "*la mere* of our esteemed Victor knows how to think. And she's right, is she not– in a simple and honest game of coin flip, each player has the same chance. So we change the rules to make the game *un peu plus interessant* . . . more interesting. Now we say that one of the players can add more coins to his stack any time he wants. Who wins now in our little game?"

"The one who can add to his stack, of course. It's too easy– there's no way he can lose since the game will go on until his adversary has no more coins." Caroline Sikes had answered.

"*Bon*!" said Armand with an approving smile. "The wise Caroline knows that the player who can add coins to his stack will always win. This is the power of the Big Stack, but our *belle* Caroline says my game is too easy so let us add one more factor to make the game relevant to *le monde bouge*– our changing world. Assume now my children that the first player, the one who can add coins to his stack, will earn a bonus from the casino depending on how long the game goes on. And the bonus gets larger the longer they play. How does the Big Stack player encourage our foolish flipper to keep playing?"

I decided to give it a try. "If I were the player with the power to add coins, I would offer to loan some coins to my opponent every time his stack got a bit low. If he signed on for the loan, he would keep playing– and that way I would earn the bonus."

"Right again is the esteemed lawyer," said Desserte. "Is he not correct? If our silly flipper takes a loan, the game will continue and our banker will get his bonus. And now when our flipper loses the game, he ends up in debt. *Sacre Dieu*, our borrower is a fool, is he not? His loss is now this big!" Armande spread his arms wide to illustrate the point. "And our banker is this big a winner, *d'accord*? What a good, good game it is if you have the Big Stack."

"Like my countrymen in France, our fool thinks he'll get ahead by borrowing. But actually he just wastes his energy. Do not sit at the bankers' table! Do not play the bankers' game! Do this to the bankers." Armand spit on the ground. "Refuse to speak to them! This is how the Blood Children will win and the Igigi of Enlil will lose. The Big Stack means nothing if we won't use their money.

"And that, my children, is the lesson from this week in Iran, is it not? People on Kish Island, refusing to play at the bankers' table. The bankers bring their bombs, and destroy the Oil Bourse, and kill people. So, *garcons et filles*, will the banker bombs work? Will we still use their money? Will we be fools, or will the thousands dead on Kish be avenged, perhaps by someone we don't even know? *Nous verrons, mes amis* . . . we shall see, my friends, we shall see."

IV.

We were living in a time of the false calm. It was like being in the eye of a hurricane– enormous storm clouds were circling around, but all was peace, and quiet, and enormous beauty in the place where we were standing. The season was summer, and in the false calm it almost seemed like we were on a camping trip at the lake. I was taking long walks in the forest every chance I could get, and needless to say, Janie and the boys were having the time of their lives swimming every day in the warm waters of Lake Ponderosa. Except for Sydney Anjau with his powers of perception, none of us knew for sure what lay ahead.

Some of the pilgrims headed for home. They thought the old life was still possible, and how could we say they were wrong? The cities had quieted down, and by outward appearances everything seemed comfortably set on the road to rebirth. The TV channels were up and running again, and the mainstream media was leading the cheers. The bankers were lending again, they told us! Buy a house, they said! Buy a car, the talking heads suggested! Your credit is good with the bankers! Economic growth was the talk of the day, and there were many who wanted to believe. Our population at the camp dipped back to 2000.

The camp was a very busy place and each of the remaining pilgrims, it seemed, had a function and purpose. In my eyes, everyone in camp was running around doing important things, making decisions, and just in general turning Shanidar into the kind of place where we would want to live for a long time to come. Everyone, that is, except me. It wasn't for lack of trying– I picked up a hammer and took a turn with the carpenters, but most of what I accomplished had to be reworked by someone who knew what he was doing. I tried helping Karen Ashley in the food service operation for a time, but my food service work had the effect of slowing things down rather than speeding them up. I wasn't much use in perimeter defense, and I couldn't really do anything at the farms since I knew nothing at all about growing crops or taking care of animals. I was still very much a lawyer, and there wasn't much use for my profession at Shanidar. A fish out of water, it seemed for a time.

Sarah Anjau was the one who came up with a solution. She had been watching my struggles with amusement, and finally she suggested that I start up a journal. Like all of us who decided to stick it out at the compound that summer, Sarah knew to the depths of her soul that the time was coming when we would change the world. So that was the start of the Randolph Blaine journals– with thanks to Sarah, I had found my place. Pretty soon I had a camp newspaper going– our pilgrims wanted to read about themselves, and be kept up to date about what was going on. My twice–weekly publication of the *Shanidar Pine Cone* filled a need.

Mostly I wrote about the people– our endless array of extraordinary and unique people. Were we on the right road? Was Shanidar truly the place of the future? Sometimes it appeared as if we were hopelessly out of step– the normal looking things we saw on TV seemed to mock our effort. We were loners, with little direct contact with the outside world, but through the *Pine Cone* I was able to help keep spirits high. There might occasionally be a few muted words questioning whether Sydney Anjau's vision would actually come to pass, but overwhelmingly we were a gathering of true believers, and the sense of shared mission was the centerpiece of our lives. My journals were easy to write . . . because this was the most extraordinary gathering of people I had ever come across in my life. Blood Children indeed!

Minnie and Caroline from the law firm had fit right in. They were both LA girls growing up, but you would never know it to see them at the camp. The two of them were enjoying every minute of their new lives, and it showed.

They were our camp administrators. Running Shanidar was a big operation, and Minnie and Caroline were the ones who took on the task. They spent most of their time in the office at the lodge– handling the money, paying bills, planning the budget, and just in general taking care of the business end of things in a highly efficient way. They did it because they could, and they handled themselves well. We were in capable hands from an administration standpoint, and the two women had Alan Butler working with them– our full time accountant on staff. Oh, and there was one more thing: Caroline, for sure, had a serious admirer that she picked up somewhere along the way. Frank Paladin– our resident tough guy from the inner city– was showing all the signs of being hopelessly in love.

Walter Kollett had become the de facto commander of Shanidar– mirroring his old job at Talon Air Force Base. It was an entirely natural thing– the job was nothing he asked for, but Walter Kollett was a leader because he knew what was needed, and how to get it done. His primary focus was compound security, and all able bodied men and women in the camp had been through his rigorous training in firearms usage and defense.

We had learned over long hours with Walter what it meant to maintain interior lines of communication, and how to set up a defensive position, and when to fall back during an attack, and when to stand your ground. Walter was teaching us something quite specific in his training sessions– it all had to do with lines of fire, and interior positions within the perimeter of the compound itself. The lake was at the back of these fallback locations, and Walter spent endless hours teaching us how to retreat from the outer perimeter to reach the bunkers and earthworks he was building in a semicircle close to the main dock area. Walter had something quite specific in mind, and his level of confidence was such that none of us questioned his strategies. Victor Desert's stepfather was a towering presence in our gathering of civilians– without him I'm quite sure our group would never have been ready when the moment of truth came.

The busiest person in camp, by far, was the indomitable Sylvia Burstein. Our resident psychiatrist from New York was in high demand– all day, every day, she would talk to pilgrims about whatever it was they wanted to talk about. For some, it was just a chance to hear a friendly and amusing voice. For others, it was to seek help in dealing with the absence of loved ones. For yet others, it was a matter of seeking advice about how to adjust to the new life at Shanidar. Sylvia Burstein welcomed one and all, and her humor and good spirits were legendary in the community.

For Sylvia, there was no looking back. No crying about the loss of her beloved New York, or her own parents who had refused to join her at the camp and were struggling to survive in the Brooklyn neighborhood where she grew up. Sylvia didn't allow our camp members to live in the past– because she refused to live in the past herself. It was all about the future with Sylvia Burstein, and every time she explained such things, the answers seemed so obvious. Many of us went away from our sessions with Sylvia wondering why we hadn't been able to figure it out for ourselves.

Our most popular figure in camp was among the last to join us. Camelhump put together shows on the baseball field once a week, often featuring Katy Hooper, who seemed to have regained something of her health and happiness in the Shanidar environment. Camelhump's real name was Lambert Kamins, and I enjoyed calling him Lambert when we spoke.

Camelhump, who always seemed to be smiling, turned out to be something much more than a singer and record producer. He took on the job of perimeter security as an assistant to Walter Kollett, and every day he was on the outer lines with a work crew– clearing lines of sight, strengthening fencing, stringing barbed wire, and doing all the other myriad tasks that Walter asked him to do. Camelhump, the LA rapper, had become Walter Kollett's right hand man. We marveled at his energy and commitment.

Barbara Langsden was another of the Southern California travelers who was blossoming in camp life. It took some time for her to get over the loss of her husband– even during her busy days as Miss Century, she had always been a wife and mother first. But Barbara had found a new life now, and it must have touched her in some very deep place to have seen her husband's action at the Bankers' Ball become a rallying point in the worldwide cry for freedom. She didn't condone what Scott had done, but she surely must have wondered sometimes whether Scott Langsden had known that his act of shooting Lawrence Yasgar would spark the movement in a way that nothing else could have done. Did he know that the lid was ready to blow? Did he sense that he was the one among millions who was destined to actually do something about the cancer of the bankers? The rest of us will never know for sure, but I suspect that Barbara Langsden had answers to such questions locked away somewhere deep inside.

Barbara worked at the farms every day. Armand Desserte had taken her under his wing and was teaching her all about raising animals and growing things out of the ground. He and Barbara were good together– his booming laughter kept her spirits high, and her human warmth was something the older man from Alsace found enormously attractive. The farms were producing for all of us, and Barbara and the Desserte family were a big part of the reason why.

Paul Cutter was our rock. The quiet man from Prospect must have been amazed to see his long dormant property reborn as a bustling small city. Could he ever have foreseen that his grand location on Lake Ponderosa would one day become our Shanidar? Could any of us have foreseen? Sydney Anjau, perhaps– but certainly not me.

Paul had no specific title or responsibilities at the camp, yet he was always among the leaders in pretty much everything that happened. He was so . . . competent. Is that the right word . . . it almost seems inadequate to properly describe the myriad contributions made by Paul Cutter.

Perhaps none of his many attributes was as important as the simple fact that Paul had lived in Prospect all his life. He was a local, and the townspeople knew and trusted him. Because of Paul, we weren't just another bunch of extremists on a frivolous adventure from California. Paul's presence gave us substance in the eyes of the neighboring community– and without that boost, much of what we were doing could never have been accomplished. Paul Cutter brought experts from town– local people who knew about water delivery, and land use, and the building trades. These people knew how to get things done, and Paul Cutter had everyone's respect– in camp and off. He had a diverse collection of skills, and his quiet confidence was something I envied. The man was entirely comfortable doing the simple everyday things that I was quite incapable of achieving.

Sydney Anjau was our spiritual leader– the man who would go down in history as the father and founder of Shanidar. Without Sydney Anjau, my family and I would still be back in Los Angeles, living on a road to nowhere. The news reports we were getting said that things had calmed down, but I knew better. The fate of Los Angeles was something I wouldn't have wished on anyone: people there were soon to die– while we at Shanidar were going to live.

I had been raised, to pretty much accept on faith the lessons of Genesis as they were taught in Sunday School. The ancient mythologies of Enki, and Ninhursag, and their creation of the Blood Children were unknown to me, and I was troubled by the new interpretations at first. Our day to day life experience tells us there are no shortcuts on the road to knowledge, so how do we improve? No self help book or magic potion is going to lead us to anything of importance, so where does transcendence come from? The people of Shanidar believed in their own powers and capabilities– but was that enough?

I looked for answers one day in an interview with Peter Trel for the *Shanidar Pine Cone*. He was the leader of our Singularity group– and the self made billionaire who was largely responsible for the creation of Shanidar as it existed in 2021. Peter Trel did what was needed– he put up money, and lots of it. In our interview, he explained the reasons why.

Trel: I did it because I knew Sydney Anjau, and I'd seen his movies, and I'd heard him speak. Sydney has transcendent perception– I saw that right away. It's so rare; and that's how we became friends.

Blaine: Transcendent perception, you say. What is it?

Trel: In simple terms, it's the capacity to know reality. To see things clearly, as they truly are. And of course, if one sees the truth, he or she will know the future. Sydney Anjau's greatest gift.

Blaine: I'm not sure I see the logic of a connection between your Singularity movement in Silicon Valley and Sydney Anjau, the Hollywood film producer. It seems like you're coming from entirely different outlooks and cultures.

Trel: And indeed we were. Which is exactly the quality that makes Sydney so special. I doubt if there is anyone else in the world who could have come to Silicon Valley and convinced eight of my brightest colleagues to leave their homes and move with him to this compound. We're here because of Sydney Anjau, and his transcendent future vision, and I suspect that's true for most of the rest of the pilgrims as well.

Blaine: It certainly is for me, but what is the connection– how does your science of Singularity intersect with the vision of Sydney Anjau?

Trel: It's not actually complicated at all. Singularity is about the engineering of life, and to us, the brain is akin to a computer. But did you know that humans, on average, use only a small part of their available brain power? So if you want to talk about achieving transcendence, and living life with genuine perception of the truth, development of our own individual potential is the obvious place to start. Think of what it would mean if the average person merely stepped up his own intellectual development . . . if we simply used our own brains, we would see a burst of human growth like nothing the world has ever experienced! That sort of change is completely within our capability right now. The only reason people are slaves is because they can't imagine for themselves what it would mean to be free.

Blaine: How does DNA fit in?

Trel: DNA is part of it, of course. Not everyone is a Sydney Anjau, and it's silly to think otherwise. But the potential for enhancement is enormous . . . for all of us. Members of our team– and many other eminent scientists, I might add– have spent a huge amount of time and focus on the use of genetics to improve and expand our human characteristics in areas of health and intelligence. And isn't that exactly what Enki is said to have done in the great mythology about his creation of the Blood Children? I don't believe that strands of DNA from thousands of years ago are the determinants of human potential today, but does any of that really matter? Isn't it enough that we're searching today for ways to enhance our knowledge and perception? That means unlocking the secrets of DNA enhancement at the same time we take the obvious first step of using our available brain power. The two go hand in hand, and once we start making progress on these simple things the rule of the Overlords will end. Remember the teachings of Enki: eat from the tree of knowledge if you want the slavery to be over.

Blaine: I take it you aren't worried about the backlash your sort of thinking is sure to generate. How many people do you think are going to be receptive to the idea that they could actually improve themselves if they simply made the effort to do it?

Trel (smiling): You're right, of course. For whatever reason, the vast majority of people aren't interested in expanding their scope of knowledge and understanding. Truth about the world we live in can be a bitter pill to swallow, and let's face it: genuine creative thinking strains the brain! It's so much easier to live in the darkness and leave well enough alone. If you try to force people to grasp their true potential, the reaction is going to be kill the messenger– they'll tell us such talk is blasphemy and perversion. Enhancement is a threat to the things people think they already know, so the concept of transcendent perception remains forever foreign to many, many people. But so what? Isn't enhanced perception exactly what we should be seeking? Think about it– what if people really could expand the perception of their own brains? And what if we find out that we're only using a small portion of our total DNA capability? Isn't Sydney Anjau living proof that transcendent perception is entirely within our reach?

Blaine: I wish I could agree with you, but it seems to me that what you're suggesting is quite impossible.

> Trel (smiling again): Are you so sure? How do you know that? We're seeing fantastic advances in our understanding of the human mind every day– it's one of the most rapidly emerging fields in modern science. Enki and Ninhursag were a bit ahead of us with their strategy for the creation of Cain and Luluwa, but as far as I'm concerned, we humans are about to learn all over again that our potential for enhancement of knowledge and perception is limitless. And once we do that, the freedom vision of the Blood Children tablets will inevitably be fulfilled.

* * *

I could go on– there are so many interesting characters in camp that I could write about . . . and will. But not right now– there's plenty of time to write later about the lovely Sarah Anjau, and our irascible genius Mark Greenlee, and the brilliant writer Raffi, and the warm and wonderful Blooms, and so many more.

I won't write their stories now because I want to be outside. I want to feel the warm summer sun, and take another swim in the soothing waters of our grand lake. So I'll close this segment of the journal with just a few short words about Theresia and Victor.

May I call them a couple? By all appearances, I think I can. Victor had been alone since his difficult split from Katy, and he looked very wounded for a time. He wasn't taking an interest in any woman– even with Theresia Anjau standing right next to him. My disengaged young colleague seemed to be missing the boat entirely.

That was the time when Robert Rossignal was pursuing Theresia with all the love and attention that she deserved from a man. Robert is a forceful figure in his own right, and for a time it seemed as though she might be interested. There was an attraction toward Robert Rossignal that was visible in Theresia, no doubt about it. But it passed– Victor Desert was the one she wanted, and in my humble opinion she had wanted Victor from the first time we met her at Hazeltine Phillips & Blaine. I don't think she ever changed her mind. She may have wavered a bit when Robert came into her life, but it wasn't enough. She was Victor's woman . . . then and now.

So what Theresia Anjau did was bide her time and wait. Victor needed to wake up, and come to her– it would never have worked the other way around. Well slowly but surely it began to happen. More than any of us, it seems, Victor Desert has changed at Shanidar. His brashness has been replaced by the sort of quiet confidence that we all want to see in our next leader. Which is what Victor Desert will surely be– our next leader. Once Sydney Anjau passes the mantle, Victor Desert will be our Enki. How strange for me to write that . . . but it's true! And Theresia will be his bride . . . that's true as well. All destined to happen in its own good time.

So on that happy note, I'll close my notebook and go enjoy these last fading rays of summer sunlight. It's been another memorable day at Shanidar.

V.

Irwin Lester was the first President since James Buchanan in pre–Civil War days to come to the presidency as a confirmed bachelor. President Lester was fussy about not being disturbed in his bedroom, and Chief of Staff Danny Abrams knew full well that his boss wasn't going to appreciate being awakened at this time of night. But there was no choice in the matter. The staffer gathered up his courage, and knocked firmly on the bedroom door.

"What is it?" An unpleasant tone had been invoked by the awakened President.

"Mr. President, we have something of an emergency going on. We need for you to come with us to the basement."

"What do you mean, the basement? Is that you, Danny? If it is, this better be something pretty damned important. I had a late night at the

Embassy Ball, and this isn't a good time for you to be knocking on my door. And what time is it, anyway? My alarm clock doesn't seem to be working."

"Mr. President, that's part of what we wanted to talk to you about. It seems that the power has gone out– all over the city. And maybe in other parts of the country as well. We don't know for sure– we're having trouble establishing communications."

Silence ensued from behind the closed bedroom door for a period of several minutes. There was definitely some urgency involved here, and Danny Abrams wasn't quite sure what he should do. But just as he was getting ready to knock again, the door opened, and Irwin Lester stood in the doorway. The President's bedroom was entirely dark, as was the White House hallway– the only light came from a flashlight in the hand of the Chief of Staff. The time was 3:20 a.m. when President Lester was led away by his Secret Service agents to a stairwell which led to the underground bunker at the residence. President Lester noticed that the entire White House was in darkness; there was an eerie silence all around.

The bunker was crowded with staffers and military personnel by the time the President arrived. The elevators in the White House were out of service– Lester and his entourage had been required to walk down more than twenty sets of steps to reach the location of the bunker deep underground. The President was breathing hard from the effort, and he sat down heavily in a chair, feeling dizzy. The President was disoriented after his long walk, and when he looked around all he could see was a room intermittently lighted by an array of flashlights. Even here– in the safest location of the nation's capital– there was no electricity. Irwin Lester felt a chill run down his spine as he strained to catch his breath.

"We've got a team of engineers looking into the lighting," said Abrams. "There's an auxiliary generator that should have kicked in by now, but for some reason it didn't. And none of our cell phones seem to be working. So we'll just have to wait a few minutes while they figure this thing out."

"What happened?" Lester's tone was impatient.

"We don't know for sure, because we don't have any communications capability in place right now. But from the early reports we got before the blackout, it appears that two rockets were launched to high altitude from ships standing off our east and west coasts. It hasn't been verified yet, but we think the rockets carried nuclear devices that were set off at an altitude of about 300 miles for the purpose of generating an EMP attack."

"EMP?" President Lester was unfamiliar with the acronym.

"Electro–magnetic pulse. It's a form of attack that can have the effect of disabling our electrical grid and devices that rely on electrical energy to operate. Some of our scientists have been saying that an attack of that sort was possible, and we think that may have been what happened. We're still waiting for confirmation– the communications system with our bases went down before we could get any sort of definitive assessment."

"Are you saying we're defenseless? That a task force of Russian bombers could be flying over the country right now dropping nuclear bombs, and we'd have no way to respond? Is that what you're telling me?" Irwin Lester was speaking in a shaky voice– he was barely able to get his words out.

"We haven't heard any reports of bombs, or any sort of air raids. But like I said before, we lost communications about an hour ago, and we haven't been able to get reports more recently than that. So we can't know for sure. If it's only an EMP attack, I think we can expect to recover fairly quickly. From all that I've heard, that sort of attack can have a big initial impact by shutting down the electrical grid, but then the power repair people will get out there and have things up and running again."

At just that moment, the overhead lights came on in the bunker. The room was filled with cheers.

President Lester didn't know what to do. The idea that he would be sitting here in an underground bunker having no way to communicate with the outside world was a scenario entirely foreign to him. And he wasn't handling it well.

"What do we do now?" the President said to no one in particular in the group of military officers and staffers that were crowded around him.

For a long moment there was no response. Then one of the high ranking military men said, "I think we should order a strike. The country is in danger, and every minute we wait makes us more vulnerable to a first strike attack against us. We need to get our planes up in the air and on their way."

"On their way to where?" asked Abrams with considerable annoyance in his voice. "We have no idea where the two rockets came from, or who's responsible, or even whether there's been any damage outside of a power outage. And we have no way to order a strike anyway– all our communications are down. Let's just keep our heads, and get some information together before we start going off half cocked."

The general who had spoken in favor of an air strike was silenced for the moment by Abrams' show of common sense. And when three engineers in oil stained overalls came into the bunker, the idea of a preemptive air strike was put aside for the moment. All eyes turned to the repairmen with hopeful looks, and the leader of the group launched into an explanation of what they had found.

"There doesn't seem to be any physical damage that we could see. It's just a power outage. But it's an outage that affects electrical devices even if they're not directly connected to the grid. That's part of the reason our cell phones don't work. The towers are out of commission, but the phones aren't working right either. Anyway, we went down to the generator room, and tried to figure out why the backup generators didn't start up automatically like they were supposed to. Somehow, this thing– whatever it is– caused the generator startup mechanism to go all haywire. So, we worked on the generators for awhile and we finally got one of them running. That's where these lights are coming from. It's a start, anyway– but there's a lot more that needs to be done."

* * *

At the same time that the President and his men were trying to figure out what happened, a collection of teams in twenty three widely separated locations across the United States and eastern Canada were moving quietly into action. Each team consisted of five or six men dressed in black for a dark night when no lights were working. Each group was traveling with similar gear– wire cutters, heavy duty lanterns, and backpacks containing an assortment of rocket propelled grenades. Each group had an RPG–7 grenade launcher to carry out the mission.

The groups were highly trained, and knew exactly what to do. It was made easy by the fact that there was no worry about detection. The EMP attack had shut down alarms, security cameras, control panels, communications devices, and other defensive systems that might have deterred entry to the electrical substations, and twenty three stations in total would come under attack on this night. The substations were mostly located in rural locations– with cars and trucks not working there was almost no risk of police or firemen appearing on the scene to try to stop the intruders. The saboteurs would be long gone before anyone became aware of what they had done.

The twenty three groups went about their tasks in a methodical way. Holes were cut in the perimeter fences at each of the substations, and the saboteurs just walked right in. There were no guards or watchmen at these automated facilities, and once inside it was a simple matter to locate the large electrical transformers that formed the operating heart of our nationwide power grid. Each of these giant transformers weighed thousands of tons, and they were filled to the top with the immense quantity of cooling oil that was needed to control the heat generated in the process of moving huge quantities of electricity along miles of overhead wires. The transformers in the twenty three substations that came under attack that night formed the core of the grid– without them, the country would have no ability to move electrical power over anything other than short distances for months or even years to come. The system couldn't operate without these giant transformers, and once they were destroyed it would take six months or longer to build each replacement unit. A small group of experts armed with rudimentary tools and weaponry was about to bring civilization as we'd known it in the United States and eastern Canada to a screeching halt.

The work was done quickly, but without haste. Each transformer was struck with a specially constructed incendiary grenade launched from the shoulder mounted RPG–7 unit. The flammable oil in the transformer would catch fire, and the saboteurs could then move on to the next transformer in line. The process was quite methodical, since there were no defensive measures that could come into play. The flooding devices that were supposed to douse transformer fires had been disabled by the EMP attack, and without fire suppressant capability, the giant electrical units were sitting ducks. The saboteurs moved quickly from one transformer unit to the next in each of the twenty three locations.

In all, a total of 295 transformers were destroyed at the substations. The entire task was completed in less than two hours, and by the time engineers had begun to figure out how to overcome the EMP effects, they began to discover that a much more serious problem had developed. A problem that was not going to be solved that night, or anytime soon. There would be no electricity flowing through the North American electrical grid for many months to come, and there was nothing any of the experts or engineers could do to change that. The country had gone dark, and it was going to stay dark until replacement transformers could be built and installed. The saboteurs had hit America at its weakest point– blowback had come with a vengeance.

The Internet was working in London as dawn was breaking through the darkness of Washington DC. The following post appeared on the London Times website:

> To: The Leaders and People of the United States of America
>
> What happened last night was payback for an unprovoked attack that killed more than 3000 innocent civilians on the free port island of Kish. You cannot expect such wrongful acts to go unnoticed . . . or unavenged. Your actions in the world have consequences.
>
> Nemesis

VI.

President Lester emerged from his White House bunker into a hot summer morning in the nation's capital. There was no mass communications capability yet, but the President wanted to get out into the streets and reassure his people that things were under control. Which of course, they weren't. America was awakening to a day with no electrical power grid– something the country hadn't experienced since horse and buggy days. And no electrical power meant no functioning civilization– it was as simple as that. No major city in America could survive even a brief power outage– there would be no food delivery, and no water, and no lights, and no air conditioning, and no elevators, and no functioning gas stations, and no television, and no Internet, and no telephones, and no refrigerators, and . . . the list goes on and on. The protests that had erupted during the days of the killing of the bankers were nothing compared to what the country was about to see now, and the flash mobs weren't waiting. No electricity meant no working security systems, and no coordinated police presence, and nobody to stop the looting. It was a good time to take the stuff you wanted.

One of the things city dwellers learned that day was that their electronic benefit transfer cards would no longer be working. That meant no food, so local supermarkets and food delivery locations were the first to fall victim to the mobs. Anyone who had been depending on the government and the bankers to put food on the table was instantly out of luck.

In the civilized world of 2021, big screen TVs and smart phones had been the focal points of modern culture. The delivery of low level entertainment and communication through functioning TVs and cellphones had never before been called into question, so it was a rude awakening when many Americans found themselves helpless, and alone, with no way to contact any of their usual sources of comfort and reassurance. The loss of TVs and cellphones caused enormous discomfort– but at least most people weren't going to start dying if they had to go without communications for awhile. Not so with the physical aspects of life.

Food needs to be delivered the old fashioned way– with trucks; and distribution systems; and outlets where people can come and get it. By noon on the first day, our entire structure of food delivery to American cities had come to a screeching halt, and even in places where food could still be found, the means of paying for it had disappeared into the mists. Nothing was working– not EBTs; not credit cards; not checks . . . nothing but old fashioned cash, and nobody had any of that anymore. The ordinary delivery of food to tens of millions of Americans in every great city suddenly and irretrievably stopped happening, and once the supermarkets, convenience stores, ATMs and gas stations had been looted, the shelves were not going to be restocked. Within a matter of days, people were starting to starve in the streets. The demand went out: "feed us!"– but there was no one to answer the call. So the riots and civil unrest escalated, and spread, and there was nothing that anyone could do to stop it.

The flash mobs made their way to major intersections to publicize their demands. At first there were still a few working people trying to move around in the cities, but assaults from the street corners put a stop to such activity within a week of the collapse. Everything shut down in our urban cores, and traffic ceased to exist. The cities belonged to random mobs, and the ghosts of happier times from the past. There would be no commerce in the cities for a long time to come– because without electricity there can be no cities.

The process of urban breakdown quickly spread across all social and economic levels– rich and poor alike were forced out of the urban zones. The outcome was the same in every large city in America– civilization as we had known it ceased to exist.

The police simply went home. Our thin blue line was overwhelmed by the sheer force of numbers, and without electricity they couldn't communicate; couldn't marshal forces; and couldn't appear in significant numbers when needed. There was nothing the police could do to stop the collapse . . . so why try? Law enforcement was a shadow on the sidelines while the cities burned to the ground.

* * *

After a time, things hit bottom and the signs of recovery began to appear. It could only happen unpredictably– recovery occurred where electric power was restored, and darkness prevailed where it wasn't. Within a short period of time there were two Americas, and it was in isolated rural communities that recovery came first. These were the places that had local access to their own sources of power– the grand urban capitals of old were out of luck because the destruction of crucial transformers meant that power couldn't be delivered over long distances.

Recovery became a patchwork process, and it wasn't fair or equitable. One city had power– a neighboring community didn't. If you were near to an electrical dam or a nuclear facility you had power; if you counted on delivery from distant locations, you didn't. A new class of people began to appear– we called them the wanderers. These were the refugees, traveling the countryside seeking new homes in cities that had power, and abandoning their former cities to the darkness where electricity wasn't available any more. The wanderers were our new American paradigm, but they were soon to learn a harsh reality. The people in cities with power didn't want them– the locals had problems enough of their own.

Millford and Prospect were among the first to get their local power grid up and running again. Millford was a river town– it had a hundred year old hydroelectric dam and power station located right in the heart of the downtown area. The power from this station was quickly diverted to local use, and as other dams up and down the rivers went local in their delivery strategy it didn't take long for the entire pacific northwest to find itself with power in abundance. There was no way to transfer extra power to California or other distant points, so the people of California migrated north. They didn't have resources, and they didn't have money– but they came anyway, and pretty soon the wanderers began to outnumber the locals. Once that happened, the wanderers started taking what they wanted. They were an invading army.

In the world of power haves and have nots, new questions were being asked. Why do we need a national electrical grid at all, the haves were asking, and the country was splitting up as this question began to be answered "we don't." The government and finance centers of Washington and Wall Street were increasingly marginalized as an emerging process of local control took hold. Local control was a foreign concept to people like President Lester and the bankers, but there was nothing they could do to stem the tide.

They didn't really see it anyway– all across America ordinary people were trying desperately to feed themselves, and find shelter, and keep their children alive, but in Washington DC and Wall Street the only topic of serious conversation was who should be bombed next. Someone had to pay for the "Night of Darkness" and it needed to be a country, not some ragtag band of terrorists calling themselves Nemesis. The issue was: which country to blame? But no one knew the answer– since there was no proof that any country was at fault. The eager warriors had no identifiable place to vent their vengeance, so there was nothing that could be done at all.

VII.

This was the night for the premiere showing of *Blood Children* at the compound. Jonathan Silverstein had rigged up a big screen on the baseball field, and the movie was about to be viewed by a real audience for the very first time. Everyone in camp was excited and making final preparations before walking over to find a place to sit. The fall night air was chilly, and the last of the daylight was almost gone. The film would be starting in less than an hour.

Walter, Camelhump and Paul Cutter were sitting at an outdoor table near the lodge, waiting for Victor to wrap up his meeting in the conference room and join them. They'd been there awhile– Victor was running late. He was going over the food service issues with Karen and her team, and the three security leaders were acutely aware that food delivery was rapidly emerging as a critical aspect of camp operations. Winter was coming soon– and the farms wouldn't be making regular deliveries anymore. Victor and Karen Ashley had much to talk about, so the three security men patiently waited their turn.

By the time Victor emerged from the lodge it was getting darker by the minute. The men greeted him warmly, and said nothing about their long wait. They knew full well that Victor Desert was simply doing what needed to be done. Hours, and days, and weeks meant nothing to Victor anymore– it was all about accomplishing the task at hand. And there were so many tasks.

"So what is it you want to show me?" asked Victor with genuine curiosity. He knew these men wouldn't bother him with anything that wasn't high priority.

Walter responded for the group. "Come with us. There's still enough light, I think." He rose from the table and led the group toward the center of camp where a new water tower recently constructed by Rossignal and one of his construction teams now stood. The tower wasn't quite completed– there was no water in the raised reservoir, and the makeshift ladder leading up to the top of the structure was only temporary.

"Come on," said Walter. "Follow me." The older man began to climb the rickety ladder, while Victor looked on with trepidation. The lawyer wasn't a great fan of heights, but he stifled his fears and made his gingerly way up the side of the structure. Camelhump and Paul Cutter joined them moments later, and the four men found themselves standing on a wooden cover which extended over the top of the reservoir.

In the center of the cover was a collection of items that were unfamiliar to Victor. Walter walked in that direction, and Victor soon saw that it was electronics gear of some sort, and what appeared to be a loudspeaker. The other item on the wooden reservoir cover was a round metal cylinder about the size of a beach ball which rested in a handmade cradle about three feet above the cover itself. The cylinder was connected to the electronics array by a bevy of wires coming out of an entry port at the top of the metal object. Victor had no idea what he was looking at.

Victor smiled at the three men in the growing darkness. "So now I find out why you built this monstrosity of a tower right in the middle of camp. More than a mere water basin, it seems."

"Exactly right," said Walter, also smiling. "We needed a tall structure that wouldn't seem out of place in the middle of camp, and the water tower idea was what we came up with. Lambert had the idea, actually." Camelhump looked pleased by Walter's acknowledgment of his contribution.

"OK– I see the electronics, and the loudspeaker, and this cylinder device. So now maybe you can tell me what it is we're looking at."

Walter Kollett became deadly serious. "These items are the centerpiece of my final stage plan for defense of the compound. The cylinder is top secret– only Sydney and the four of us know it's here, and it's essential that we keep it that way. This evening at the film showing I'm going to explain to the pilgrims about the last line of defense near the lake, and this siren device here is a part of the plan." Walter pointed to the loudspeaker as he spoke. "What I don't plan to tell the campers is what Paul and I have been seeing on our daily visits outside camp. Something big is going on, and I don't like the looks of it. People are gathering in Prospect– we're seeing a lot of cars from out of town. Paul, maybe you can bring Victor up to date on what you're learning."

Cutter picked up the report. "I try to get into town every day to find out from the locals whether there's anything unusual going on. And Walter and Camelhump take a look around from the air in the helicopter. What we're seeing is a buildup. A bunch of new people are gathering in Prospect, and all around the area at various camping locations. A few women are in the group, but it's mostly men. I've seen a number of them in town– and they're wanderers . . . thugs . . . just the type of people that would be interested in what we're doing here at the compound."

"Do you think they've targeted us?" asked Victor.

"No doubt about it. Walter and Lambert are seeing people gathered in the forest areas just down the road from camp, and more of these wanderer types are showing up every day. They're getting ready to do something– and we're the ones they're after."

"They're looking for food," said Walter Kollett. "And a place to hang out. But most of all, they're going to want our women. More appear every day, and they're moving closer and closer to the compound."

"How many are there?"

"We can't tell for sure, since they're spread out and it isn't entirely clear that they're all part of a single group anyway." Paul Cutter was looking at Walter for confirmation as he spoke. "But my estimate is that there may be five thousand that we're seeing so far. And more coming." Walter nodded his head in agreement.

"Five thousand!" Victor was stunned by the scope of the threat. It wasn't entirely unexpected; but nevertheless it was chilling for Victor to actually be confronted with the prospect of an imminent attack. Five thousand angry men– with more coming every day! The population of the camp was only two thousand, and nearly half of them were women and children. It was Victor's worst nightmare; but he maintained his composure and asked the obvious question: "So what do we do?"

Walter spoke for the group. "Well the first thing is, we try to keep our people from panicking. That's why I'm planning to give a talk to the group tonight before the movie. I'll tell them something about what Paul and I have seen, and about the new defense strategies I have in mind. Except for one thing . . . this cylinder we're looking at. I'm telling you about it, but no one else."

"Go for it." Victor was ready to listen.

"First is the siren. I've been teaching people since we first got here about the strategy of using the lake to protect our backs in the event of an attack on the compound. I'll be making that point again tonight– we have to be disciplined in our defense, or the whole thing will fall apart. We need to hold defensive lines, and maintain interior lines of communication. If we need to give ground from the perimeter, we can fall back to the predesignated defensive positions that we've set up inside the camp. And finally, we can go to the lake if we're in danger of being overrun. That's where the siren comes in."

"How do you plan to use it?" Victor asked with an intense look on his face.

"I'll be overhead in the helicopter with my team of shooters. We'll be able to see the entire field of battle, and I'll know if we need to fall back into our final lines of defense. If we reach that point, I'll set off the siren using remote control from the JetRanger." Walter showed Victor a radio transmitter device about the size of a cell phone. "This transmitter will send the signal to activate the siren. And trust me, people will be able to hear it anywhere in the camp. The thing really puts out some noise."

"What happens then?"

"When the siren goes off, that's the signal for everyone to move in an organized retreat down to the docks. The Seawelanna will be there to take people across the bay to the Spinnaker property. They'll need to get on board and get the other boats launched as quickly as possible once the siren sounds. I have people assigned to captain every boat. Robert Rossignal will take the Seawelanna, and some of the younger guys will operate troop transports. We'll have enough space for everyone, but it will take two trips. So the women and children go across first– as soon as the attack starts. Then the boats come back to pick up the men."

"Some of our women won't like that. They'll want to fight for the camp with the men."

"I know– but this is the way it's going to be. I have a final defense in mind, and there isn't enough room on the boats for everyone to leave at once. It's going to be women first . . . then men."

Victor wasn't following the logic. "OK. So what's the final defense? Once we all get across to Spinnaker, the main camp will be theirs and we'll never get it back. Spinnaker doesn't have any road access– we'd never survive the winter over there. I don't understand the strategy of falling back, and giving up the camp."

Walter smiled broadly. "Somehow I knew you were going to say that. And I have an answer for you . . . something I haven't told you about until now." Victor could see that Paul and Lambert were looking at Walter in a relaxed way. They were enjoying the moment, so whatever it was that Victor's stepfather was about to say, they already knew about it.

Victor sighed, and smiled, and said in a resigned voice. "OK. I'm ready. You've obviously got something cooked up– so let me hear it."

Walter gave it to him straight. "See that cylinder there?" Walter was pointing to the metal beach ball object in its cradle. "That's a neutron bomb. I picked it up over at the air force base from a very dear friend of mine. They have about thirty of them on the base, and he figured Uncle Sam wouldn't miss one any time soon, and anyway we needed it here at the compound a hell of a lot more than they need it at the base."

Victor was having trouble processing what Walter had just told him. "A nuclear weapon? Here? Sitting right there in front of us?"

Walter looked pleased with himself. "Yep. I selected it myself. Looks pretty good in its new home, doesn't it?"

"So what do we do with it?" asked Victor. "Blow up the entire region– not to mention killing ourselves across the bay at Spinnaker?"

Walter was looking at his bomb fondly. "Oh, I wouldn't worry about that. This is a neutron bomb, not a high impact fission device. It's a tactical weapon– not the kind of bomb people use to blow up cities. The whole purpose of a weapon like this is to kill people with a massive dose of neutron radiation within a small geographic range of the explosion, but at the same time do only minimal damage to structures and surrounding facilities in the area. Once we leave the camp and set this thing off, everyone for about a mile around ground zero will be wiped out, but the camp itself will mostly be intact, and across the bay at Spinnaker we'll be fine."

In an instant Victor saw the beautiful simplicity of Walter's plan. A neutron bomb that would kill the intruders but leave the camp standing. Walter had set things up to draw the wanderers in, and get them all gathered around the center of camp at the base of the water tower. Then . . .

"What about blast, and radiation?" asked Victor. "Won't we be making the camp uninhabitable?"

"Not at all," said Walter. "This sort of weapon doesn't destroy buildings outside of a very small radius, and it doesn't leave harmful radiation. The bomb will certainly take out this tower when it goes off, and maybe the lodge and the main dormitory since they're the closest structures. But I think the rest of the camp will be OK. And the radiation will dissipate within a few days. So if everything goes as planned, we should be able to come back from Spinnaker within a week or so. And one thing is for sure– once we set this thing off, the word will spread, and no one else will be attacking us anytime soon. Setting off this bomb is our final line of defense– not just for this fight, but forever."

Victor looked at the beach ball device for a long time without saying anything. When he finally spoke again, he was as abrupt as Walter had been. "Got it. Anything else?"

"A couple of last things," said Walter. "First, I'm going to give you this radio transmitter. I have another one in the JetRanger. If anything happens to me during the firefight, you'll have to make the decision about setting off the bomb. Once you put things in motion by pushing that button, the siren will sound off for three minutes. Then it will go quiet, but there's a timer that will be working. The timer is set to blow the bomb one hour after the siren stops. That's how long you and the campers will have to get down to the boats, get over to Spinnaker, and hopefully get to the far side of the ridge over there just in case this thing has a bigger punch than advertised. I'm confident it doesn't by the way– I've seen these things tested at the base and they're actually quite precise. But just in case, take people across the ridge and lay down on the ground once you get to Spinnaker."

"What's the blast going to look like?" asked Victor.

"It will be pretty good sized– like an artillery shell. Everyone close to ground zero will be killed right away in the blast itself. People further out will die in a day or two from neutron poisoning. Some might last a bit longer– up to a week or so. But they'll be in no condition to be fighting us any more, that's for sure."

Victor marveled at Walter's plan. Bringing this weapon to Shanidar would be the salvation of the camp. The attackers would be gathered around and celebrating when the bomb went off– they would never know what hit them. "I like it." said Victor.

"Good," said Walter. "So we're ready. Oh, and one more thing. Lambert here is in charge of the rear guard group. They're going to be very key. The idea is that Lambert and his small team will hold off the attackers so the boats have their chance to get away clean. Then Lambert and his team will use Paul's Chris Craft to make their own escape when the main boats are safely away."

Victor realized that Walter had just described what in all likelihood would be a suicide mission. Surely Walter and Camelhump realized that the rear guard would never get out alive with the full firepower of the attackers focused in on them.

"I want to be part of the rear guard team," Victor said to Camelhump. Walter and his team looked at one another for a long moment. Then they nodded their heads in agreement.

VIII.

A baseball field on a chilly November night isn't exactly a location of choice for the premiere screening of a major Hollywood feature film, but under the circumstances it would have to do. Victor and the security team had spent a few minutes putting away the temporary ladder so no one would climb up the water tower, and they were the last to arrive for the event. The projector was set up near home plate, and the makeshift screen was just in front of second base– the pilgrims were using the grandstand bleachers for seating. With the exception of the perimeter guards, everyone in camp was here, so a lot of the campers had brought lawn chairs and blankets and were spread out on the infield grass. It was a festive evening at Shanidar.

Jonathan Silverstein was tinkering busily with his projection equipment while the crowd was gathering. Raffi Gutierrez– our young Callien– had taken a seat far off to the side down the left field line . . . alone. She was nervous about the opening, of course, but the young screenwriter knew she had written a great script. Once Walter and his group arrived, Adrian Garfinkle walked onto the field to make introductions.

"Good evening to all of you . . . and thank you for coming out on this special night. In a very real sense, the film we're going to see tonight was the start of a long journey that one way or another brought all of us together in this unique place. The making of the movie *Blood Children* was a defining event– it certainly was for me as a young lawyer in Los Angeles dealing with a movie production for the first time in my life. But there's a sense of sadness about the film too– we remember Harlan Bloom who you'll see on the screen tonight, but who died so tragically during the filming. To his parents who are with us, I say thank you . . . it was a pleasure for me to know your son, even if briefly. His performance in this movie is his great legacy to all the rest of us.

"You'll see some familiar faces on the screen. Our own Theresia Anjau in the role of Ninhursag, and Sarah Anjau as the young Naamah. Hollywood stars– both of them– living here in this time when there is no more Hollywood. Strange to think about, isn't it? We're watching tonight one of the last true Hollywood movies that ever will be made. So to Jonathan Silverstein the producer, and Raffi Gutierrez the screenwriter, I say thank you for your creation. The last of its kind . . . and I'm quite certain, the best.

"Let me now introduce a speaker who has some important camp news to share with you. Please listen carefully– what Walter Kollett has to say tonight is something we all need to know. Walter . . ."

Walter Kollett took the field, and talked for a few moments about the new security features, and how the defense was structured to work. He explained to the pilgrims yet again about the need to fall back in a disciplined way, and he talked about the siren. Walter spoke with an urgency that was impossible to miss: "When you hear the siren, move quickly and immediately to the lake and get on board the Seawelanna or one of the transport boats. And I mean immediately! Maintain discipline . . . don't panic, or run . . . but waste no time in getting to the boats. The siren is your signal to break off the fight– so do it! The boats will take you across the bay to Spinnaker where you'll be safe. Don't worry about what's going to happen after that . . . all I can tell you is that there will be some very unhappy intruders. I'll ask you to trust me about what I just said, so please . . . get to the boats when you hear the siren! Thank you, and now let's enjoy the film."

Many of the campers had taken the occasion of this *Blood Children* premiere to get dressed up. Did it matter that they would be sitting in bare metal bleachers at the baseball field? Not to these pilgrims– it was a special night in this pieced together outdoor theater, and the campers had risen to the occasion.

The screen displayed an advertising still from the movie. The promo featured a strong looking Harlan Bloom outfitted in the ancient dress of Enki flanked by a serene Sarah Anjau as Naamah and the fiery Theresia Anjau as Ninhursag. Then the screen went dark, and the field lights went out. The music score by Henry Thoreson was bold and uplifting– I tried to keep out of my mind that the composer had died in the first of the Los Angeles riots. The opening credits flashed onto the screen against a background of red cloth signifying the robes of the gods. The movie was underway.

Victor Desert and I were watching together, with the Kolletts and Paul Cutter seated in the bleacher row above us. I was caught up afresh in the grand story almost as though I hadn't been living with the project for a year. Jonathan Silverstein had shown me an early version of the film trailer, and on one occasion back in the editing process Victor and I had joined Theresia for a partial showing of one of the segments they were then working on. But the finished property was different– it opened with a meeting of the Council of the Gods and seemed to grow from there. It struck me as the film played out just how timely the themes of *Blood Children* truly were in the modern world. The original author had written the twelve tablets 4500 years before, yet his overriding vision of a slave race breaking free from their Overlord masters was something that we at the compound were living on this very day.

The film was nearing its end. A burdened and obviously exhausted Noah sat at the stern of the Ark remembering his earlier days with the beautiful young Naamah. The skies had begun to clear, and the waters were receding. Noah's great journey was nearing its end– he had carried his family and their precious cargo through the flood; there would soon be time for a rest. Noah was remembering when the young Naamah had first told him her story so many years before. It was a flashback scene– a youthful Noah was listening to Sarah Anjau as Naamah explained how their son Japheth would carry the line of Enki and the Blood Children forward to all the nations. Naamah told her husband about the creation and fall of Cain, and how she was the descendent of Enki and Ninhursag through Luluwa . . . the highest born of all. Noah's beautiful wife, he learned that night, was a descendent of the gods, and it was she, not he, who carried the line that would one day lift mankind above the level of slaves. Noah learned that he was Eljo, but he didn't care– the enchantress Naamah had won his heart after the death of his first wife, and he accepted that his child with Naamah was his son of the high blood. The flashback scene dissolves to Noah as an old man on the Ark being helped into bed by Ham and Shem after he has had too much to drink. Japheth looks at his sleeping father fondly– he already knew that the line of the Blood Children would be carried forward through him. The screen went dark, and the audience burst forth with heartfelt applause.

Adrian introduced Sydney Anjau to the crowd. Everyone stood, and gave the founder a standing ovation. Most of the pilgrims were at this place because of Sydney Anjau– they knew full well what their fates would have been if he hadn't intervened in the way that he did. Sydney Anjau was their leader, and the crowd cheered and clapped for long minutes before sitting down to hear his words.

"Adrian said this all started with *Blood Children* for him, and I guess the same can be said for me. Oh, I had made other films before . . . some of them quite successful. But the film we've seen tonight is something different from anything I've ever done. It started with the Callien tablets, and they've been brought to the screen by way of a script from our very own Callien, Raffi Gutierrez. I thank my daughters, of course, and Harlan Bloom, and so many more people who were involved that I can't even name. Many of them aren't with us tonight, but we will honor their work by appreciating and enjoying their film."

Sydney Anjau's tone changed. He was pensive now . . . and speaking from the depths of his soul. "Let me say a few words to all of you about how it is that we came to be here. Many of you credit me with special perception in seeing the future, and finding this place, and gathering us here, but actually it was no great insight at all. Just a matter of simplifying my mind, and seeing clearly what the future would bring.

"Well the time has come to look forward with clarity yet again. I see difficult things ahead . . . there are people out there who hate us, and envy our commitment to a civilized life. People who want what we have– and are willing to kill to take it. Walter Kollett is right– a difficult battle is coming. Be ready, and be strong, and never forget that you are the Blood Children . . . the one great hope for a better world once the darkness of this moment is over.

"My time is nearly done. I'll soon be leaving you, but there's nothing to fear. You will survive . . . because you must survive. So I say good night to all of you, and goodbye. The future is yours . . . and yours alone."

Sydney walked slowly away in the direction of the left field stands, where he took a seat next to Raffi Gutierrez. The two of them spoke in low voices, and Sydney's arm was around the shoulders of his beloved Callien. They were smiling as they shared this private moment, but Sydney Anjau looked like a very old man with the youthful Raffi at his side. Many of the pilgrims wept . . . they knew now that a difficult time lay ahead and their leader would not be with them for long. Would they survive? They didn't know. And even as the pilgrims made their way back to their cabins and dormitories, thousands of wanderers were moving closer to the perimeter of the camp. The battle for Shanidar was soon to begin.

IX.

The growing throng of wanderers in the Prospect area didn't seem to have any sort of central command. Paul Cutter spoke to some of the newcomers on his visits to town, and what he learned from their candid comments chilled him to the core. The single thing that unified the wanderers was their hatred and envy of us. These weren't protesters like the Level Z people who had appeared on the scene after Lawrence Yasgar was killed. The activists back then had been looking for justice– these wanderers weren't like that at all. They were here to take . . . and to kill. The throng gathering around our compound had no concerns about the bankers, or the government, or the future, or anything else. They only wanted what we had– and they were here to get it for themselves

Most of the wanderers had traveled north from California. That was where things were the worst. Tens of millions of people– out of money, and out of hope. This was the moment that Ivana Bartell had warned Victor about on that night of the Bankers' Ball– the Eljo were coming for us, just as Ivana had said that they would.

When wanderers had first started showing up at the compound in groups of two or three, we had been able to give them some food, and perhaps a night of shelter, before sending them on their way. The early wanderers didn't seem all that different from us– displaced people trying to survive in a radically changing world. But soon the tone of the visitors changed, and any similarities to the Blood Children disappeared into the mists. These later visitors were desperate, and demanding. The wanderers saw that we had something, and they didn't, so after a time we were turning them away at gunpoint. It worked for awhile– but every week, it seemed, more of the lost souls were around.

The wanderers became increasingly degenerate in manner and appearance. They openly carried handguns and assault rifles– their most precious possessions– and it wasn't unusual for skirmishes to break out between one faction and another in the areas around the perimeter of the compound. The locals in Prospect couldn't handle them any more than we could– the wanderers had taken over the town. There were so many of them now– and there was no one in authority in Prospect with the power to stop them. If they wanted something in a store, they took it, and the merchant said not a word. If they decided to shoot off their guns on a city street, they did it . . . and the outnumbered local police stayed in their patrol house. The wanderers could do as they pleased in Prospect . . . but that wasn't enough for them. Shanidar was the prize; the wanderers had heard stories of endless wealth and beautiful women locked behind the barbed wire fencing and steel gates. They were making their plans . . . but so were we.

* * *

I was in my assigned defensive position on the western perimeter when the assault began. They came at night . . . as we knew they would. The wanderers had no concern about the element of surprise– their plan was to win with brute force, or not at all. They knew the numbers were heavily in their favor– it was simply a matter of testing the perimeter defenses at various locations until something gave way. And once they breached the barbed wire . . .

Our lines were thin– there was a lot of perimeter to protect. The strategy was that if a concerted attack was made at one location, we would move defenders to the threatened area fast and blunt the effort. Walter and his team of shooters in the JetRanger would let us know where the reinforcements were needed most. At first, the wanderers were disorganized, and their attacks were flimsy– little more than random gunfire, and a few approaches to the wire in places where the surrounding forest provided close cover for the attackers. Walter was in the JetRanger with his shooters, and our airpower gave us all the advantage we needed in the early going. Whenever the wanderers would venture out of the forest, the marksmen on the JetRanger would find them, and drive them away. The high powered JetRanger searchlight exposed the attackers, and signaled us on the inside where there were targets in the open. We easily held our own, and after a time the initial assault petered out entirely. Camp casualties were minimal– eleven wounded and no one killed. Walter landed the helicopter for refueling and reported to Sydney and the ground leaders on what he had seen.

"There are at least 4000 of them within close proximity to the wire. They've surrounded the entire camp, but they don't appear to have any ability to communicate from one location to another. Nothing they did appeared organized to me."

"I agree," said Anjau. "But this first effort was just to test us. Their forces are here, and the attacks will continue either until we break their will, or they get inside the wire. There's no turning back for these people– they've come too far, and they have nothing left to lose."

Paul Cutter reported on the transfer of our women to the safety of Spinnaker Retreat across the bay. "Rossignal is back now, and he said it went without incident. There are no wanderers on the Spinnaker side. We've left the women some handguns, but for now at least we're counting on inaccessibility for their protection."

"OK," said Walter. "Our biggest risk is that they develop some leadership and coordination. I haven't seen anything that looks like a centralized command post, but I'm assuming there's someone in charge over there. The next attack will be stronger than what we've seen so far. They can afford to take casualties– we can't."

"Is everything in readiness at the water tower?" Sydney Anjau asked the question that was on all of our minds.

Walter Kollett smiled grimly. "I tested the unit yesterday– it's ready to go. These people are going to get quite a shock if they manage to break in."

At just that moment one of our 50 caliber machine guns near the entry gate erupted with a chattering noise. The second assault had begun, and Walter moved quickly to the JetRanger. I heard the whirring of the rotor as I ran to my position on the western wire, and caught a brief glimpse of the helicopter rising, with its searchlight shining on the open ground below.

In only a matter of moments, I was in the fight of my life. Victor Desert was at my side, and a major assault was emerging directly in front of my location. A solid wave of men had run from the surrounding forest, and they had reached the wire and were cutting their way in when Walter appeared overhead in the helicopter. Walter's presence was enough– the attackers were taking fire from air and ground, and the wire was soon piled with their bodies. They broke and ran– the perimeter had held.

I heard a fresh wave of machine gun fire from the main gate area to the north. Walter banked the JetRanger in that direction, leaving our sector in darkness. I wished for the light . . . heavy fire was coming our way from the surrounding forest, and the best we could do was fire blindly into the trees. We were doing all that we could, but there were a lot more guns on their side of the battle. The fire was so heavy that we couldn't raise our heads above the earthwork bunker, and two of our men were hit near my position. The attackers had found the range.

I watched as the searchlight from Walter's helicopter lit up the area of the main gate to the north. Then, suddenly, the light was gone. Either he had turned it off out of caution, or one of the attackers had found the mark and shot it to pieces. There were ground based searchlights in the gate area, but they weren't nearly as effective as the helicopter light. I began to develop a sinking feeling as the shooting increased in intensity– not just at my location, but all around the camp.

They were striking at multiple locations now; and at the same time. Walter could only be in one place with his JetRanger, but we needed him everywhere, and the outnumbered defenders on the ground were finding themselves increasingly on their own. The attackers made multiple assaults on my position during this second attack, and the fighting was fierce, and in close quarters. I emptied my magazine again and again, but still the attack continued. This was to the death.

Suddenly a red flare was launched from an area outside the camp to the north. Then another. The attack stopped at the sight of the flares, in what was obviously a prearranged plan. Walter stayed in the air, and none of us moved away from our defensive positions on the ground. We knew this was only a temporary reprieve. The enemy was regrouping, and another attack was soon to come. But where? And from how many? There was nothing to do but wait in the eerie silence. It was the calm before the storm.

Reinforcements came up from the area near the lake to fill in some gaps near my position. Frank Paladin was among them, and he greeted me with a grim smile.

"Having fun?"

I looked at him with a fierceness I had never felt before. "Like shooting fish in a barrel."

"Ah," said the detective, "but how many fish are out there? That's what we all want to know."

"Walter said there are several thousand, but that's not really going to mean much as long as the wire's intact. We're holding our own." At just that moment Walter's helicopter flew directly overhead. I could see that his searchlight was blown out, but Walter's shooters were still firing shot after shot into the surrounding woods. These overhead assaults from our shooters were surely taking a toll.

Suddenly a blast of fire appeared from the forest to my right. It was a surface to air missile– and it was right on target. The JetRanger fluttered in the air and spun in a sideways direction as the force of the missile struck home. Walter tried to pull up the nose and regain control, but he was too close to the ground. The JetRanger crashed with a loud thud into the cleared area between the barbed wire and the surrounding forest. In an instant a swarm of attackers was on the fallen craft, and I could see them pulling Walter and his shooters from the wreckage. They hauled the bodies back into the forest, and I hadn't been able to tell if Walter and his shooters were dead or alive. But either way, the helicopter was gone, and it had been the one factor that had somewhat evened the battle.

Victor Desert joined me at my position along the perimeter. "Get ready. They're going to come again soon, and this time– without Walter and the JetRanger– I think they're going to get in. When you hear the siren, go immediately to the lake and get on a boat. We're getting ready to evacuate."

I nodded my understanding, and Victor moved on to the next location to spread the word.

Long minutes went by– a half hour maybe. All was quiet, except for some sporadic gunfire from the other side of the compound. I saw a stirring in the forest and prepared for the next assault. But that wasn't what it was. There was a yell from an unseen attacker, "Hey in there. We're sending you a gift! Your helicopter crew– here they are! We're giving them back to you."

Walter and his three shooters came running out of the forest in the direction of the wire. But they never got there. About halfway across the cleared area, the unseen attackers in the woods opened fire. Walter and his men fell to the ground in a wave of bullets, and there they lay . . . without moving. Our commander was dead.

X.

The stillness of the night didn't last for long. A green flare went up from somewhere deep in the forest near the main gate. Then a second . . . and a third. I felt a dizziness, like time was standing still. But then with a great yell the wanderers came on the attack again, and this time they truly meant business. There was no longer a helicopter gunship to worry about, and they knew by now that our ground based fire from semi–automatic weapons simply wasn't good enough to stop a determined assault from multiple locations. It only took a few minutes for the attackers to force their way inside the perimeter wire at my location, and judging by the noise, they were getting in at other places as well. There could be no stopping the assault now. We had lost, and it was exactly at that moment when I heard the siren go off. Victor Desert had started the countdown.

I yelled to the others in my location to pull back, and was soon making my way along a narrow pathway through the trees in the direction of the lake. After passing through the interior line of defense that was manned by Camelhump and his team, I reached the water's edge and boarded the Seawelanna. I was one of the early arrivals since my location on the wire was close to the dock area– but a steady stream of retreating men was making their way in my direction.

The cruise ship was soon fully loaded, and Robert Rossignal at the helm ordered the lines to be cast off. We were underway– the remaining men in the camp would use the transports that were waiting along the shoreline.

The interior lines of defense had been carefully planned by Walter Kollett. In order to mount a broad based attack, the wanderers would need to go through a wooded area with thick brush that impeded their progress. Better and easier to follow the pathway which ran directly to the dock through the trees, but that route drew the attackers squarely into the line of fire from our rear guard contingent. Camelhump and his volunteers were waiting patiently, and whenever an attacker appeared they put up a withering fire with 50 caliber machine guns. Finally, the last of our retreating men were at the shoreline, and the transport boats were beginning to load.

After a few minutes the transports were safely away, and it was only the fifteen rear guard volunteers that were left in the camp, with Victor and Sydney Anjau among them. The attackers were being held at bay by machine gun fire, but now the moment had come for the rear guard to make their final escape.

A rear guard retreat under close fire is one of the most difficult of all military maneuvers, but Camelhump and his group had no choice in the matter– either they make their way to the Chris Craft now, or they die at the final line of defense. Camelhump ordered the evacuation, and it turned quickly into disaster. The attackers saw that their prey was escaping, and they renewed their assault with all the force they could muster against the small group of rear guard shooters. Five of the guard fell on the beach, and two more on the dock near the Chris Craft. Would any get away?

Maurice Desserte was the driver designated to pilot the Chris Craft. He stood at the controls and fired up the engine with a great roar as the surviving rear guard members stumbled into the waiting boat. Victor was the last to board, firing back at the attackers every step of the way. Just as he reached the side of the Chris Craft he took two bullets, but he managed to fall into the boat on top of an injured Sydney Anjau who was lying on the floor. Maurice spun the wheel and the boat left the dock and began to pick up speed.

At just that instant, a bullet caught him squarely in the back of the head, and Maurice fell to the bottom of the boat as if hit by a steel bar. The Chris Craft spun out of control, and for an instant was pointed back toward the camp area and the guns of the wanderers. Victor Desert was bleeding heavily from his wounds, but he managed to grab the wheel and set the boat on the right course toward Spinnaker. The group was soon out of firing range, and the wanderers on the shoreline had no way to follow.

Victor fell unconscious in the bottom of the boat next to Maurice Desserte, and Camelhump took the wheel. Everyone on the Chris Craft was injured or dead– it was a ship of the damned, but somehow with Camelhump at the helm they made their way across the bay to the Spinnaker dock, and safety. Theresia and Katy were attending to Victor's wounds on the dock when he regained consciousness. He pulled the two women close to him. "It's going to explode in minutes," he said in a rasping voice. "Tell everyone to move behind the ridge and lay flat on the ground."

"What's going to explode?" asked Katy.

"The bomb. Walter Kollett's bomb on top of the water tower. It's about to go off. Move everyone behind the ridge, now! There's only a few minutes left."

Theresia had no idea what Victor was talking about, but she recognized the urgency in his voice. "Over the hill," she yelled. "Now! Get behind the ridge and lay flat on the ground. Victor says there's a bomb about to go off. Get ready!"

Armand Desserte and three of his family members brought a stretcher for Victor, who was lying on the dock. It was only a short hike up the gentle rise– it couldn't really be called a hill– and once at the top, the ground sloped away from Shanidar and Silver Bay in the opposite direction. After a few short steps down the backside slope Shanidar disappeared completely from view. The pilgrims would be safe here.

We were gathered, and waiting, but nothing had happened. Only the leaders were in the know– Walter Kollette's secret had held. Minutes dragged by, and the only sounds were the groans of wounded men. Whatever it was we were waiting for didn't seem to be coming.

Camelhump moved close to Paul Cutter and whispered to him, "Walter said he tested it, but what kind of testing can you actually do with a neutron bomb? Small nukes like this are tricky– what shall we do if the thing doesn't go off? Maybe it's a dud . . ."

BOOM. A loud noise, and a momentary flash of light came from across the bay. The leaves on the trees along the ridgeline fluttered gently in a fresh, unnatural, breeze, but there was no other effect that we could feel or see. Paul Cutter ordered us to maintain our positions on the ground– we could satisfy our curiosity later when the danger of radiation had fully passed.

After an hour of waiting on the chilly ground, Paul and two of his lieutenants made their way cautiously to the top of the ridge. They had field glasses, and they examined the scene across the bay in the light of a few fires burning at the camp. The main lodge was on fire and several tall pine trees. Paul was looking for anyone alive in the visible areas of the camp.

"Do you see any people?" I asked shakily.

Paul was scanning the camp with his field glasses. "Nobody. I don't see a single person standing. Either they've gone back into the forest, or they're all dead. No way to tell."

Paul called the pilgrims together and brought the group up to date.

"As you all know, we've suffered a terrible assault from a roving army of wanderers. Walter Kollett has been killed, and many more. We're taking a census right now to find out who's missing. I think we can assume that anyone left on the other side of the bay is dead.

"Walter Kollett is one of the people who lost his life, but he gave us a great gift. About a month ago, he installed a special kind of bomb on top of the water tower. Only a handful of the leaders knew about the bomb– it was essential to Walter's plan that word of the weapon not get out, and it didn't.

"Walter's final plan of defense was the evacuation which brought us all here to Spinnaker. He knew very well that we couldn't defend the camp against a force of thousands– and that's what we faced tonight. Thousands of angry men– all bent on our destruction. They thought they had won; that the camp belonged to them. They were celebrating, but Walter Kollett had left his calling card behind. By all appearances it did its work exactly as Walter would have wanted."

"Where did he get the bomb?" One of the younger men had asked the question that was on the minds of many– but Paul Cutter wasn't going to reveal that part of the secret.

Instead he said, "I think it's better if we don't ask that question. Walter had his own resources, and far be it from me– or any of us– to get overly involved in the way he did what he did. It's better if we don't actually know. The secret of where Walter Kollett got the bomb will die with him."

"How is Sydney Anjau doing?" asked a voice from the back.

Karen Ashley spoke up. "Not well, I'm afraid. He took three bullets, and he's in a coma. The doctors are with him now, and they're moving him into the field hospital as soon as he's ready."

Paul Cutter continued with his briefing. "Walter's instructions were that we should stay here at Spinnaker for at least a week before returning to Shanidar. That will allow some time to pass and give any radiation an opportunity to clear. Obviously we'll take readings before we go back in– and we'll need to find out if any of the attackers have survived and are hanging around in the compound general area. In a couple of days, we'll send a team up the lake by boat to circle around behind the camp and approach it from the other side. They can take a look, and let us know. By that time, we should be able to get some readings on how hot the camp is, and whether any of the wanderers are still in the neighborhood. I'm hopeful they'll all be dead . . . or gone."

Those words, coming from the gentle and warm–hearted Paul Cutter, were shocking to me. But he had become a changed and tougher man, and so had I. Our world wasn't the same anymore– and that's just the way it was. Whether we liked it or not.

XI.

Victor had been sleeping. He awakened to find a smiling Katy Hooper seated at the side of his rumpled bed in the makeshift hospital. "Hello sleepyhead," she said.

Victor looked around the unfamiliar room, trying to get his bearings. Then he remembered– that terrible night of the battle. "How long have I been out?"

"Two days. But it's all right– you needed it."

Victor tried to get to a sitting position, but a wave of pain swept over him from the effort and he lay back on the bed again. Katy spoke in a soothing voice, "You're hurt, but the doctors say you're going to be OK. Don't try to move around yet."

"What happened? The last thing I remember is running down the dock and falling into Paul's boat on top of Sydney Anjau."

"You got shot. Once in the left shoulder and the other in the right side just above your hip. But you were lucky– no bones broken and the bullets seem to have passed through without damaging any internals. You lost a lot of blood. That's why you've been out, the doctors say."

"Is Sydney all right?"

"He fades in and out of a coma, and I'm afraid he's hurt badly. He took a bullet in the stomach, and at his age that's a tough thing to have happen. Sydney is strong, but even with all his great will, he's barely hanging on. Arthur and Courtney are with him."

"And the wanderers?"

"All gone, it seems. Paul has been to town checking up on things, and it looks like the few that survived have disappeared. The camp is empty. Paul's waiting for a go–ahead from you to send a team in and get some radioactivity readings."

"Well that's easy enough– tell him to go ahead."

Katy fluffed up Victor's pillows and smoothed out his rumpled bedding.

"Where's Theresia? Is she all right?"

Katy smiled at her patient. "Theresia is fine. She and I have been taking turns watching over you. She's sleeping right now– I can wake her if you'd like. I'm sure she'll be pleased that you're awake."

Victor thought for a moment, but then he realized that he was about to fall asleep again himself. "No, don't bother her. I'm sure she needs her rest as much as I do." Victor's eyes were beginning to close. "Just tell Paul . . ." Then he was asleep again.

Paul Cutter personally led the group of four men to test the compound that afternoon. They had radiation suits and geiger counters, but it turned out that neither was necessary. The radiation after only three days was at an acceptably low level except for the area directly beneath the location where the water tower had stood. The bomb had performed amazingly well– killing the attackers, but causing relatively minimal damage to the surrounding area. The lodge had suffered heavy damage, and probably wasn't salvageable, and there were some burned out areas in the nearby forest. But the new dormitory had survived, and the cabins on the Cutter property were out of the blast area entirely. Eagle Nest was far enough away that it hadn't suffered any blast damage at all.

Everywhere Paul looked, the ground was littered with dead bodies. Mostly the attackers– Paul found at least two thousand dead in the camp itself, and as many more would later be located in the surrounding forest areas. Just as Walter had foreseen, the wanderers had gathered in the central courtyard area near the water tower when the bomb went off. Those in close proximity to the blast had been killed instantly. Others in the surrounding areas further from the blast location had taken longer to die as the neutron damage to their bodies did its insidious work.

Paul found many dead defenders as well– mostly in the perimeter positions. Walter Kollett's body was at the perimeter fence not far from the wreckage of his JetRanger, with three of his gunnery crew. The other helicopter shooter had died in the crash.

Paul found the body of Mark Greenlee in the area near the main gate. The great scholar had been shot seven times. The man who had started it all– Greenlee's discovery of the Callien tablets was the triggering event for all of us. A uniquely talented historian and scholar– dead on the ground at Silver Bay on Lake Ponderosa.

There were many more. Men from all walks of life who had come to the compound to start again after Level Z. Two of the Singularity group were dead– the camp's greatest scientists had joined in defense of the compound . . . and paid the ultimate price.

Samuel Bloom's body was found over on the Eagle Nest side near a great gashed opening in the perimeter barb wire. By all appearances, Bloom and a small group had fought hand to hand with the attackers as they entered the camp through their hole in the wire. Many were dead at that location, and it was with a heavy heart that Paul Cutter turned away from the sickening carnage and led his men back to the waiting speedboat. Two of the rear guard unit lay dead on the dock near where the Chris Craft was tied up.

Cutter was there with Theresia when Victor woke up for the second time. The woman gave Victor a gentle kiss, and Paul smiled about as broadly as anyone had seen him smile ever. He gave a report about his visit to the camp and the disappearance of the wanderers, then he left the young couple alone.

"Would you help me?" Victor asked. "I'd like to stand up and walk around for a few minutes."

"Of course. It would do you good if you think you're ready." Theresia took hold of Victor's arm and lifted him to a sitting position on the bed.

She had placed a cane against the wall, and she brought it to him. Victor rose to his feet unsteadily, placing his weight on the cane while he caught his breath. Theresia took a firm hold on his good arm to steady him, and after a few moments, Victor was ready to take his first halting step. Then another. And another. He made it to the door, and took a seat outside in a chair on the porch. He was totally out of breath, but Victor and Theresia both knew that his recovery had now officially begun.

"You have a bad shoulder and a torn up area above your hip," said Theresia. "It's no wonder you're a bit slower than usual. But give it a little time; let it heal; and don't try to do everything at once." Theresia brought Victor a pillow and fussed over him as he sat in the chair.

Victor and Theresia sat for awhile, saying nothing. He enjoyed her closeness, and the sunshine of the fall morning. Theresia's arms were folded, and she seemed almost catlike in her contentment as she looked out over the deep blue water of the lake. A gentle breeze rustled the overhead pine trees. "I wonder if we'll ever live in a city again," she said.

Victor took a long time to answer; he seemed to be almost dozing. "Do you think you'll ever want to?"

"Not anytime soon," said Theresia. "It's going to be horrible for awhile, and we're in the right place while this ongoing catastrophe plays itself out. I think we can make it here. Make a life, I mean. But someday I'm going to miss it. The people . . . and always having something to do, some place to go. Making a film– that's the kind of thing you need a city for. We could never have shot *Blood Children* without all the dozens and dozens of talented support people. Specialists . . . you know what I mean? We have a wonderful group in our camp community, but we're small. There are so many artistic and creative skills and capabilities we're not going to have."

One of the doctors walked out and greeted Victor warmly. She was obviously pleased to see him up and about. Victor sat quietly again for awhile. Then he said, "I agree with you about making it here. And we'll have some artists in camp . . . you'll see. Do you remember the words of Plato: 'At the touch of love, everyone becomes a poet.'"

Theresia laughed heartily. "Got me with that one. But who was talking about love?"

"Maybe I was," said Victor. "Shakespeare: Love comforteth, like sunshine after rain. Maybe some talk about love can be a good idea every once in awhile."

Theresia looked at him sharply. "Like now?"

"Like right now," said Victor. "I love you, you know. I have from the very first– although I didn't know it for awhile. To the extent I understand what love is at all, it's because of you. I'm learning . . . and what I'm coming to know is that love is the only happiness there is in life when you get right down to it. I love you Theresia . . . and I want you to be my wife."

Theresia was smiling, "Is that a proposal?"

"Absolutely . . . and made to you without any hint of a doubt or second thought. So you better say yes, or I'm liable to suffer a terrible relapse in my recovery process."

"Blackmail, eh. Well you don't need it. Of course I'll marry you. Marriage, yes– what did one of the writers call it: the supreme felicity of life . . . something like that. Who wrote that, Victor?"

"Mark Twain. One of the true freedom lovers in American history, by the way."

"He'd go well in this camp."

Victor sat quietly again. So he had done it! He'd asked Theresia to marry him, and she had said yes. It had been coming to Victor for awhile, but something at the compound always seemed to interfere. Now it was done, and Victor felt as if a great weight had been lifted from his shoulders. His spirits soared as he thought about this wonderful woman and the life they would lead together. Love rejoices! It frees us from all the weight and pain of life. Victor was in love . . . he rejoiced.

Walking back to his bed with Theresia holding his uninjured arm for support, Victor asked about her father.

"Not well. He's delirious most of the time, and fading. He's been asking for you. I think it's the only thing that's keeping him alive."

* * *

Sydney Anjau had been moved to one of the cabins higher up the hill than the makeshift Spinnaker hospital. Theresia and Victor walked together to the cabin later that afternoon, and soon they stood above the bed of their stricken leader. The cabin was dark– blankets covered the windows to keep out the glaring afternoon sunlight.

Sydney was sitting upright in the bed, but he appeared to be sleeping when the couple entered the cabin. His face was drawn, and seemed as white as his hair. Yet somehow he sensed the presence of the visitors, and his eyes opened with a start. "Kill them all, Victor. They'll kill us if you don't. Kill them all– leave none alive."

Sydney's eyes were open very wide. "It had to be like this, of course. We must survive the Eljo before we can even begin the battle against Enlil and the Igigi. It's not our choice, but it's to the death." Then Anjau spoke the words from Deuteronomy in the Old Testament:

"And they smote all the souls with the edge of the sword. There were not any left to breathe."

"And all the cities of those kings did Joshua take, and he utterly destroyed them, as Moses the servant of the Lord commanded."

The words seemed to exhaust the injured man. He put his head back against his pillow and closed his eyes again.

Victor leaned down to speak softly to the leader. "They're all gone, Sydney. We killed them, and chased them away– and they won't be coming back. Paul Cutter has seen it with his own eyes . . . the compound is safe."

Anjau nodded his head slightly, with approval. "You must take my place, Victor. I won't live to see Shanidar again. It falls now to you to reach out for the grand future of our Blood Children that I will never see. There is so much trouble ahead, but you can overcome. This is our moment! The moment we've been waiting for. It's here now for you, Victor. For you, and for Theresia and Sarah, my beloved daughters. Lead the way, Victor . . . the children of Enki will follow."

"Theresia and I are to be married, Sydney. We'll have children of our own soon . . . your line is not going to die."

Anjau smiled weakly, and lay quietly for several minutes. Victor and Theresia waited at the side of the leader's bed. Finally he spoke, "You'll have a daughter, Victor. A beautiful daughter– the child of the gods. The daughter of Enki and Ninhursag . . . just as the tablets of Callien foretold. You have my full support, Victor. Go now, and tell the others. Prepare well– more of the darkness is yet to come."

Sydney closed his eyes again. Victor and Theresia left him alone with a watchful nurse and made their slow way back to the hospital.

"He's nearly gone," said Theresia.

"I'm afraid so."

"But what a wonderful life he lived. My father did so many things, Victor. I wonder if we can even come close to living our lives as fully and richly as he did."

Victor was walking very slowly, leaning on his cane for support with each step. But he knew that this was the time for reassuring words. "We will have a wonderful life of our own, Theresia. Not the same as your father's, of course. He lived in different times– and different ways. But wonderful in our own way. I'm certain of it."

Theresia placed her hand on his and gave it a gentle squeeze. “His final prophesy– that we’ll have a daughter. I wonder if he truly knows, or whether he’s just delirious. My father’s greatest talent was seeing the future– maybe he’s done it again, for us.”

“He’s always been right before,” said Victor, “so why would we doubt him about this? And having a daughter sounds terrific to me.” Theresia squeezed Victor’s hand in agreement.

Sydney Anjau died that night.

XII.

Joanne Kollett took charge of the arrangements. Walter and Sydney would be placed in the Desserte mausoleum in Millford– and their fallen soldiers Mark Greenlee, and Samuel Bloom, and Maurice Desserte would be buried right outside. Honored guests, at the last Desert Hotel.

Joanne asked Victor to say a few words to the mourners at the cemetery, and fortunately Paul Cutter had the foresight to arrange for a loudspeaker. More than ten thousand people showed up for the services. They came from everywhere, and they covered the lawn at the middle terrace in front of the Desserte property for as far as the eye could see.

Many of them were in uniform. Talon Air Force Base had turned out in force to honor its former commander. Others were common people– arriving from miles around to pay their respects to the legendary Sydney Anjau. The spirit of Shanidar was in the air.

Victor had chosen his words carefully.

> Another day has come again,
> As time moves surely on–
> But nothing now seems quite the same,
> To know that they are gone.

The loss cannot be measured now,
The void cannot be filled–
And though someday the grief may fade,
Their mark will live on still.

After the readings, Colonel Roosevelt Tuckerman came up to Victor Desert. "May I speak to you for a moment?" The two men went around to the far side of the mausoleum where they found a quiet place alone to talk.

"As you probably know, I was quite close to your stepfather. Walter Kollett was my mentor– he's the reason I'm the commander at Talon today. Without Walter, my command never would have happened."

Victor was gracious. "Thank you for coming– we all feel the same way about Walter. My mother was fortunate to find him– they had a warm and loving life together."

"Quite so, I'm sure. And as you can perhaps understand, it was very distressing to me when persons higher than me in the chain of command started asking unpleasant questions about where Walter might have gotten his hands on a nuclear weapon of the sort that has been rumored to have gone off at your compound in Silver Bay. I found it quite troubling– these officers appeared to be investigating the possibility that Walter might somehow have gotten his weapon from Talon. Do you grasp my point?"

"I do."

"So naturally, I wanted to assure my superiors that the base which I currently command– and which your stepfather formerly commanded– was not involved in any sort of explosion event that might have occurred at the Shanidar compound. I wanted to make sure that Walter's good name wasn't dragged though the mud– so I did my own detailed investigation to determine if there was any possibility that he might have somehow gotten his hands on a tactical nuclear weapon of the sort that we maintain at Talon. Such weapons, as I'm sure you'll understand, are highly prized by terrorists, and as a result, those of us to whom such weapons are entrusted must be vigilant at all times to ensure that they don't fall into the wrong hands. Do you understand what I'm saying?"

"Perfectly."

"So when my superiors from Washington DC raised the suspicion that Walter might have acquired a nuclear device from the arsenal at Talon, it became a matter of immediate concern and high priority to me. I'm sure you can relate to that– the military chain of command must be respected and adhered to at all times in my profession."

"I understand."

"So I undertook a thorough investigation of our records at Talon to make certain that our inventory of tactical weapons was entirely accounted for."

Victor was beginning to grasp what Roosevelt Tuckerman was leading up to. "That certainly sounds like a prudent thing to do under the circumstances."

"Thank you. Of course I'm not suggesting that a nuclear device actually was used during the unfortunate attack on your community. We at Talon have no opinion one way or the other on the question whether you set off a nuclear device– that is a matter entirely outside of our jurisdiction. What is within our jurisdiction, however, is the determination whether any of our weapons might have fallen into the wrong hands– and specifically, whether Walter Kollett might have somehow gotten possession of a neutron tactical weapon from our inventory at the base."

"Of course . . . you would want to know that." Victor knew what was coming, but he waited patiently for Colonel Tuckerman to make the point in his own way.

"Quite so. And what I wanted to tell you is that– following a thorough review of our records– we concluded that all of our nuclear arsenal is fully and properly accounted for. None of our devices are missing . . . so as far as we're concerned, Walter Kollett is not under suspicion at the base in any way. Do you understand what I'm saying?" Colonel Tuckerman was looking closely at Victor as he spoke those words.

"I understand perfectly. And I appreciate your telling me this. It's comforting to know that my stepfather– a man I consider to be a part of my family– is not under any sort of suspicion from your organization. And I'm sure it was a relief to you as well to find there was no misappropriation of your inventory."

Roosevelt Tuckerman smiled for the first time. "Exactly. There was no misappropriation. So we've closed out the investigation where Walter is concerned. And let me add one additional point. If you find yourself again in a circumstance where your community faces a threat of the sort that you recently dealt with, feel free to call upon me for assistance. I'll be happy to do anything within my power to help you maintain your mission. What you are doing meant a lot to Walter– he talked to me about you, and Sydney Anjau, and your compound, on a number of occasions. Our officers and many of our enlisted men are sympathetic with your goals– both Walter and Sydney Anjau had strong and committed followers on the base. I can tell you that I was happy to help Walter when he came to me before, and I would be happy to do the same if it becomes necessary for you to come to me again in the future. Do you understand what I am saying?"

"Indeed," said Victor, "and if I may add a final point. We found that Walter's security plan for the compound worked exactly the way he said it would. He had a particular strategy in mind, and he chose his tools carefully and well. I'm sure he appreciated any help that you were able to give him, and I can say with no doubt in my mind at all that it is entirely as a result of Walter and your good offices that our group survived the attack and deterred our adversaries. So I hope you'll understand me when I say we are most appreciative for whatever help it was that you were able to give to Walter. It was quite literally a matter of life and death for a large number of people, and things worked out just as he said they would."

"I understand, and thank you." With those words, Colonel Tuckerman was gone.

Walter Kollett was quite a man, Victor thought to himself. A man with some very helpful friends.

* * *

Two days later was Thanksgiving at Spinnaker, and the pilgrims had prepared a grand outdoor feast. They would be crossing the lake to Shanidar on the following day.

Victor explained to the pilgrims about his discussion with the Colonel. He told them about the complete disappearance of the wanderers, and how the word had spread regarding their successful defense of the camp. No future attacks were anticipated, Victor said. He told the people of Shanidar that work crews had completed the unpleasant task of removing the bodies and debris from the main camp area, and he talked about the coming winter, and how everything remained on track in their planning for heat, and food, and shelter in the challenging days ahead. Then, finally, Victor Desert said this:

"The most powerful revolutions start quietly, in the shadows, where societies in decline fear the words of the visionaries. But people who insist on liberty will succeed, and will get as much as they have the intelligence and the courage to take. Fantasy! Lunacy! All revolutions are called that . . . until they happen. Then they become inevitability. So the way to support a revolution is to make it your own.

"We have it within our power to begin the world over again. Our Overlords have not heard the voices of the people for generations, but they are soon to find that those voices can be much, much louder than they care to think about. Our revolution will be one of better ideas, not guns, so let us all remember:

> The new world is as yet behind the veil of destiny.
> In our eyes, however, its dawn has been unveiled.

"Sydney Anjau spoke to me just prior to his death. He said that he wanted me to fill his place as the leader of the camp, and I agreed to do so to the very best of my ability. I'm not Sydney Anjau– far from it– but I will do my best. That's all I can do . . . and my commitment to you is that my best is what you'll receive.

"Sydney Anjau said one other thing to me on the day of his death. As most of you already know, Theresia Anjau and I will soon be married– the first of what I hope will be many marriages within our Shanidar community.

"Sydney told us something from his deathbed when Theresia and I gave him the news about our marriage plans. He said that our first child would be a daughter, and Sydney Anjau was never wrong about such things. So we've decided what the name of our daughter will be, and we've drawn from the ancients:

Her name will be Luluwa."

THE STORY CONTINUES

BLOOD CHILDREN
The Temple of Nippur

BLOOD CHILDREN
Daughter of the Gods

ONE DIFFERENCE PRESS
Publisher
www.onedifferencepress.com

www.ingramcontent.com/pod-product-compliance
Lightning Source LLC
Chambersburg PA
CBHW022134170626
46807CB00005B/1941